HINGES
MEREDITH MCCLAREN

BOOK 2
PAPER TIGERS

"MANY THANKS TO ALL THE IMPS AND ODDS, WHO PUSHED, POKED, AND PRODDED ME ALONG."

- MEREDITH MCCLAREN

IMAGE COMICS, INC.

ROBERT KIRKMAN - CHIEF OPERATING OFFICER
ERIK LARSEN - CHIEF FINANCIAL OFFICER
TODD MCFARLANE - PRESIDENT
MARC SILVESTRI - CHIEF EXECUTIVE OFFICER
JIM VALENTINO - VICE-PRESIDENT

ERIC STEPHENSON - PUBLISHER
COREY MURPHY - DIRECTOR OF SALES
JEFF BOISON - DIRECTOR OF PUBLISHING PLANNING & BOOK TRADE SALES
JEREMY SULLIVAN - DIRECTOR OF DIGITAL SALES
KAT SALAZAR - DIRECTOR OF PR & MARKETING
EMILY MILLER - DIRECTOR OF OPERATIONS
BRANWYN BIGGLESTONE - SENIOR ACCOUNTS MANAGER
SARAH MELLO - ACCOUNTS MANAGER
DREW GILL - ART DIRECTOR
JONATHAN CHAN - PRODUCTION MANAGER
MEREDITH WALLACE - PRINT MANAGER
BRIAH SKELLY - PUBLICITY ASSISTANT
RANDY OKAMURA - MARKETING PRODUCTION DESIGNER
DAVID BROTHERS - BRANDING MANAGER
ALLY POWER - CONTENT MANAGER
ADDISON DUKE - PRODUCTION ARTIST
VINCENT KUKUA - PRODUCTION ARTIST
SASHA HEAD - PRODUCTION ARTIST
TRICIA RAMOS - PRODUCTION ARTIST
JEFF STANG - DIRECT MARKET SALES REPRESENTATIVE
EMILIO BAUTISTA - DIGITAL SALES ASSOCIATE
CHLOE RAMOS-PETERSON - ADMINISTRATIVE ASSISTANT
IMAGECOMICS.COM

FIRST PRINTING
ISBN: 978-1-63215-524-5

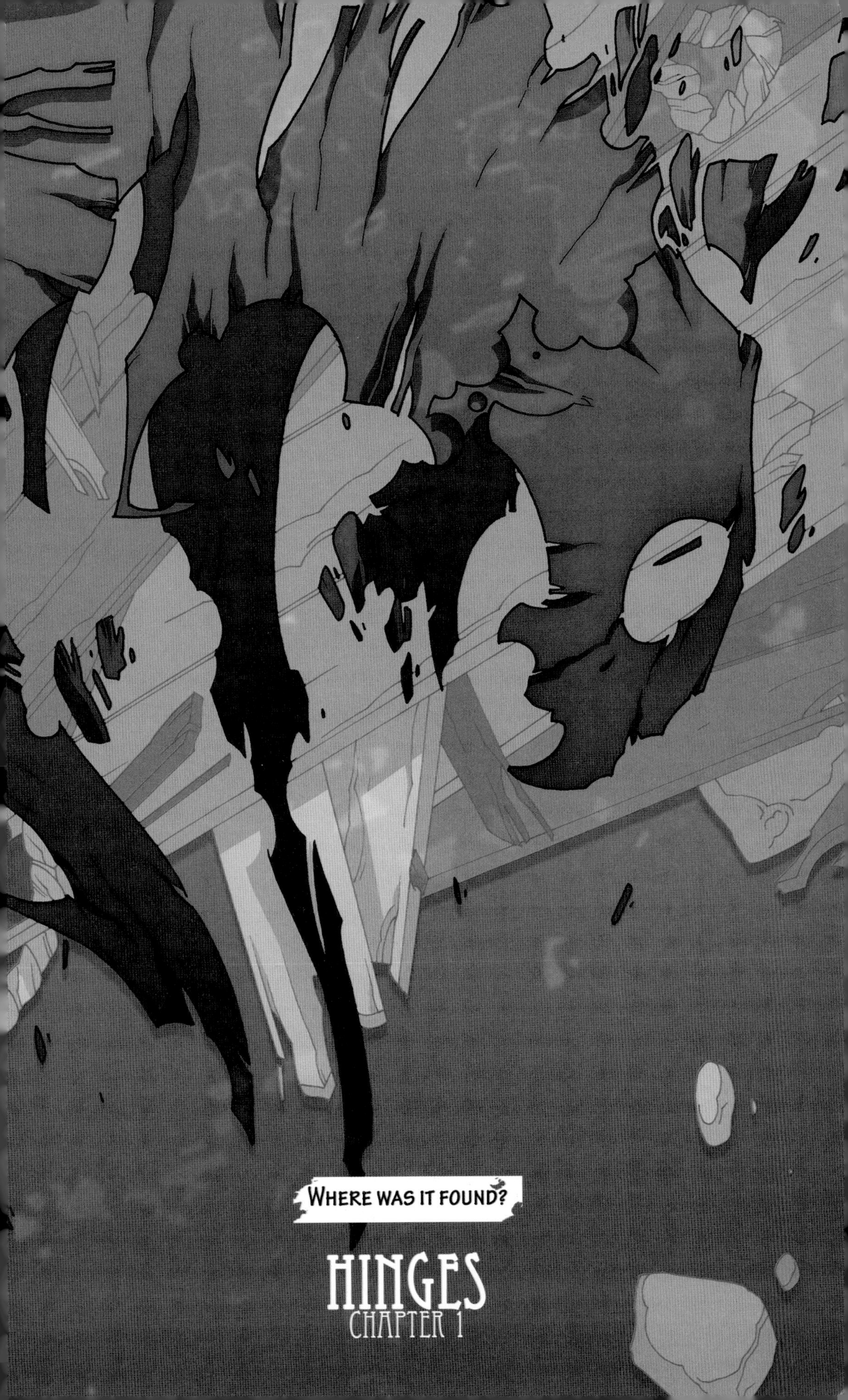
WHERE WAS IT FOUND?
HINGES
CHAPTER 1

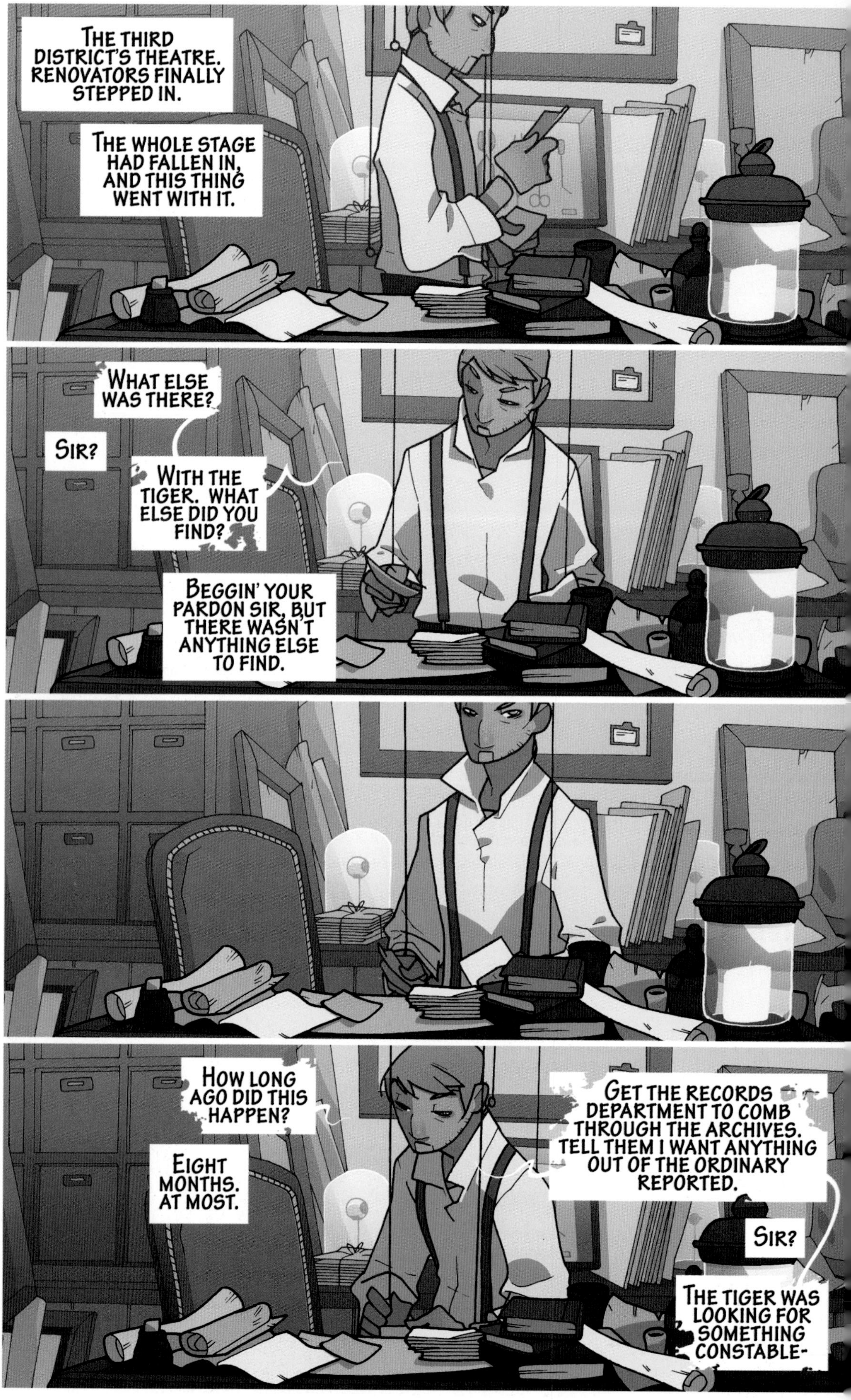
THE THIRD DISTRICT'S THEATRE. RENOVATORS FINALLY STEPPED IN.
THE WHOLE STAGE HAD FALLEN IN, AND THIS THING WENT WITH IT.
WHAT ELSE WAS THERE?
SIR?
WITH THE TIGER. WHAT ELSE DID YOU FIND?
BEGGIN' YOUR PARDON SIR, BUT THERE WASN'T ANYTHING ELSE TO FIND.
HOW LONG AGO DID THIS HAPPEN?
EIGHT MONTHS. AT MOST.
GET THE RECORDS DEPARTMENT TO COMB THROUGH THE ARCHIVES. TELL THEM I WANT ANYTHING OUT OF THE ORDINARY REPORTED.
SIR?
THE TIGER WAS LOOKING FOR SOMETHING CONSTABLE-

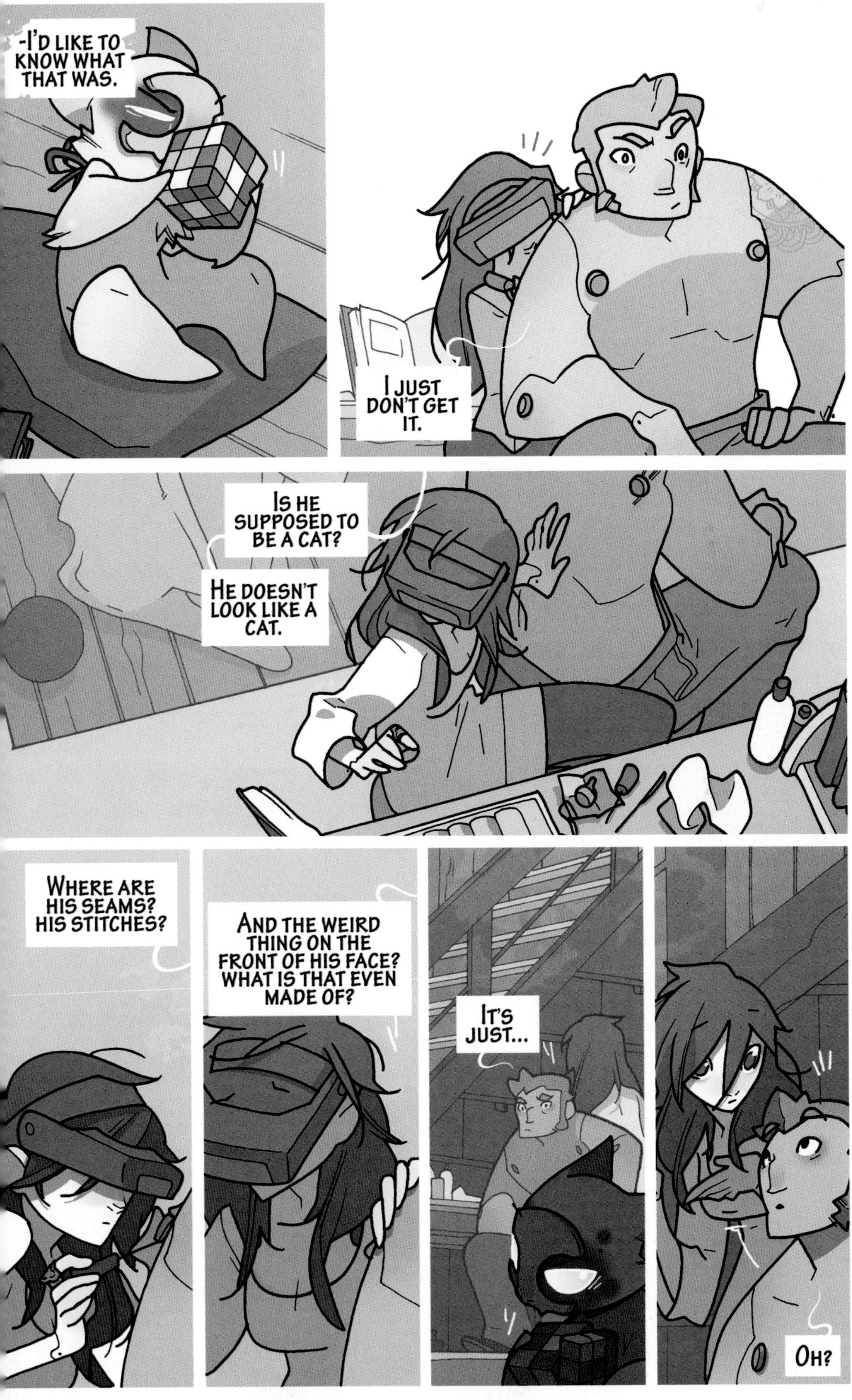
-I'D LIKE TO KNOW WHAT THAT WAS.
I JUST DON'T GET IT.
IS HE SUPPOSED TO BE A CAT?
HE DOESN'T LOOK LIKE A CAT.
WHERE ARE HIS SEAMS? HIS STITCHES?
AND THE WEIRD THING ON THE FRONT OF HIS FACE? WHAT IS THAT EVEN MADE OF?
IT'S JUST...
OH?

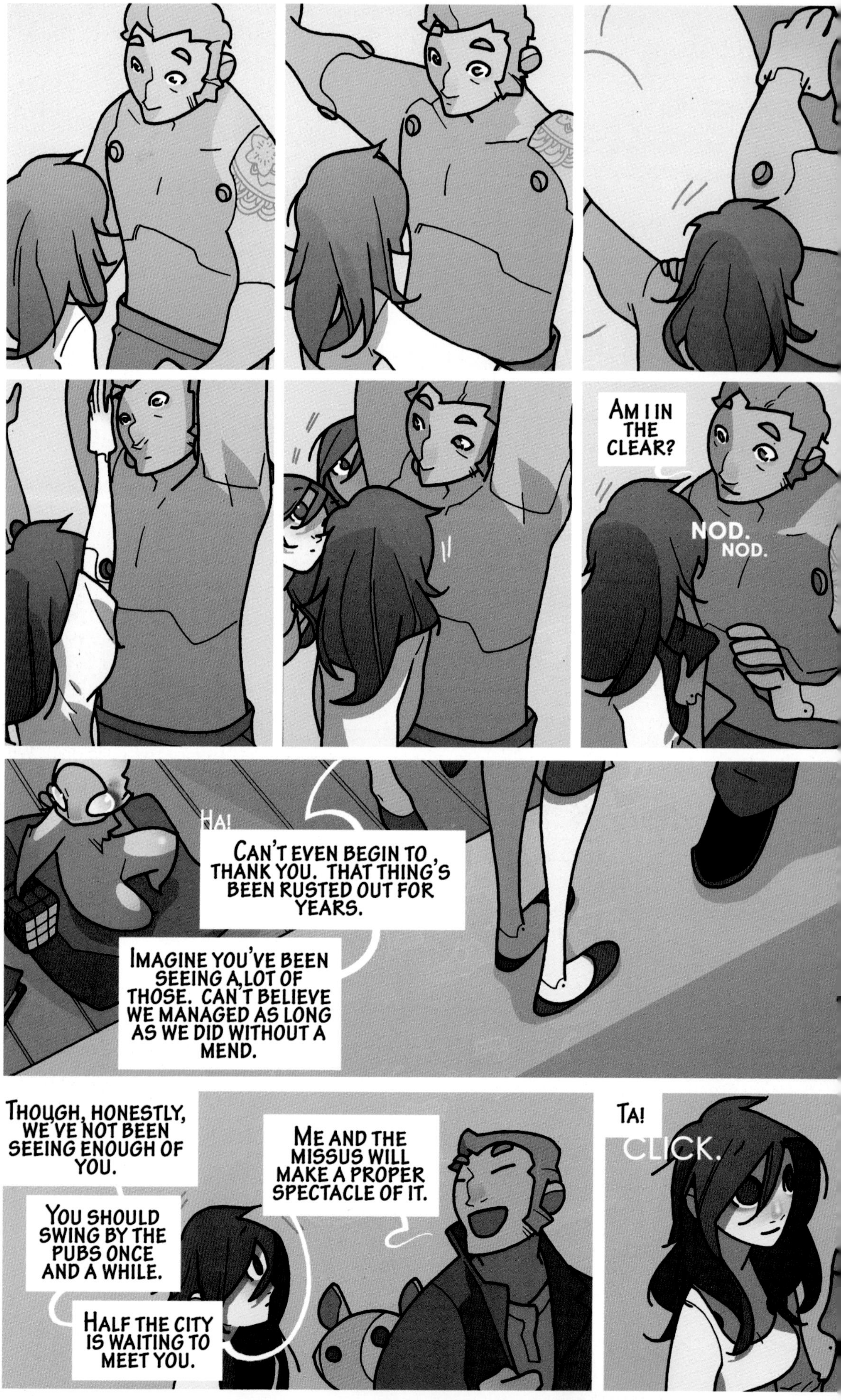
AM I IN THE CLEAR?
NOD.
NOD.
HA!
CAN'T EVEN BEGIN TO THANK YOU. THAT THING'S BEEN RUSTED OUT FOR YEARS.
IMAGINE YOU'VE BEEN SEEING A LOT OF THOSE. CAN'T BELIEVE WE MANAGED AS LONG AS WE DID WITHOUT A MEND.
THOUGH, HONESTLY, WE'VE NOT BEEN SEEING ENOUGH OF YOU.
YOU SHOULD SWING BY THE PUBS ONCE AND A WHILE.
HALF THE CITY IS WAITING TO MEET YOU.
ME AND THE MISSUS WILL MAKE A PROPER SPECTACLE OF IT.
TA!
CLICK.

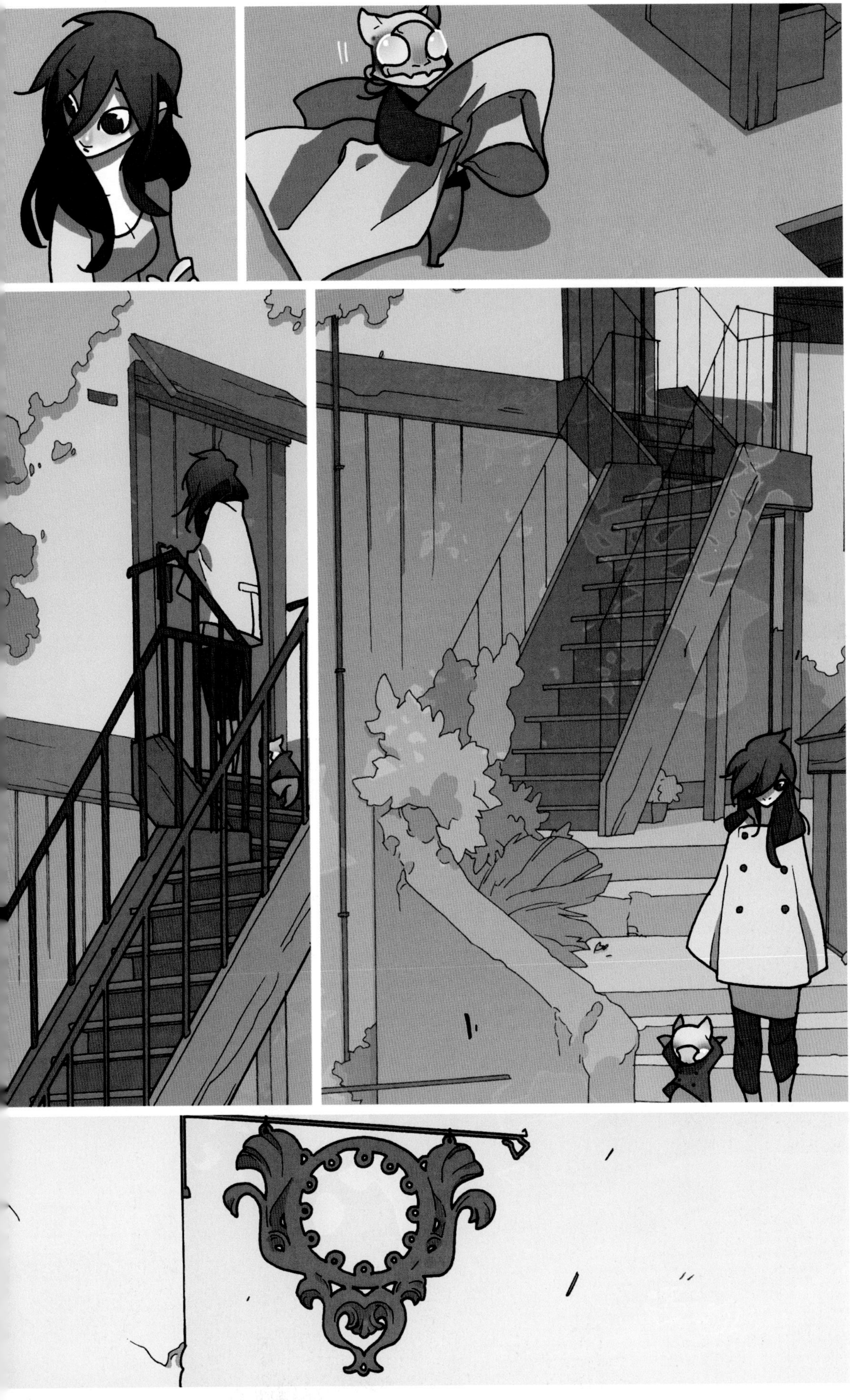

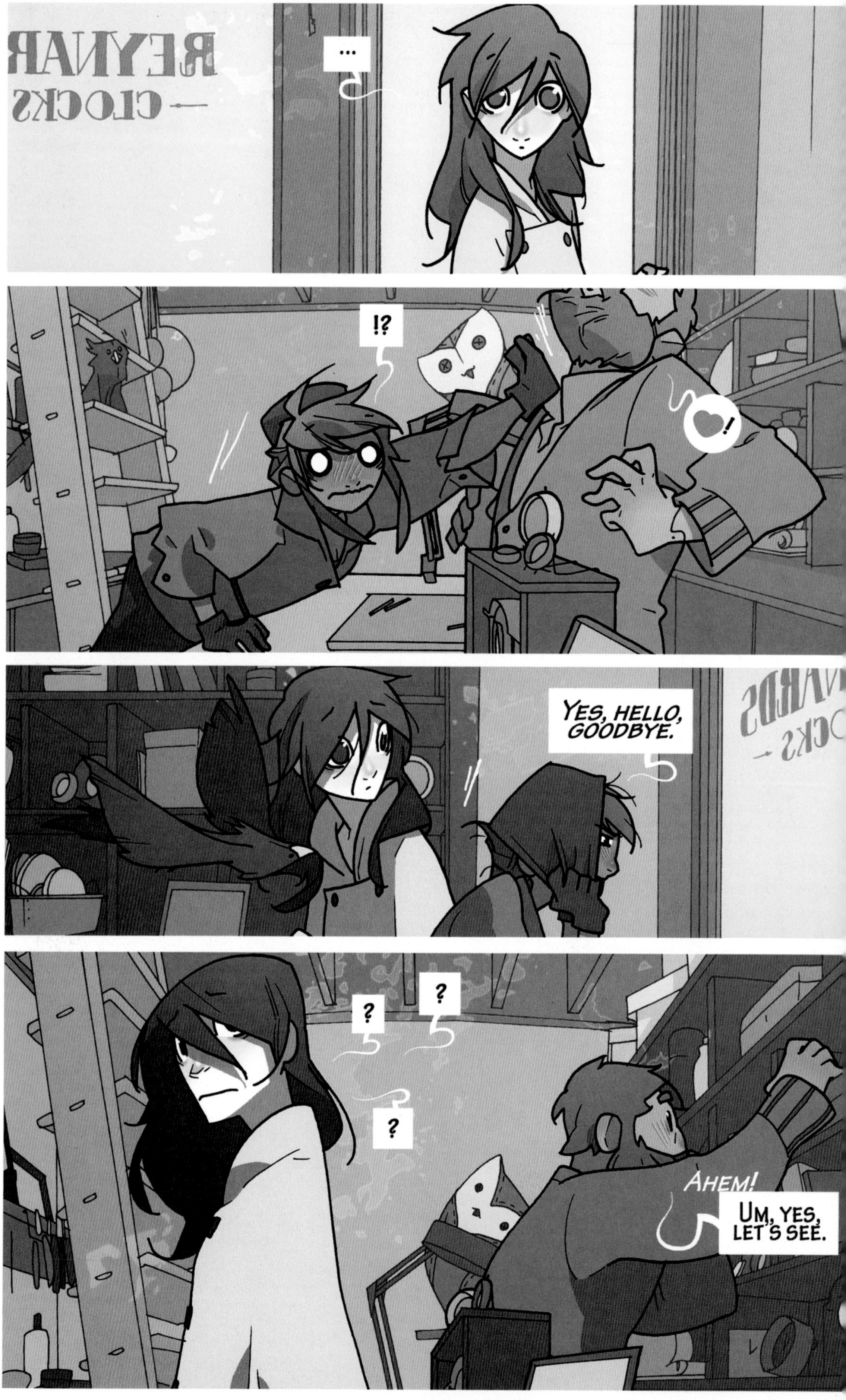
...
!?
!
YES, HELLO, GOODBYE.
?
?
?
AHEM!
UM, YES, LET'S SEE.

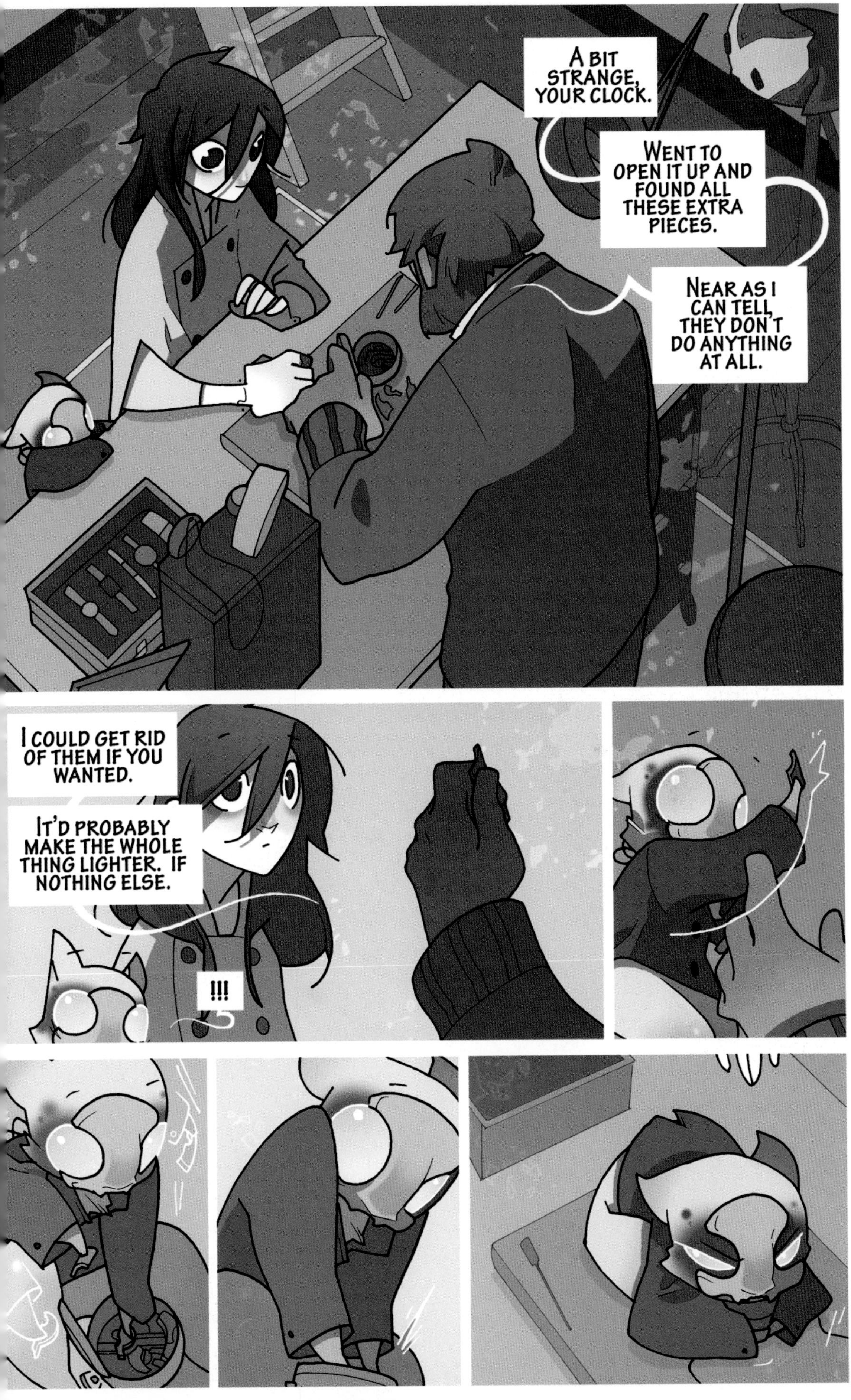
A BIT STRANGE, YOUR CLOCK.
WENT TO OPEN IT UP AND FOUND ALL THESE EXTRA PIECES.
NEAR AS I CAN TELL, THEY DON'T DO ANYTHING AT ALL.
I COULD GET RID OF THEM IF YOU WANTED.
IT'D PROBABLY MAKE THE WHOLE THING LIGHTER. IF NOTHING ELSE.
!!!

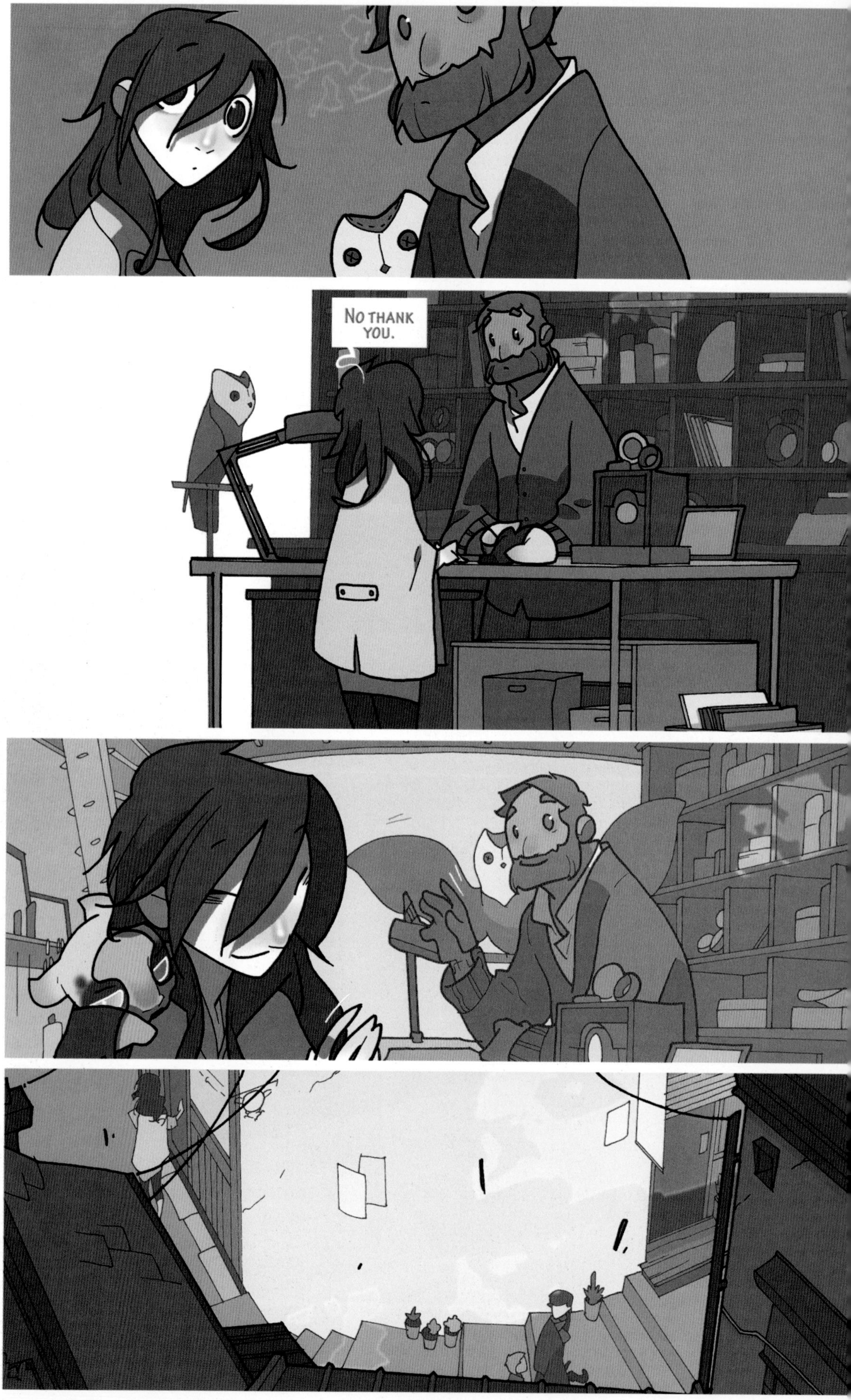
NO THANK YOU.

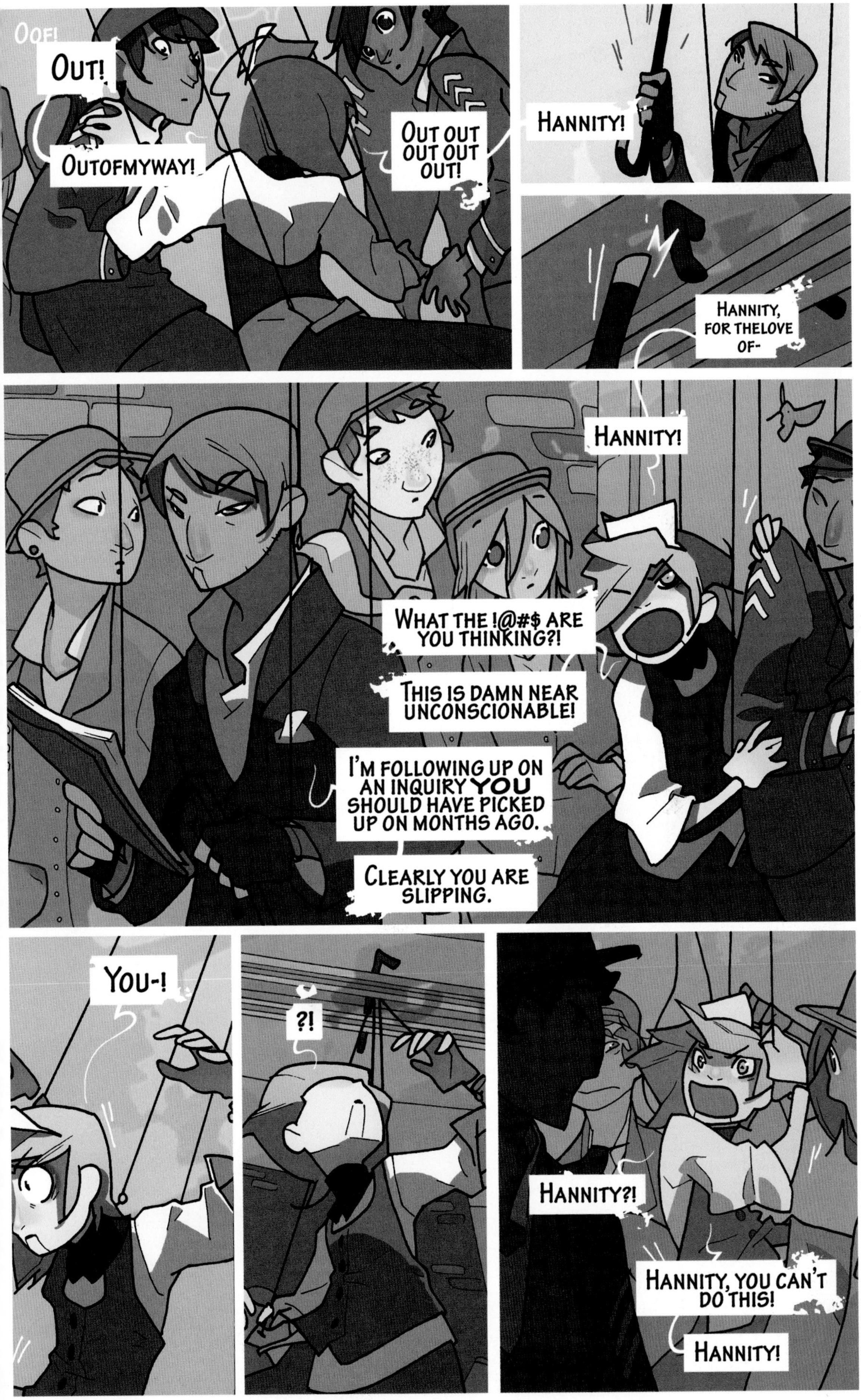
OOF!
OUT!
OUTOFMYWAY!
OUT OUT OUT OUT OUT!
HANNITY!
HANNITY, FOR THELOVE OF-
HANNITY!
WHAT THE !@#$ ARE YOU THINKING?!
THIS IS DAMN NEAR UNCONSCIONABLE!
I'M FOLLOWING UP ON AN INQUIRY YOU SHOULD HAVE PICKED UP ON MONTHS AGO.
CLEARLY YOU ARE SLIPPING.
YOU-!
?!
HANNITY?!
HANNITY, YOU CAN'T DO THIS!
HANNITY!

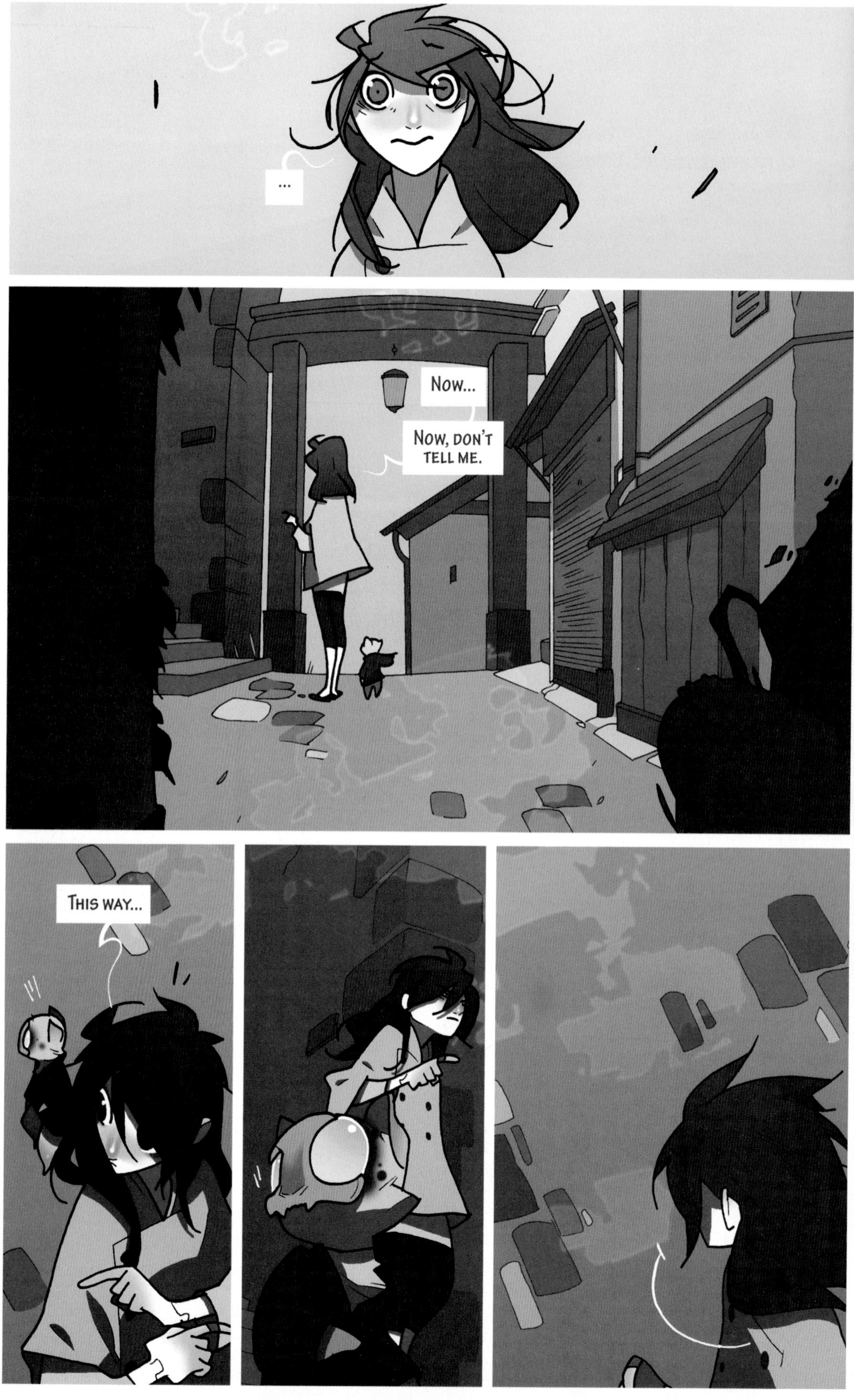
...
Now...
Now, don't tell me.
This way...

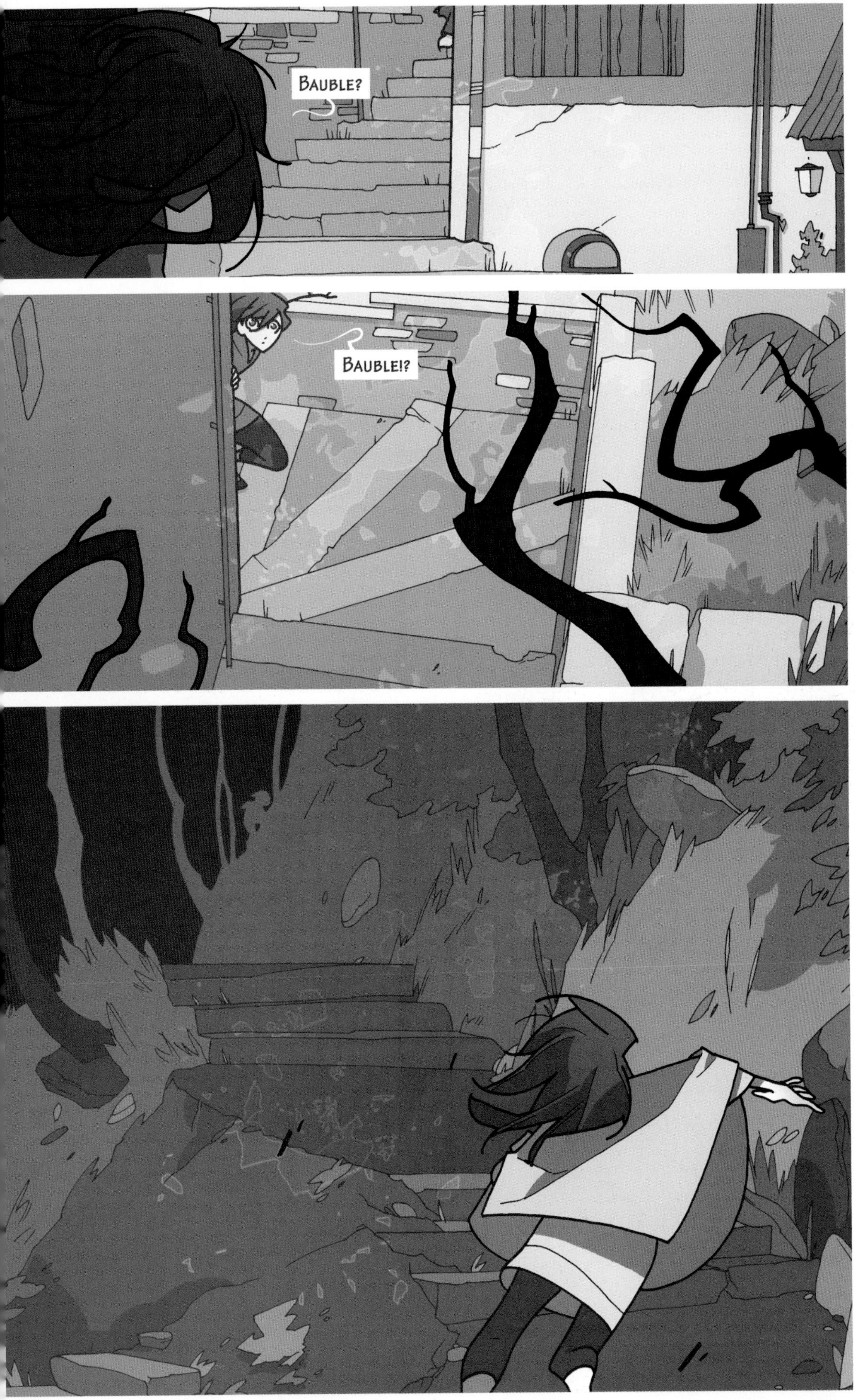
BAUBLE?
BAUBLE!?

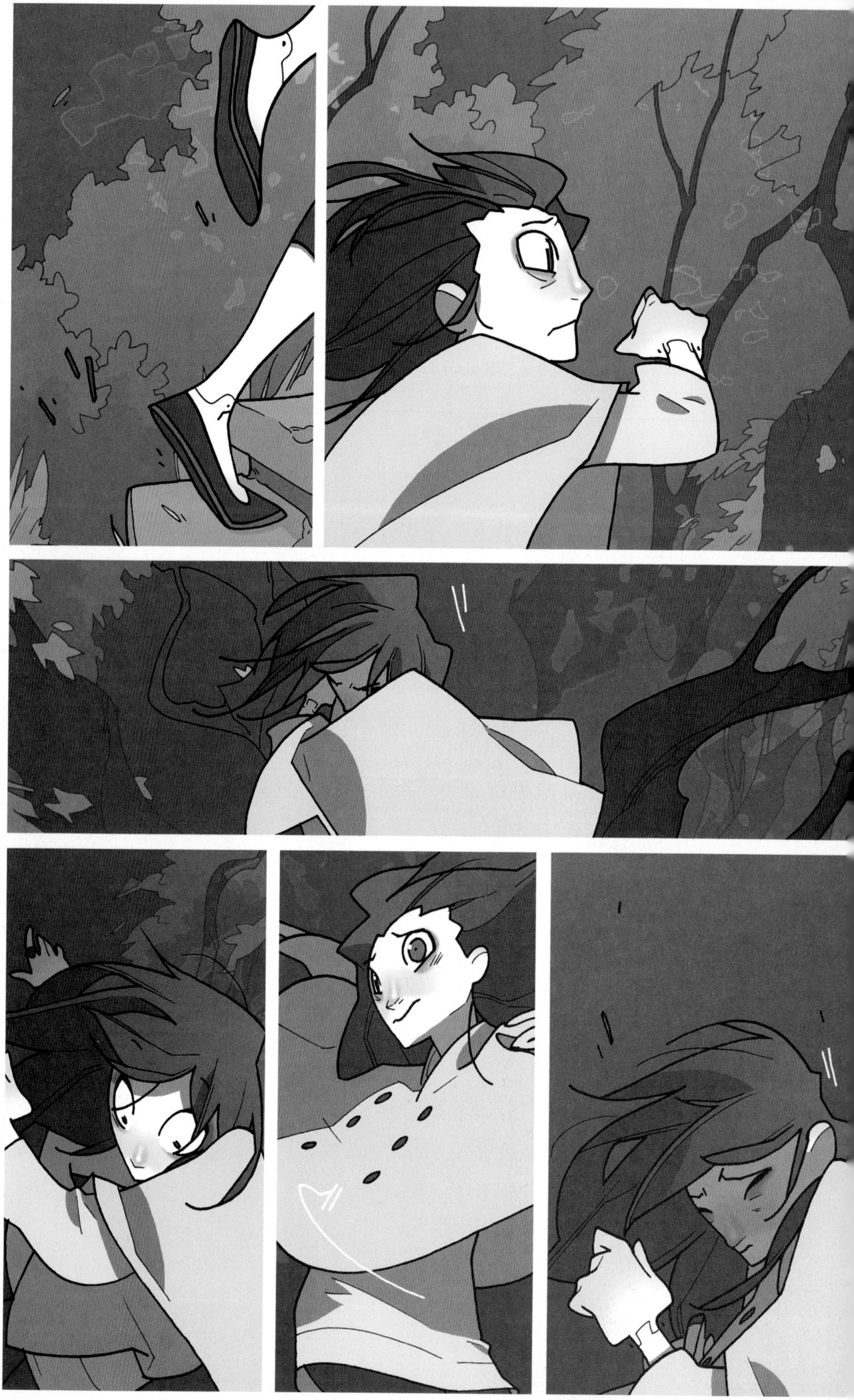

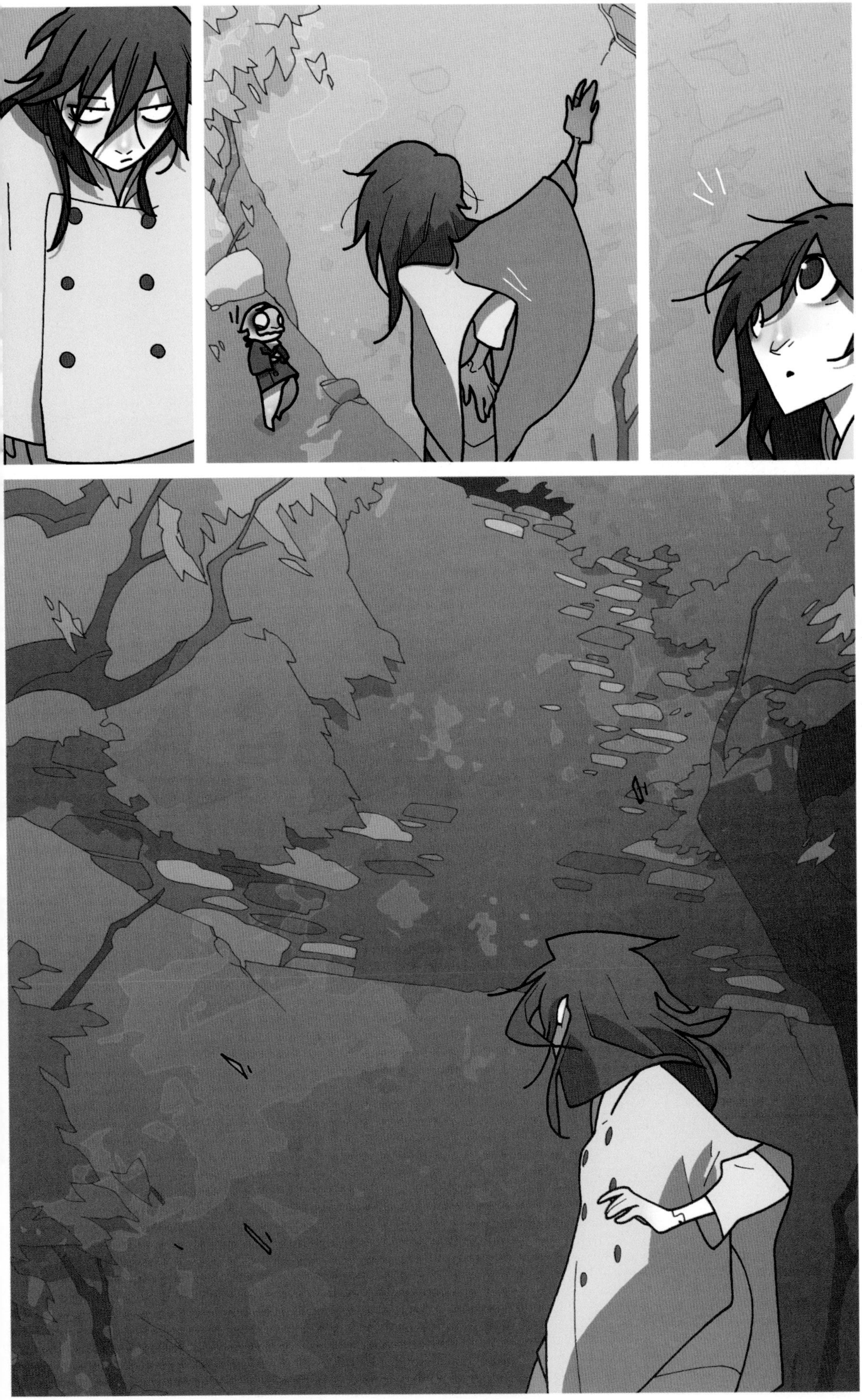

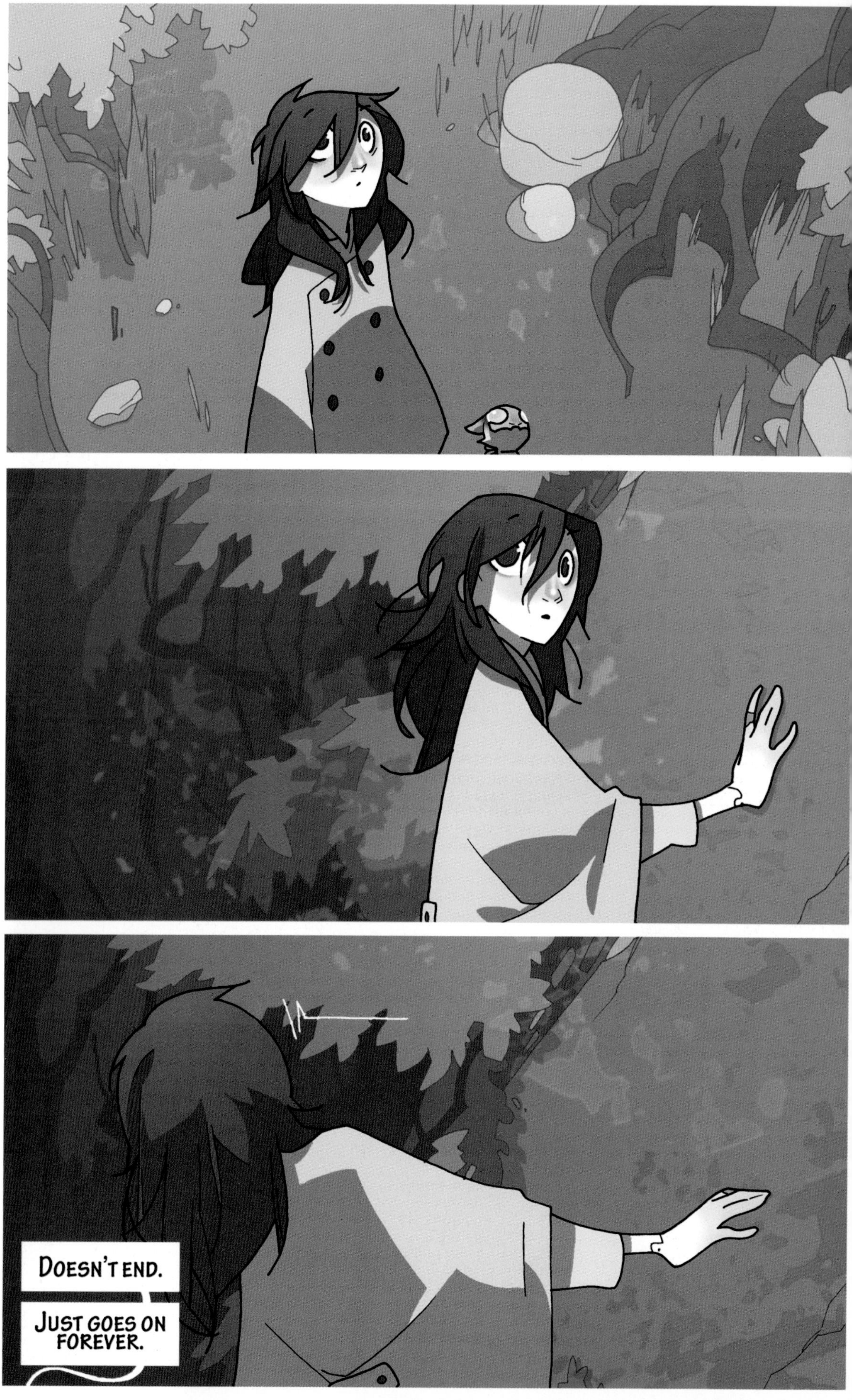
DOESN'T END.
JUST GOES ON FOREVER.

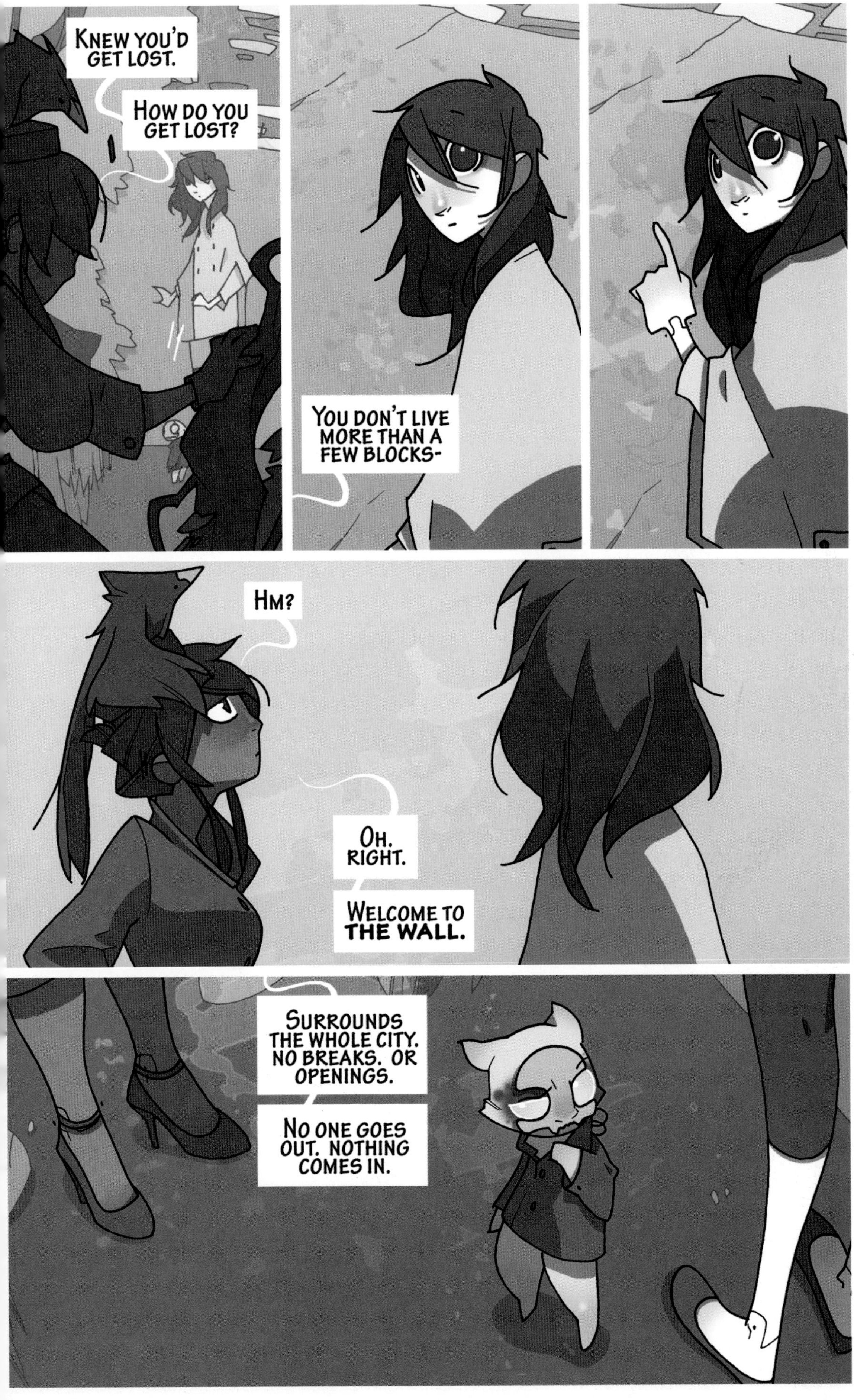

KNEW YOU'D GET LOST.
HOW DO YOU GET LOST?
YOU DON'T LIVE MORE THAN A FEW BLOCKS-
HM?
OH. RIGHT.
WELCOME TO THE WALL.
SURROUNDS THE WHOLE CITY. NO BREAKS. OR OPENINGS.
NO ONE GOES OUT. NOTHING COMES IN.

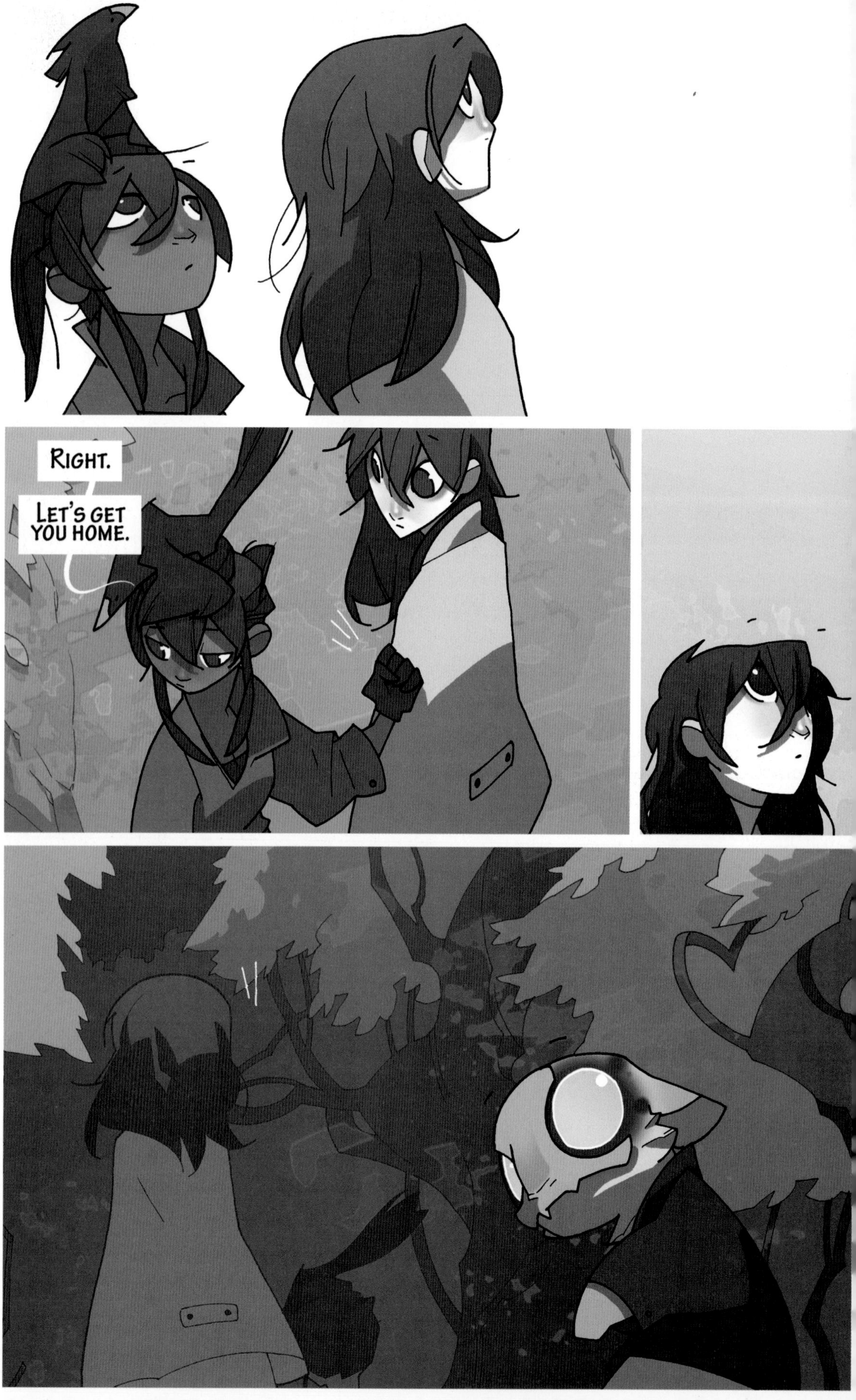
RIGHT.
LET'S GET YOU HOME.

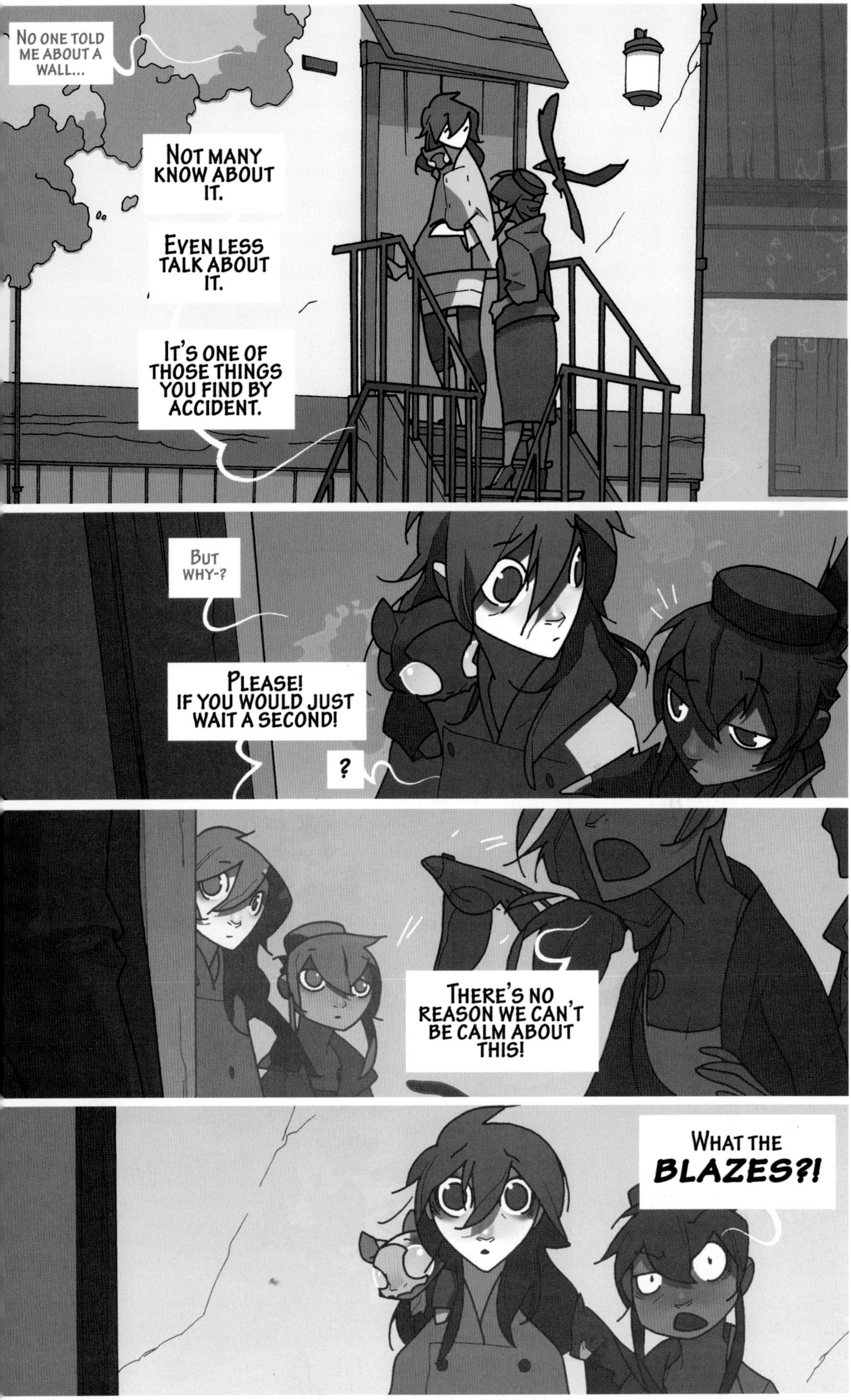
No one told me about a wall...
Not many know about it.
Even less talk about it.
It's one of those things you find by accident.
But why-?
Please! If you would just wait a second!
?
There's no reason we can't be calm about this!
What the BLAZES?!

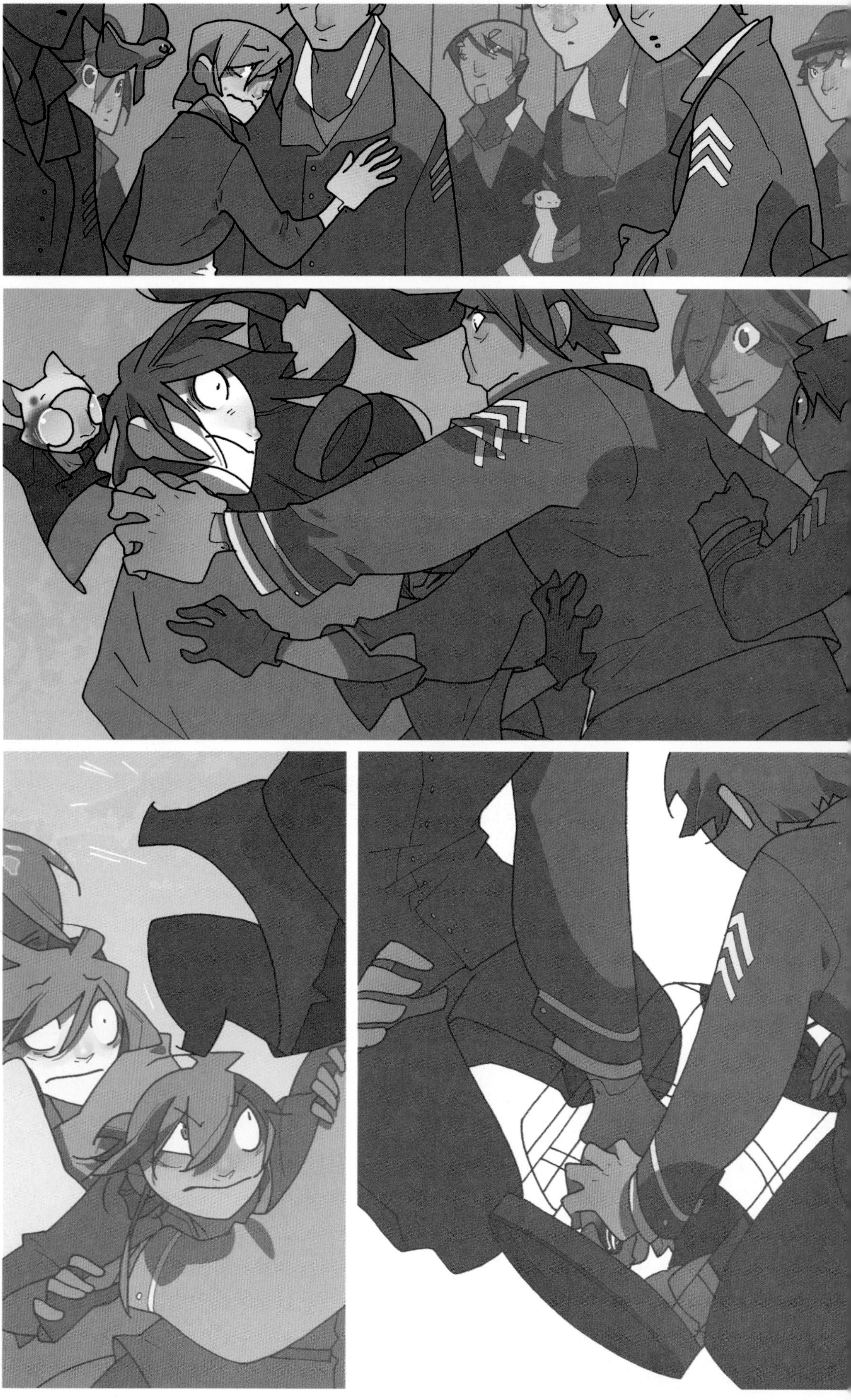

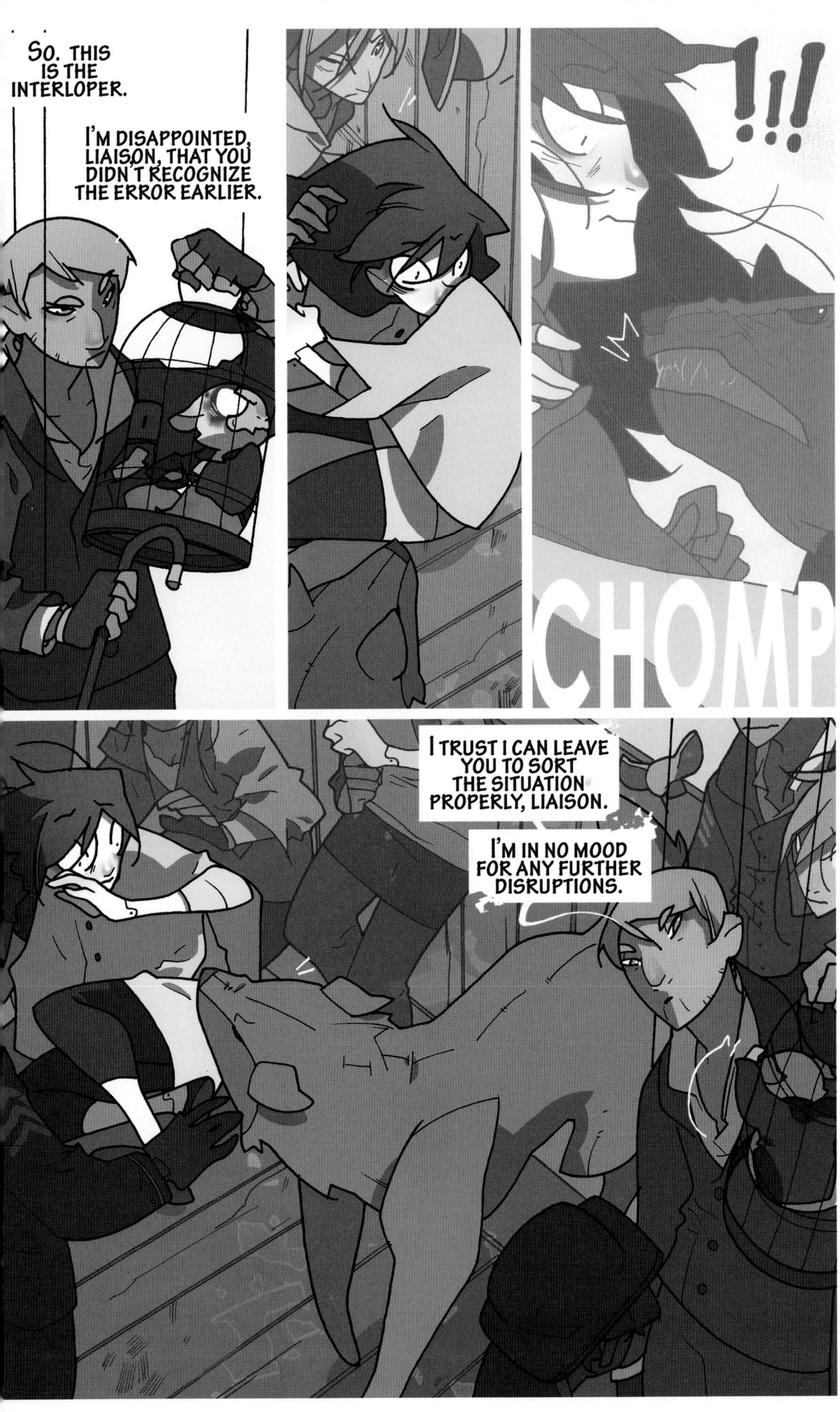

SO. THIS IS THE INTERLOPER.
I'M DISAPPOINTED, LIAISON, THAT YOU DIDN'T RECOGNIZE THE ERROR EARLIER.
!!!
CHOMP
I TRUST I CAN LEAVE YOU TO SORT THE SITUATION PROPERLY, LIAISON.
I'M IN NO MOOD FOR ANY FURTHER DISRUPTIONS.

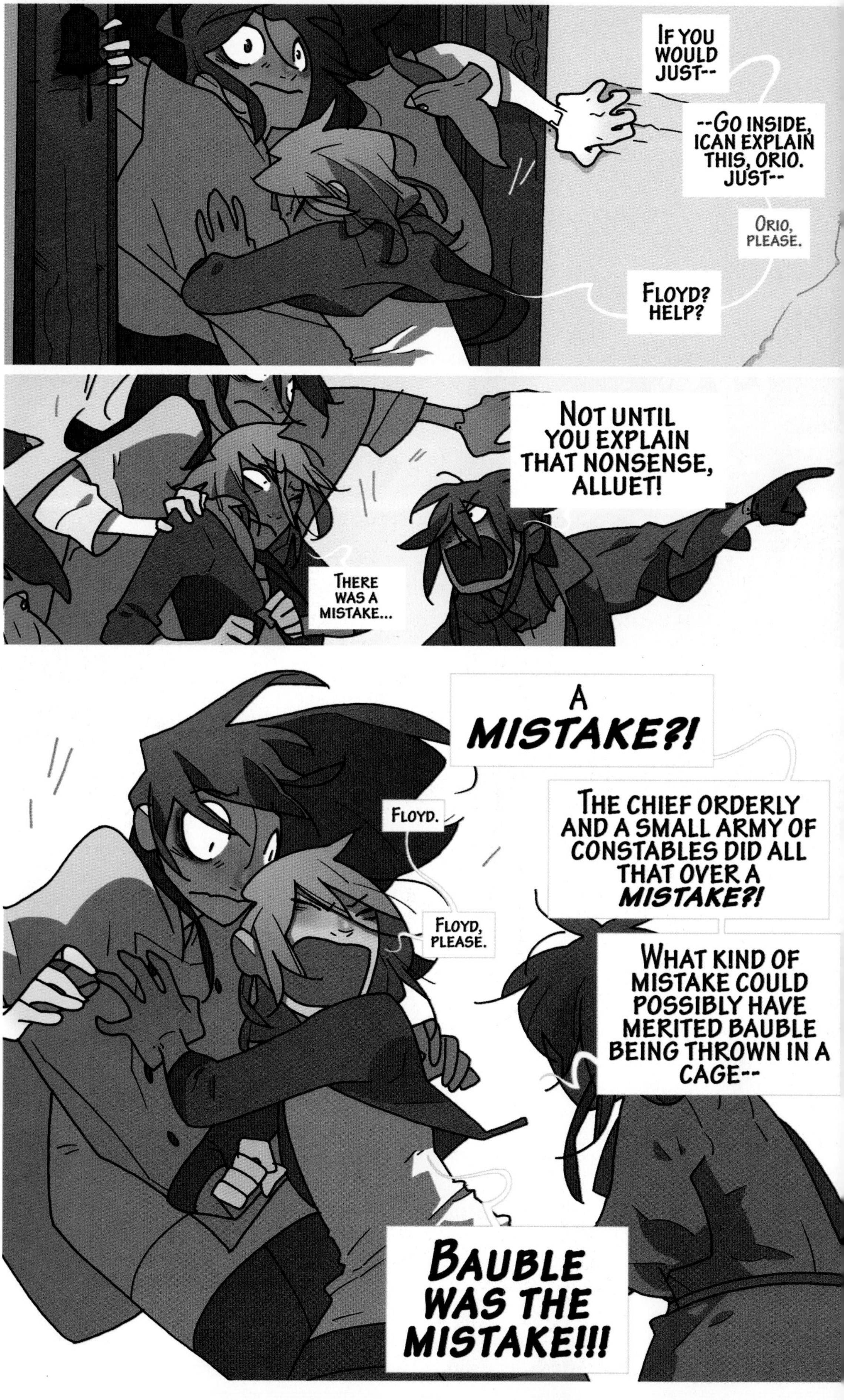

If you would just--
--Go inside, ICAN explain this, Orio. Just--
Orio, please.
Floyd? Help?
Not until you explain that nonsense, Alluet!
There was a mistake...
A MISTAKE?!
Floyd.
The chief orderly and a small army of constables did all that over a MISTAKE?!
Floyd, please.
What kind of mistake could possibly have merited Bauble being thrown in a cage--
Bauble was the mistake!!!

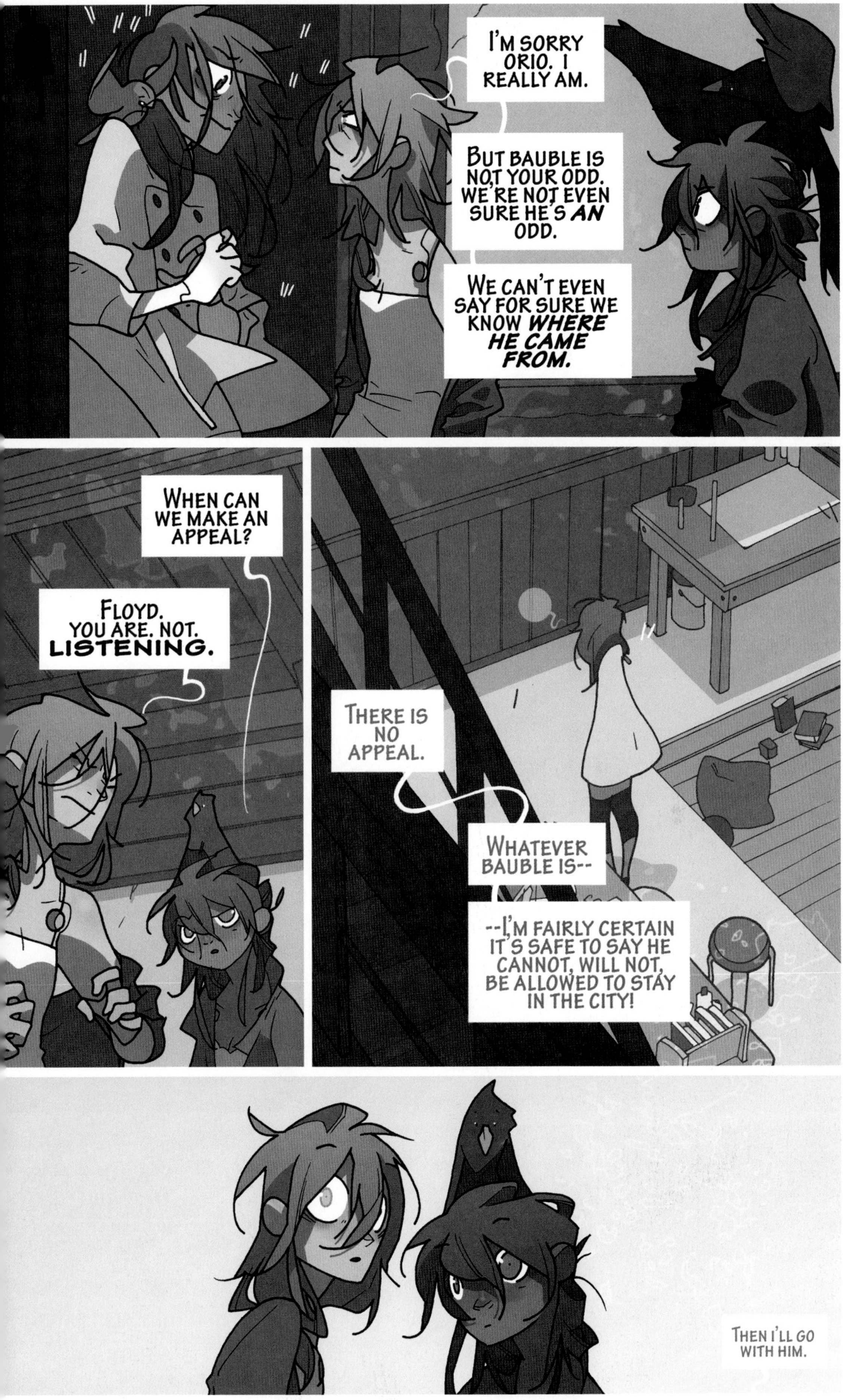
I'M SORRY ORIO. I REALLY AM.
BUT BAUBLE IS NOT YOUR ODD. WE'RE NOT EVEN SURE HE'S *AN* ODD.
WE CAN'T EVEN SAY FOR SURE WE KNOW ***WHERE HE CAME FROM.***
WHEN CAN WE MAKE AN APPEAL?
FLOYD. YOU ARE. NOT. **LISTENING.**
THERE IS NO APPEAL.
WHATEVER BAUBLE IS--
--I'M FAIRLY CERTAIN IT'S SAFE TO SAY HE CANNOT, WILL NOT, BE ALLOWED TO STAY IN THE CITY!
THEN I'LL GO WITH HIM.

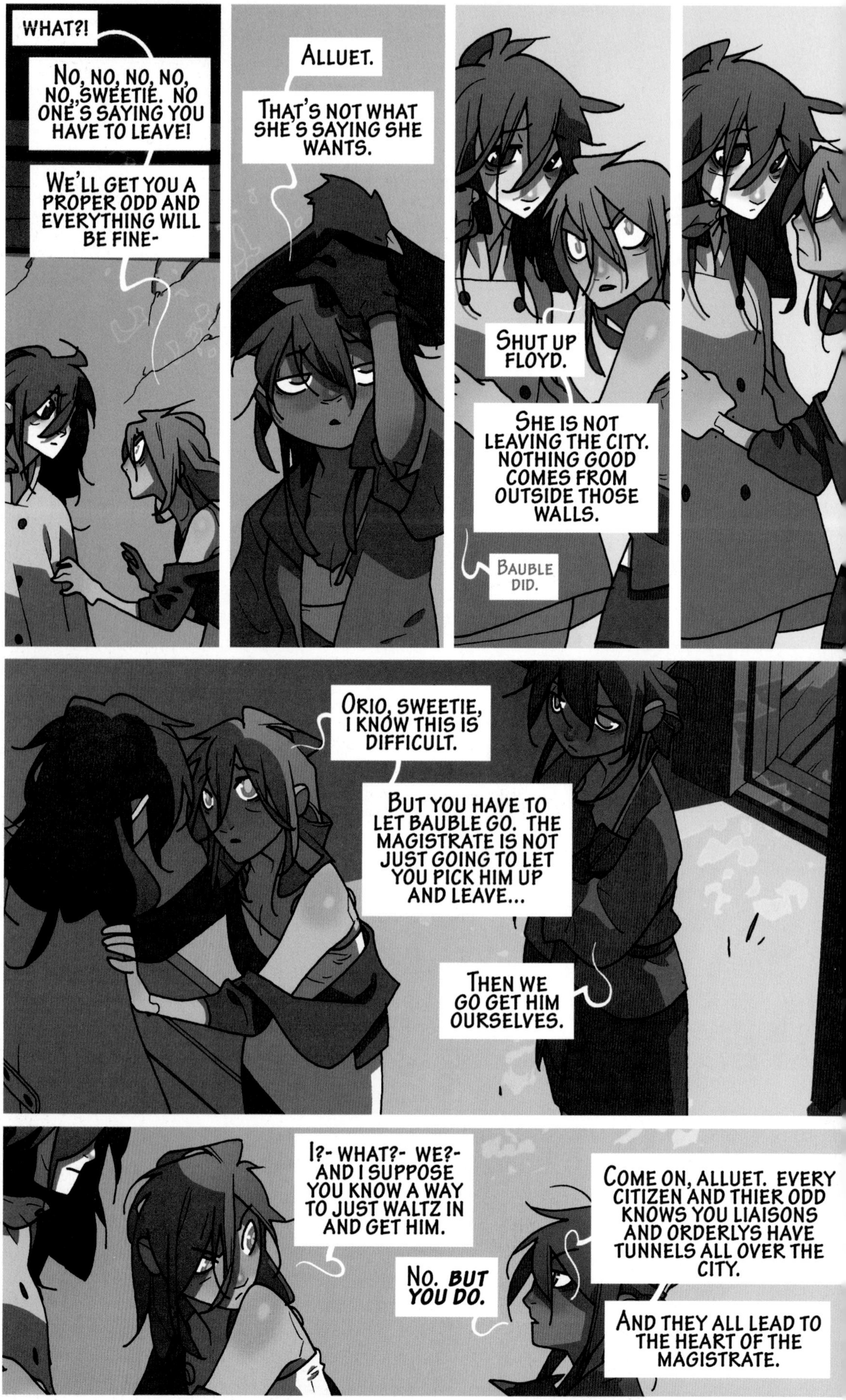
WHAT?!
NO, NO, NO, NO, NO,,SWEETIE. NO ONE'S SAYING YOU HAVE TO LEAVE!
WE'LL GET YOU A PROPER ODD AND EVERYTHING WILL BE FINE-
ALLUET.
THAT'S NOT WHAT SHE'S SAYING SHE WANTS.
SHUT UP FLOYD.
SHE IS NOT LEAVING THE CITY. NOTHING GOOD COMES FROM OUTSIDE THOSE WALLS.
BAUBLE DID.
ORIO, SWEETIE, I KNOW THIS IS DIFFICULT.
BUT YOU HAVE TO LET BAUBLE GO. THE MAGISTRATE IS NOT JUST GOING TO LET YOU PICK HIM UP AND LEAVE...
THEN WE GO GET HIM OURSELVES.
I?- WHAT?- WE?- AND I SUPPOSE YOU KNOW A WAY TO JUST WALTZ IN AND GET HIM.
NO. BUT YOU DO.
COME ON, ALLUET. EVERY CITIZEN AND THIER ODD KNOWS YOU LIAISONS AND ORDERLYS HAVE TUNNELS ALL OVER THE CITY.
AND THEY ALL LEAD TO THE HEART OF THE MAGISTRATE.

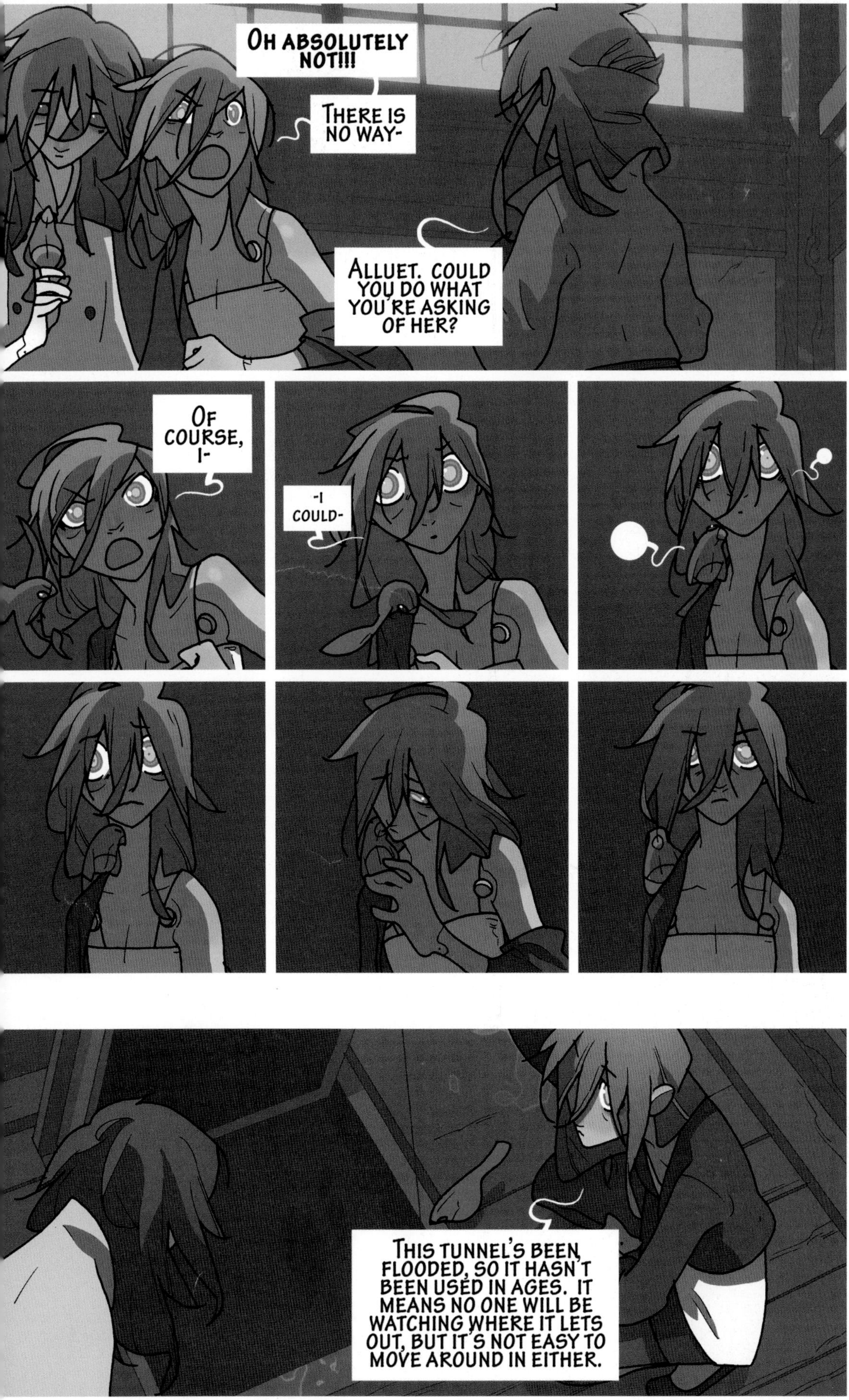
OH ABSOLUTELY NOT!!!
THERE IS NO WAY-
ALLUET. COULD YOU DO WHAT YOU'RE ASKING OF HER?
OF COURSE, I-
-I COULD-
THIS TUNNEL'S BEEN FLOODED, SO IT HASN'T BEEN USED IN AGES. IT MEANS NO ONE WILL BE WATCHING WHERE IT LETS OUT, BUT IT'S NOT EASY TO MOVE AROUND IN EITHER.

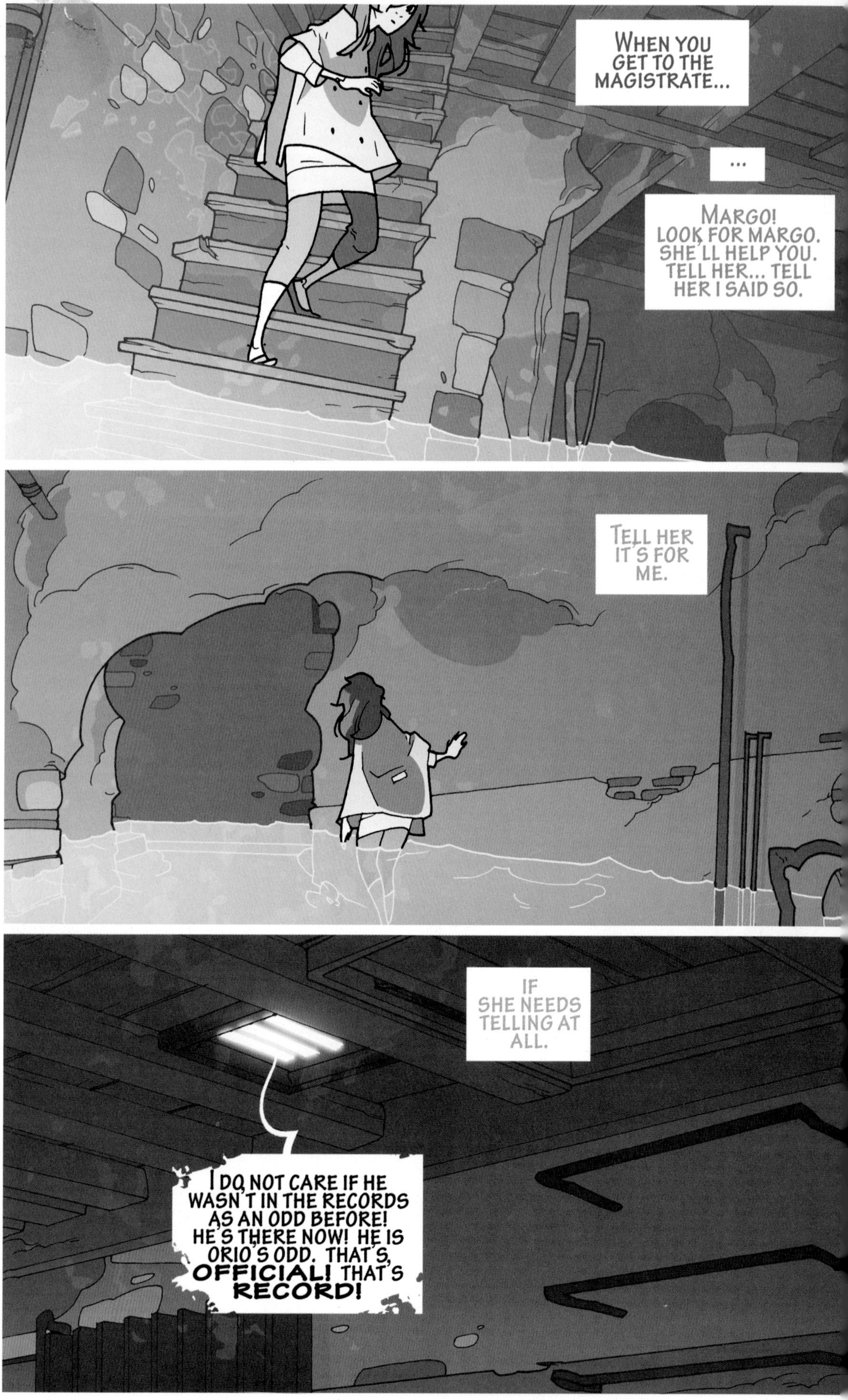
WHEN YOU GET TO THE MAGISTRATE...
...
MARGO! LOOK FOR MARGO. SHE'LL HELP YOU. TELL HER... TELL HER I SAID SO.
TELL HER IT'S FOR ME.
IF SHE NEEDS TELLING AT ALL.
I DO NOT CARE IF HE WASN'T IN THE RECORDS AS AN ODD BEFORE! HE'S THERE NOW! HE IS ORIO'S ODD. THAT'S OFFICIAL! THAT'S RECORD!

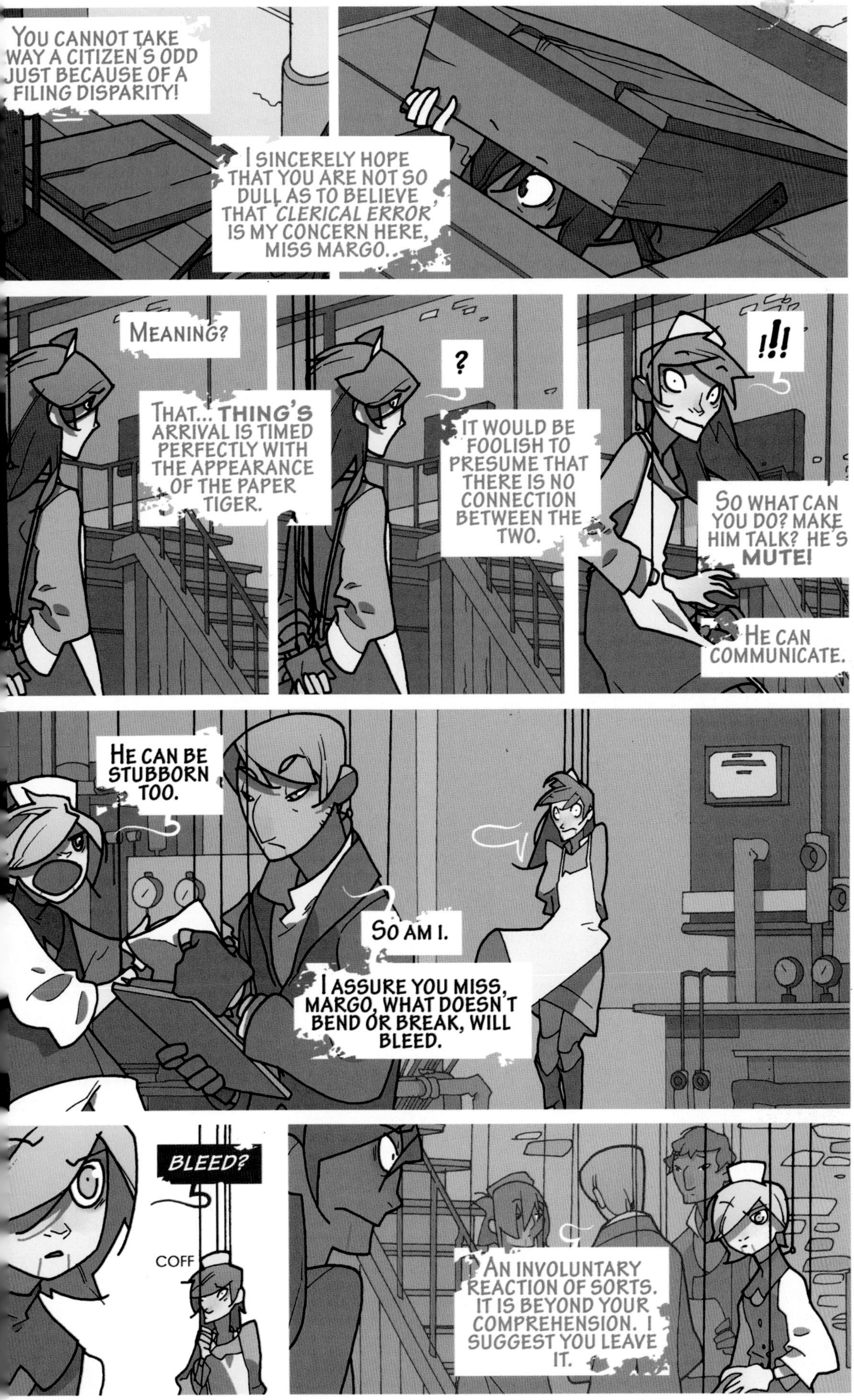

YOU CANNOT TAKE WAY A CITIZEN'S ODD JUST BECAUSE OF A FILING DISPARITY!
I SINCERELY HOPE THAT YOU ARE NOT SO DULL AS TO BELIEVE THAT 'CLERICAL ERROR' IS MY CONCERN HERE, MISS MARGO.
MEANING?
THAT... THING'S ARRIVAL IS TIMED PERFECTLY WITH THE APPEARANCE OF THE PAPER TIGER.
?
IT WOULD BE FOOLISH TO PRESUME THAT THERE IS NO CONNECTION BETWEEN THE TWO.
!!!
SO WHAT CAN YOU DO? MAKE HIM TALK? HE'S MUTE!
HE CAN COMMUNICATE.
HE CAN BE STUBBORN TOO.
SO AM I.
I ASSURE YOU MISS, MARGO, WHAT DOESN'T BEND OR BREAK, WILL BLEED.
BLEED?
COFF
AN INVOLUNTARY REACTION OF SORTS. IT IS BEYOND YOUR COMPREHENSION. I SUGGEST YOU LEAVE IT.

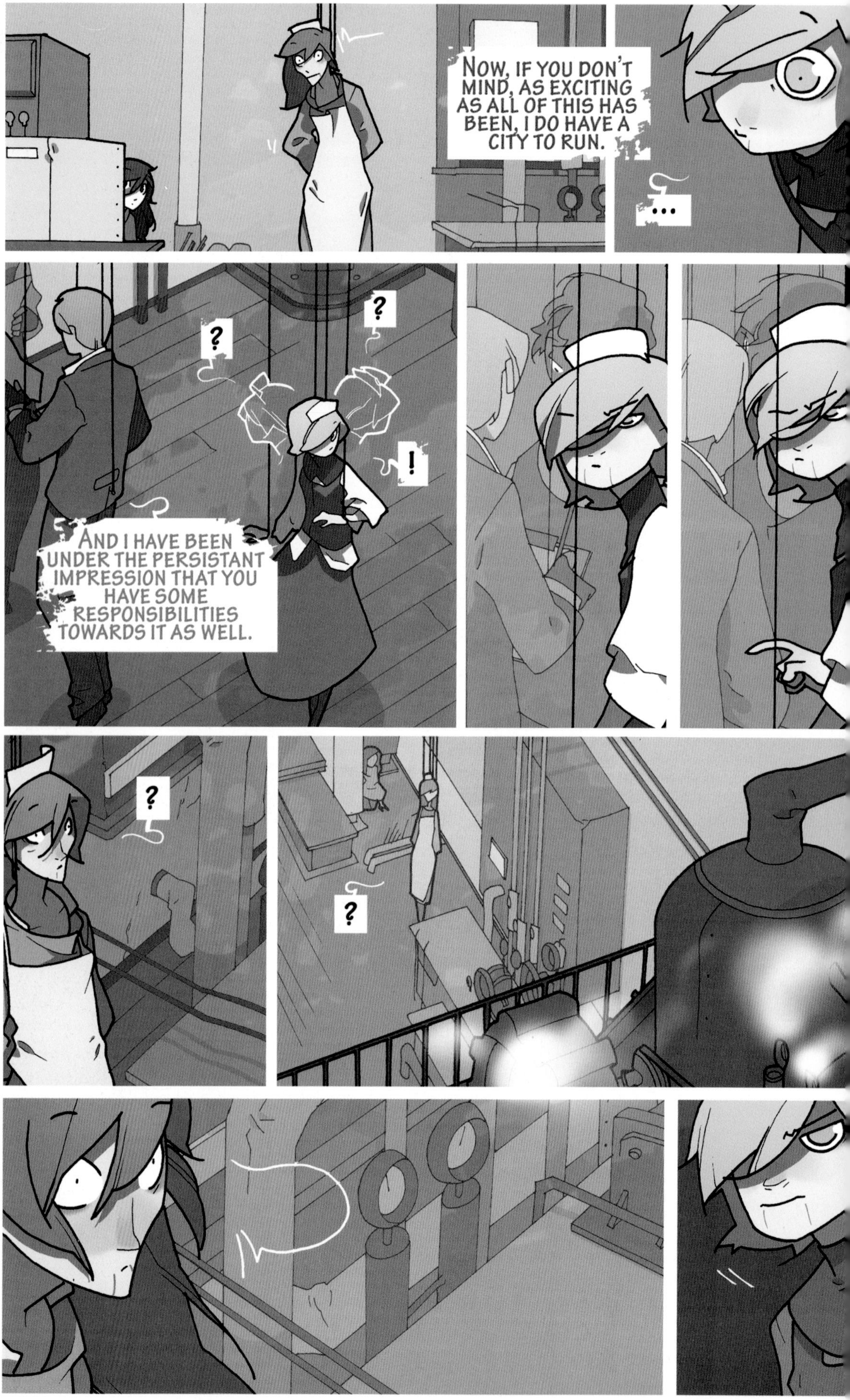
Now, if you don't mind, as exciting as all of this has been, I do have a city to run.
...
?
?
!
And I have been under the persistant impression that you have some responsibilities towards it as well.
?
?

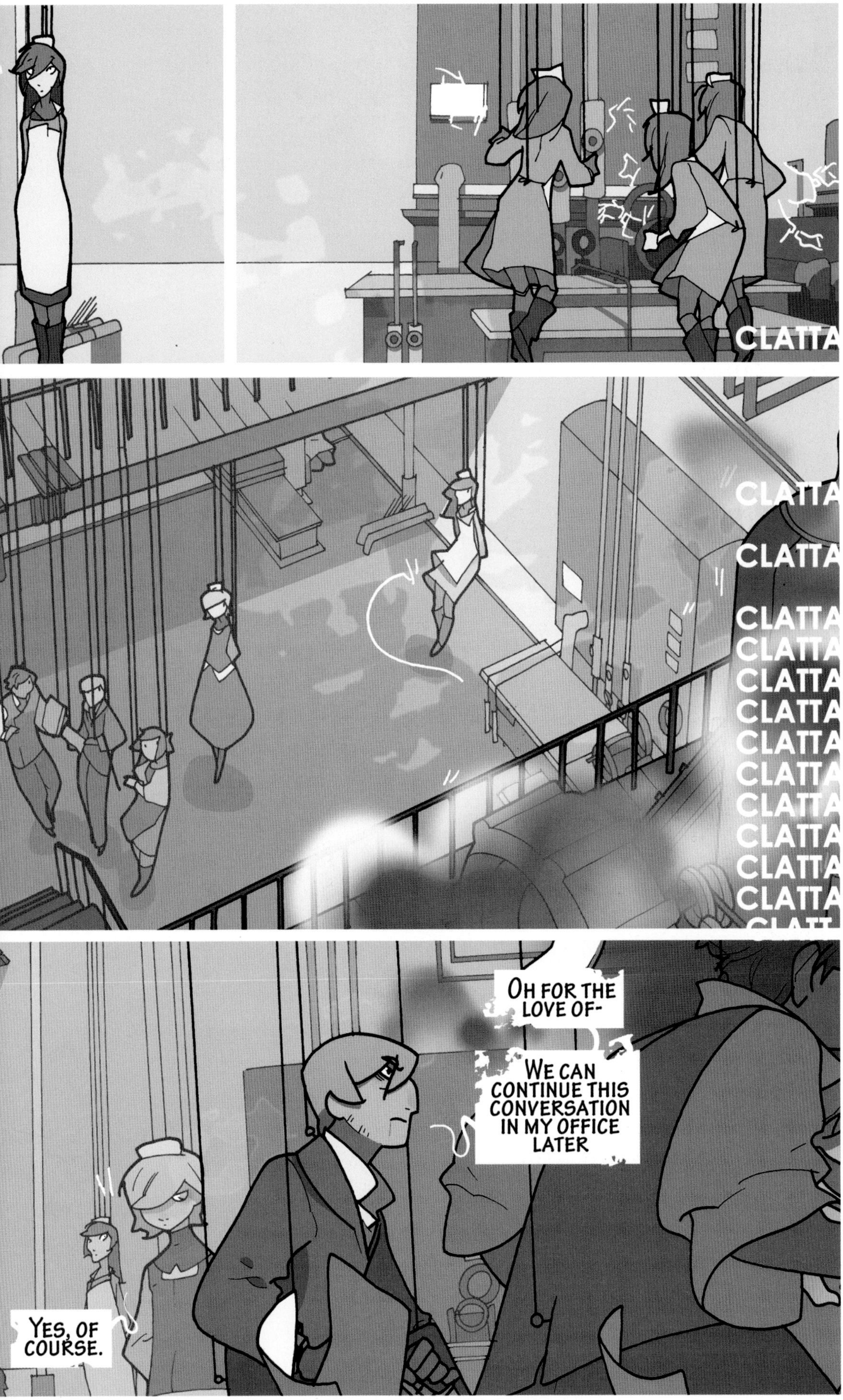
CLATTA
CLATTA
CLATTA
CLATTA
CLATTA
CLATTA
CLATTA
CLATTA
CLATTA
CLATTA
CLATTA
CLATTA
CLATTA
CLATTA
OH FOR THE LOVE OF-
WE CAN CONTINUE THIS CONVERSATION IN MY OFFICE LATER
YES, OF COURSE.

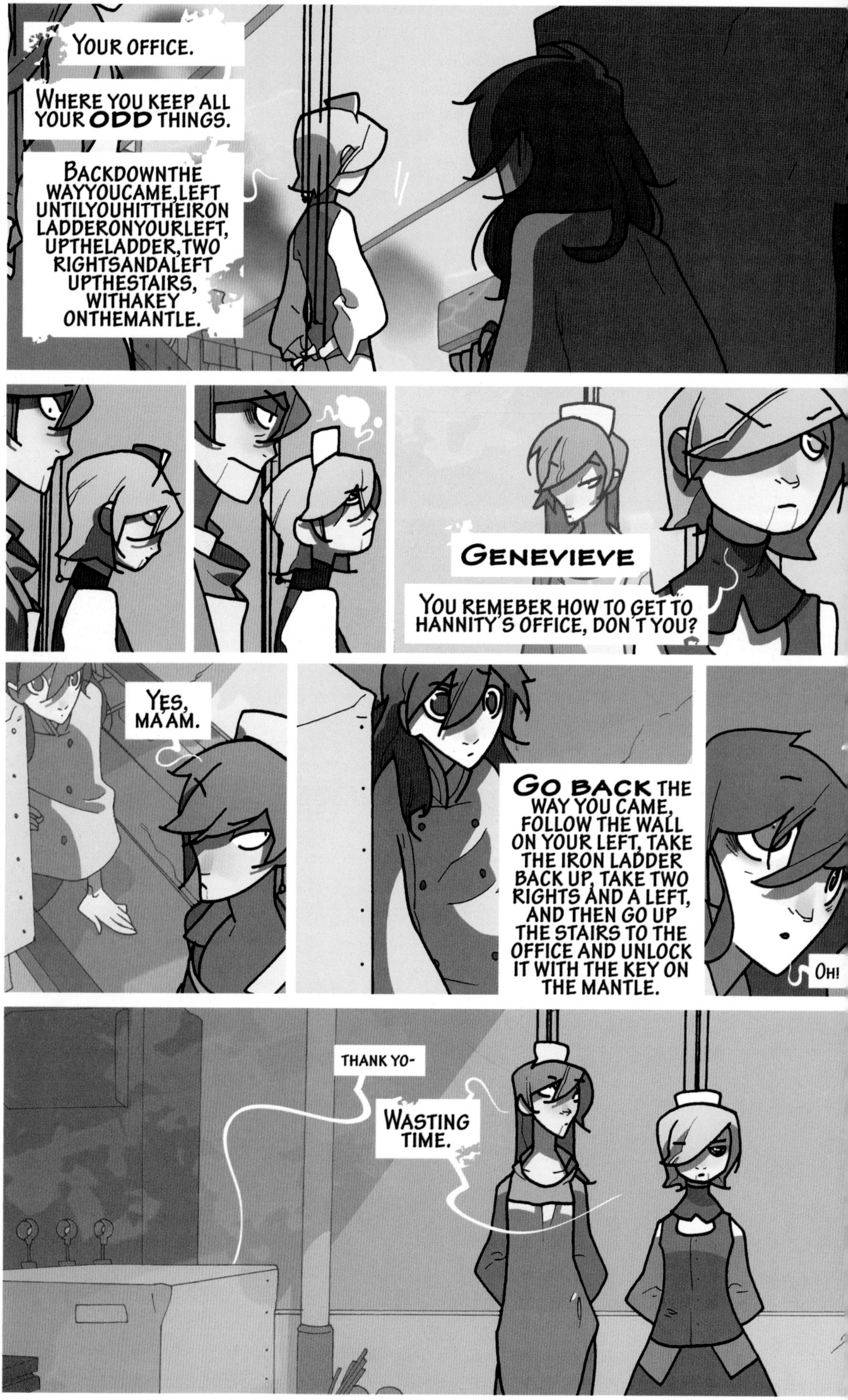

YOUR OFFICE.
WHERE YOU KEEP ALL YOUR ODD THINGS.
BACKDOWNTHE WAYYOUCAME,LEFT UNTILYOUHITTHEIRON LADDERONYOURLEFT, UPTHELADDER,TWO RIGHTSANDALEFT UPTHESTAIRS, WITHAKEY ONTHEMANTLE.
GENEVIEVE
YOU REMEBER HOW TO GET TO HANNITY'S OFFICE, DON'T YOU?
YES, MA'AM.
GO BACK THE WAY YOU CAME, FOLLOW THE WALL ON YOUR LEFT, TAKE THE IRON LADDER BACK UP, TAKE TWO RIGHTS AND A LEFT, AND THEN GO UP THE STAIRS TO THE OFFICE AND UNLOCK IT WITH THE KEY ON THE MANTLE.
OH!
THANK YO-
WASTING TIME.

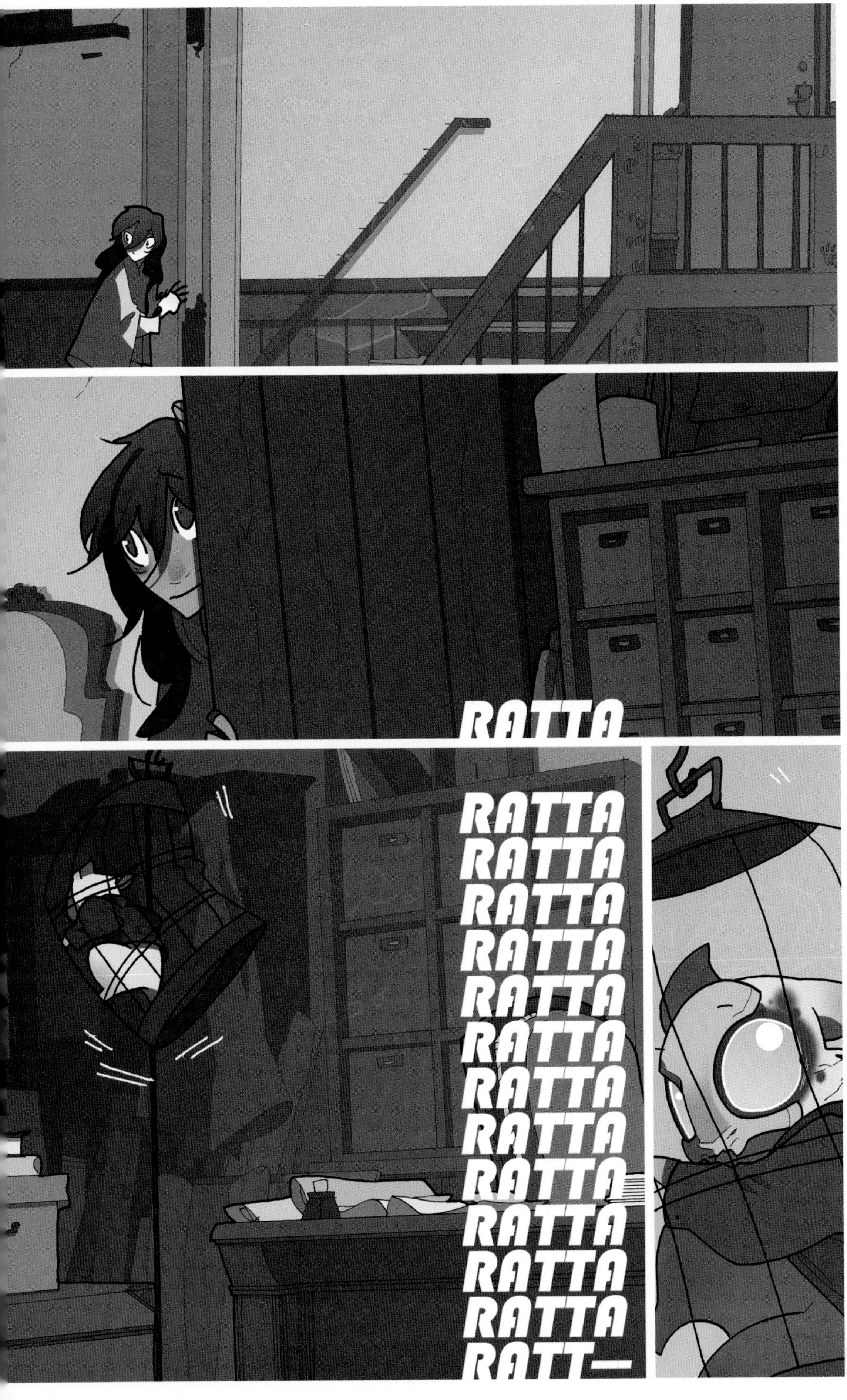
RATTA
RATTA
RATTA
RATTA
RATTA
RATTA
RATTA
RATTA
RATTA
RATTA
RATTA
RATTA
RATTA
RATT—

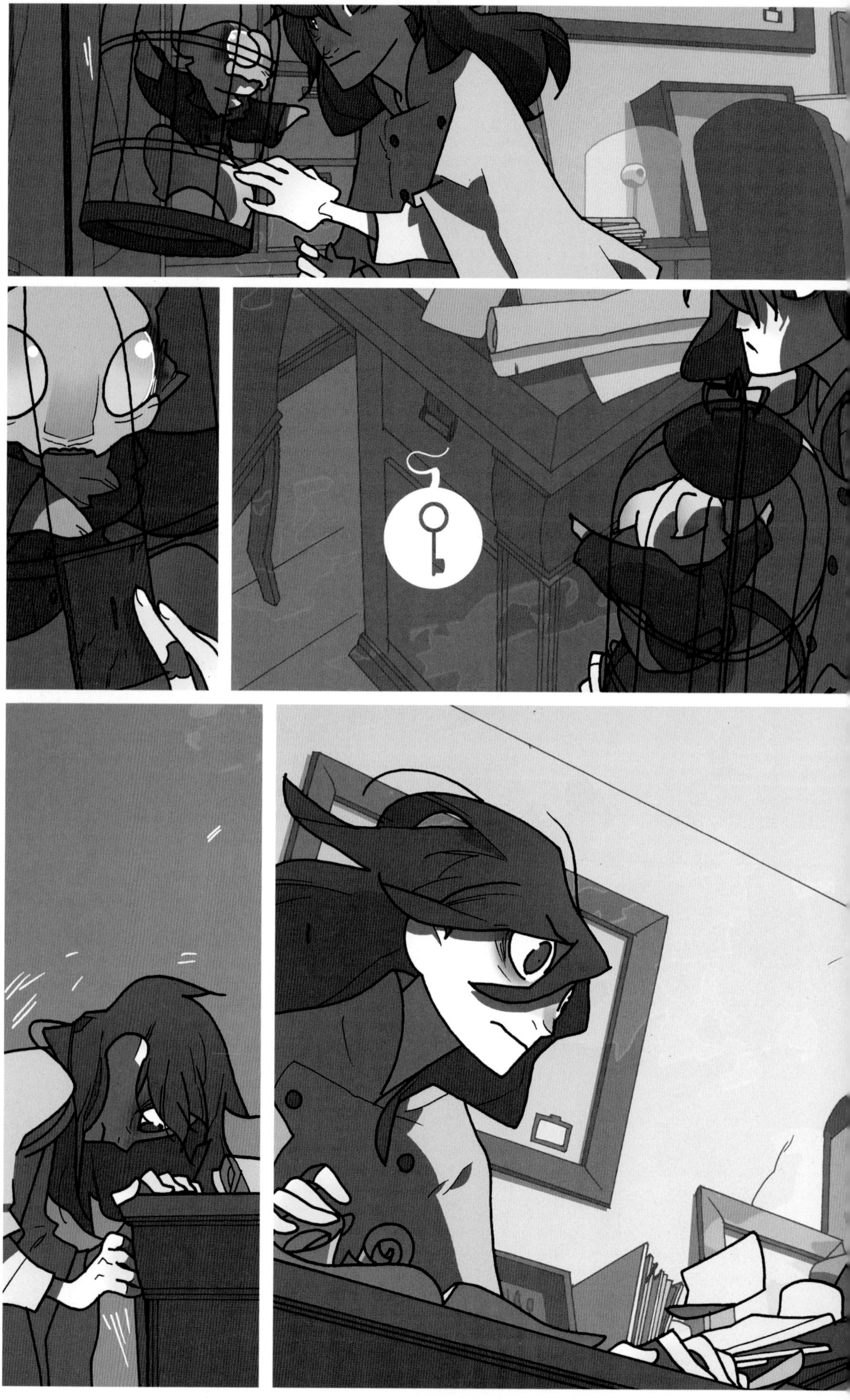

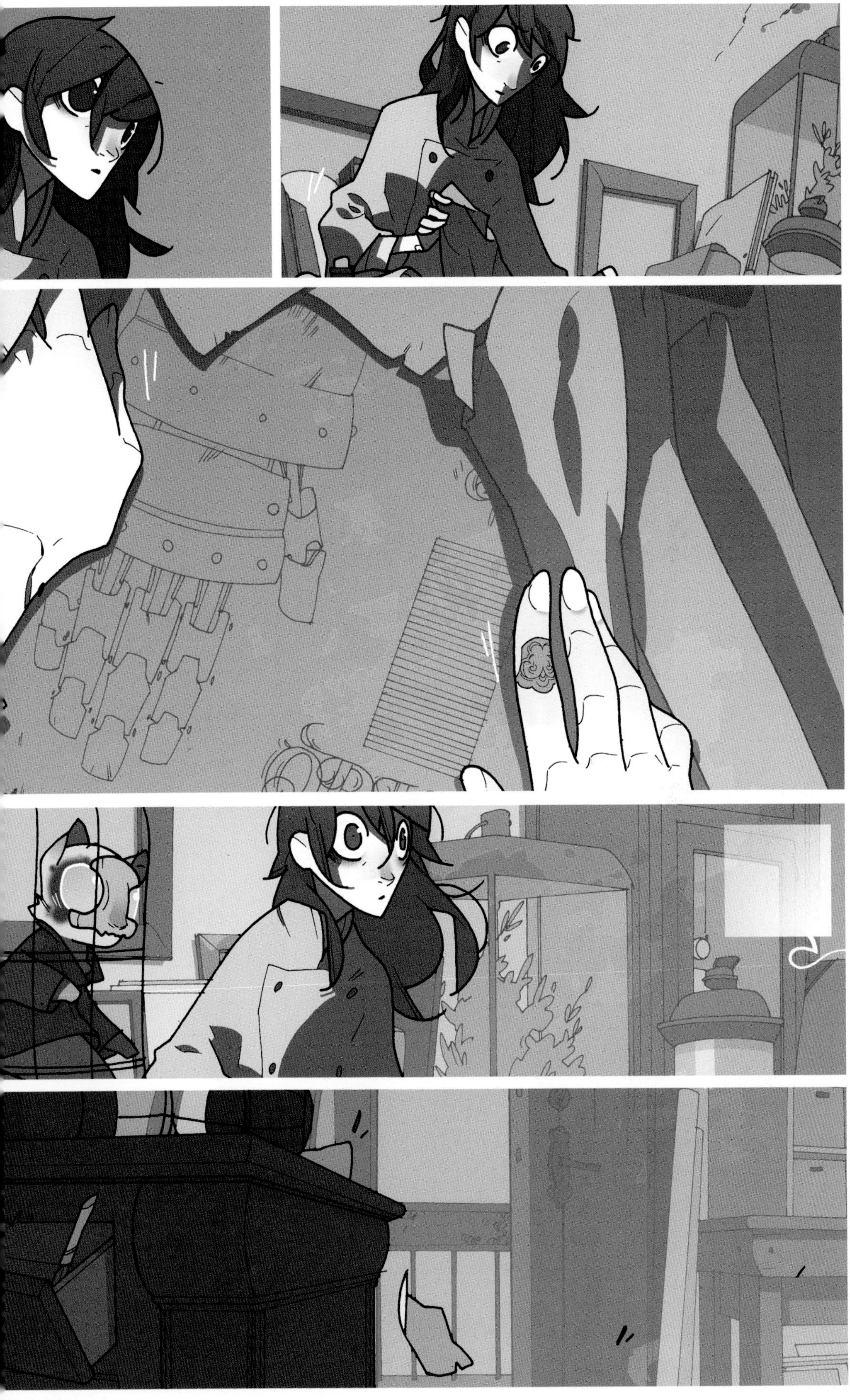

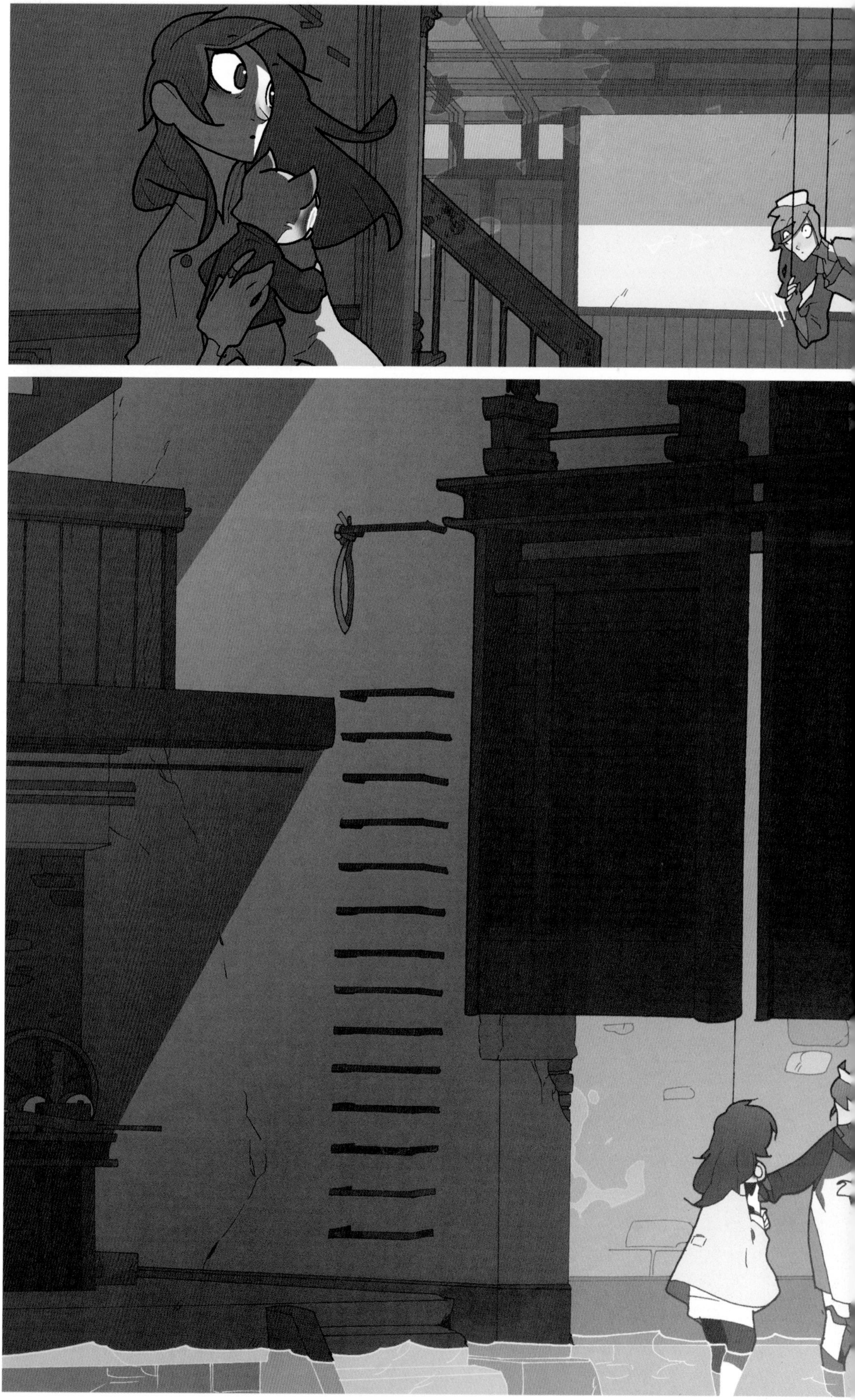

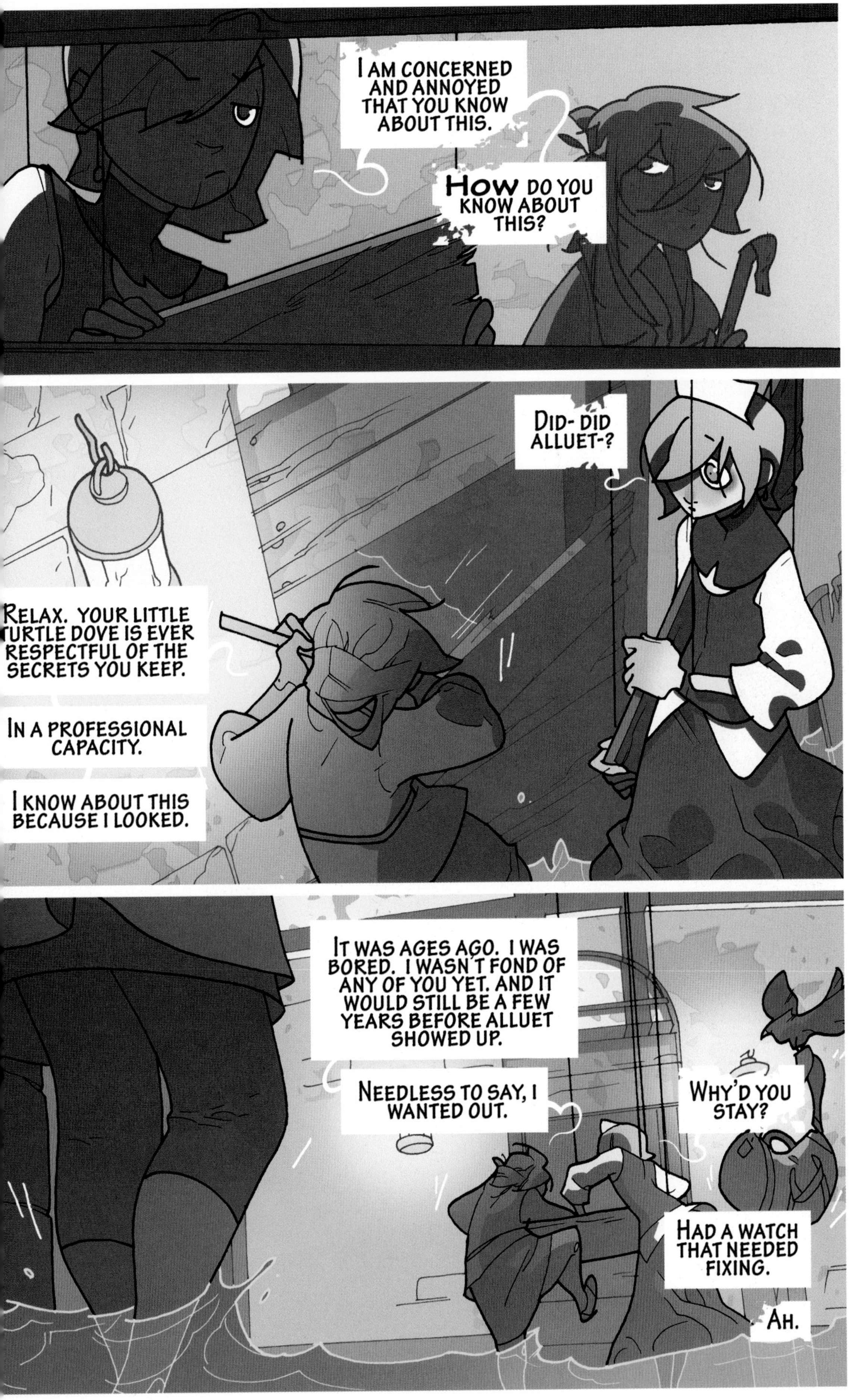
I AM CONCERNED AND ANNOYED THAT YOU KNOW ABOUT THIS.
HOW DO YOU KNOW ABOUT THIS?
DID- DID ALLUET-?
RELAX. YOUR LITTLE TURTLE DOVE IS EVER RESPECTFUL OF THE SECRETS YOU KEEP.
IN A PROFESSIONAL CAPACITY.
I KNOW ABOUT THIS BECAUSE I LOOKED.
IT WAS AGES AGO. I WAS BORED. I WASN'T FOND OF ANY OF YOU YET. AND IT WOULD STILL BE A FEW YEARS BEFORE ALLUET SHOWED UP.
NEEDLESS TO SAY, I WANTED OUT.
WHY'D YOU STAY?
HAD A WATCH THAT NEEDED FIXING.
AH.

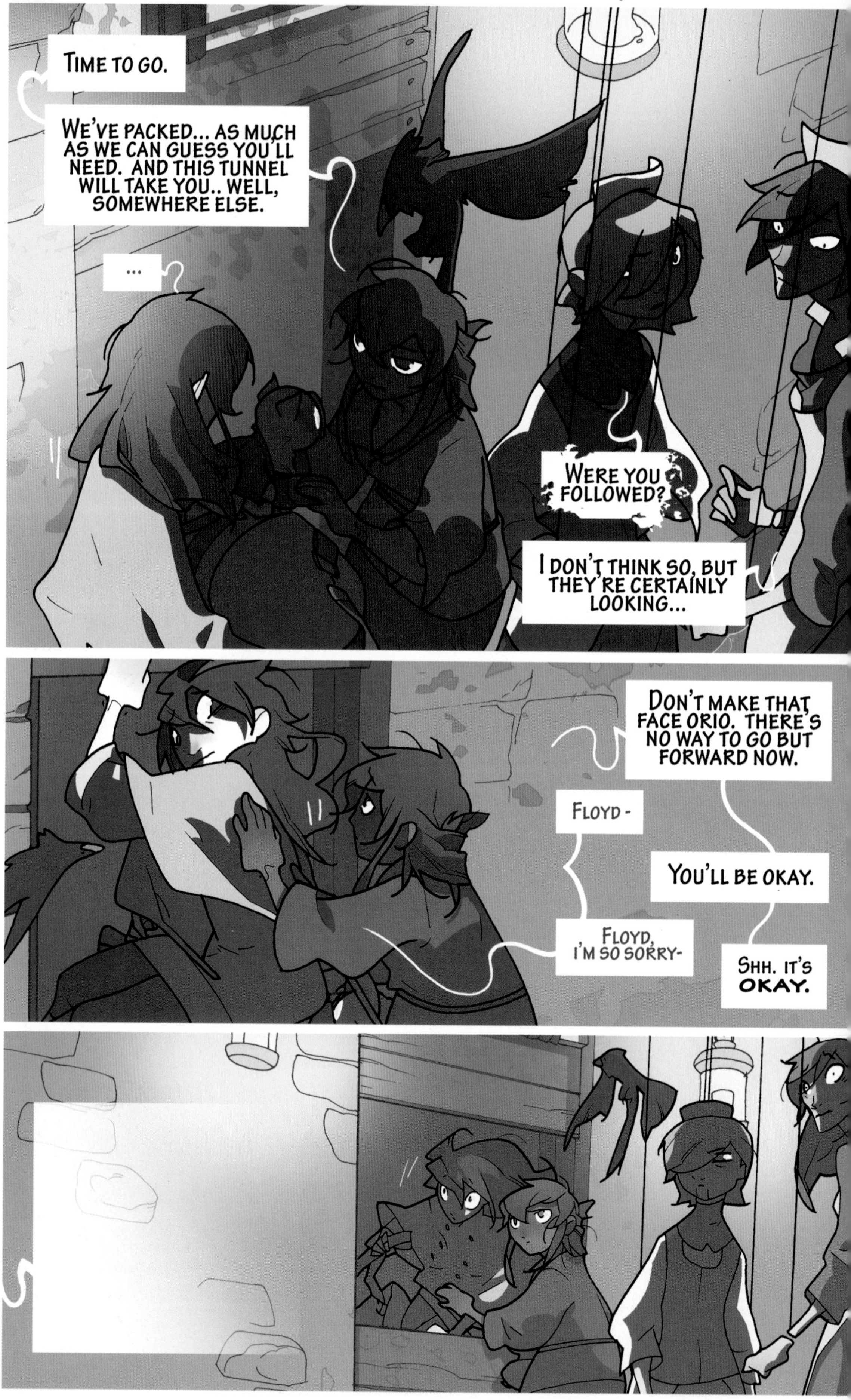
TIME TO GO.
WE'VE PACKED... AS MUCH AS WE CAN GUESS YOU'LL NEED. AND THIS TUNNEL WILL TAKE YOU.. WELL, SOMEWHERE ELSE.
...
WERE YOU FOLLOWED?
I DON'T THINK SO, BUT THEY'RE CERTAINLY LOOKING...
DON'T MAKE THAT FACE ORIO. THERE'S NO WAY TO GO BUT FORWARD NOW.
FLOYD -
YOU'LL BE OKAY.
FLOYD, I'M SO SORRY-
SHH. IT'S OKAY.

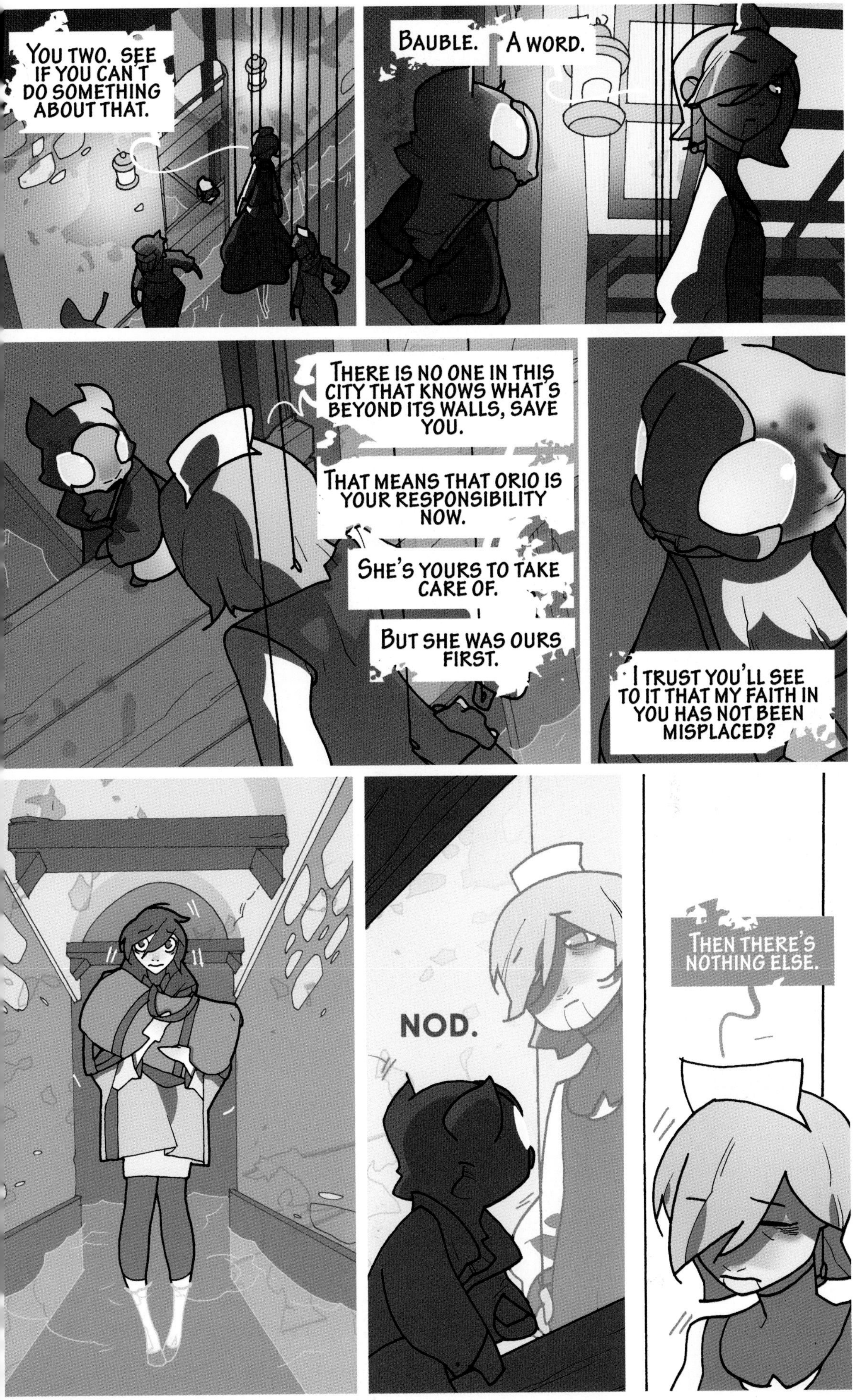

YOU TWO. SEE IF YOU CAN'T DO SOMETHING ABOUT THAT.
BAUBLE.
A WORD.
THERE IS NO ONE IN THIS CITY THAT KNOWS WHAT'S BEYOND ITS WALLS, SAVE YOU.
THAT MEANS THAT ORIO IS YOUR RESPONSIBILITY NOW.
SHE'S YOURS TO TAKE CARE OF.
BUT SHE WAS OURS FIRST.
I TRUST YOU'LL SEE TO IT THAT MY FAITH IN YOU HAS NOT BEEN MISPLACED?
NOD.
THEN THERE'S NOTHING ELSE.

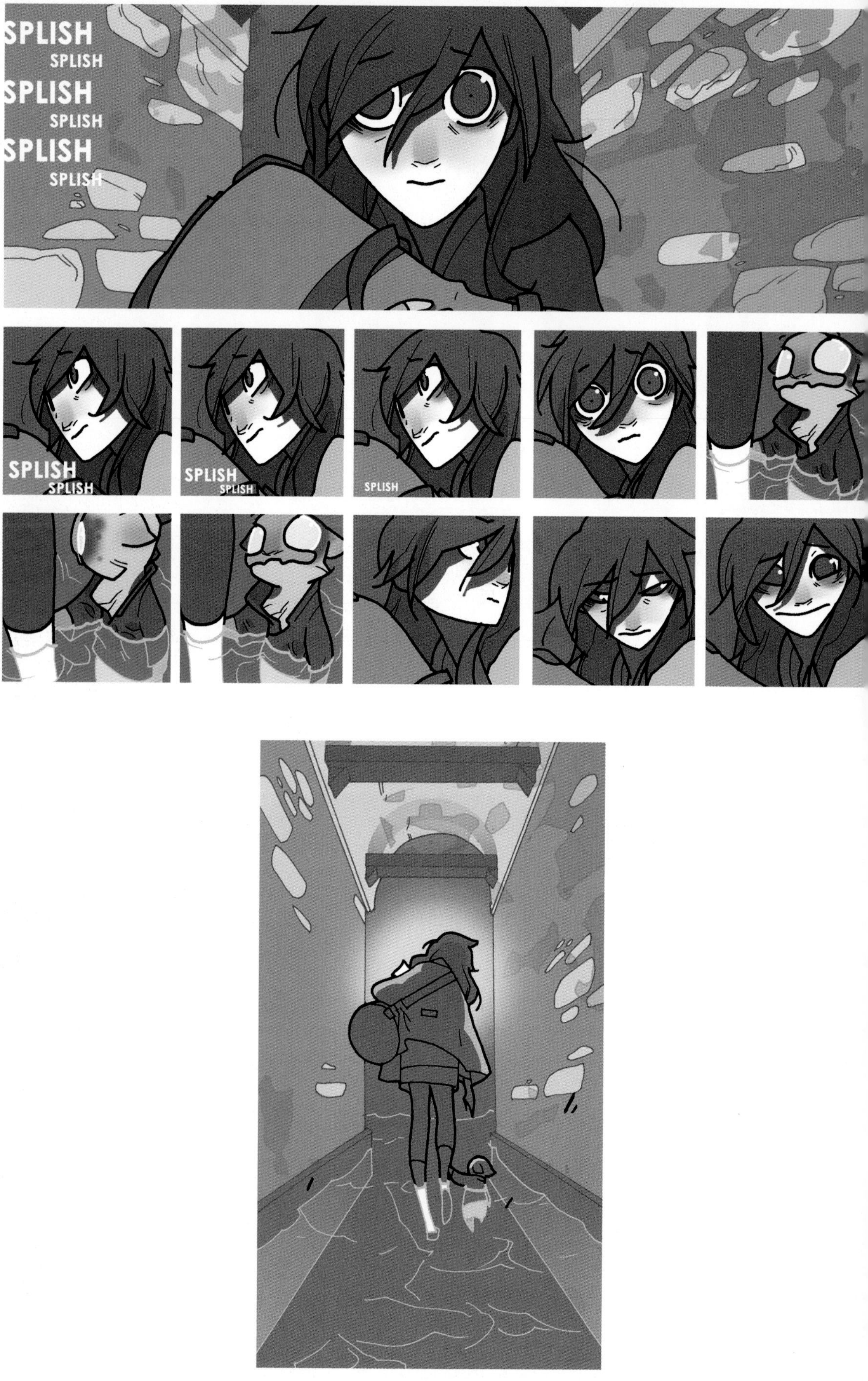
SPLISH
SPLISH
SPLISH
SPLISH
SPLISH
SPLISH
SPLISH
SPLISH
SPLISH
SPLISH
SPLISH

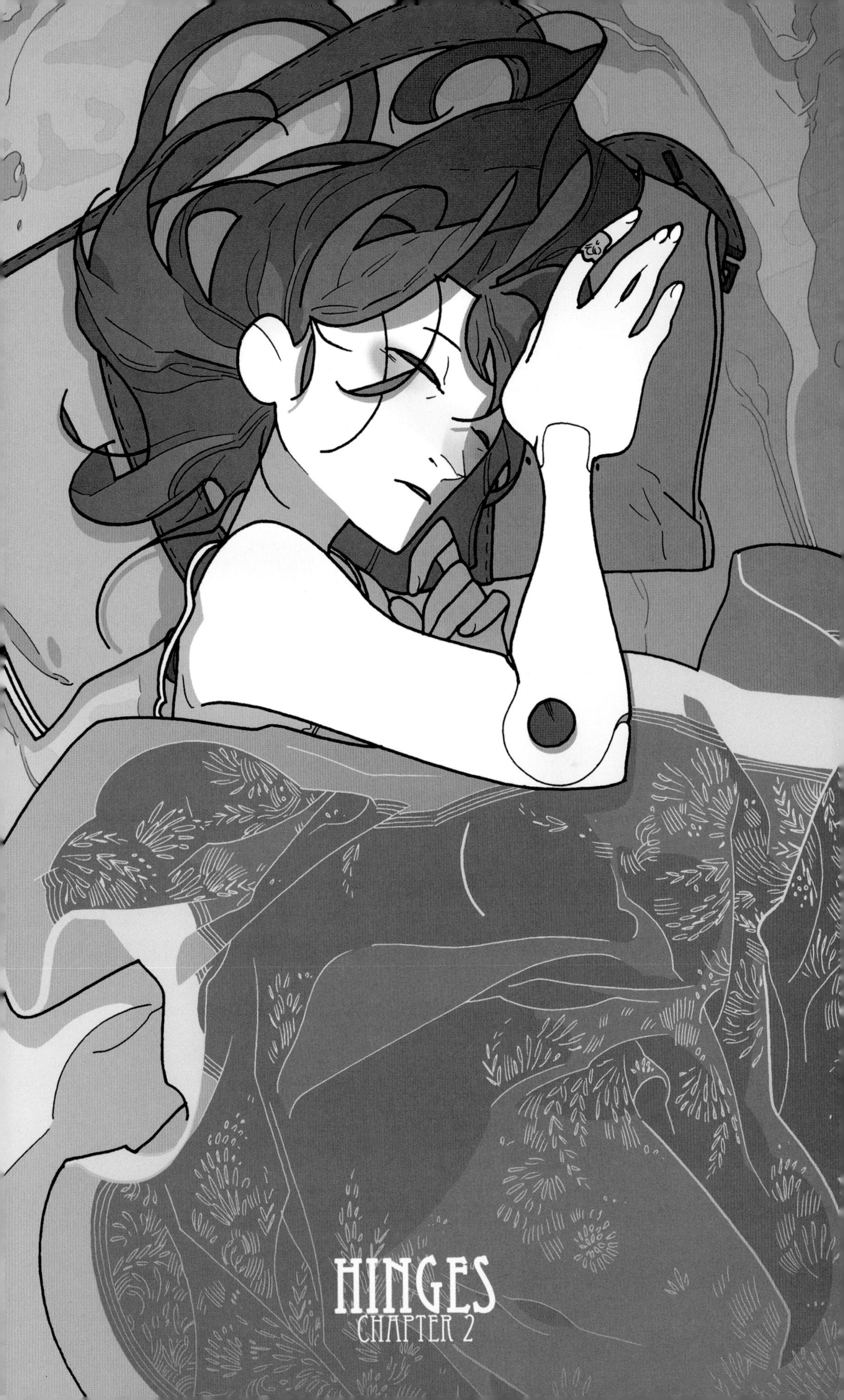
HINGES
CHAPTER 2

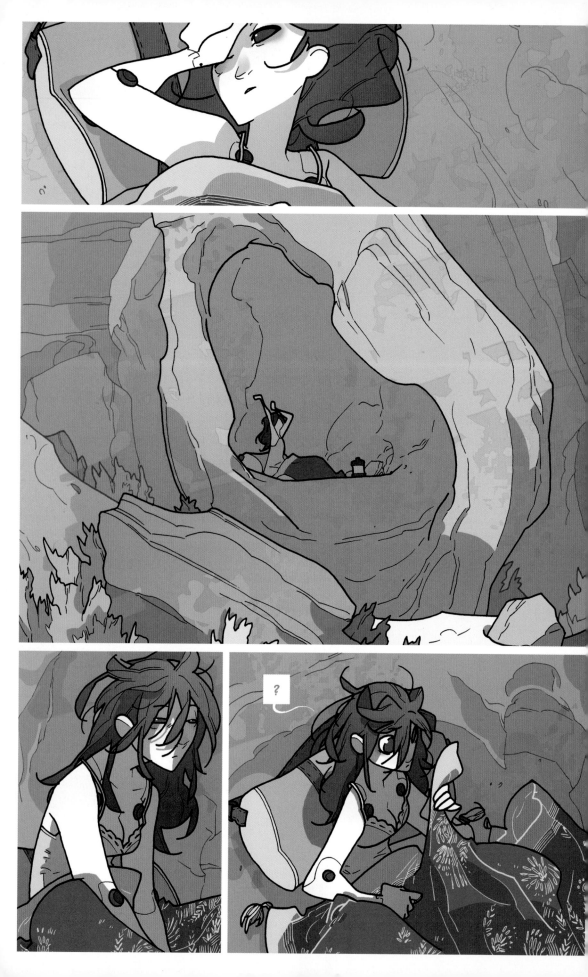

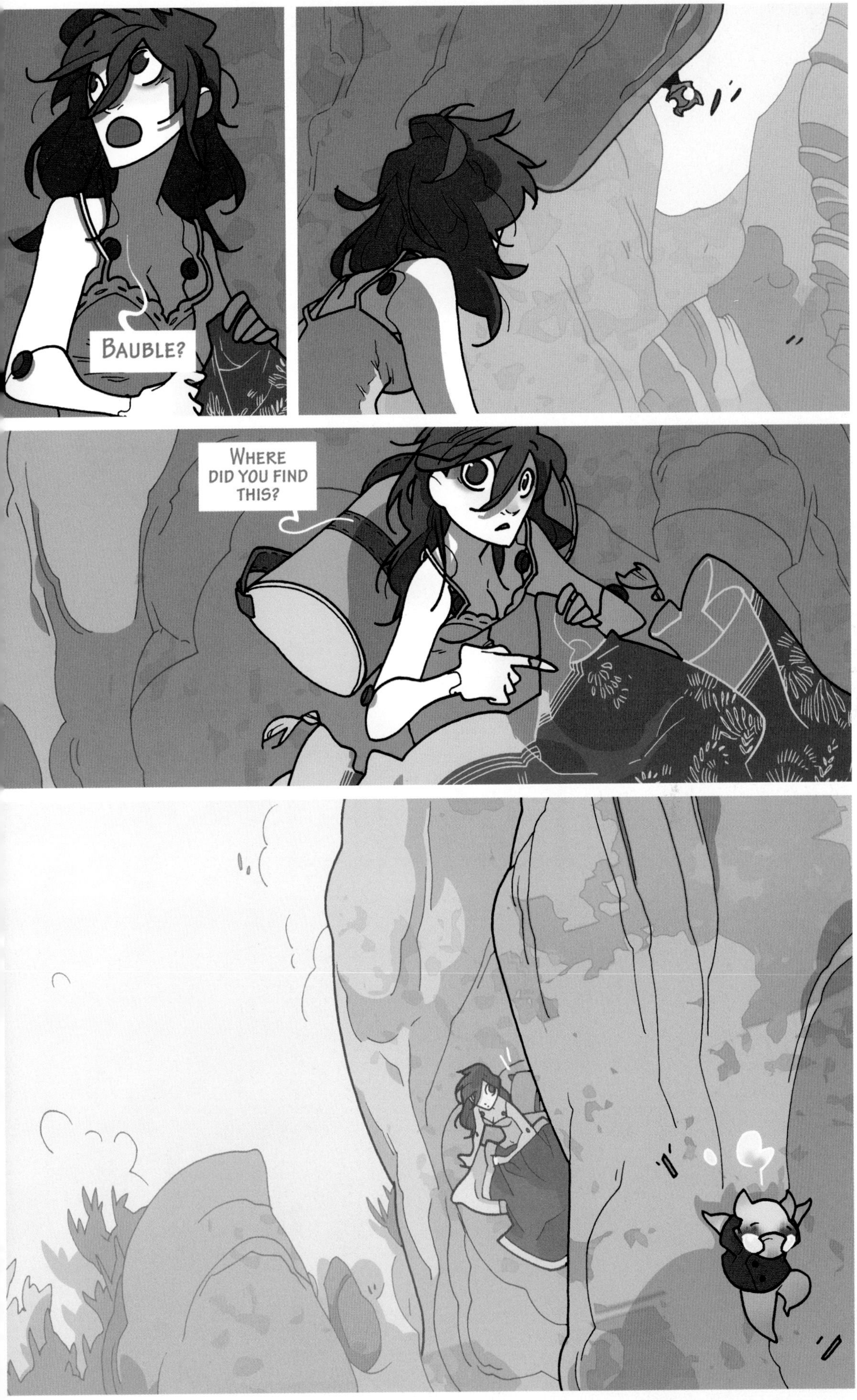
BAUBLE?
WHERE DID YOU FIND THIS?

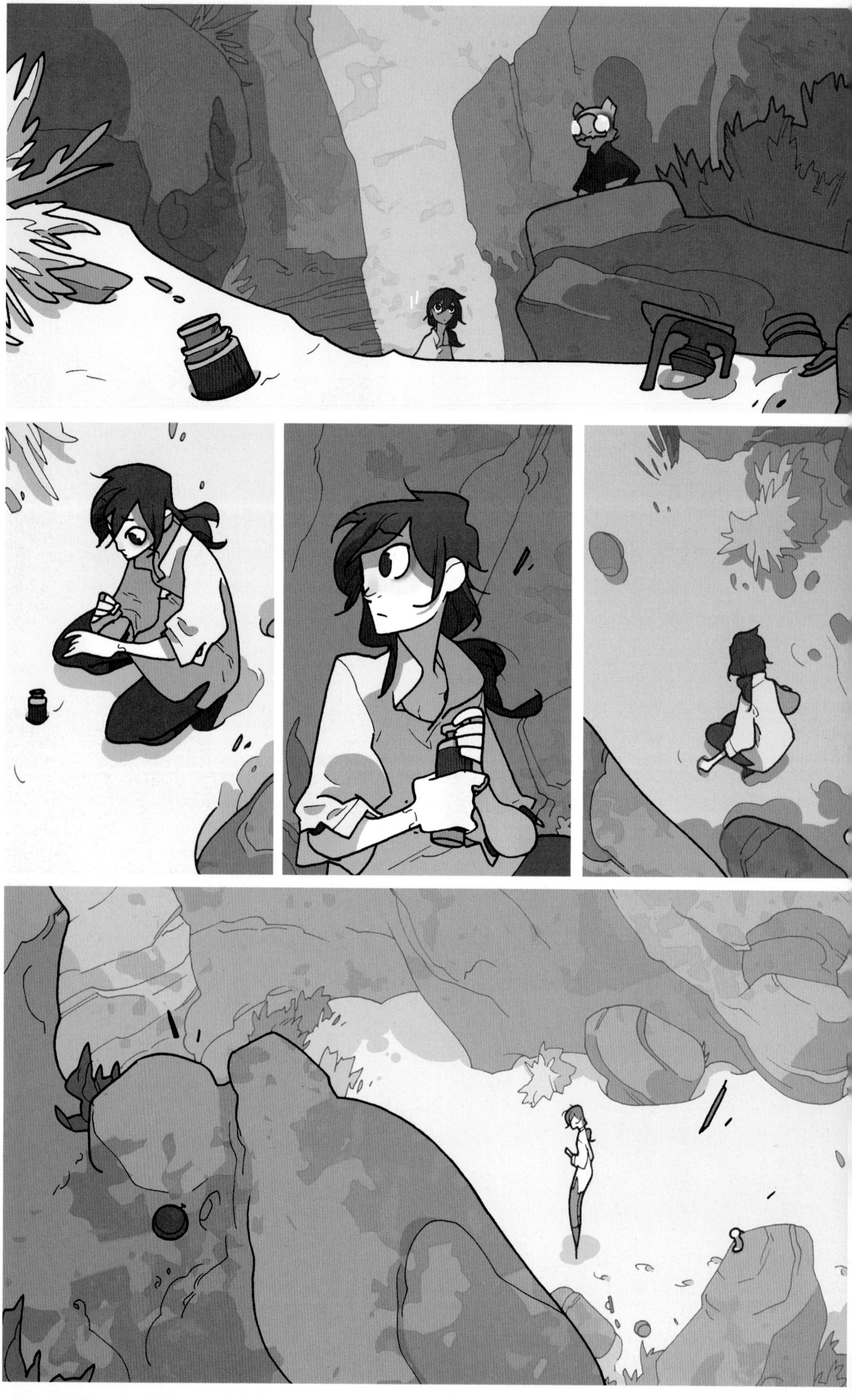

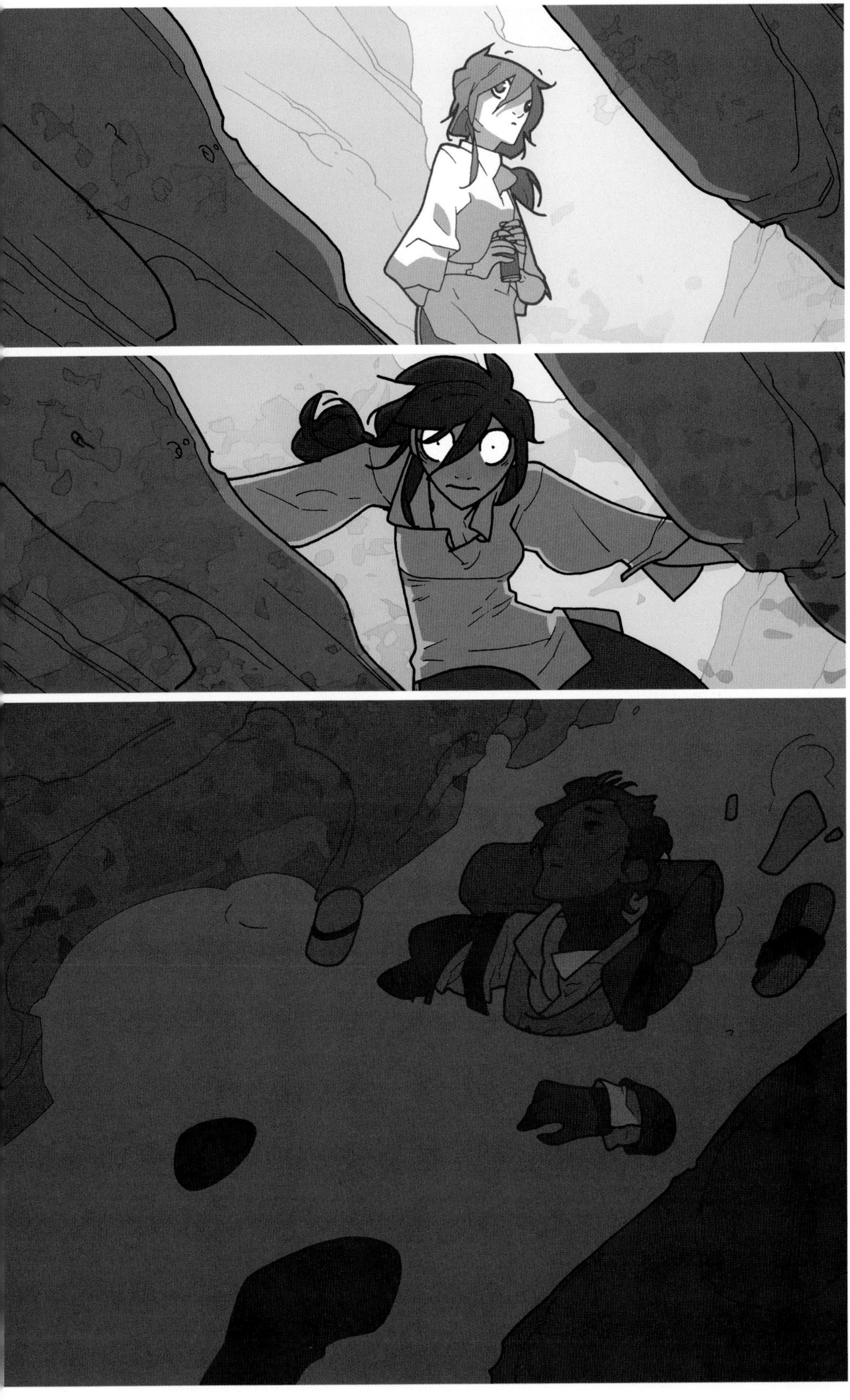

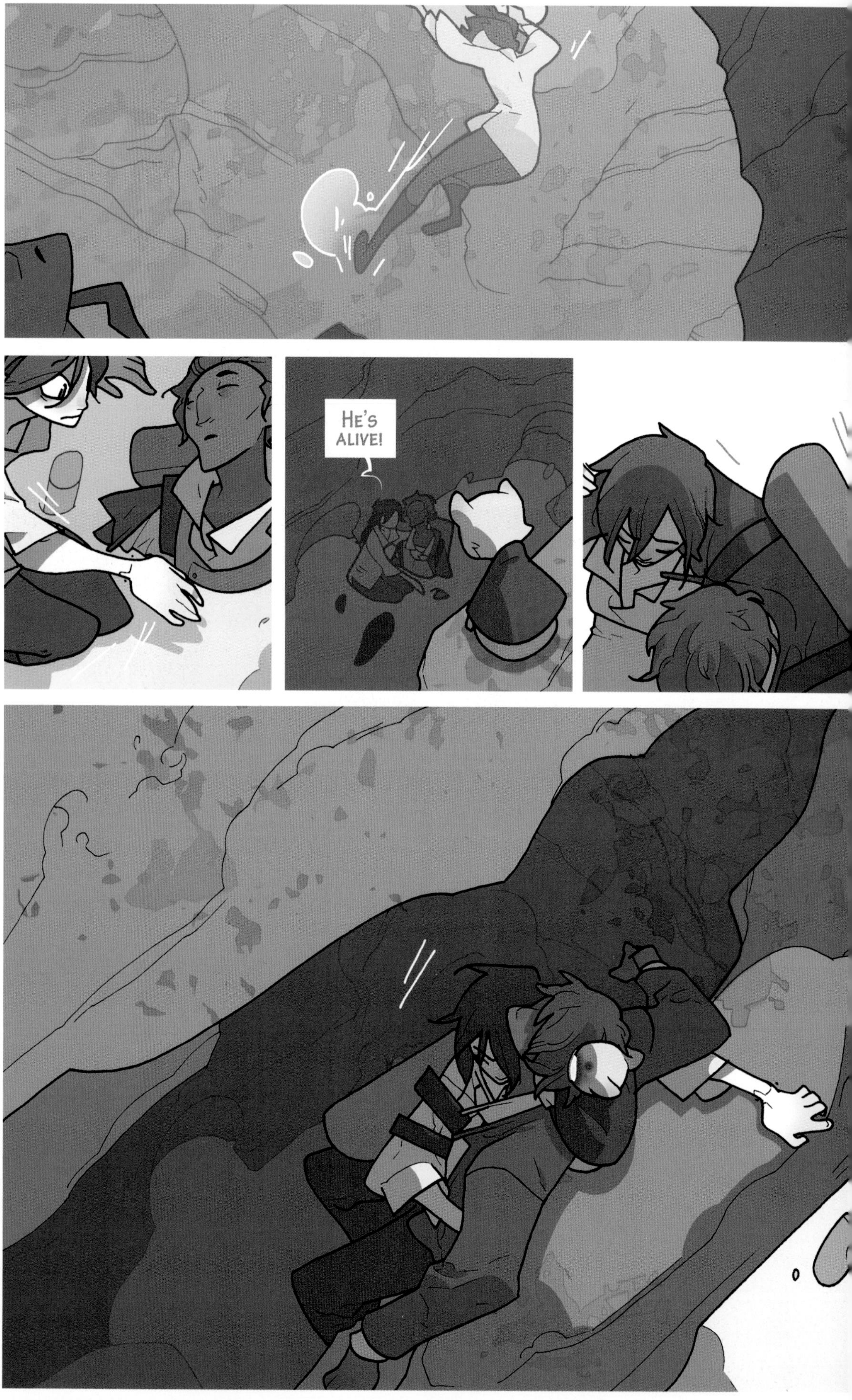
HE'S ALIVE!

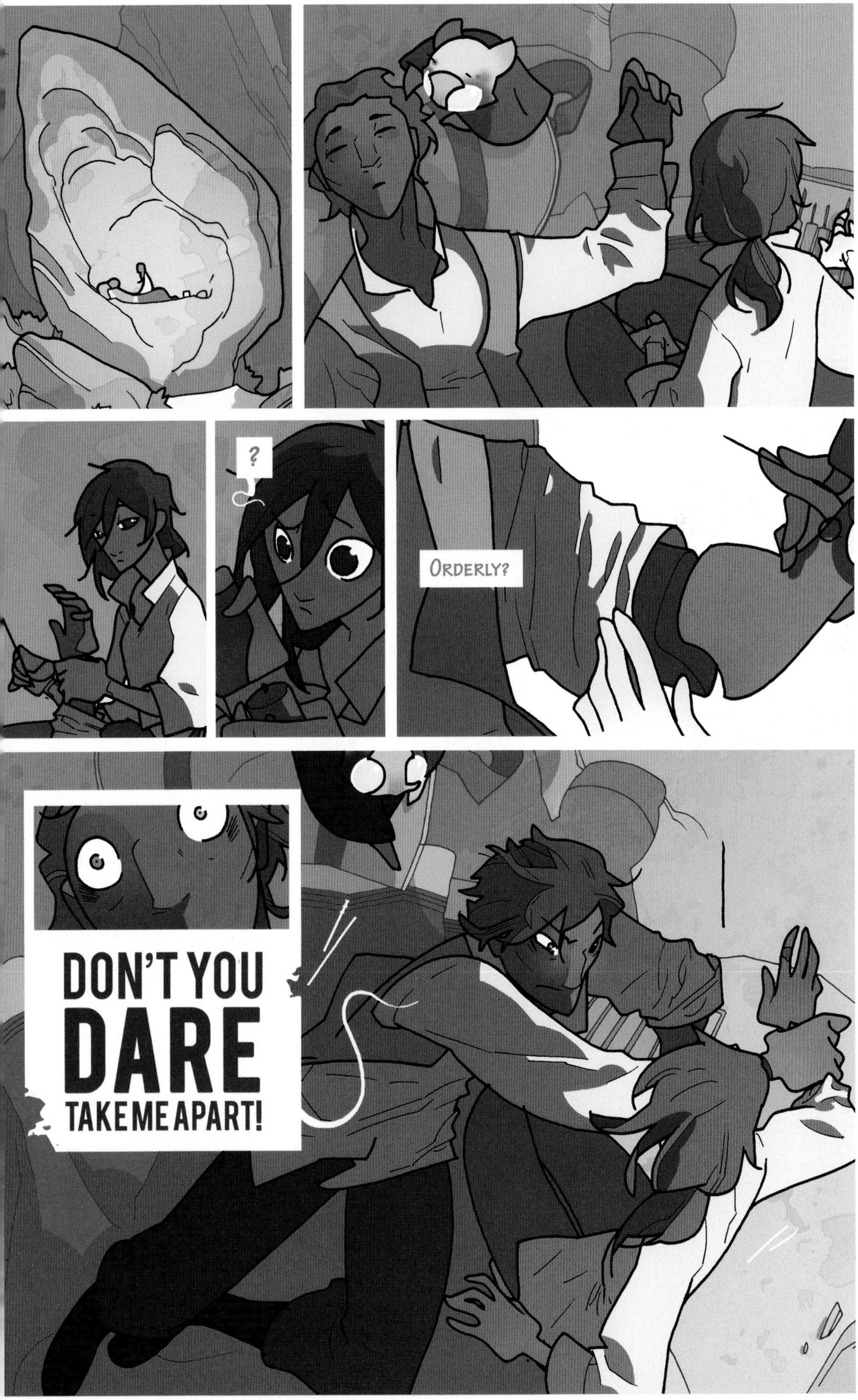
?
ORDERLY?
DON'T YOU
DARE
TAKE ME APART!

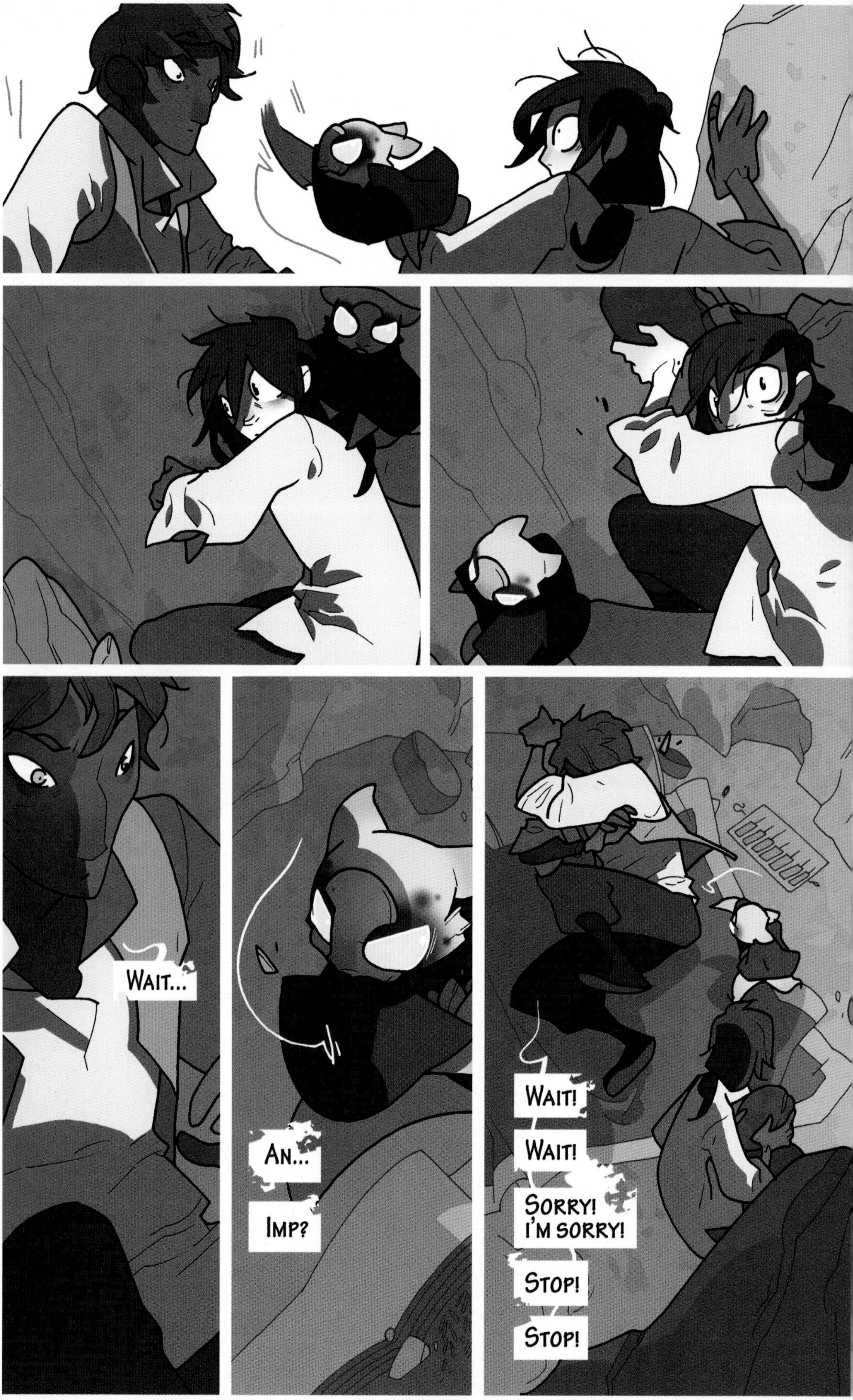
WAIT...
AN...
IMP?
WAIT!
WAIT!
SORRY! I'M SORRY!
STOP!
STOP!

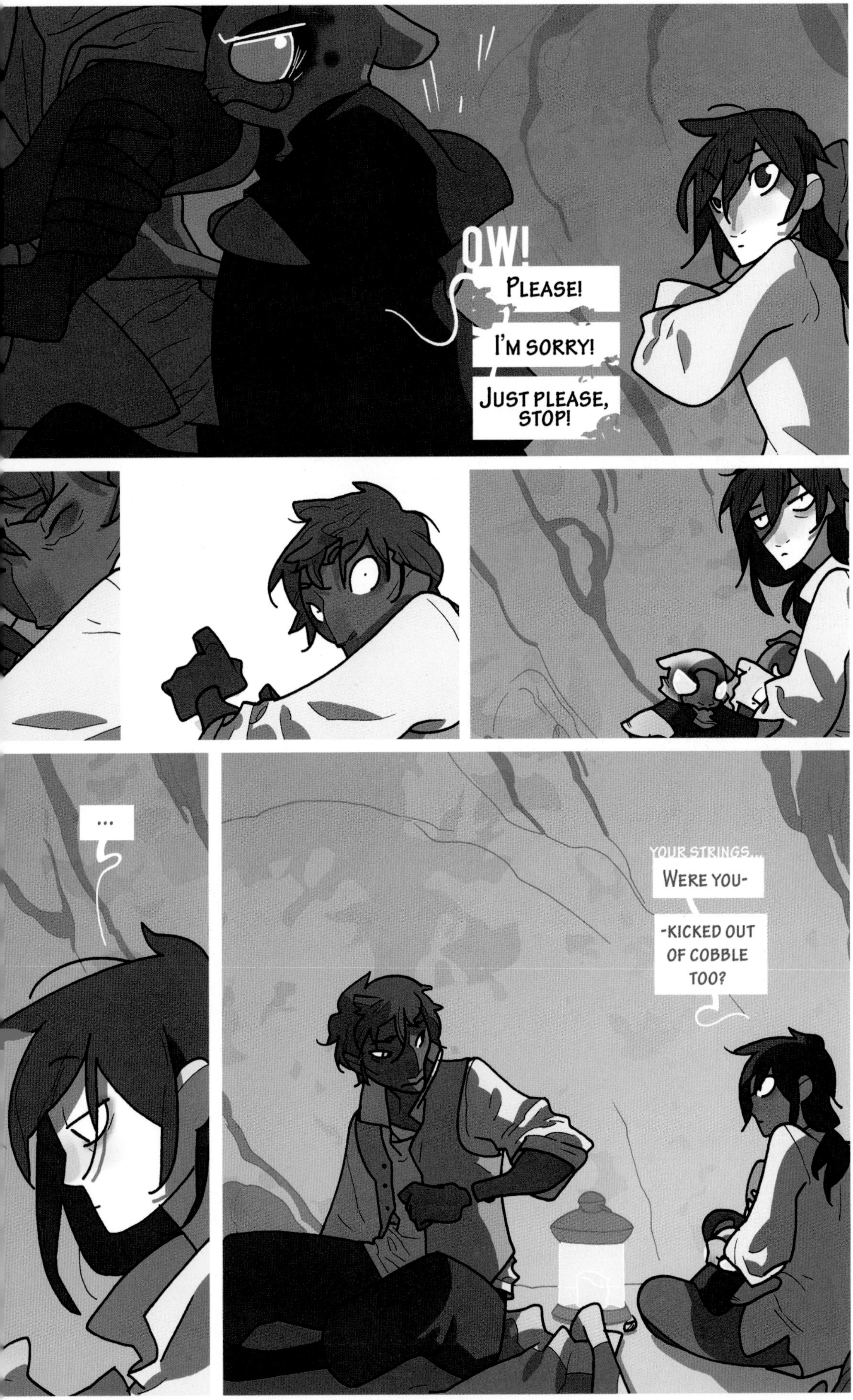
OW!
PLEASE!
I'M SORRY!
JUST PLEASE, STOP!
...
YOUR STRINGS...
WERE YOU-
-KICKED OUT OF COBBLE TOO?

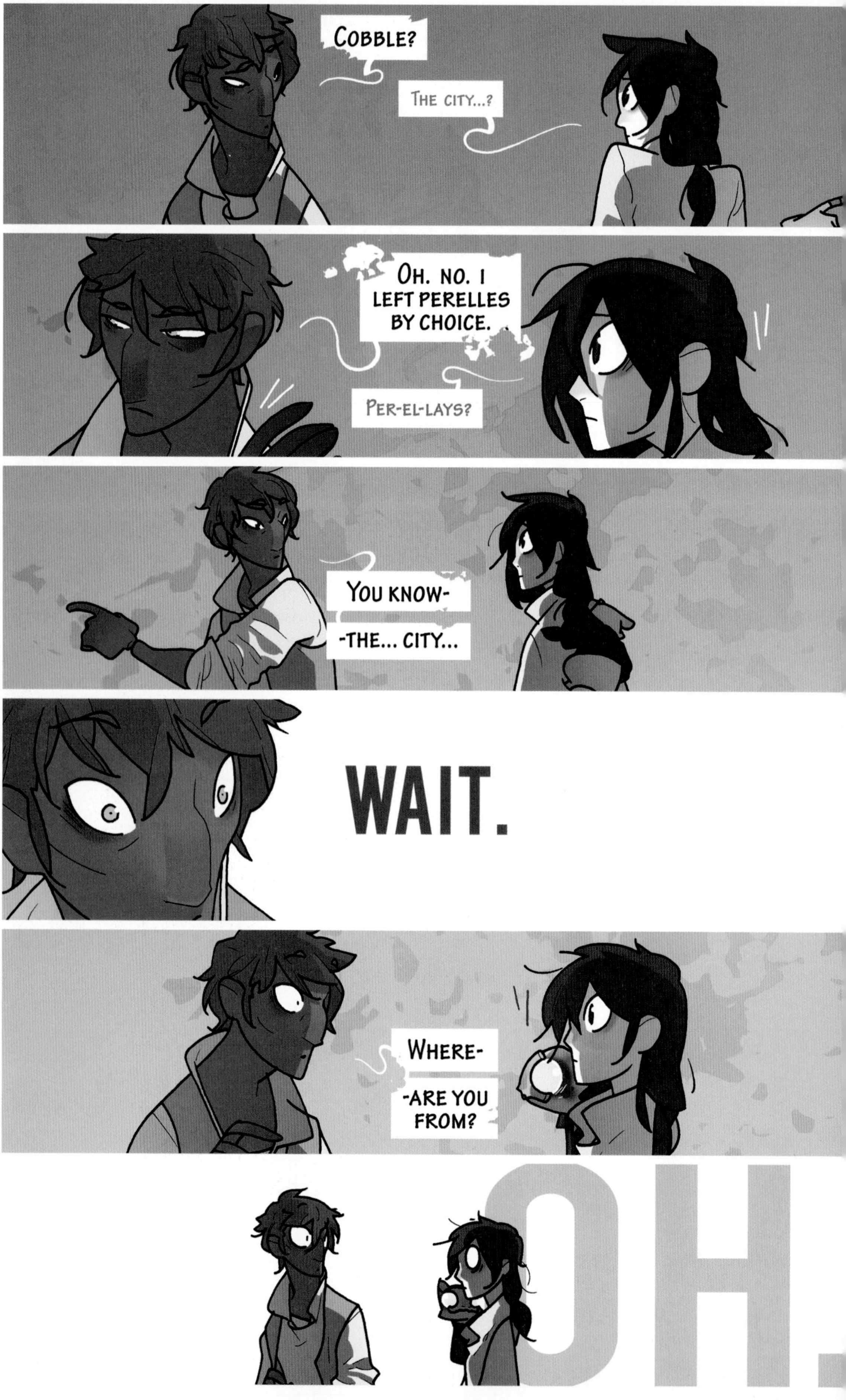
COBBLE?
THE CITY...?
OH. NO. I LEFT PERELLES BY CHOICE.
PER-EL-LAYS?
YOU KNOW-
-THE... CITY...
WAIT.
WHERE-
-ARE YOU FROM?
OH.

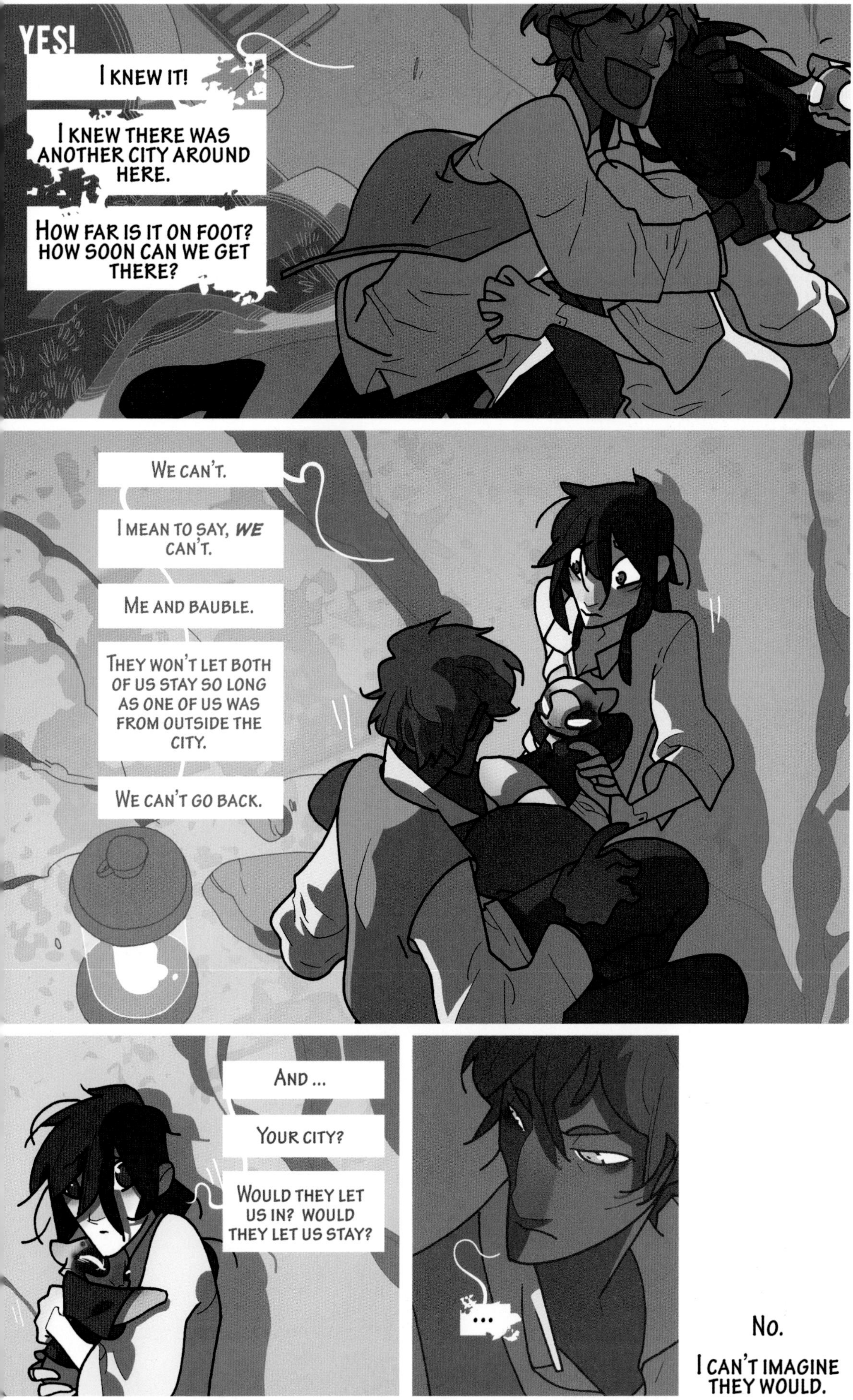
YES!
I KNEW IT!
I KNEW THERE WAS ANOTHER CITY AROUND HERE.
HOW FAR IS IT ON FOOT? HOW SOON CAN WE GET THERE?
WE CAN'T.
I MEAN TO SAY, *WE* CAN'T.
ME AND BAUBLE.
THEY WON'T LET BOTH OF US STAY SO LONG AS ONE OF US WAS FROM OUTSIDE THE CITY.
WE CAN'T GO BACK.
AND ...
YOUR CITY?
WOULD THEY LET US IN? WOULD THEY LET US STAY?
...
NO.
I CAN'T IMAGINE THEY WOULD.

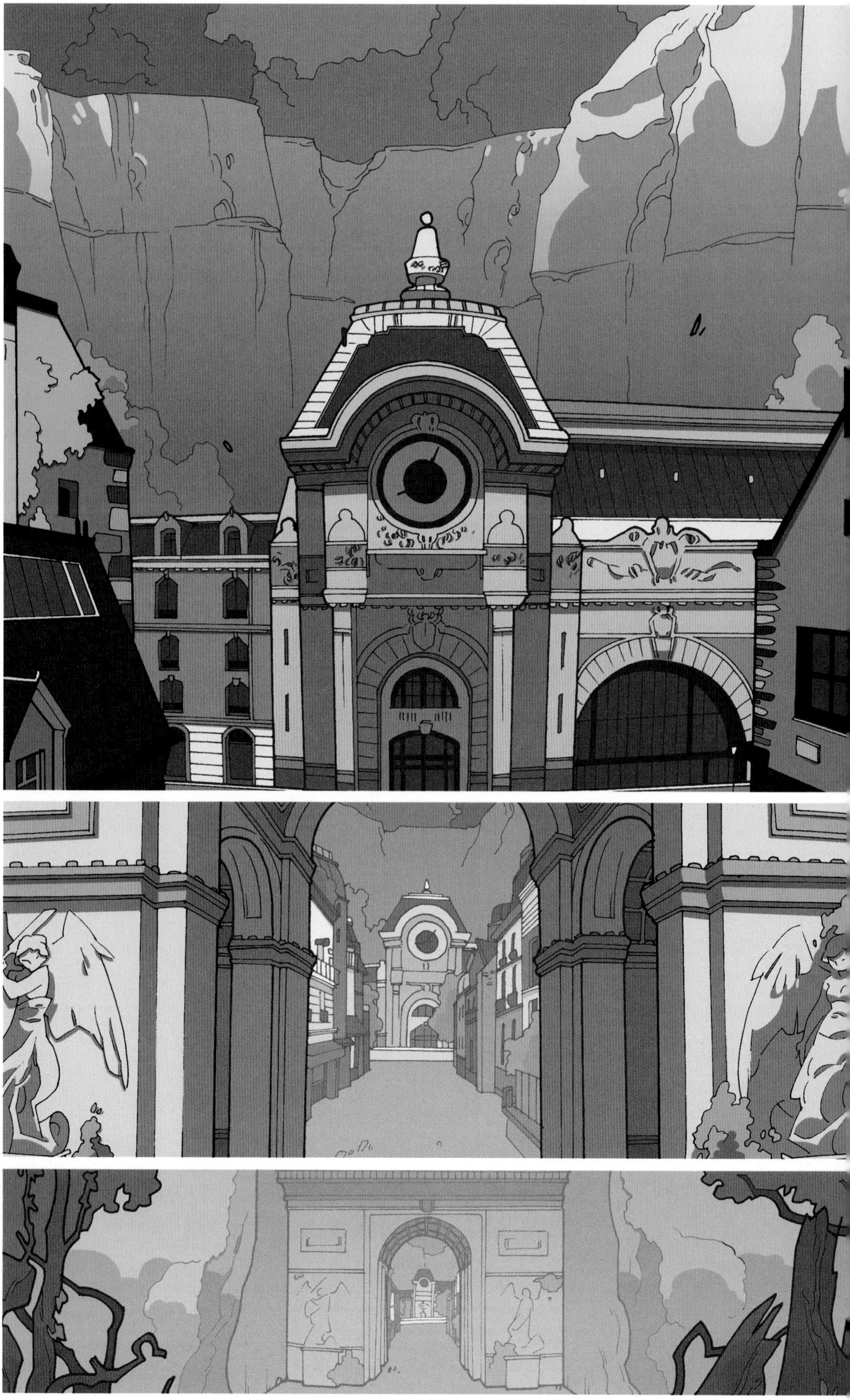

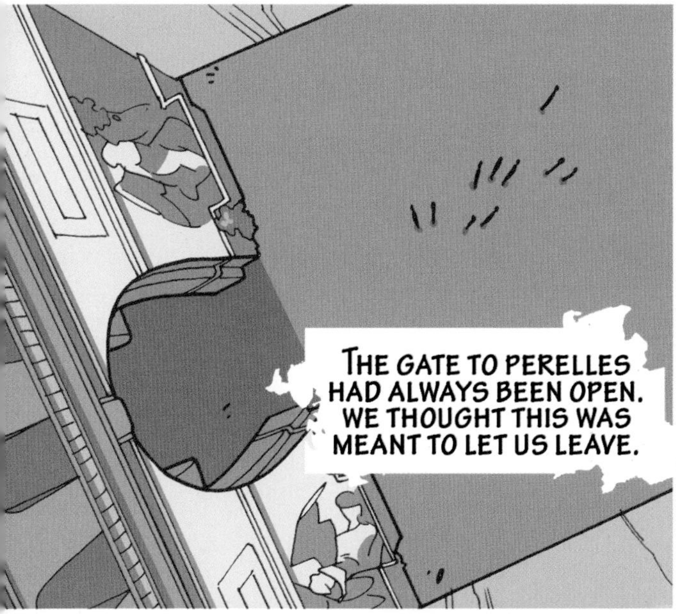
THE GATE TO PERELLES HAD ALWAYS BEEN OPEN. WE THOUGHT THIS WAS MEANT TO LET US LEAVE.

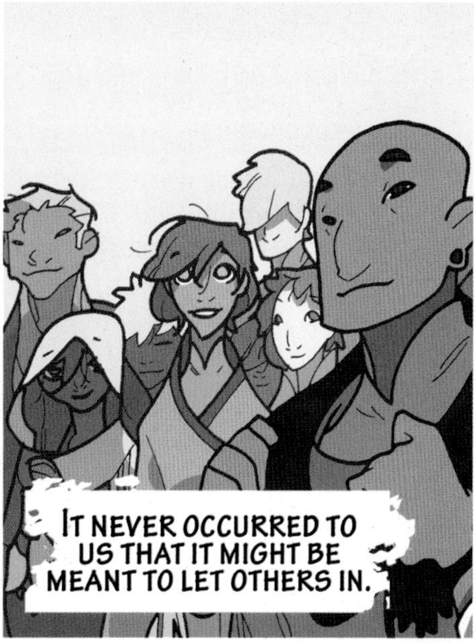
IT NEVER OCCURRED TO US THAT IT MIGHT BE MEANT TO LET OTHERS IN.

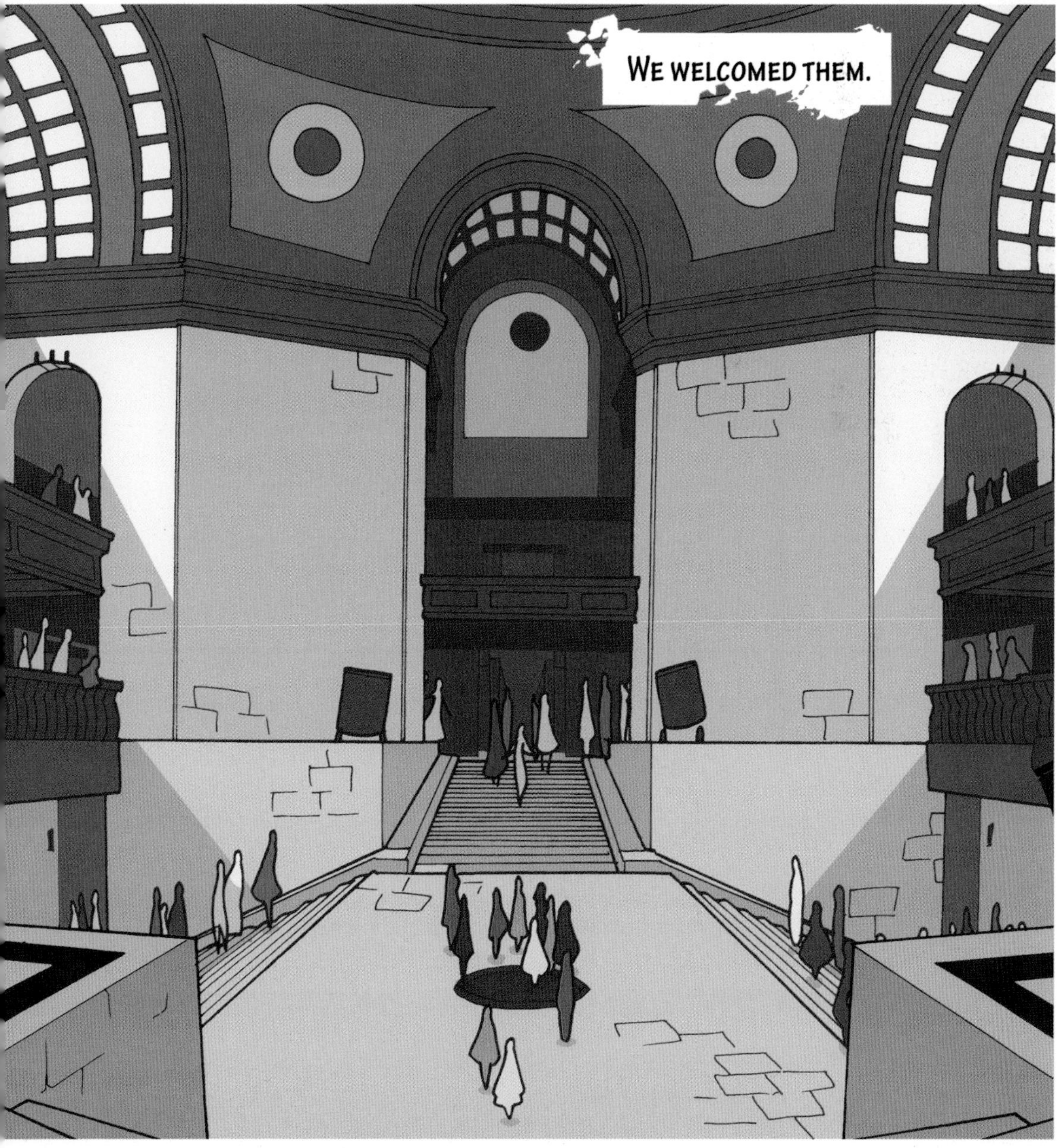
WE WELCOMED THEM.

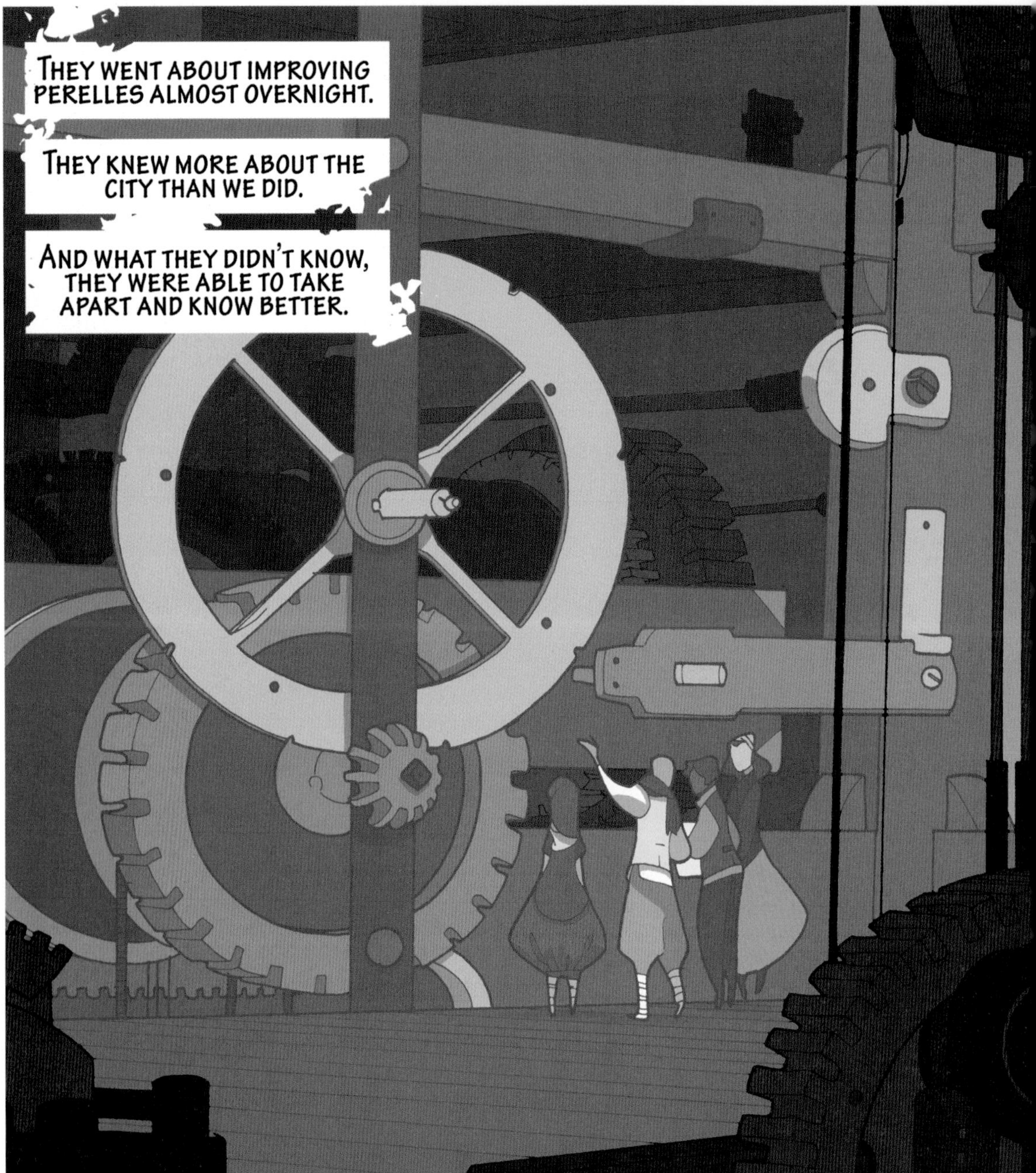

THEY WENT ABOUT IMPROVING PERELLES ALMOST OVERNIGHT.
THEY KNEW MORE ABOUT THE CITY THAN WE DID.
AND WHAT THEY DIDN'T KNOW, THEY WERE ABLE TO TAKE APART AND KNOW BETTER.

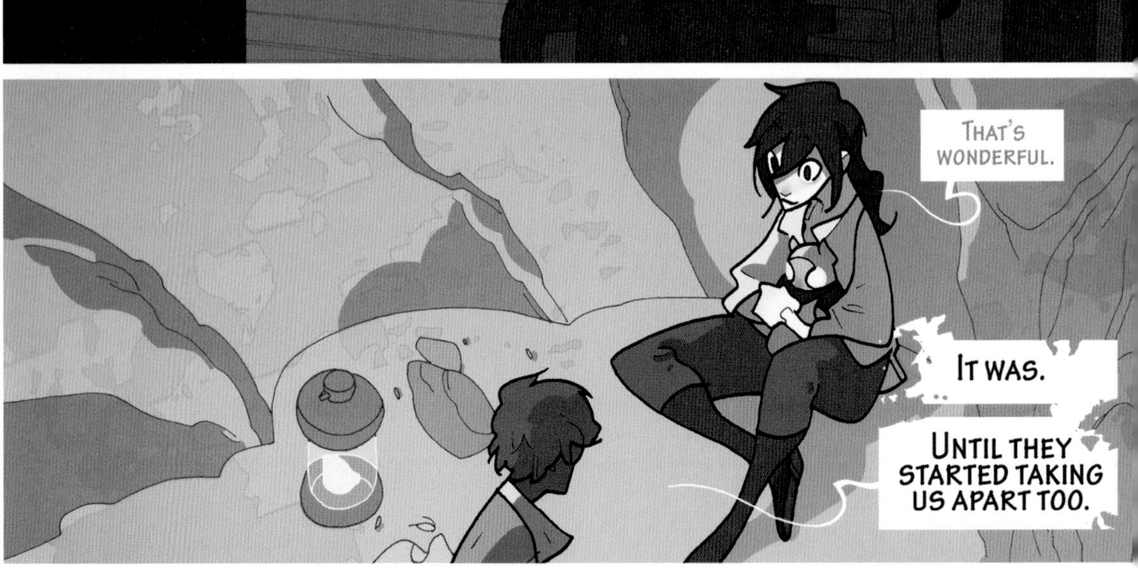

THAT'S WONDERFUL.
IT WAS.
UNTIL THEY STARTED TAKING US APART TOO.

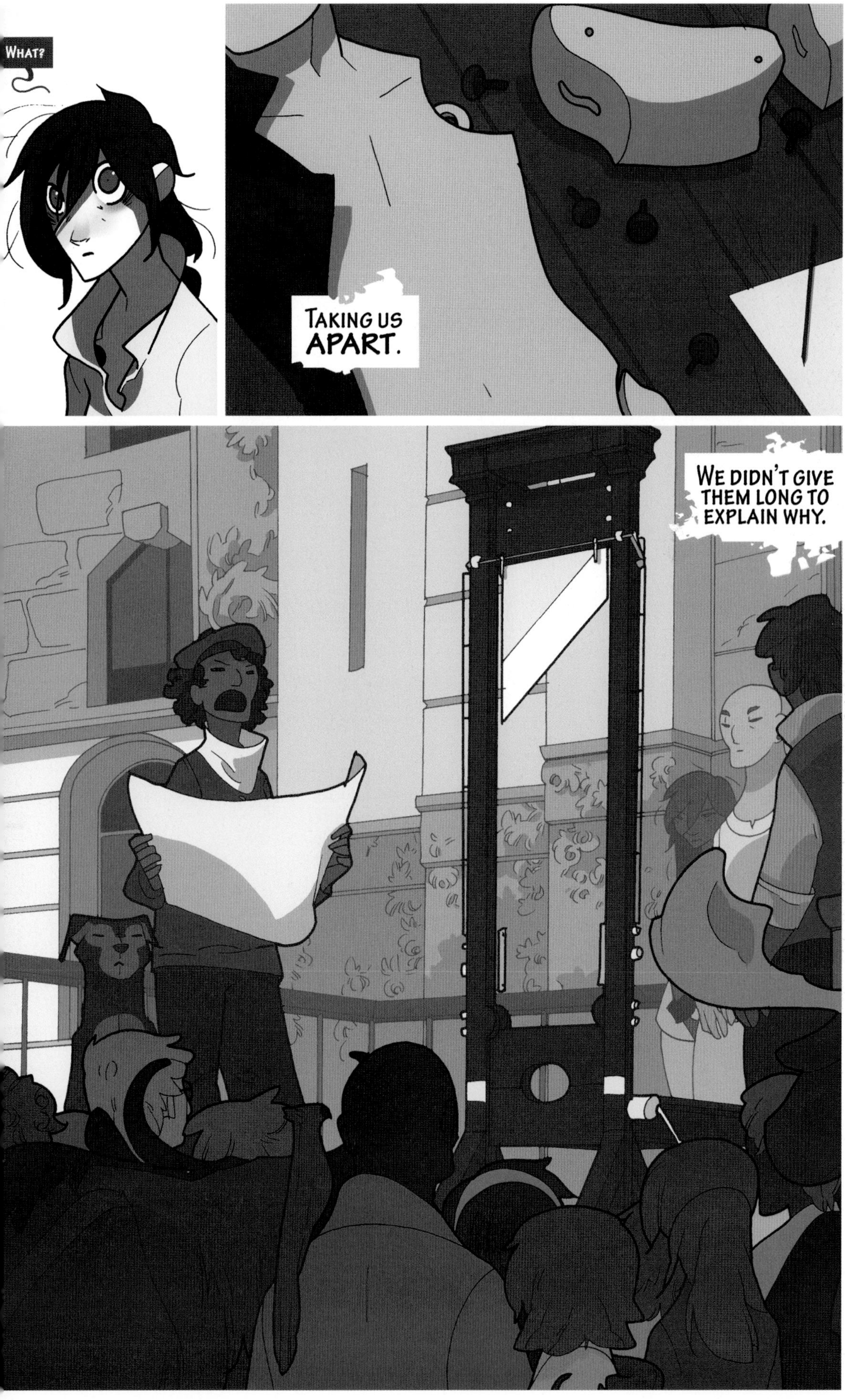
WHAT?
TAKING US
APART.
WE DIDN'T GIVE
THEM LONG TO
EXPLAIN WHY.

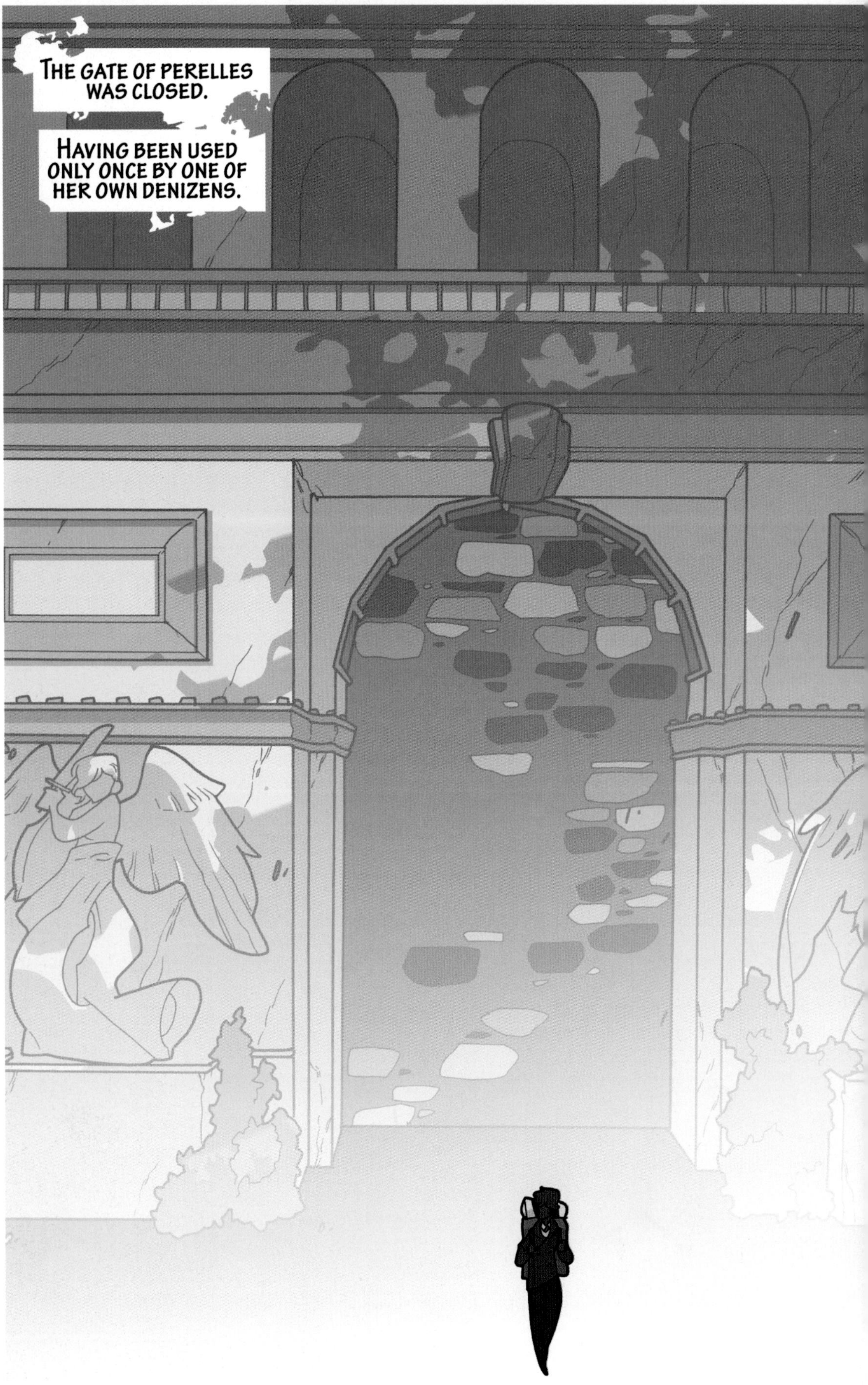
THE GATE OF PERELLES WAS CLOSED.
HAVING BEEN USED ONLY ONCE BY ONE OF HER OWN DENIZENS.

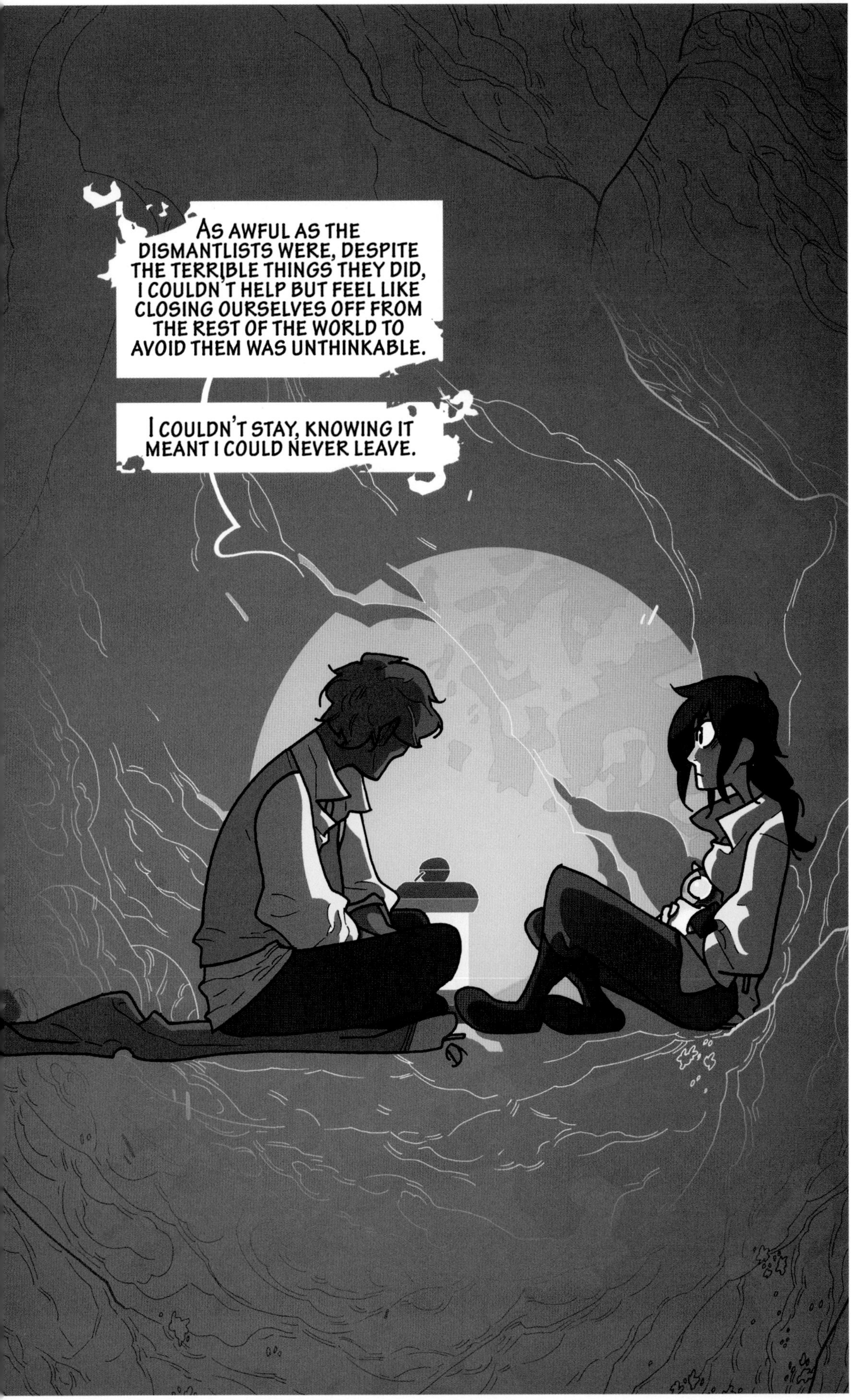
As awful as the dismantlists were, despite the terrible things they did, I couldn't help but feel like closing ourselves off from the rest of the world to avoid them was unthinkable.
I couldn't stay, knowing it meant I could never leave.

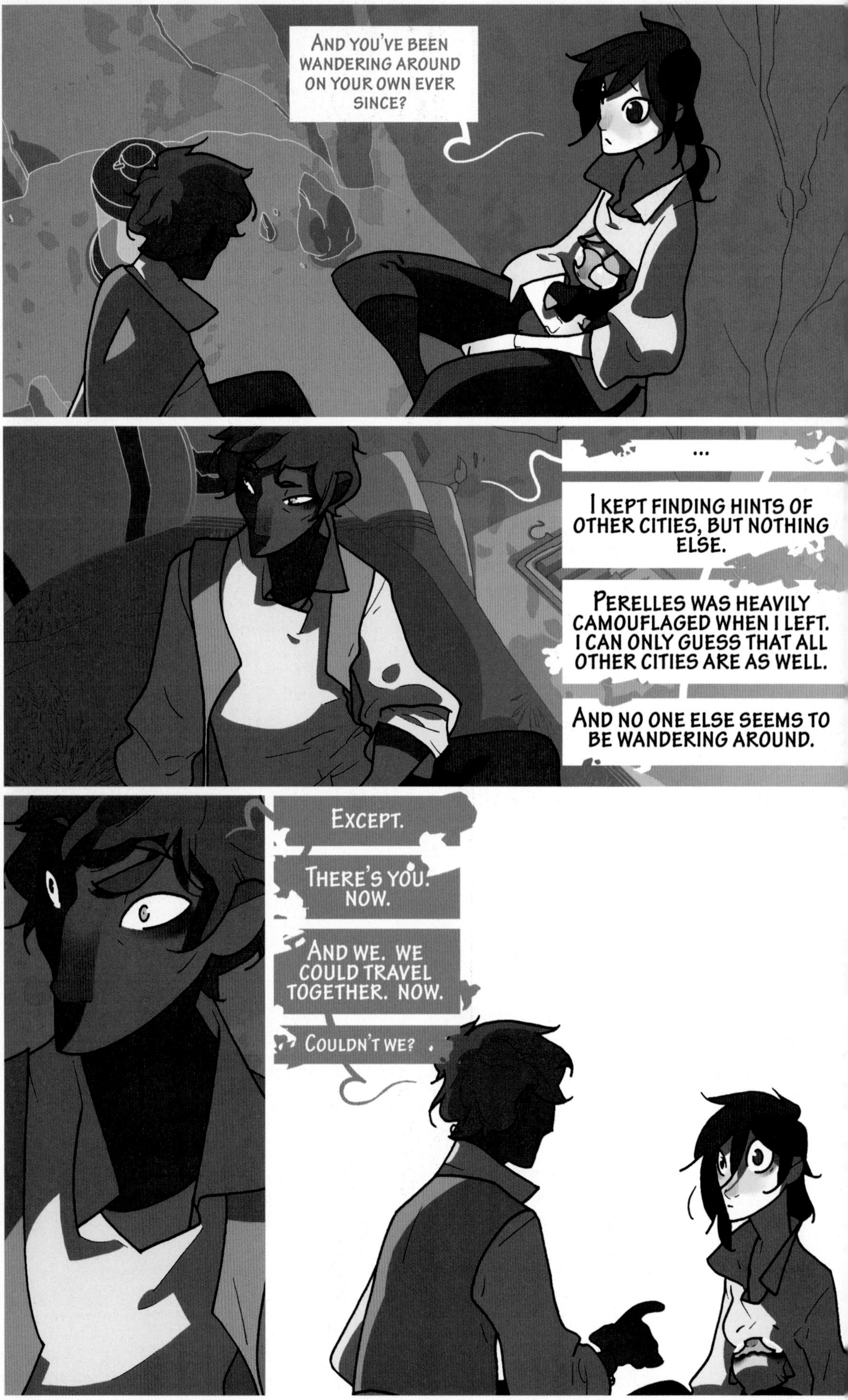
And you've been wandering around on your own ever since?
...
I kept finding hints of other cities, but nothing else.
Perelles was heavily camouflaged when I left. I can only guess that all other cities are as well.
And no one else seems to be wandering around.
Except.
There's you. Now.
And we. We could travel together. Now.
Couldn't we?

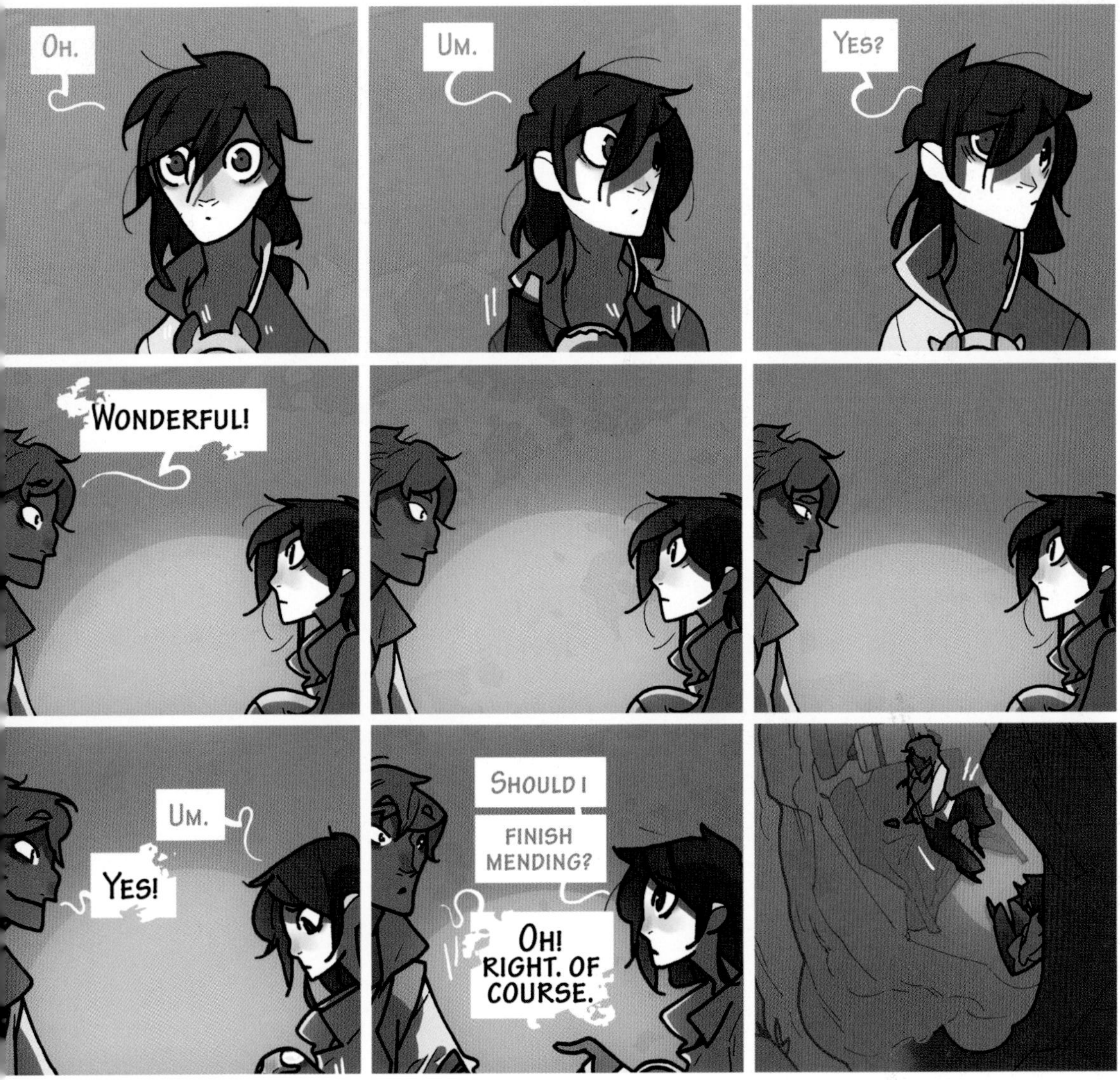
OH.
UM.
YES?
WONDERFUL!
UM.
YES!
SHOULD I
FINISH MENDING?
OH! RIGHT. OF COURSE.

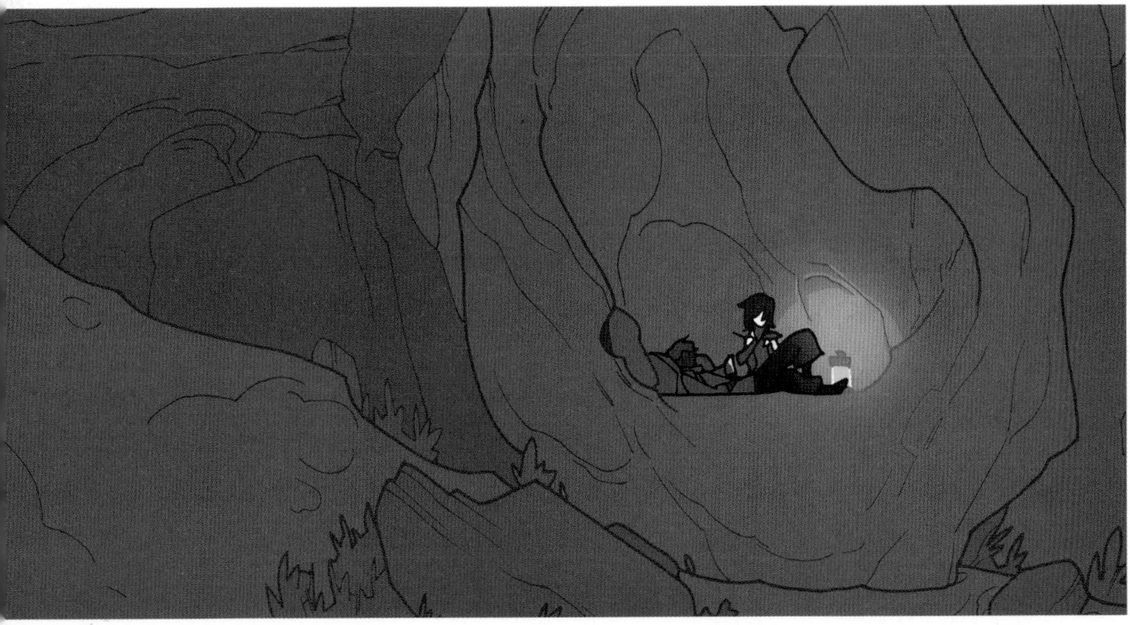

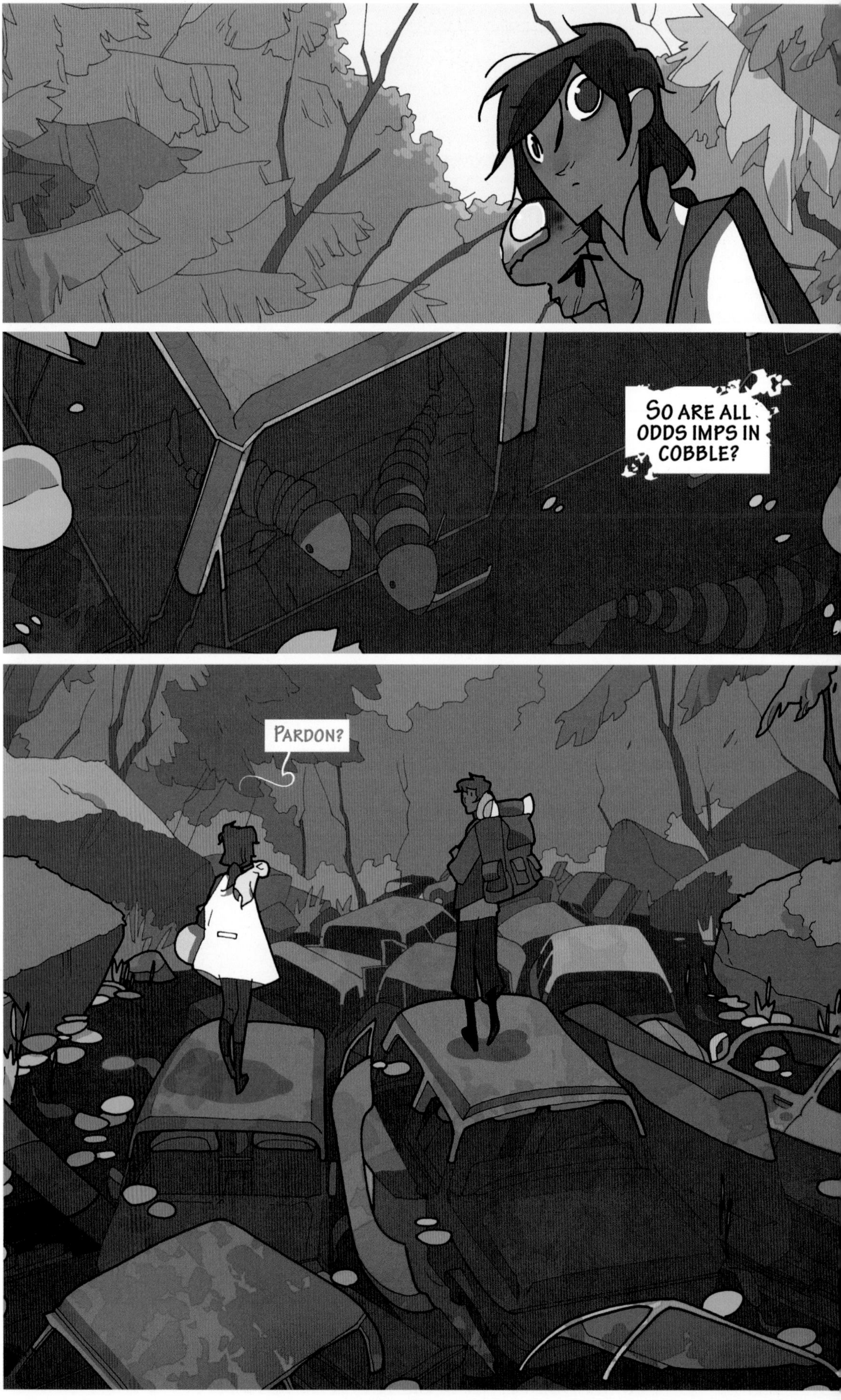
So are all odds imps in cobble?
Pardon?

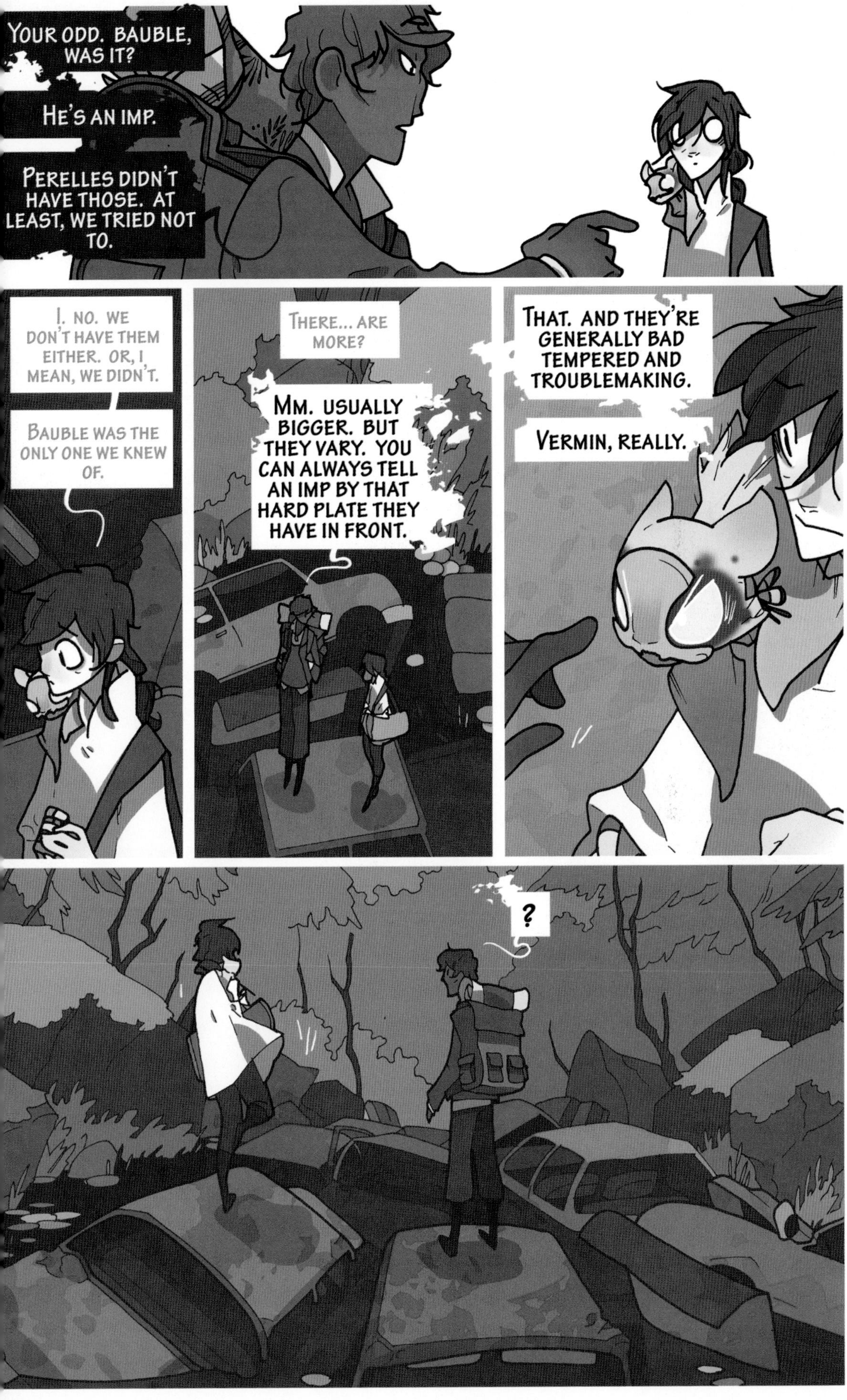

YOUR ODD. BAUBLE, WAS IT?
HE'S AN IMP.
PERELLES DIDN'T HAVE THOSE. AT LEAST, WE TRIED NOT TO.
I. NO. WE DON'T HAVE THEM EITHER. OR, I MEAN, WE DIDN'T.
BAUBLE WAS THE ONLY ONE WE KNEW OF.
THERE... ARE MORE?
MM. USUALLY BIGGER. BUT THEY VARY. YOU CAN ALWAYS TELL AN IMP BY THAT HARD PLATE THEY HAVE IN FRONT.
THAT. AND THEY'RE GENERALLY BAD TEMPERED AND TROUBLEMAKING.
VERMIN, REALLY.
?

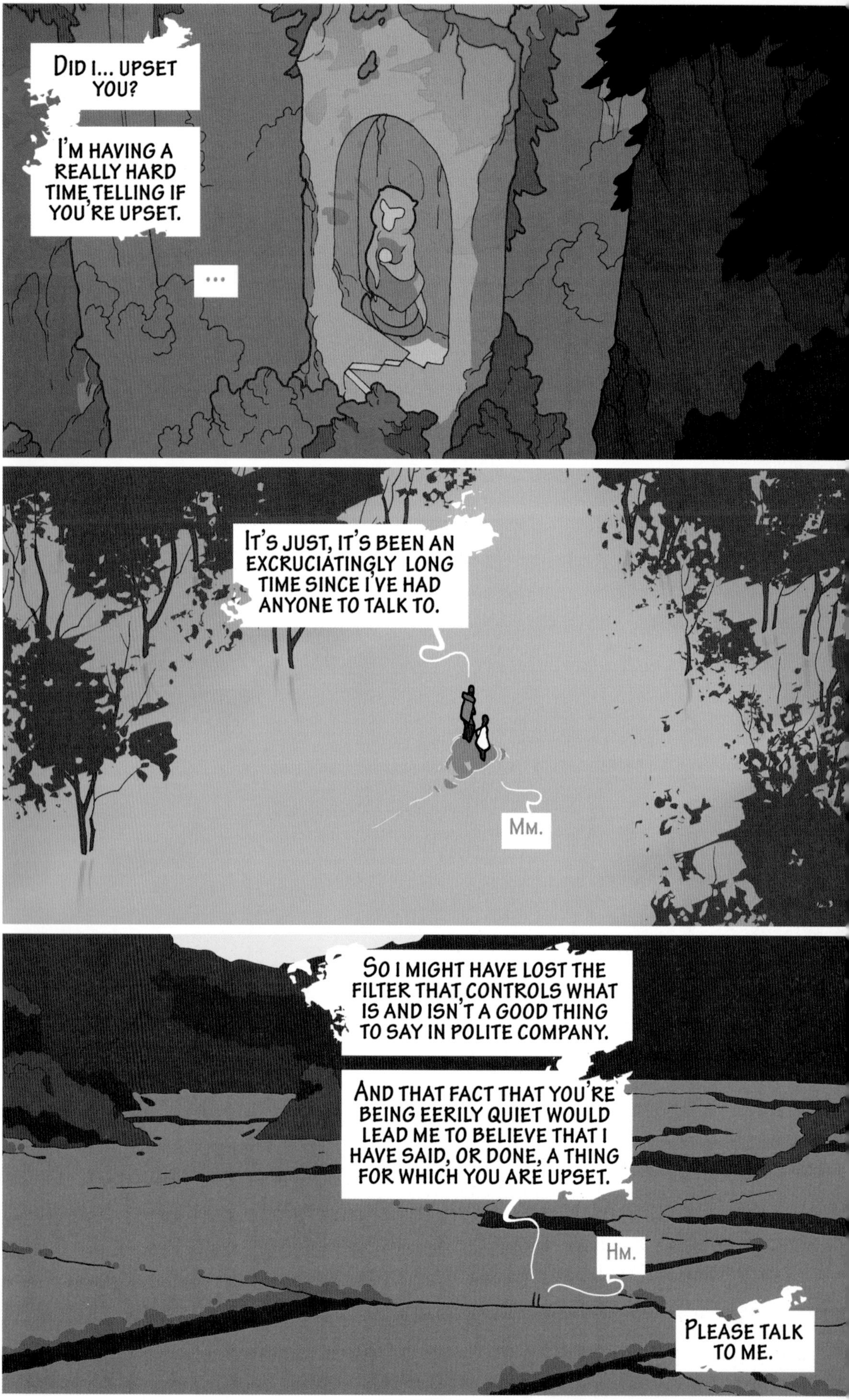
Did I... upset you?
I'm having a really hard time, telling if you're upset.
...
It's just, it's been an excruciatingly long time since I've had anyone to talk to.
Mm.
So I might have lost the filter that, controls what is and isn't a *good* thing to say in polite company.
And that fact that you're being eerily quiet would lead me to believe that I have said, or done, a thing for which you are upset.
Hm.
Please talk to me.

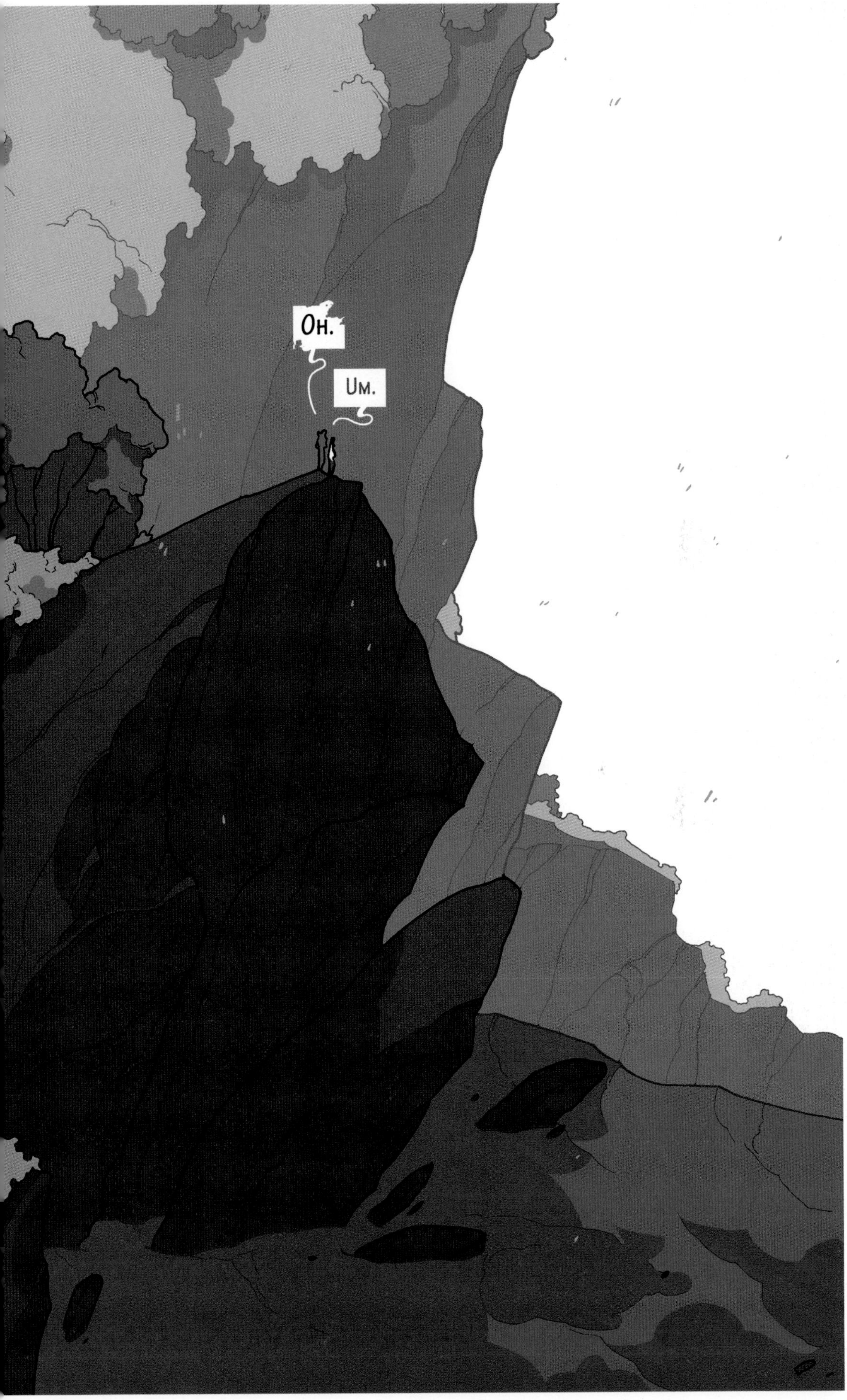
Oh.
Um.

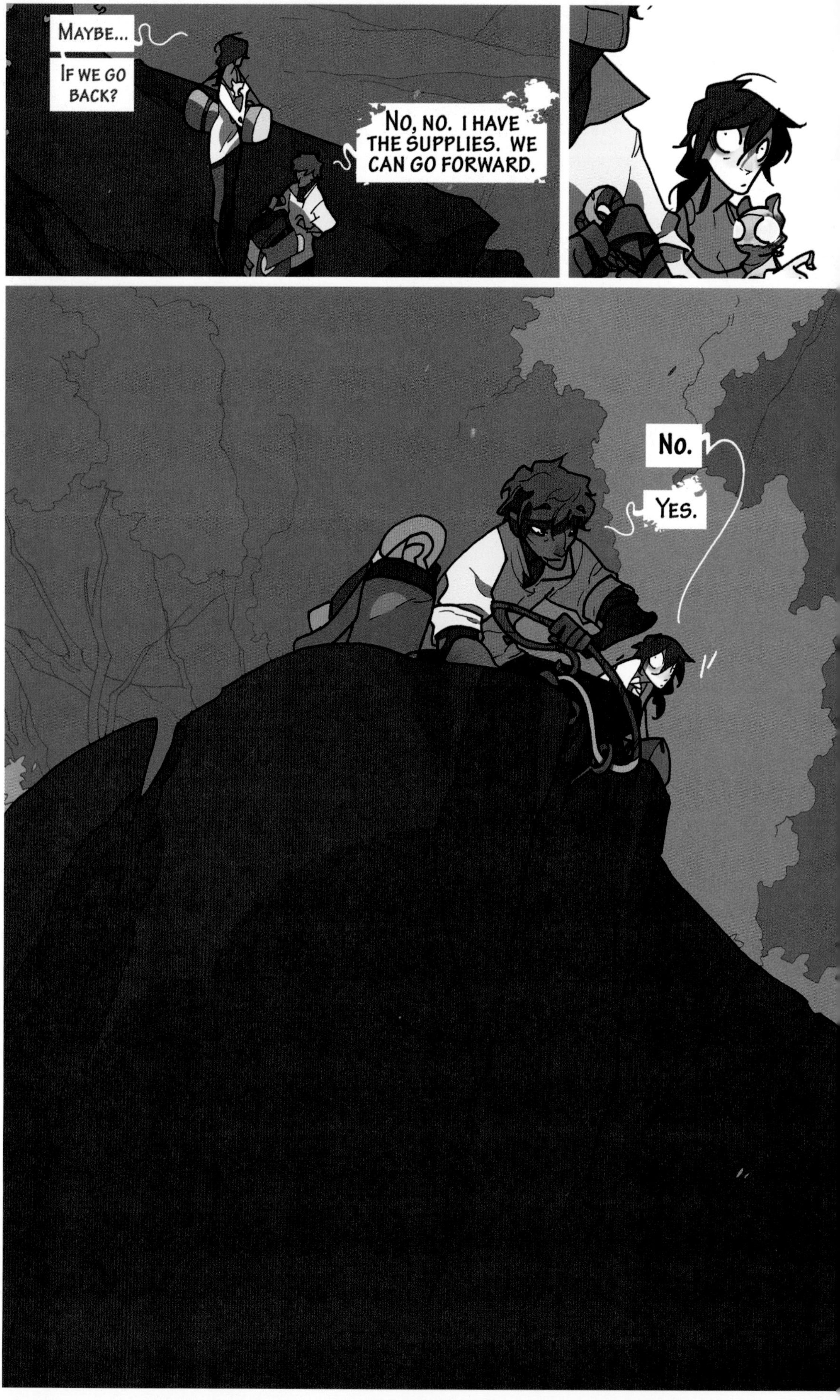
Maybe...
If we go back?
No, no. I have the supplies. We can go forward.
No.
Yes.

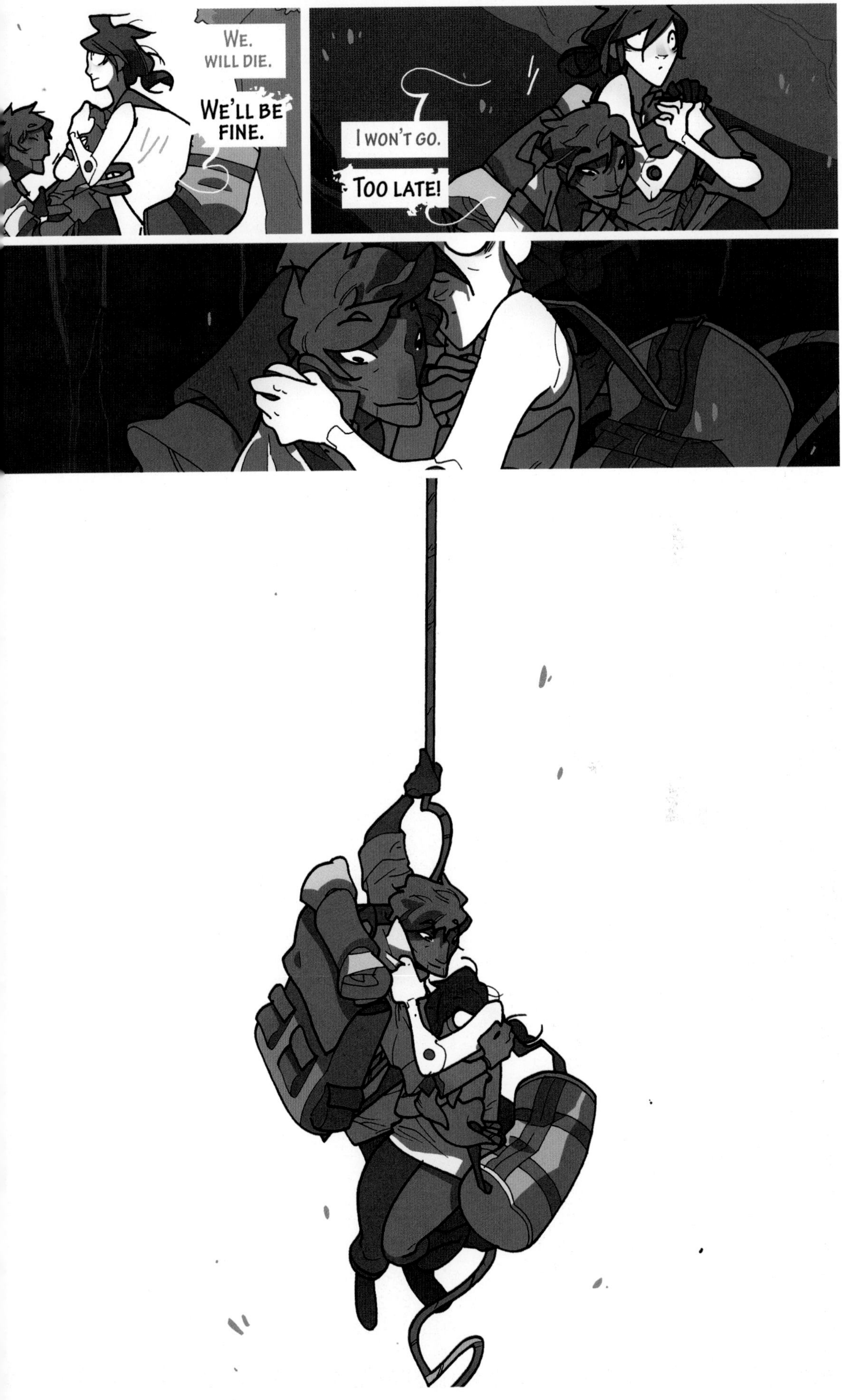
WE.
WILL DIE.
WE'LL BE FINE.
I WON'T GO.
TOO LATE!

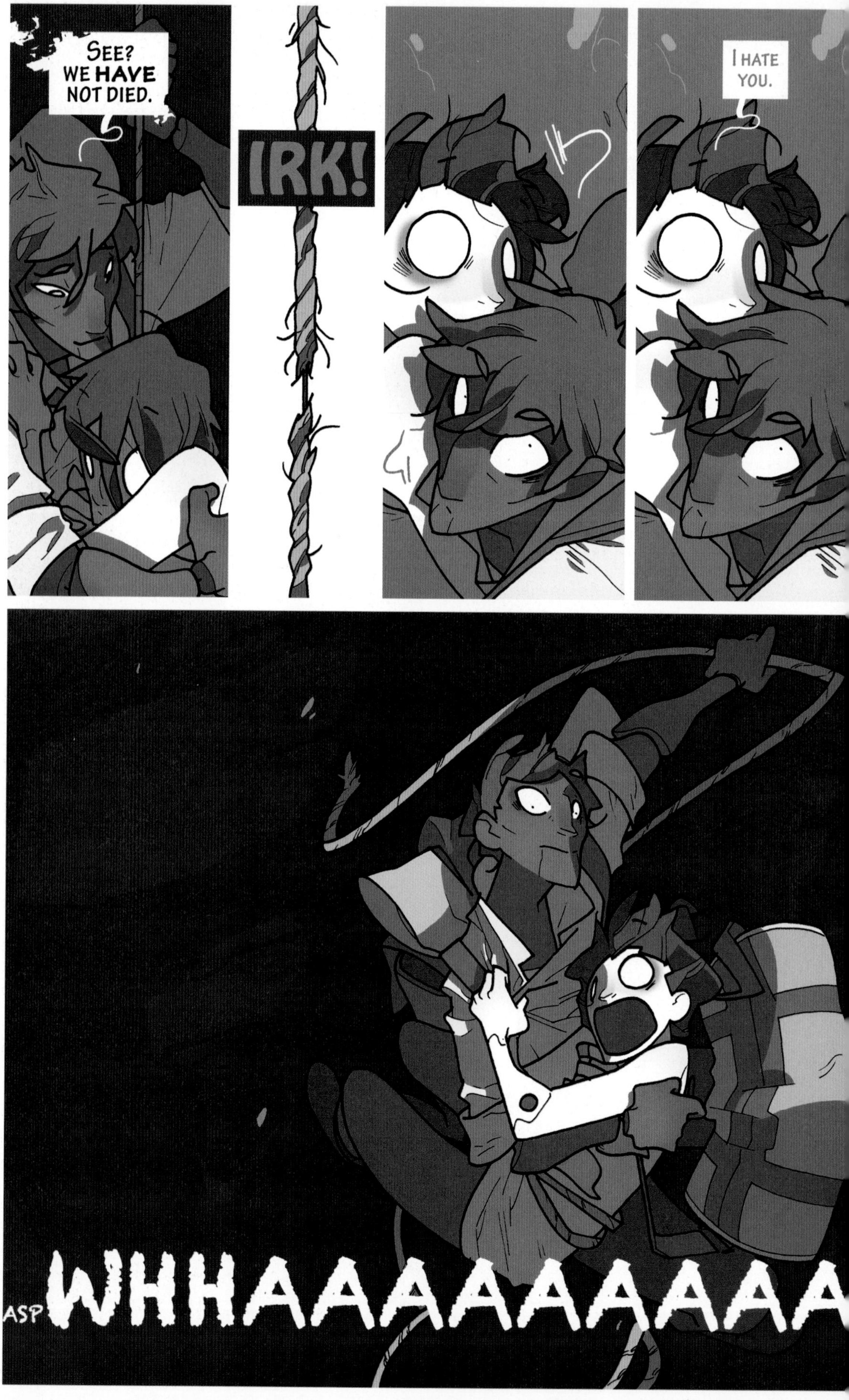
See?
We HAVE
not died.
IRK!
I hate
you.
ASP WHHAAAAAAAAAA

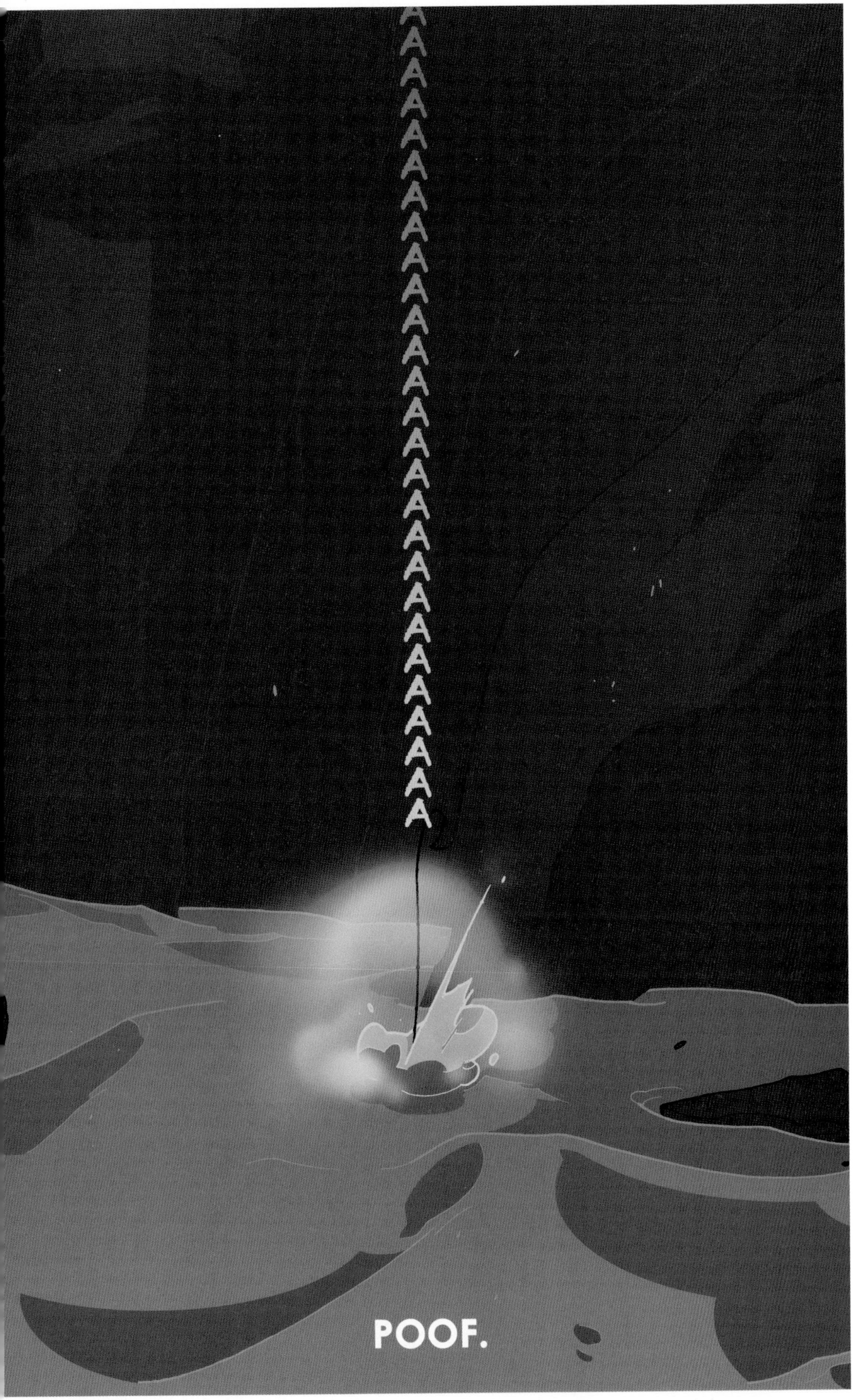

AAAAAAAAAAAAAAAAAAAAAAAAAAAAAAAA
POOF.

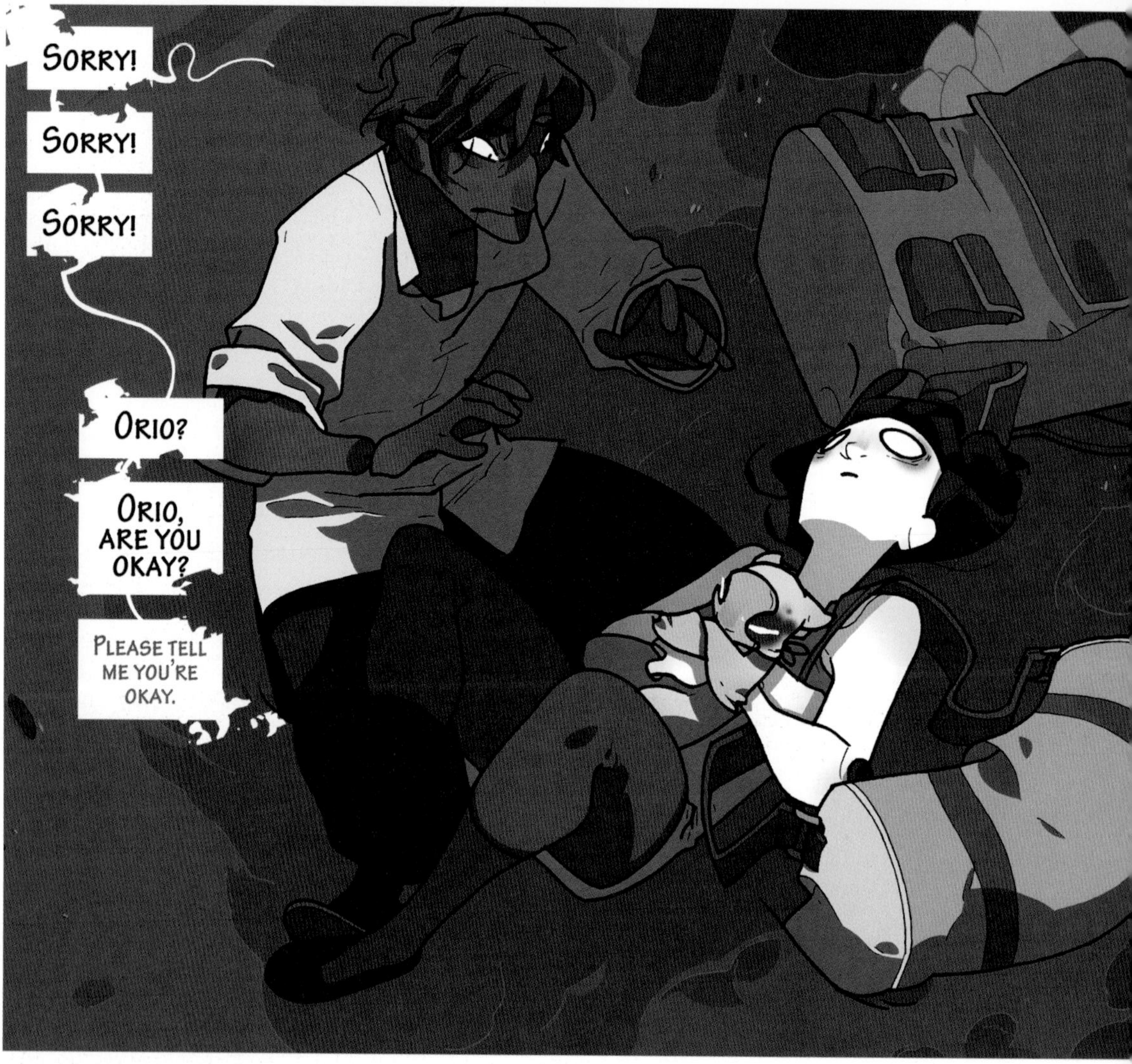
Sorry!
Sorry!
Sorry!
Orio?
Orio, are you okay?
Please tell me you're okay.

Hah.

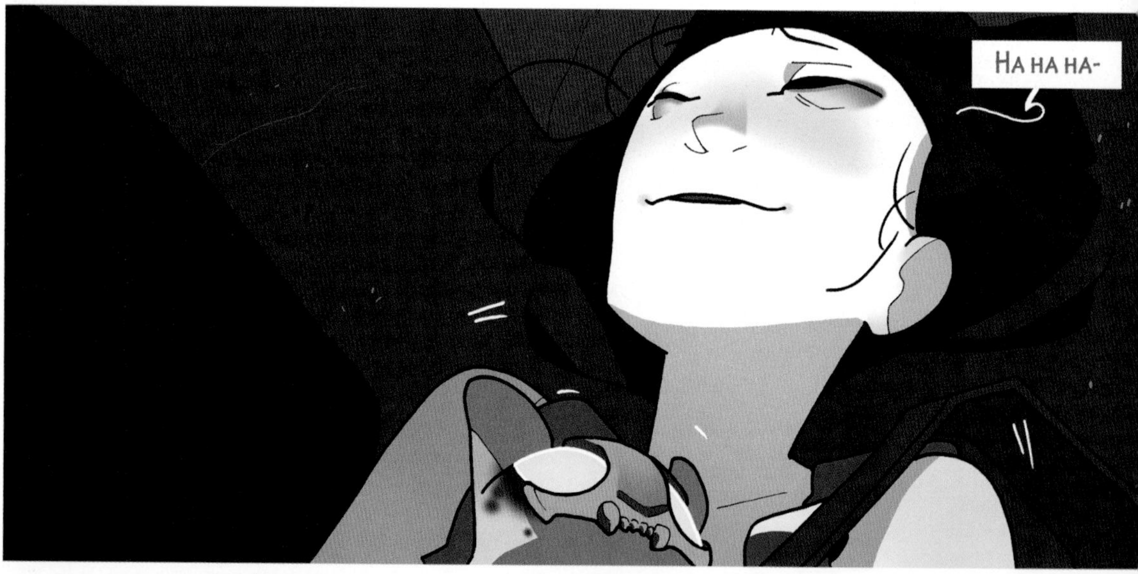
Ha ha ha-

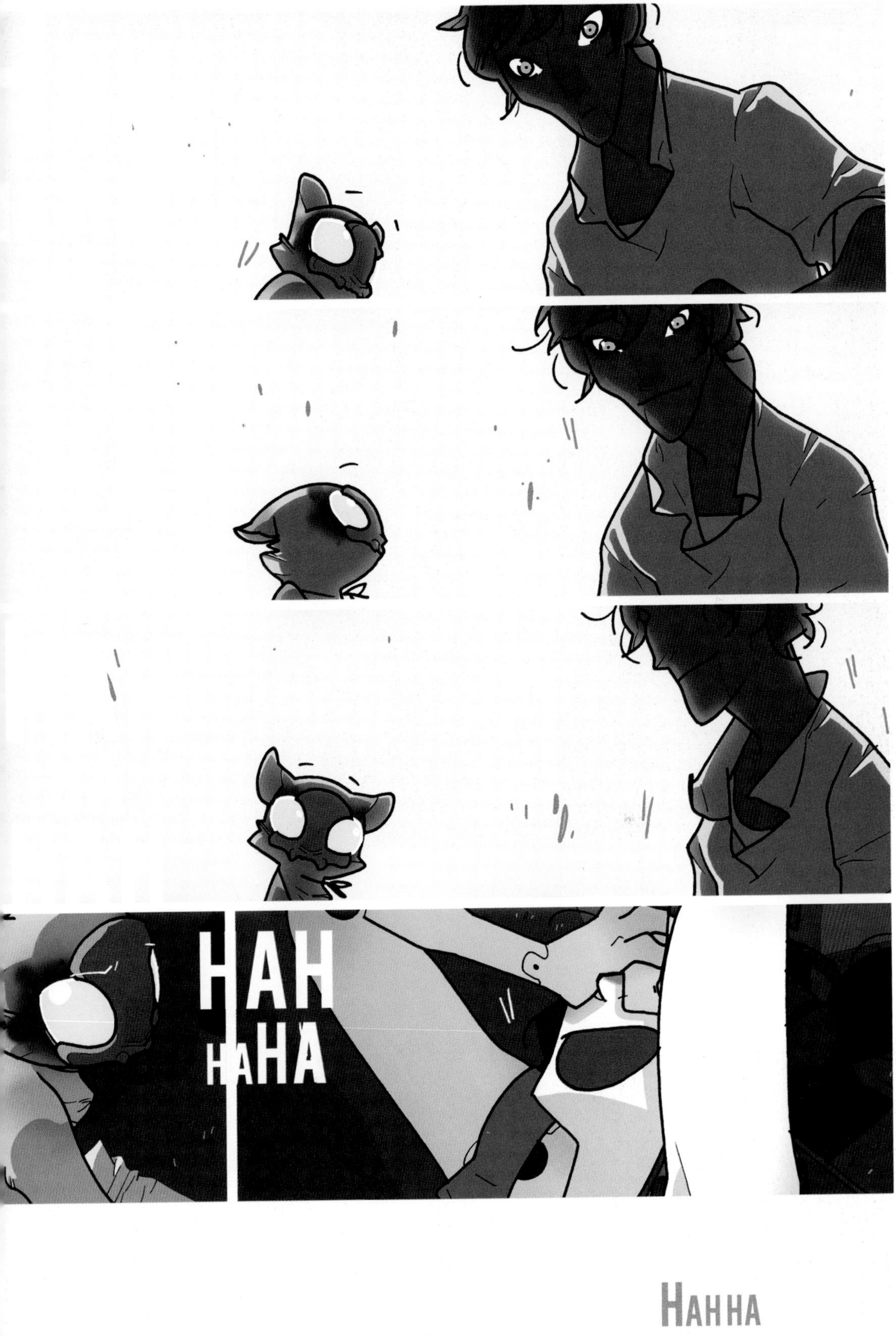
HAH
HaHA
HAHHA
HA

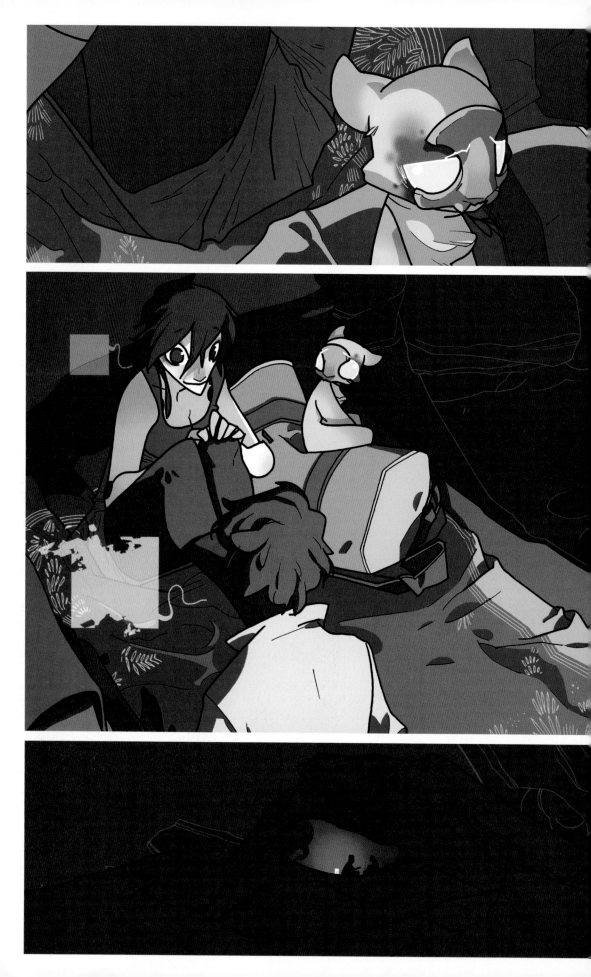

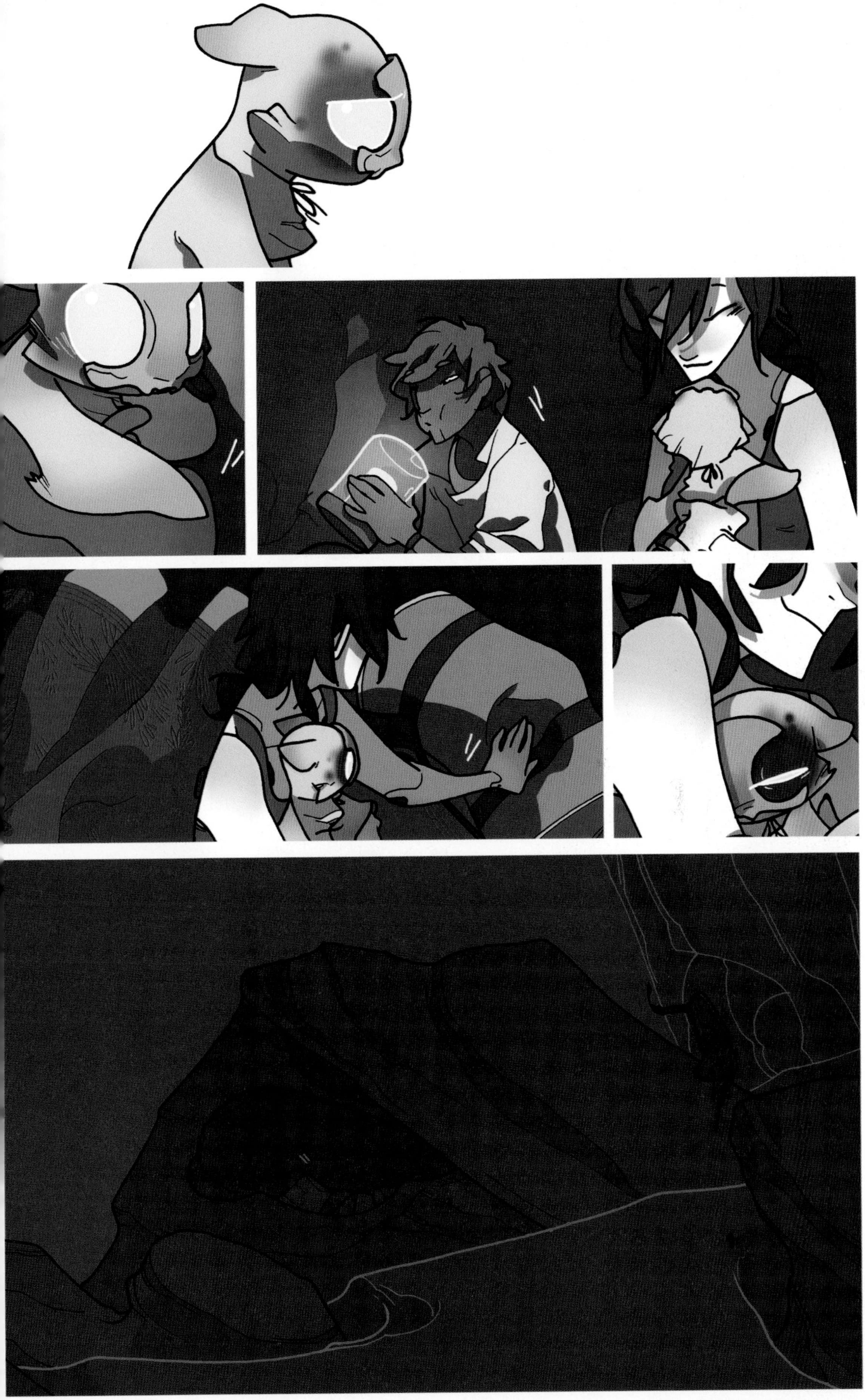

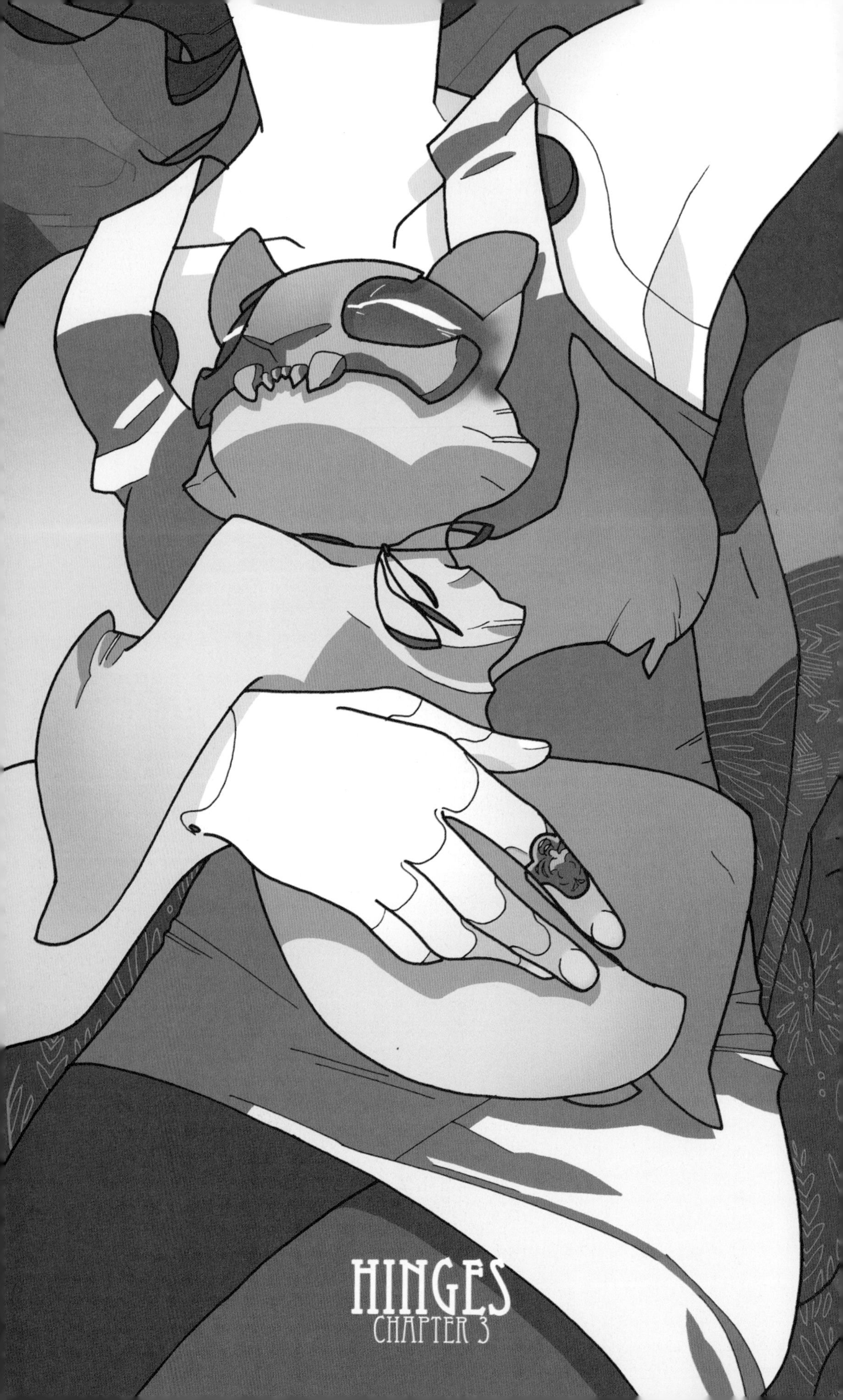

HINGES
CHAPTER 3

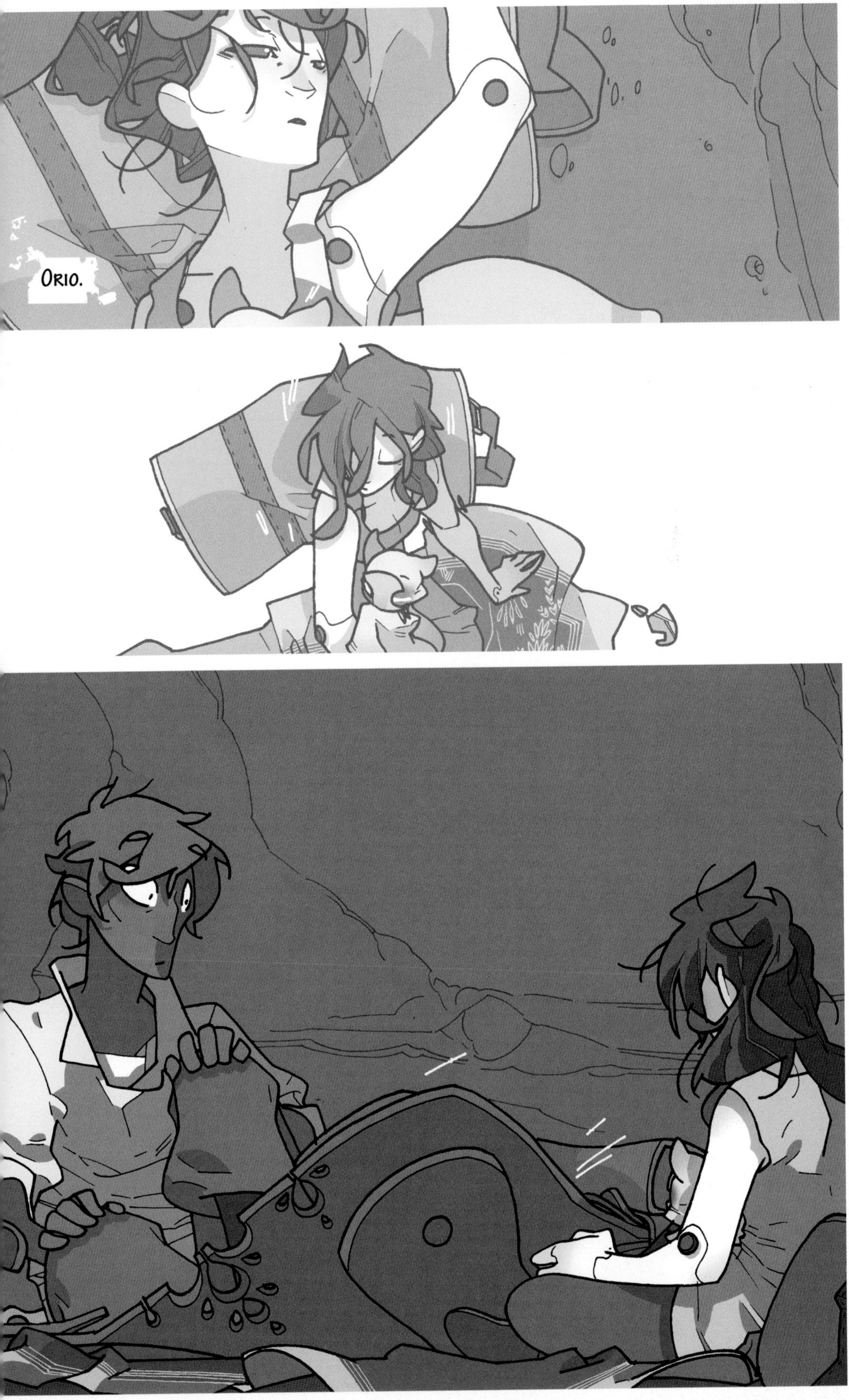
Orio.

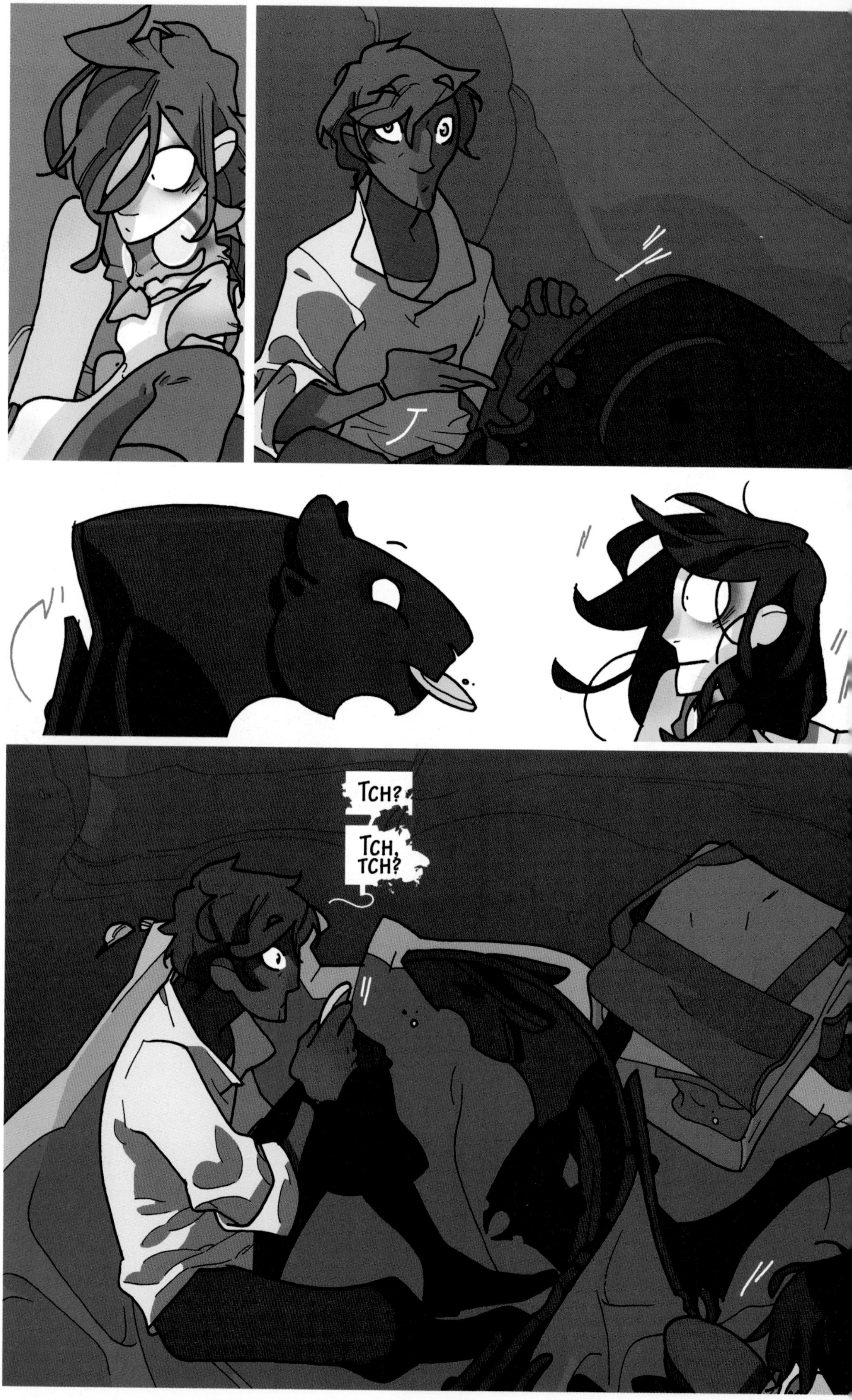

TCH?
TCH, TCH?

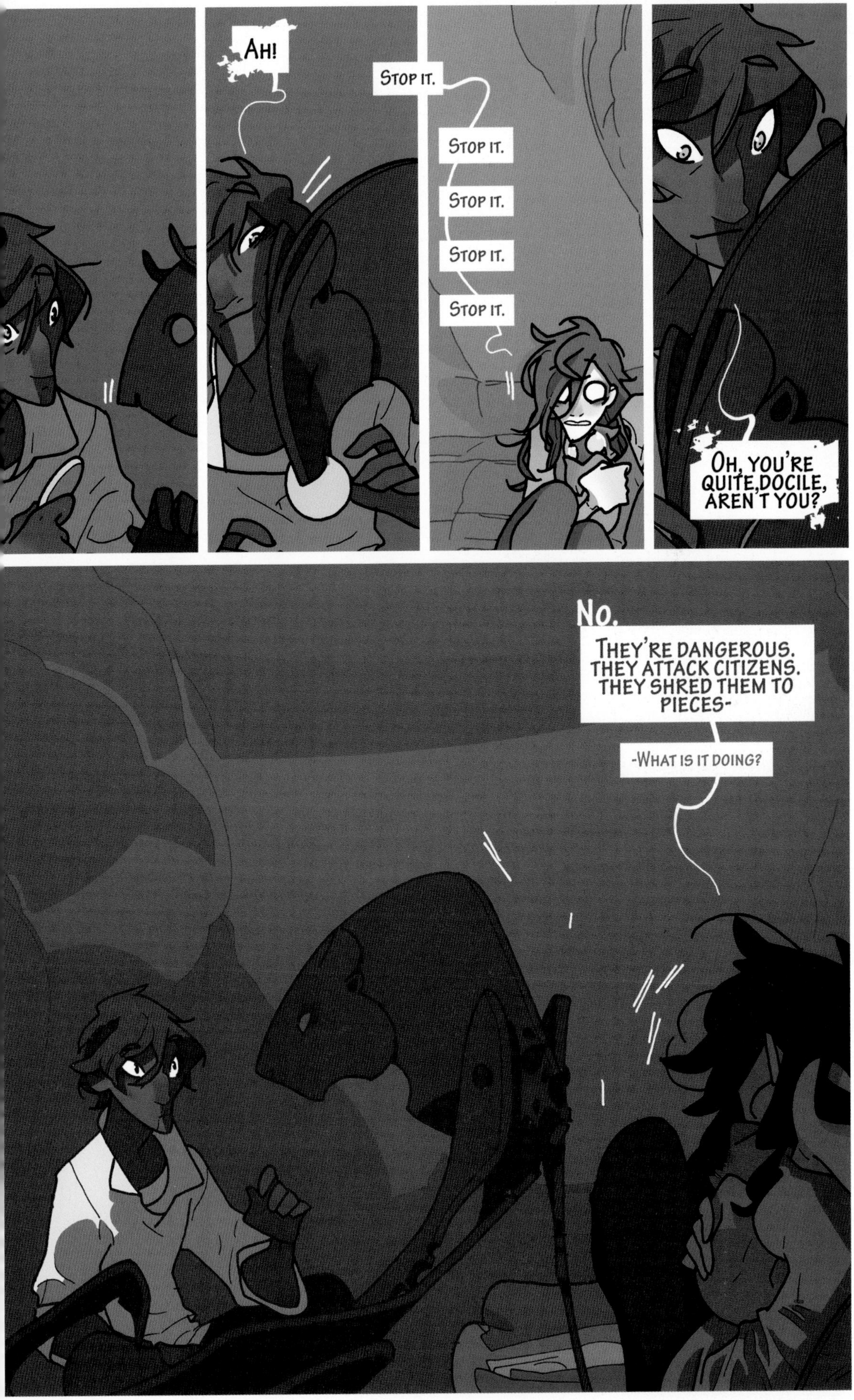
Ah!
Stop it.
Stop it.
Stop it.
Stop it.
Stop it.
Oh, you're quite,docile, aren't you?
No.
They're dangerous. They attack citizens. They shred them to pieces-
-What is it doing?

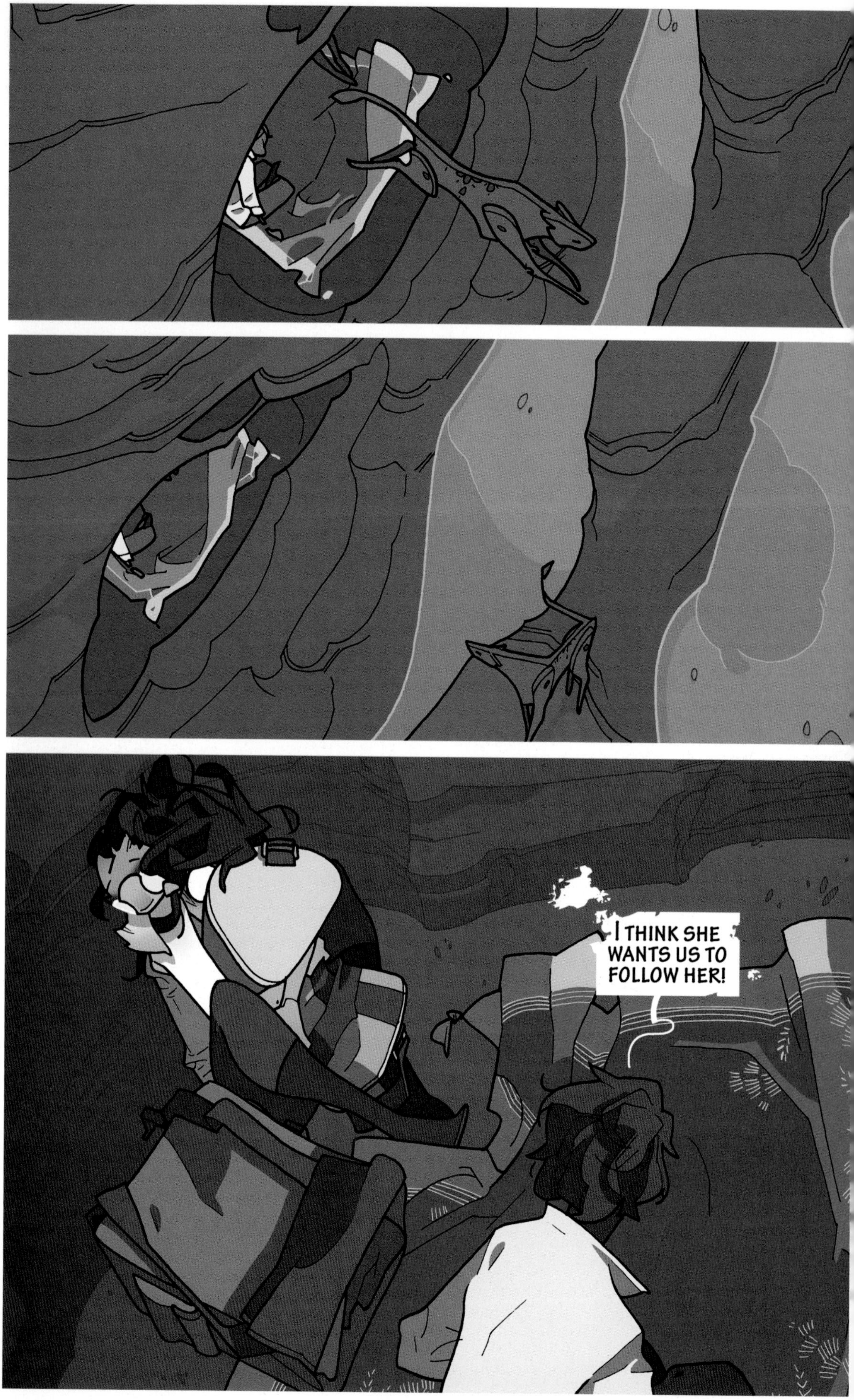
I THINK SHE WANTS US TO FOLLOW HER!

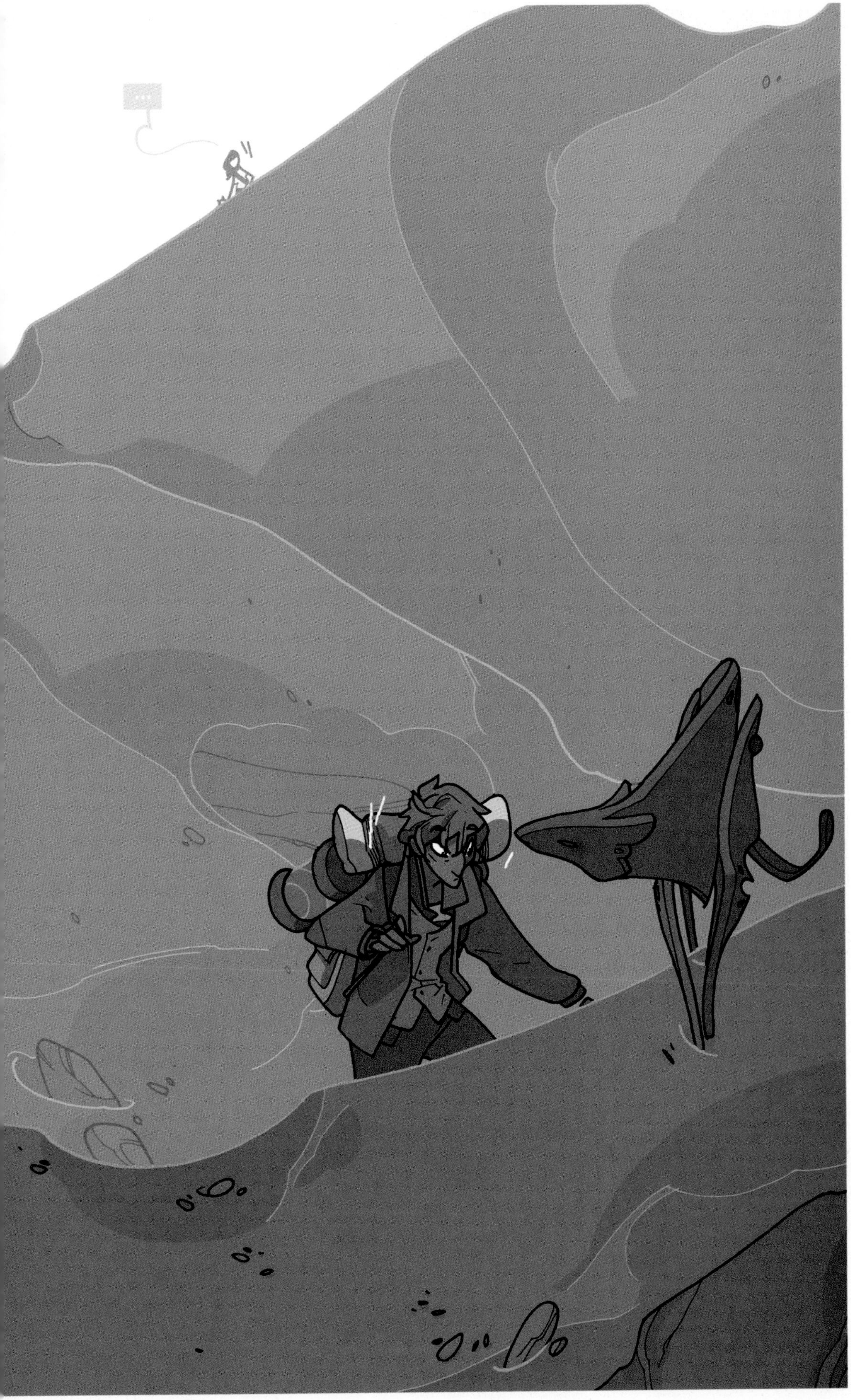
...

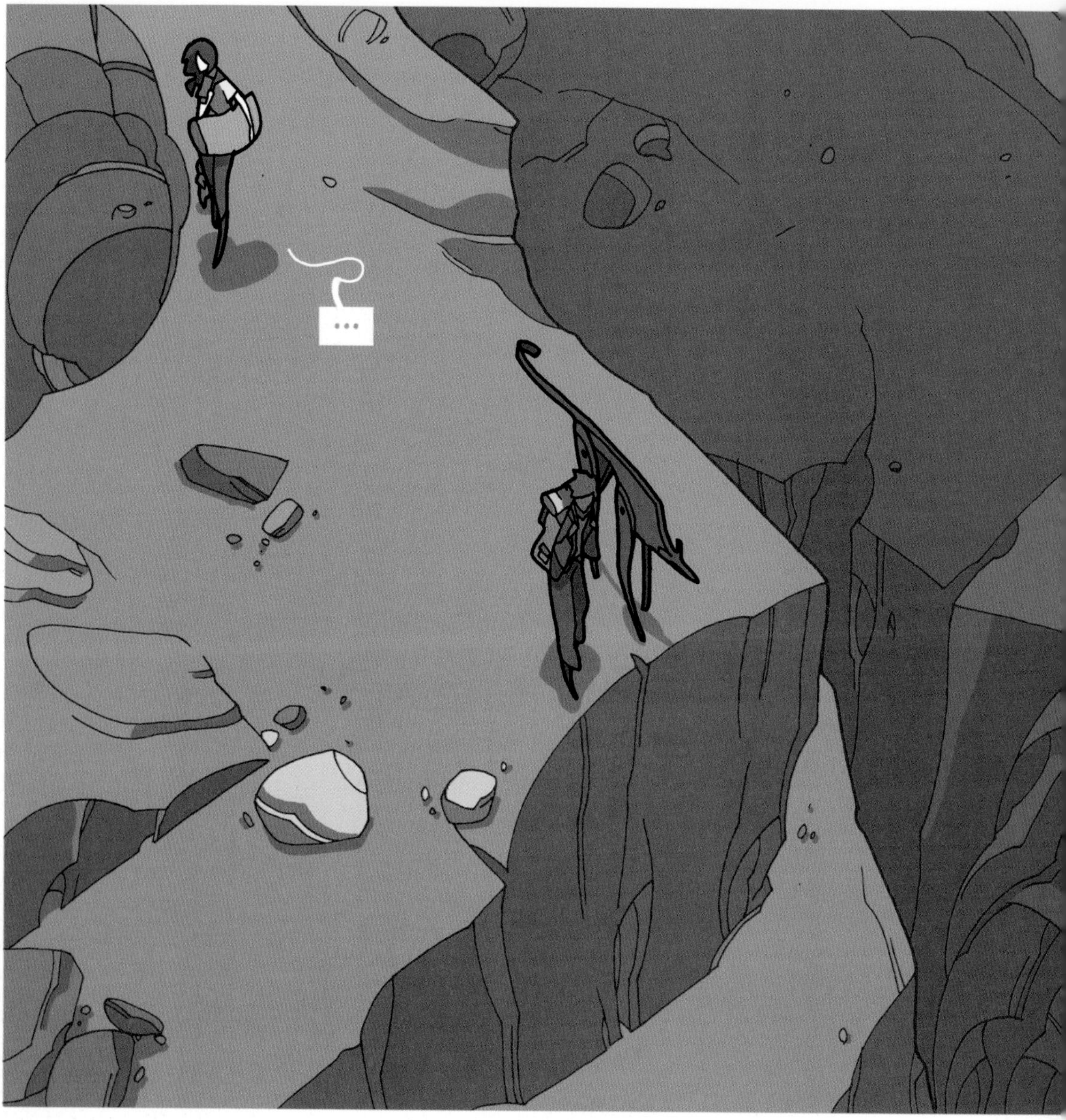
...

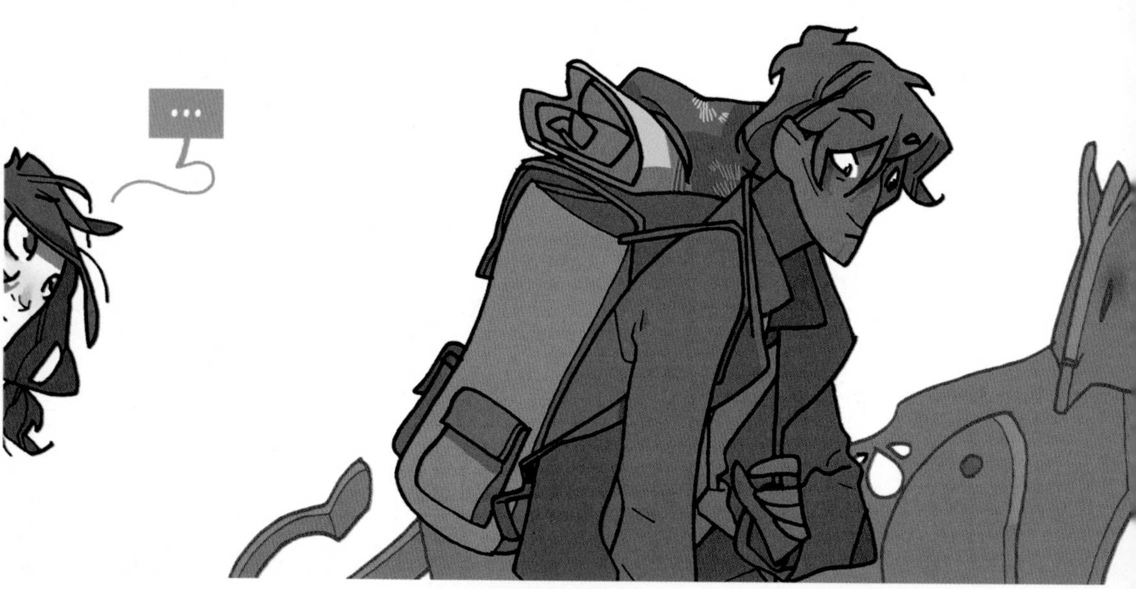
...

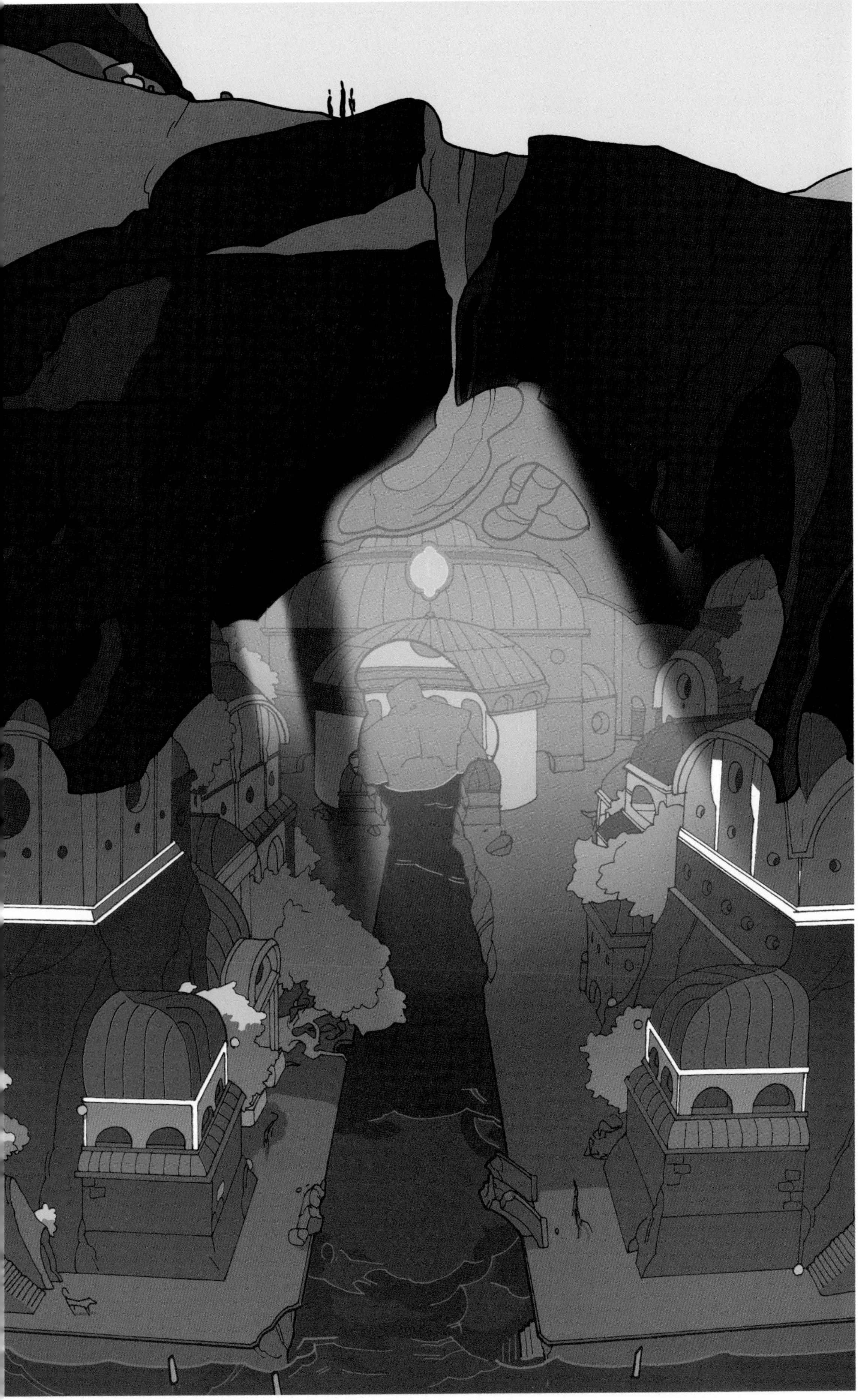

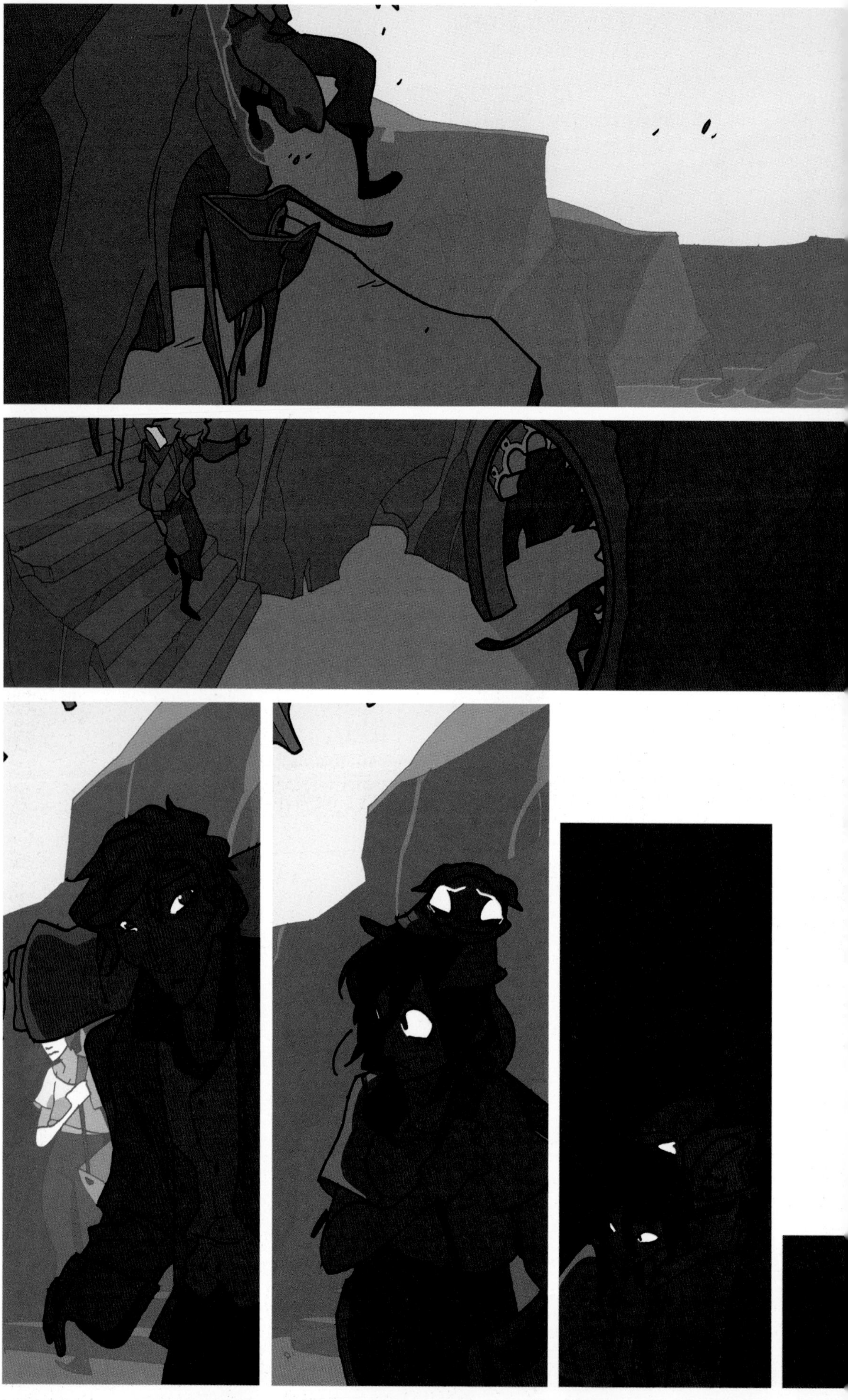

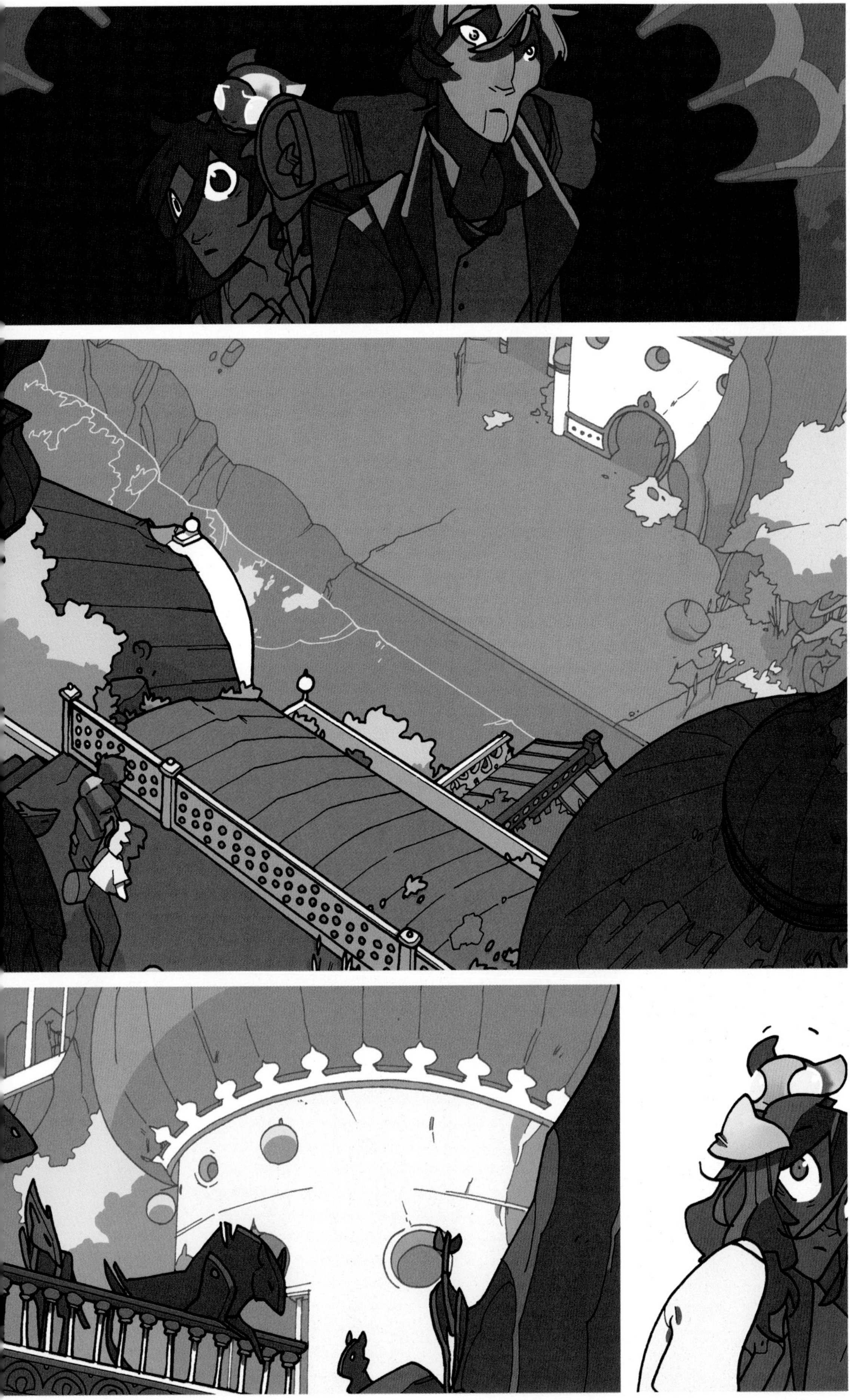

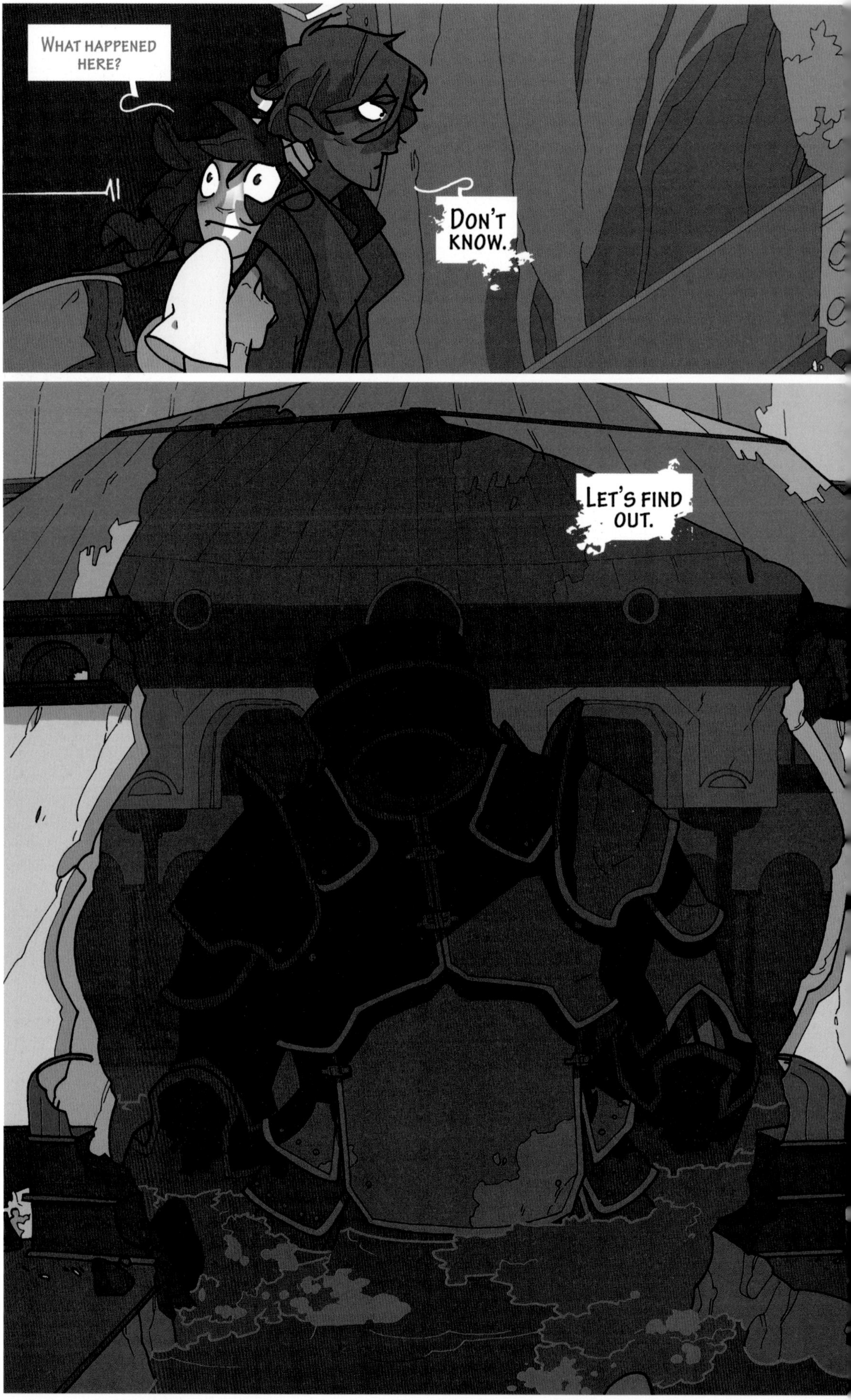
What happened here?
Don't know.
Let's find out.

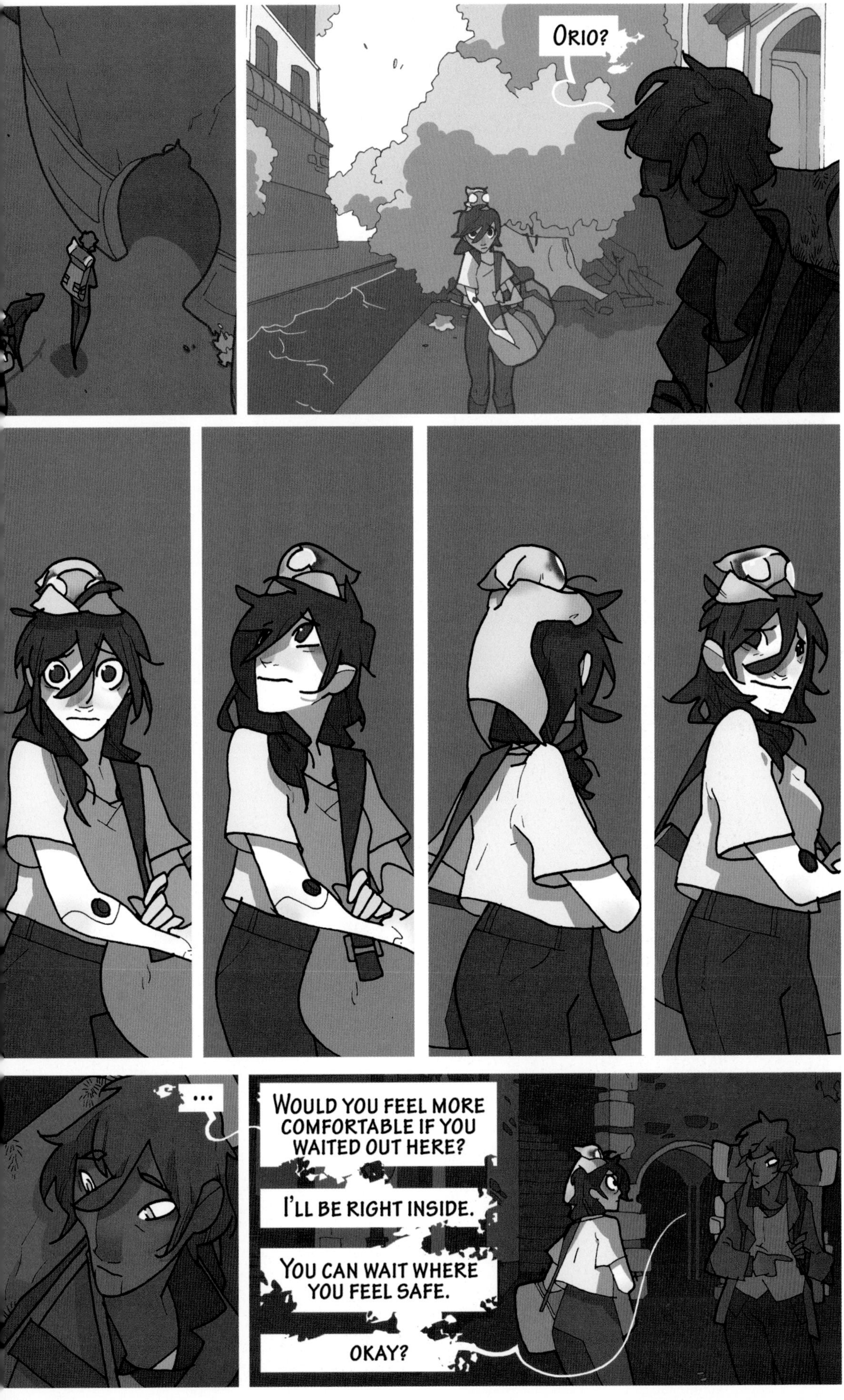

ORIO?
...
WOULD YOU FEEL MORE COMFORTABLE IF YOU WAITED OUT HERE?
I'LL BE RIGHT INSIDE.
YOU CAN WAIT WHERE YOU FEEL SAFE.
OKAY?

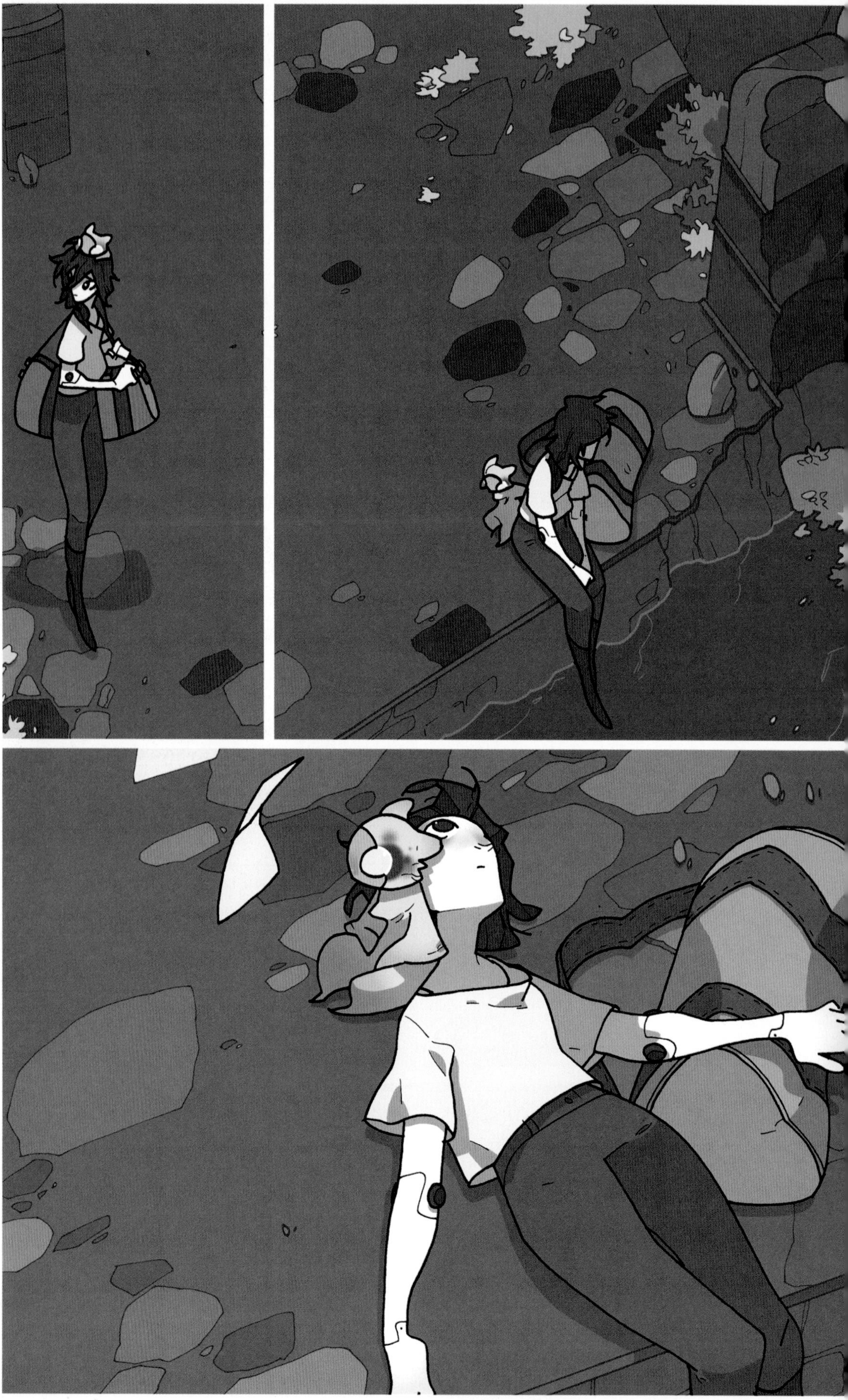

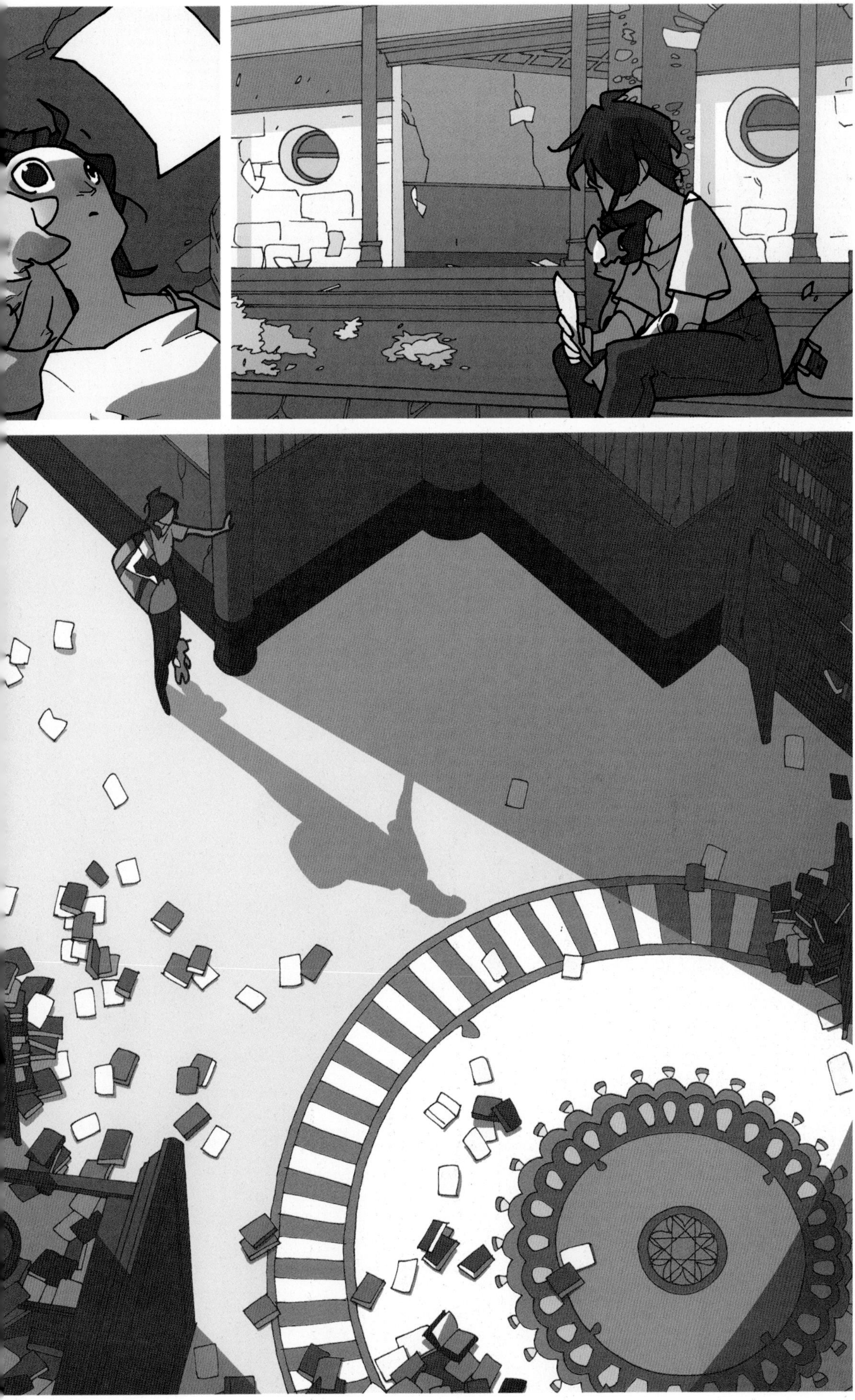

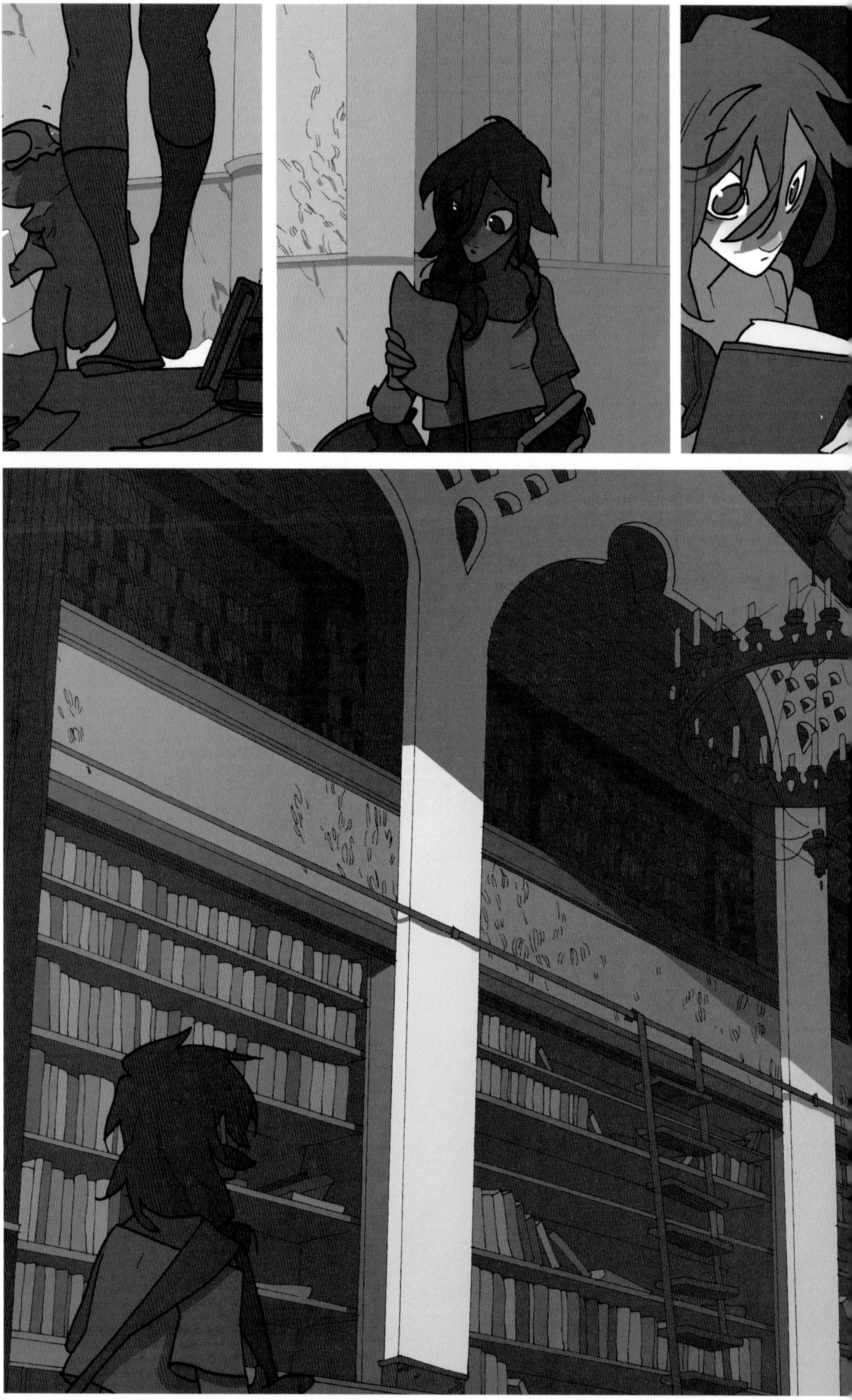

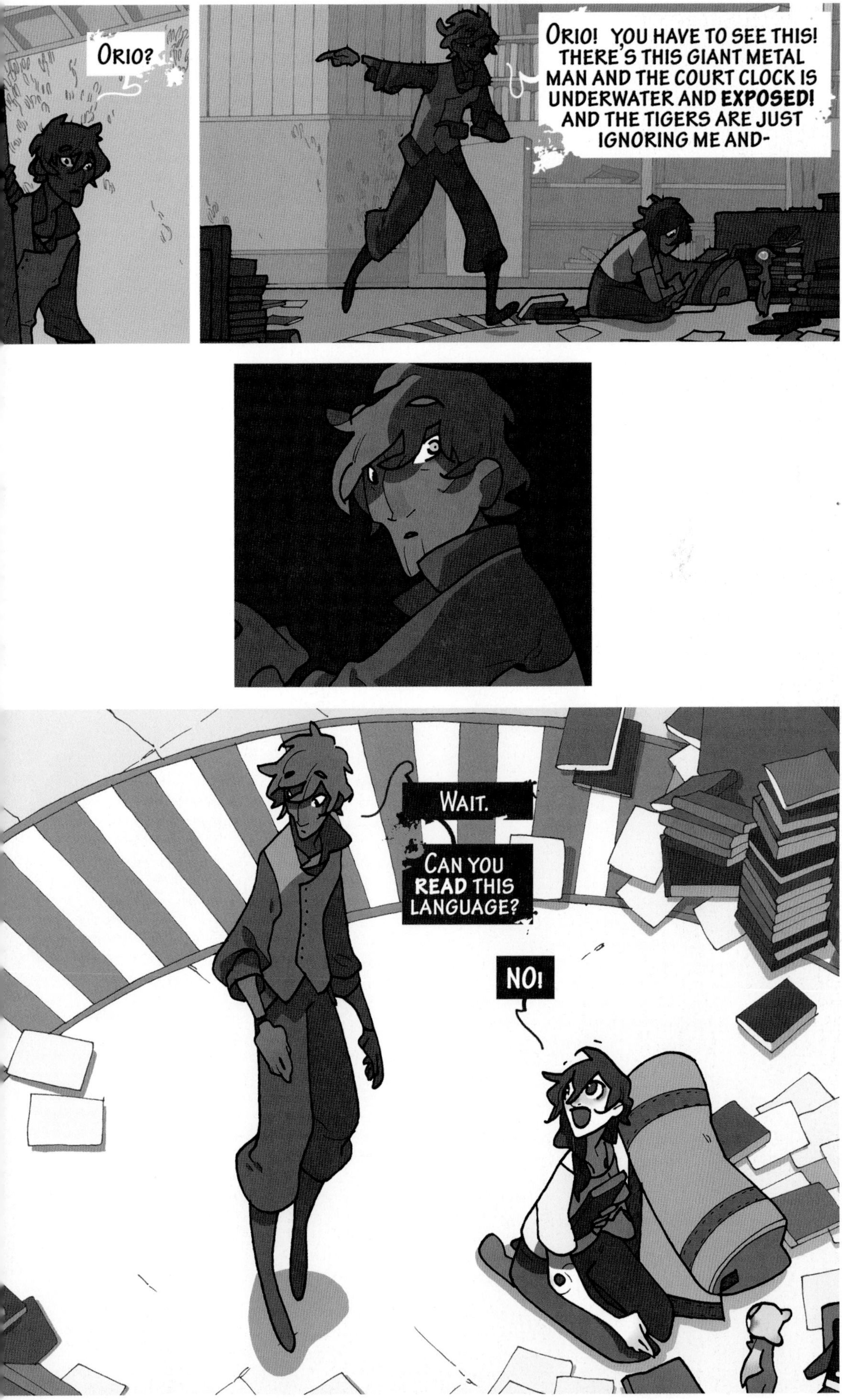
Orio?
Orio! You have to see this! There's this giant metal man and the court clock is underwater and **exposed!** And the tigers are just ignoring me and-
Wait.
Can you **read** this language?
NO!

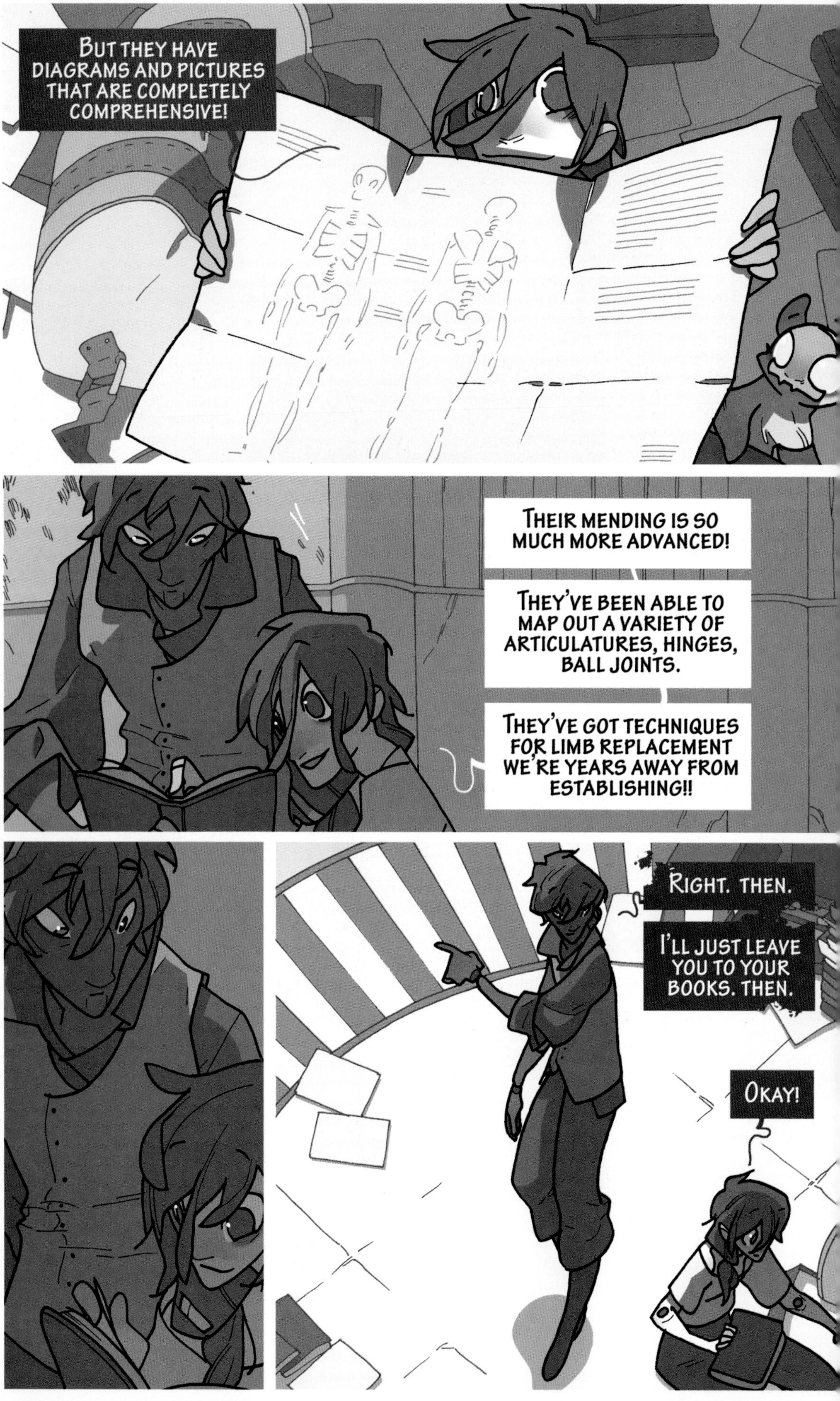
But they have diagrams and pictures that are completely comprehensive!
Their mending is so much more advanced!
They've been able to map out a variety of articulatures, hinges, ball joints.
They've got techniques for limb replacement we're years away from establishing!!
Right. Then.
I'll just leave you to your books. Then.
Okay!

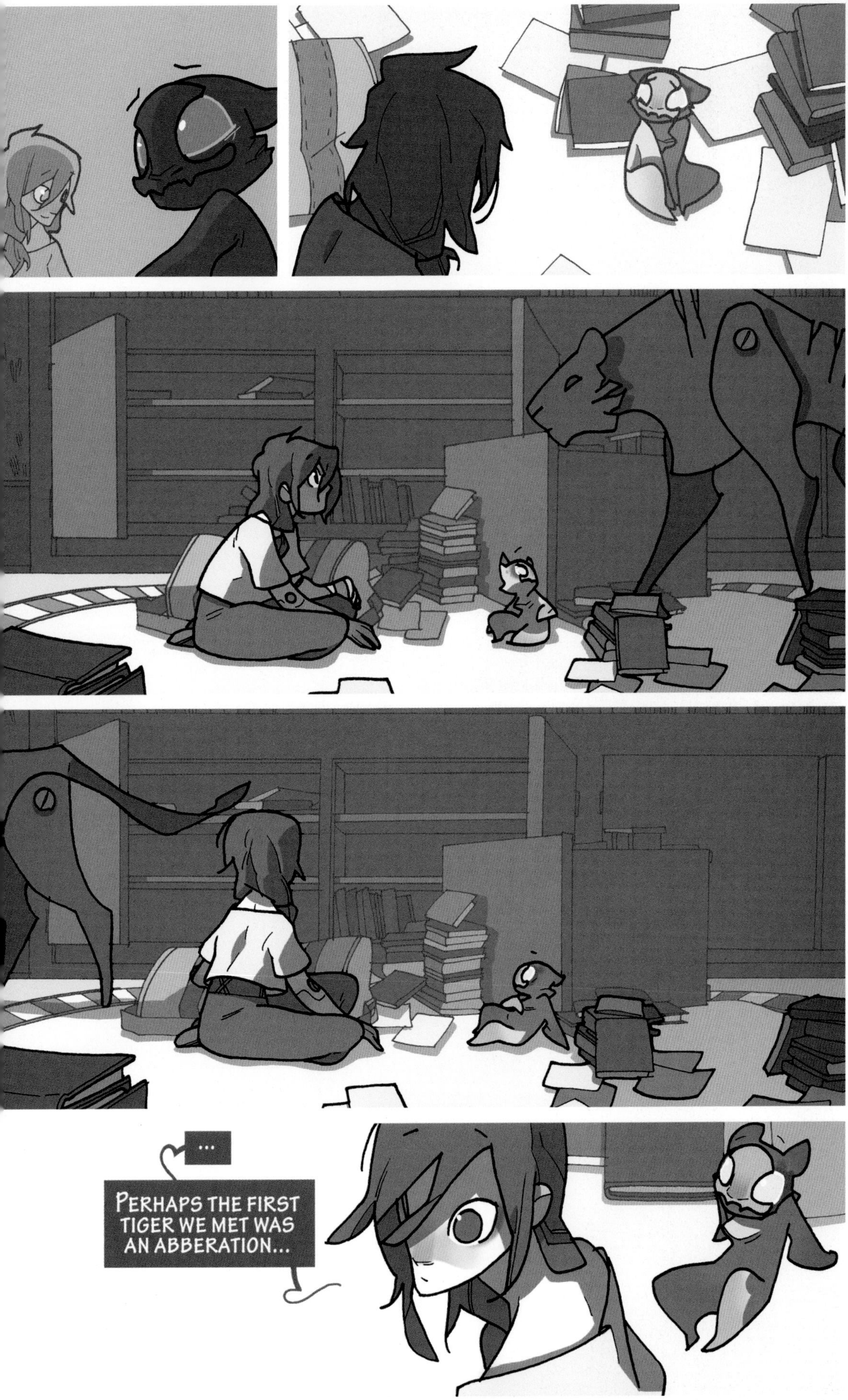
...
Perhaps the first tiger we met was an abberation...

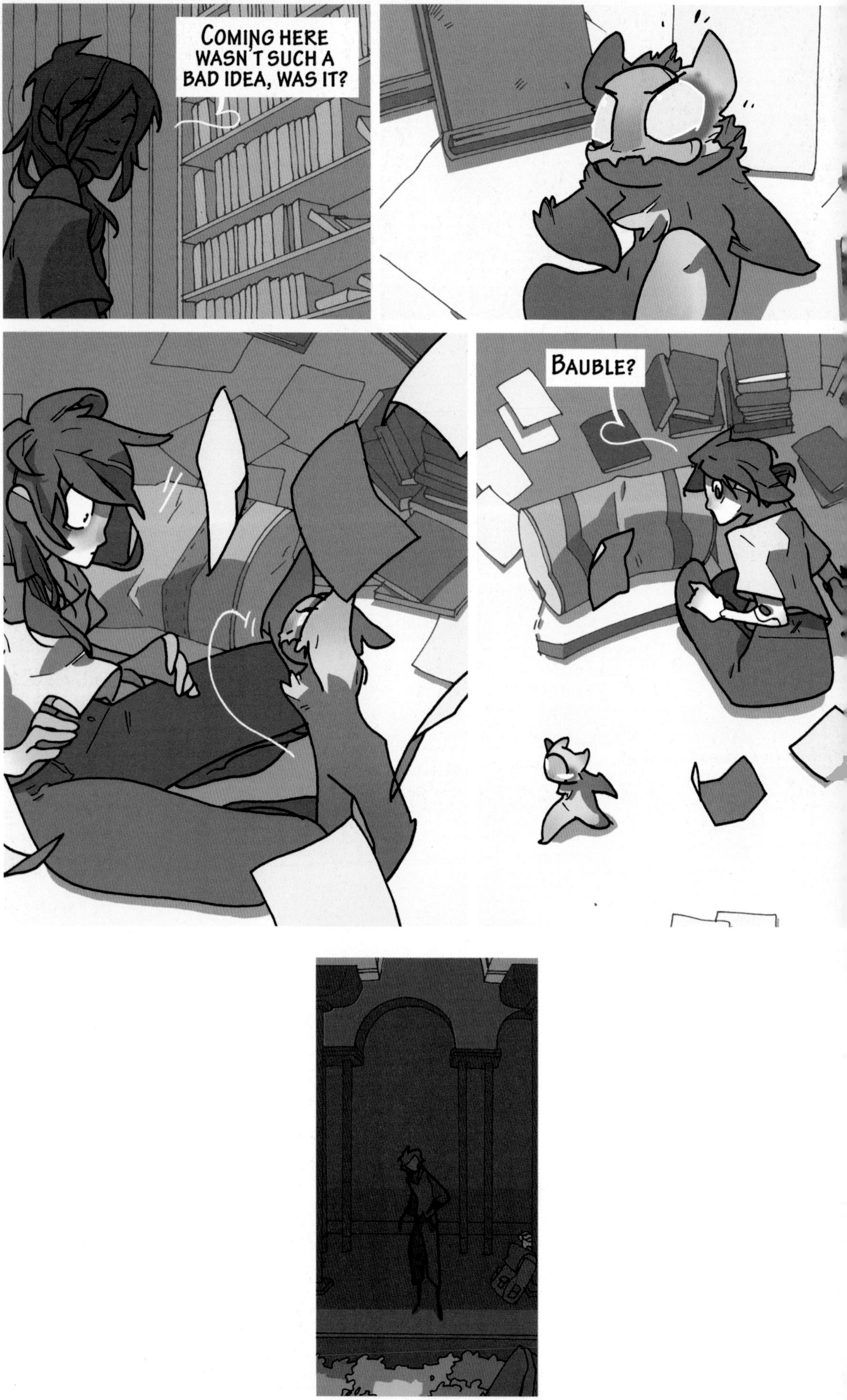
COMING HERE WASN'T SUCH A BAD IDEA, WAS IT?
BAUBLE?

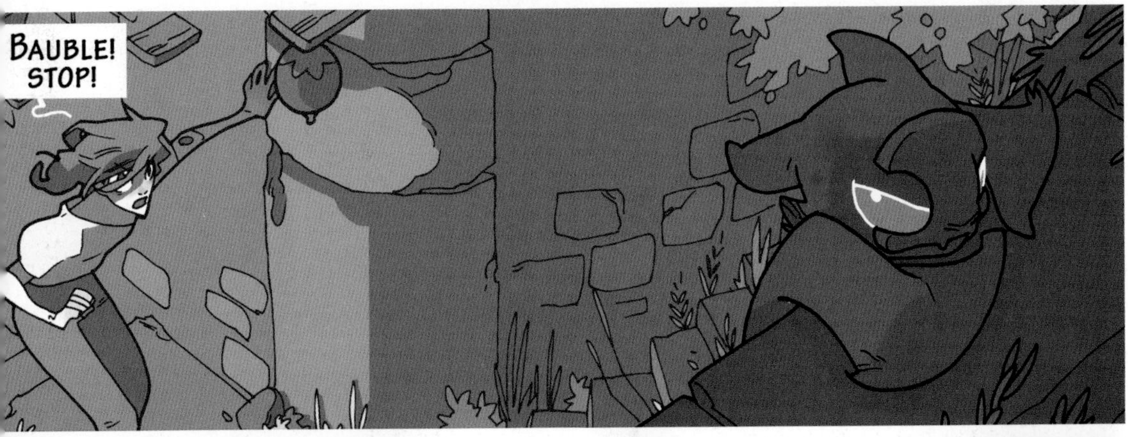
BAUBLE! STOP!

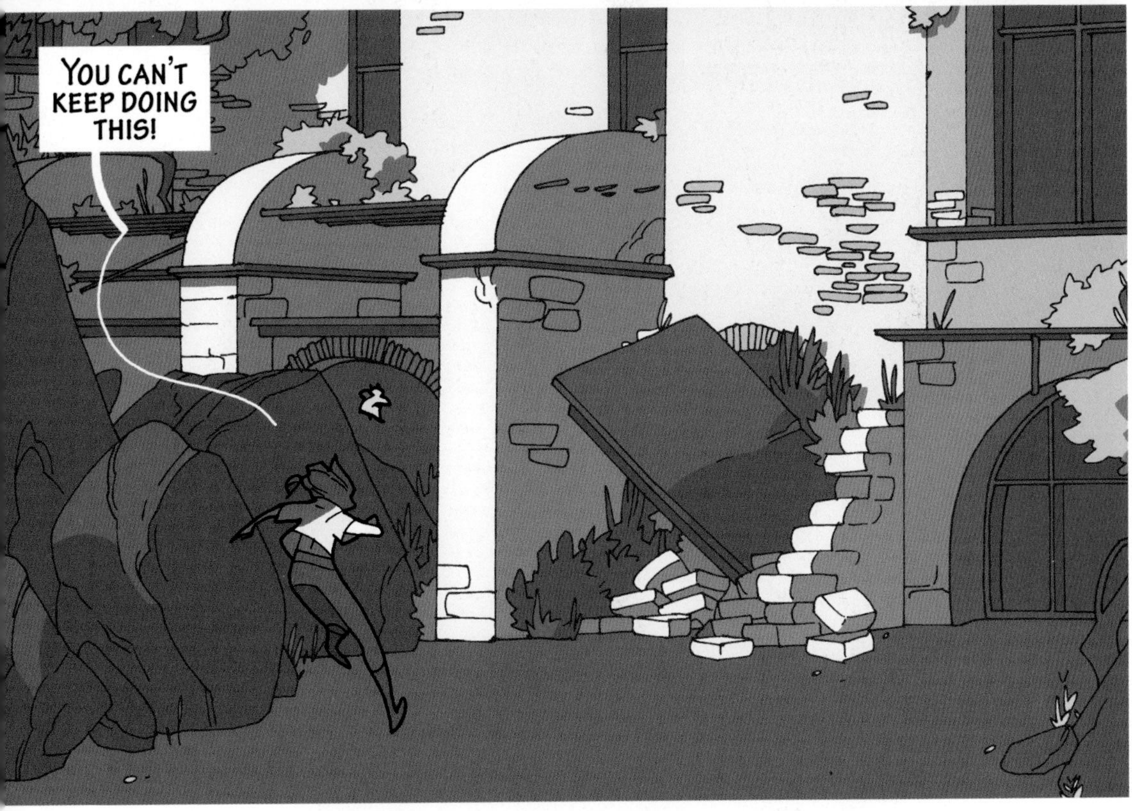
YOU CAN'T KEEP DOING THIS!

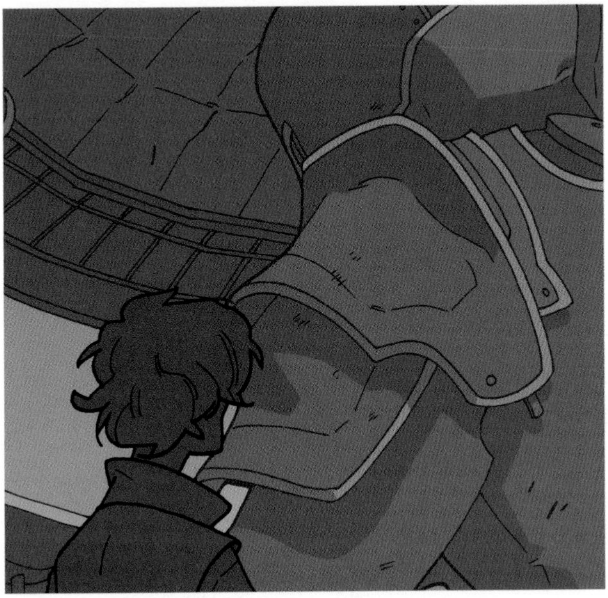

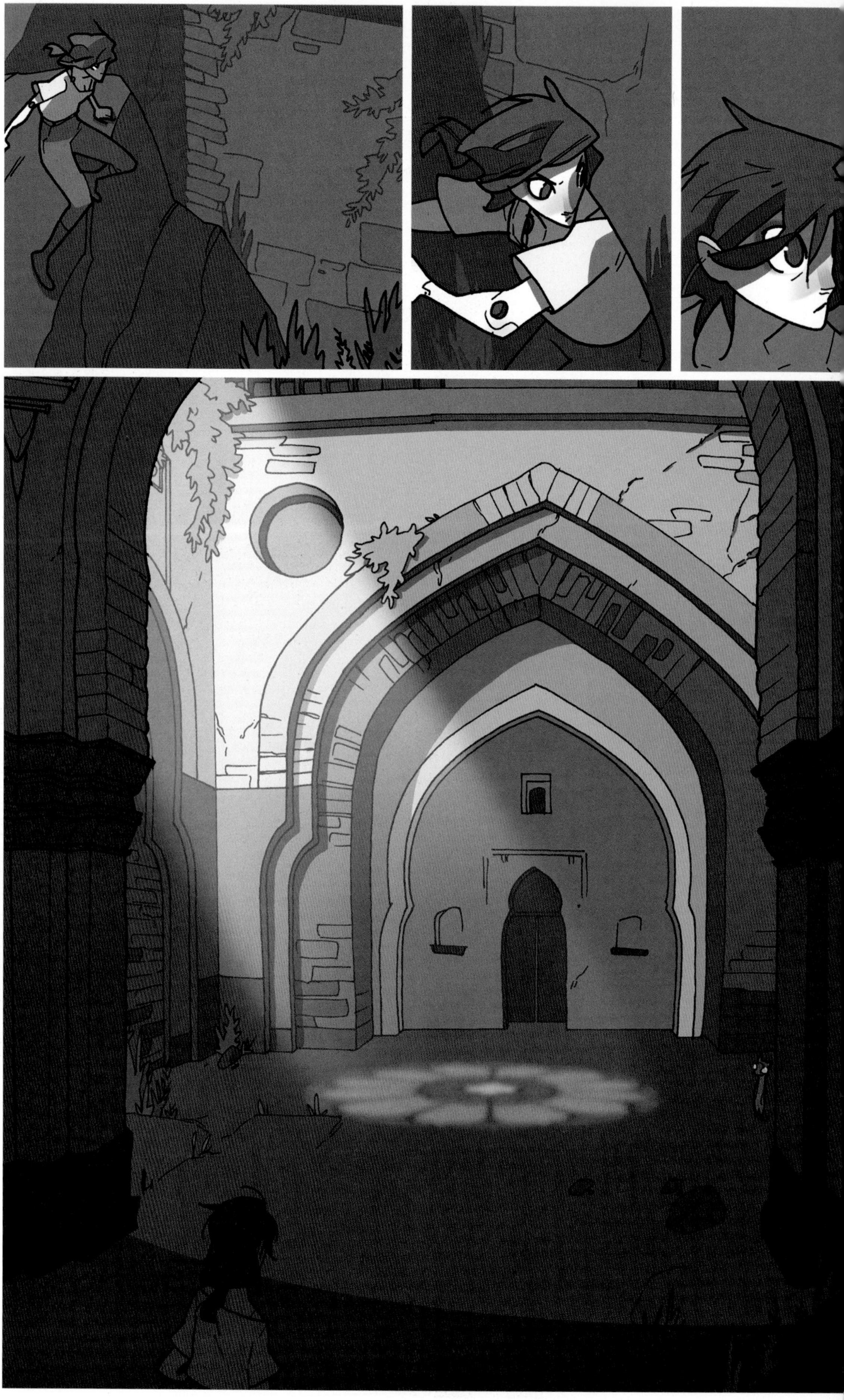

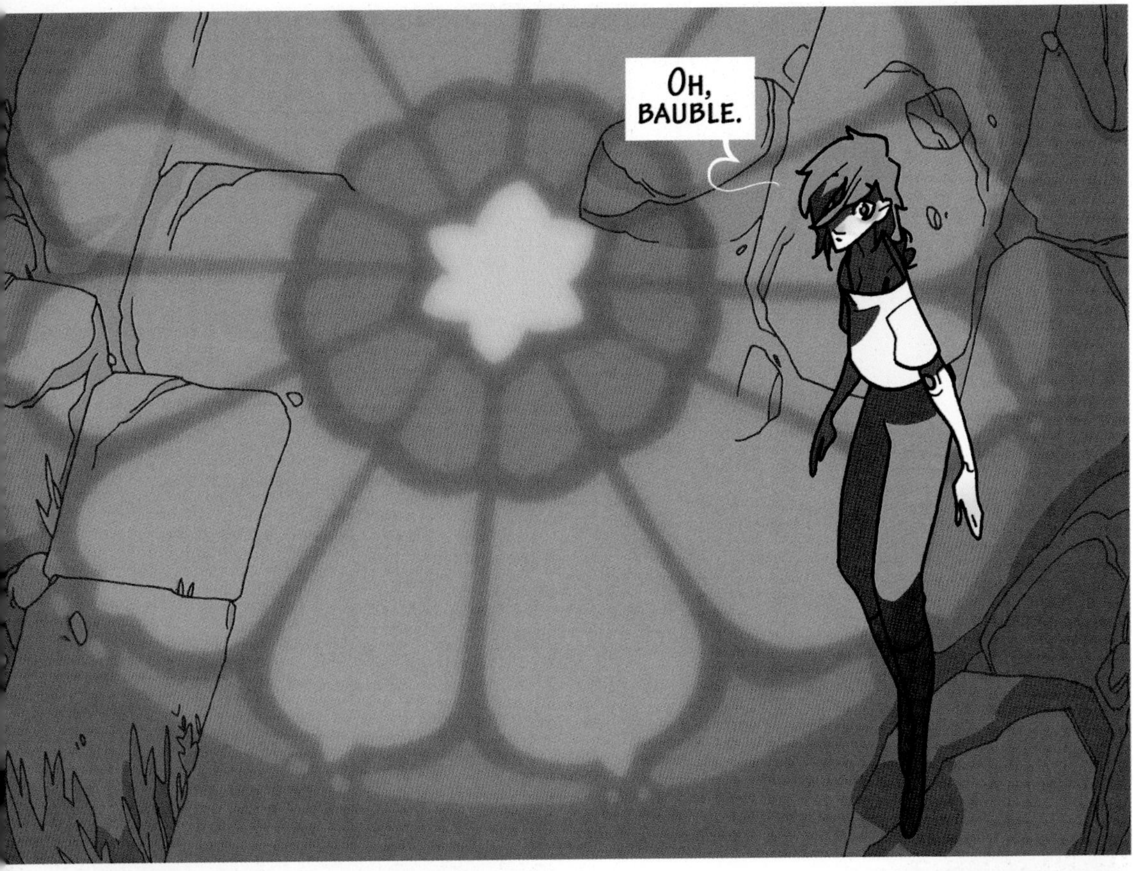
OH, BAUBLE.

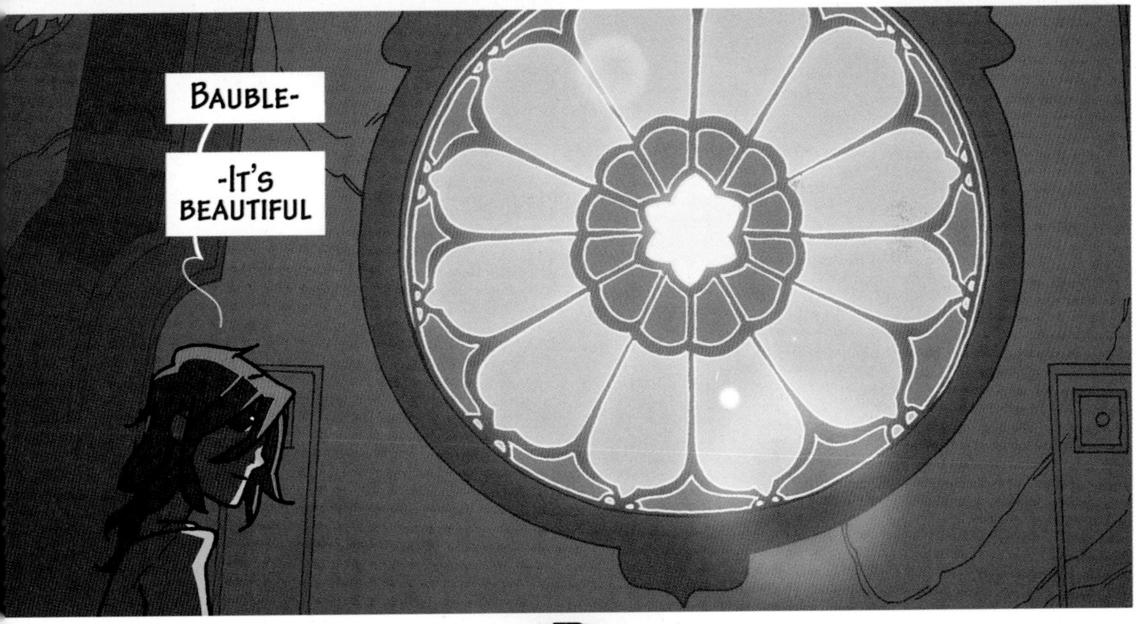
BAUBLE-
-IT'S BEAUTIFUL

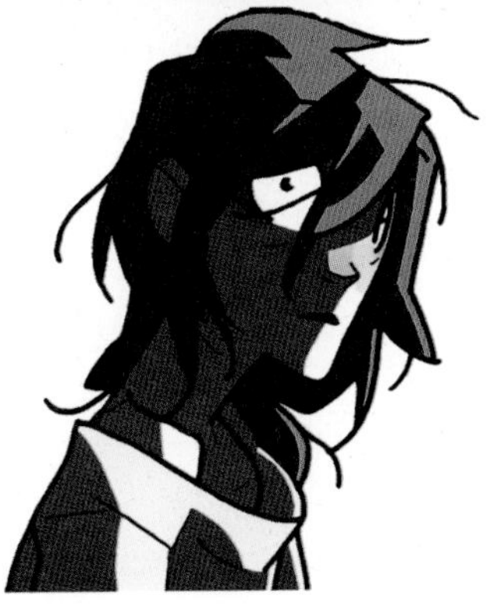

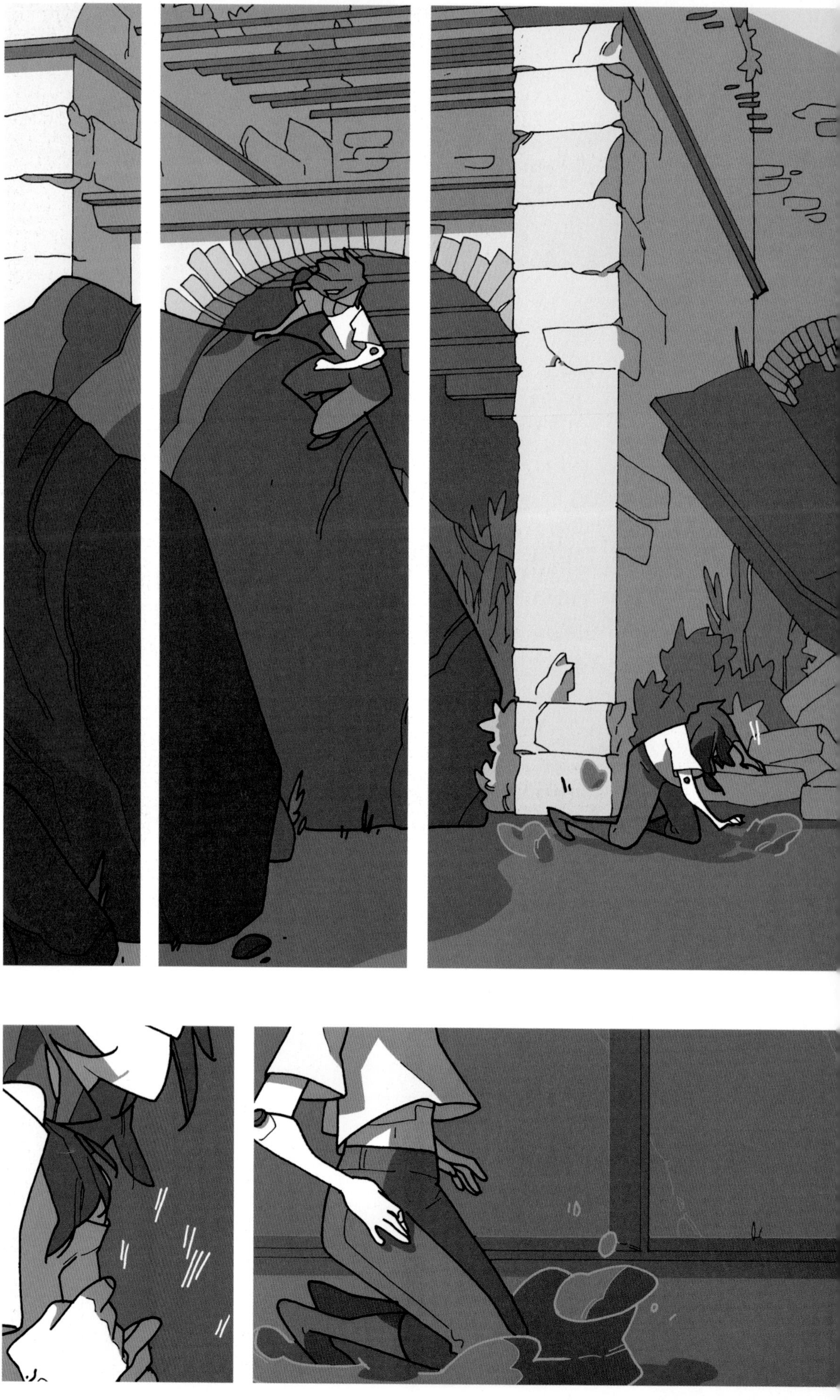

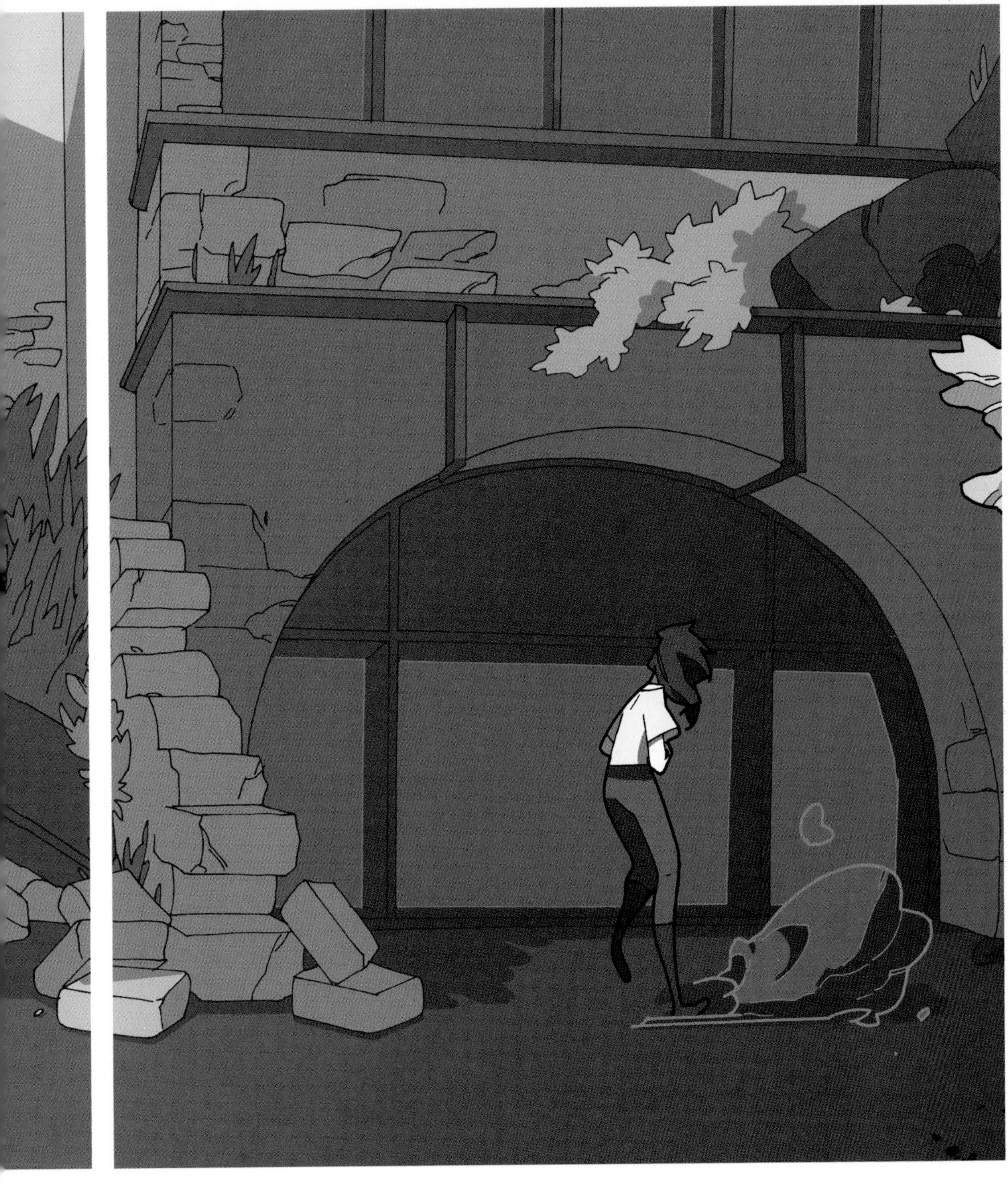

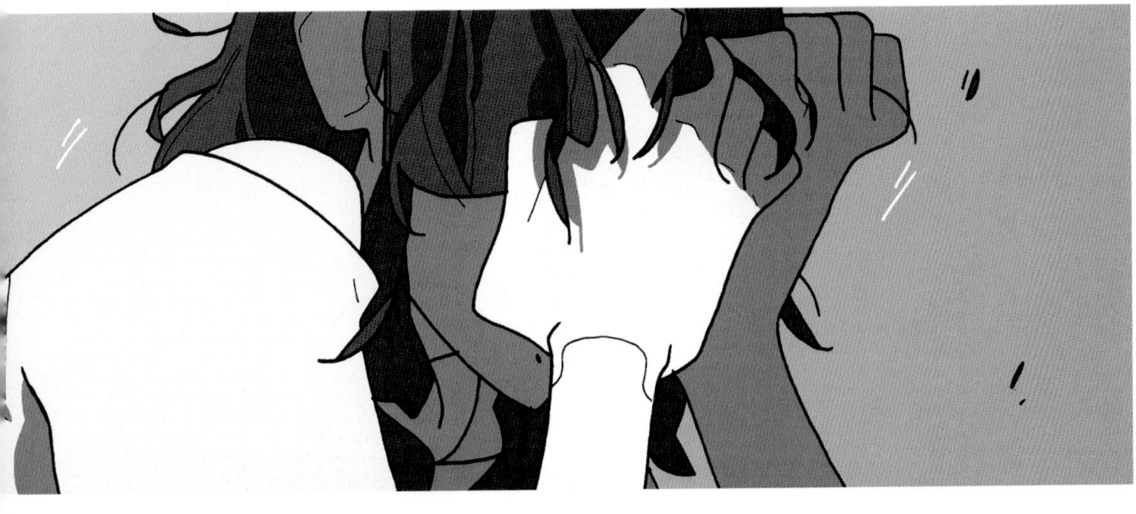

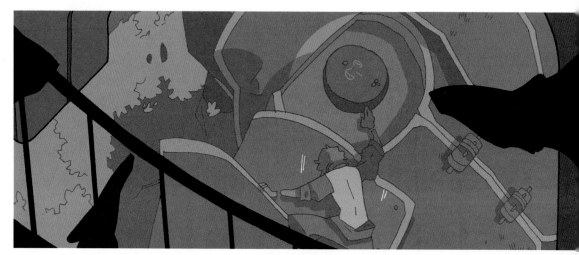

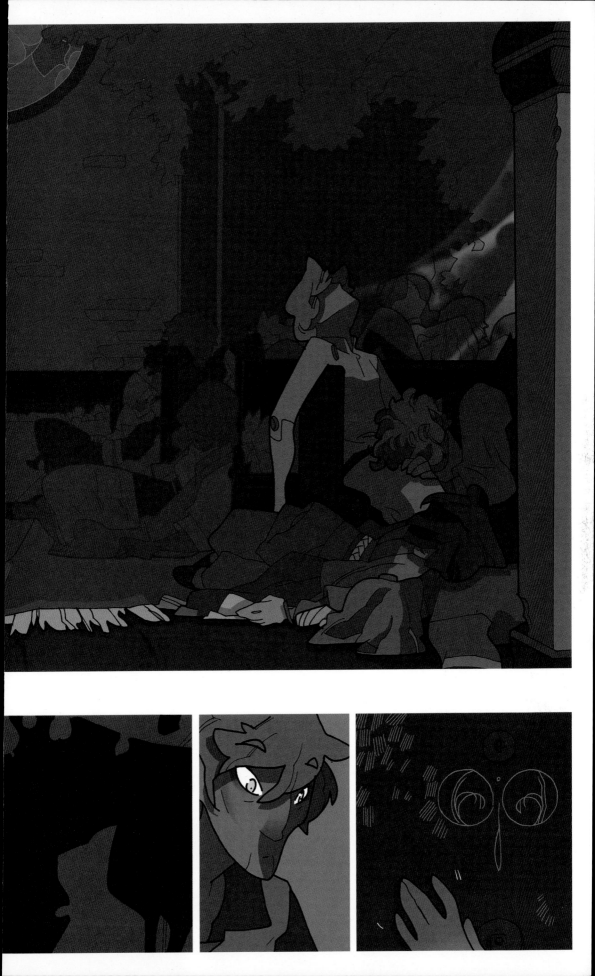

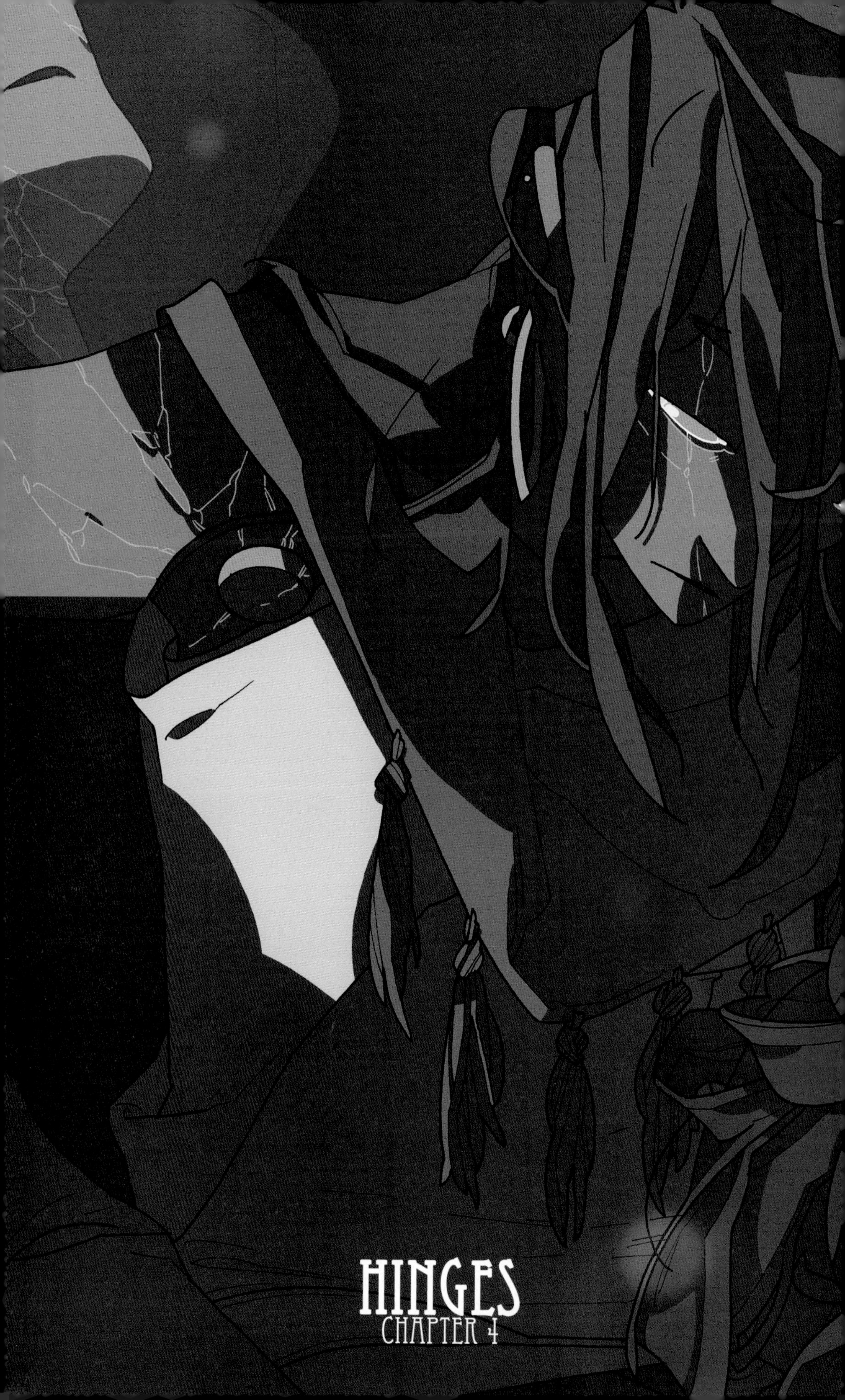
HINGES
CHAPTER 4

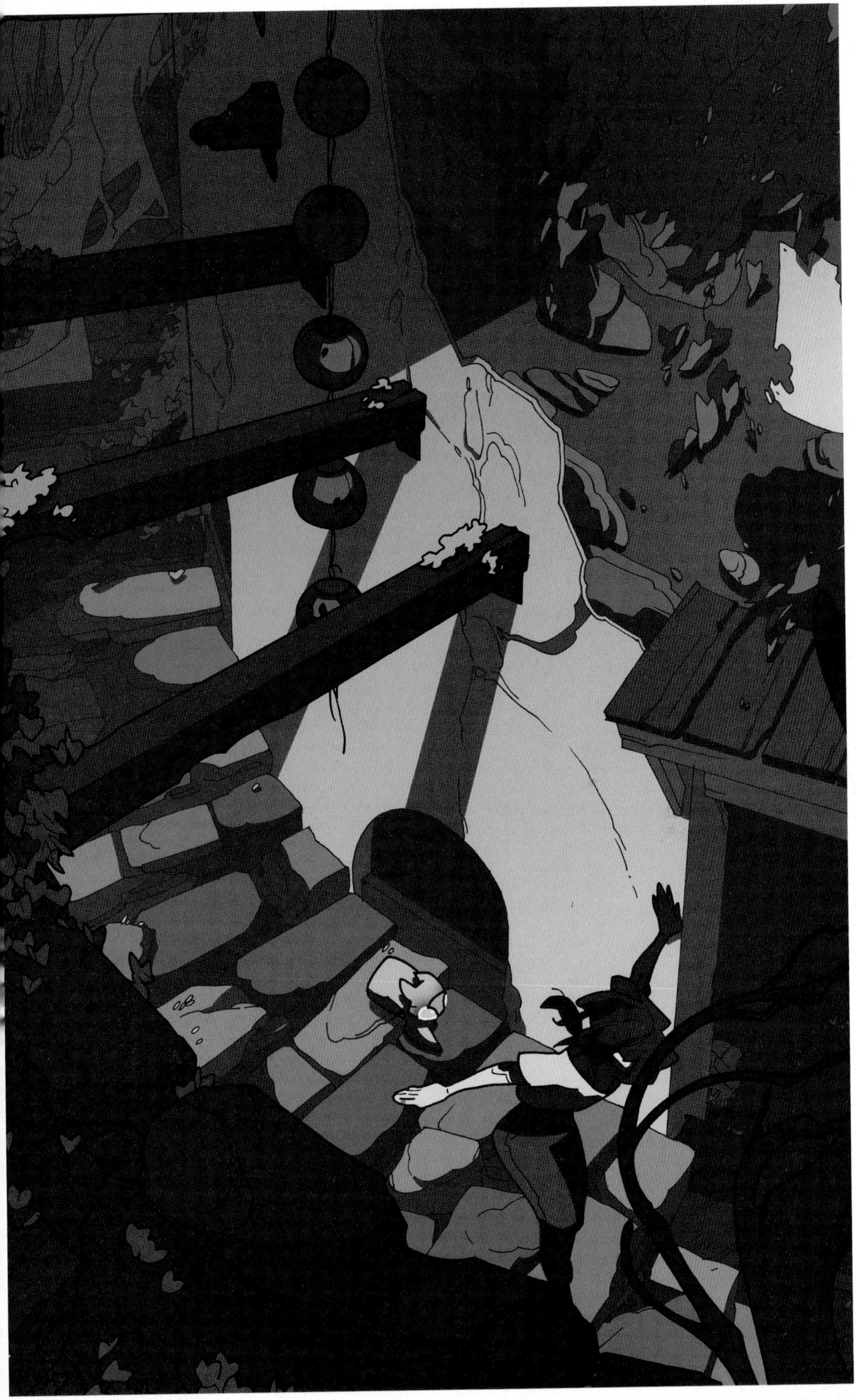

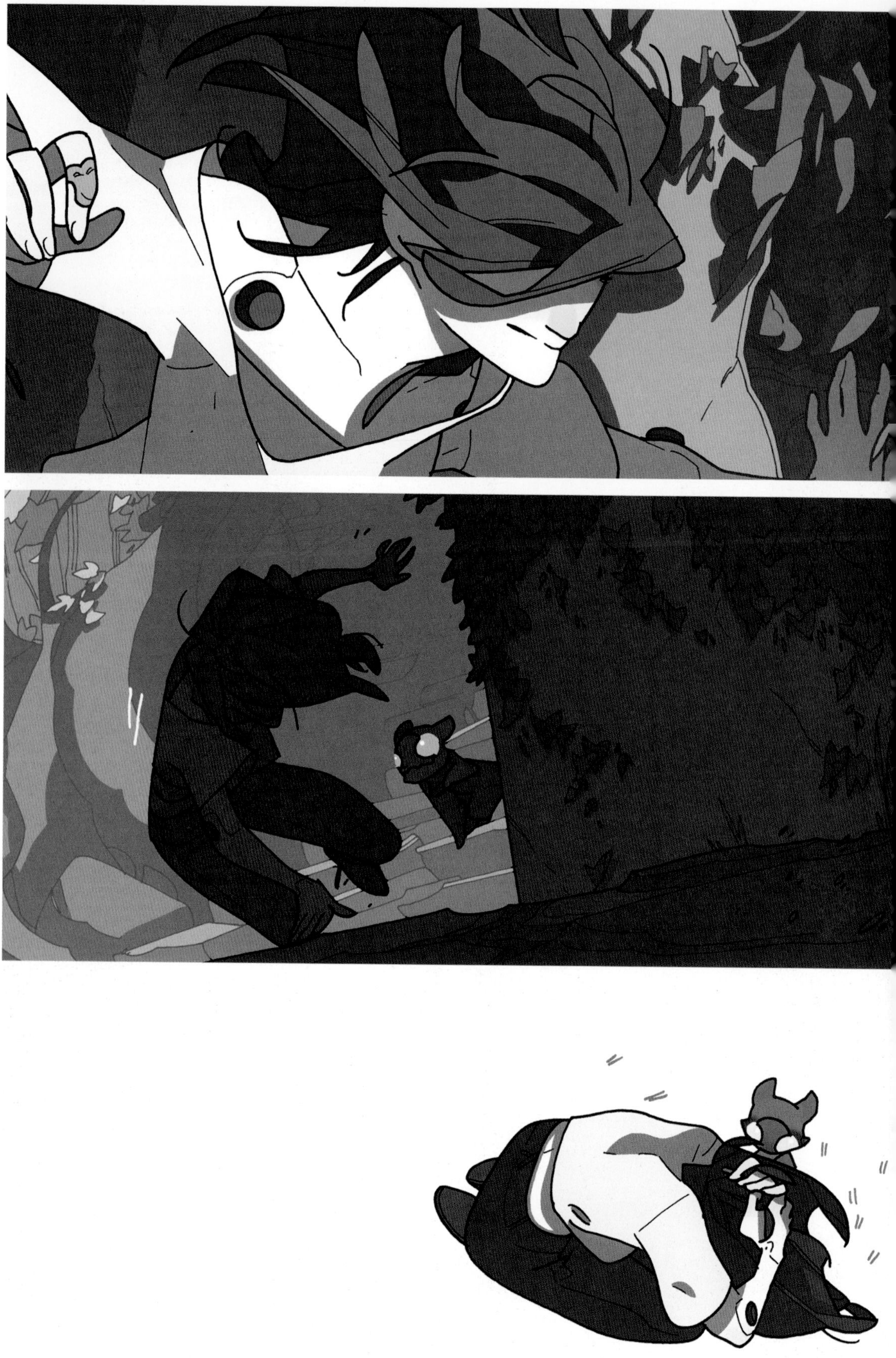

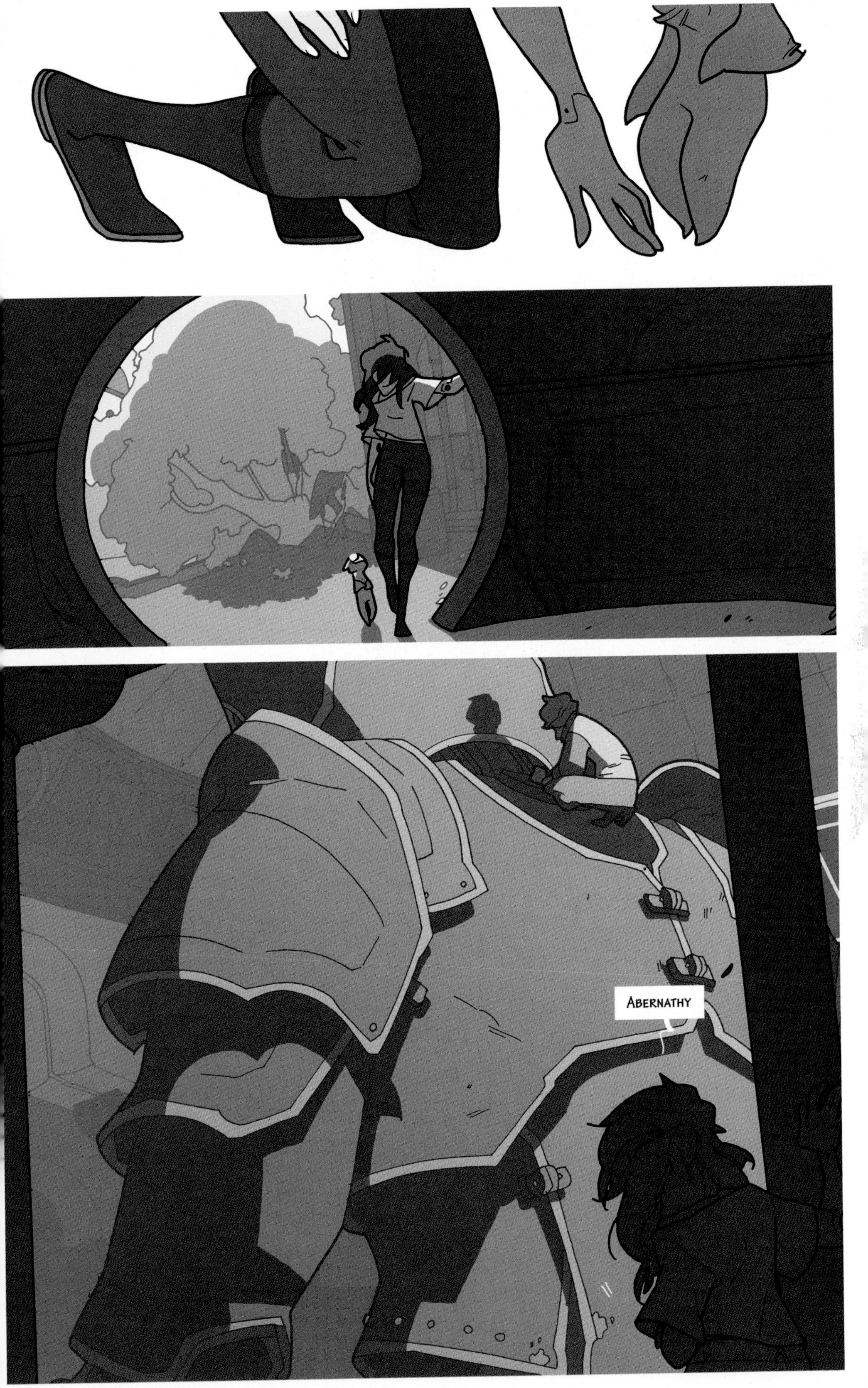
ABERNATHY

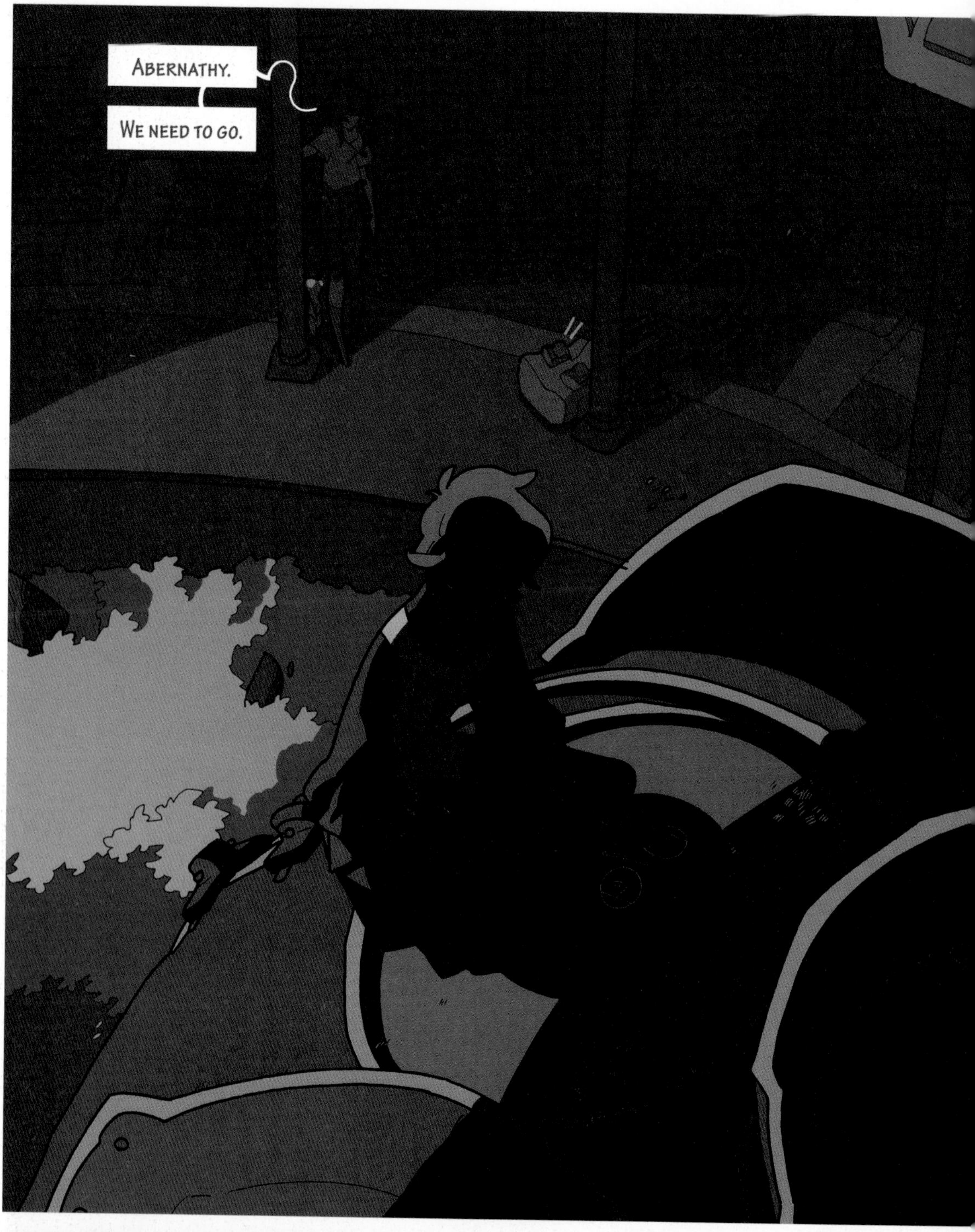
ABERNATHY.
WE NEED TO GO.
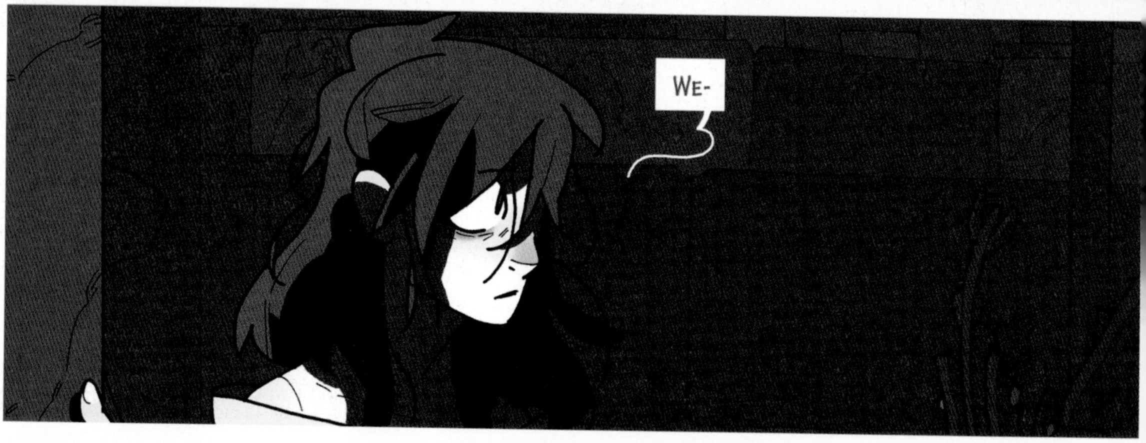
WE-

WHAT DID YOU DO?

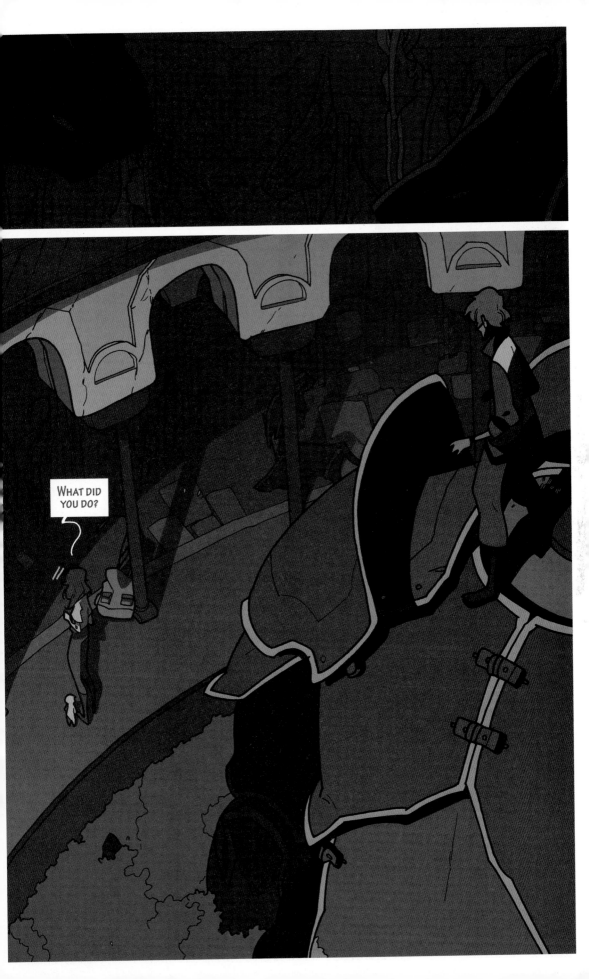

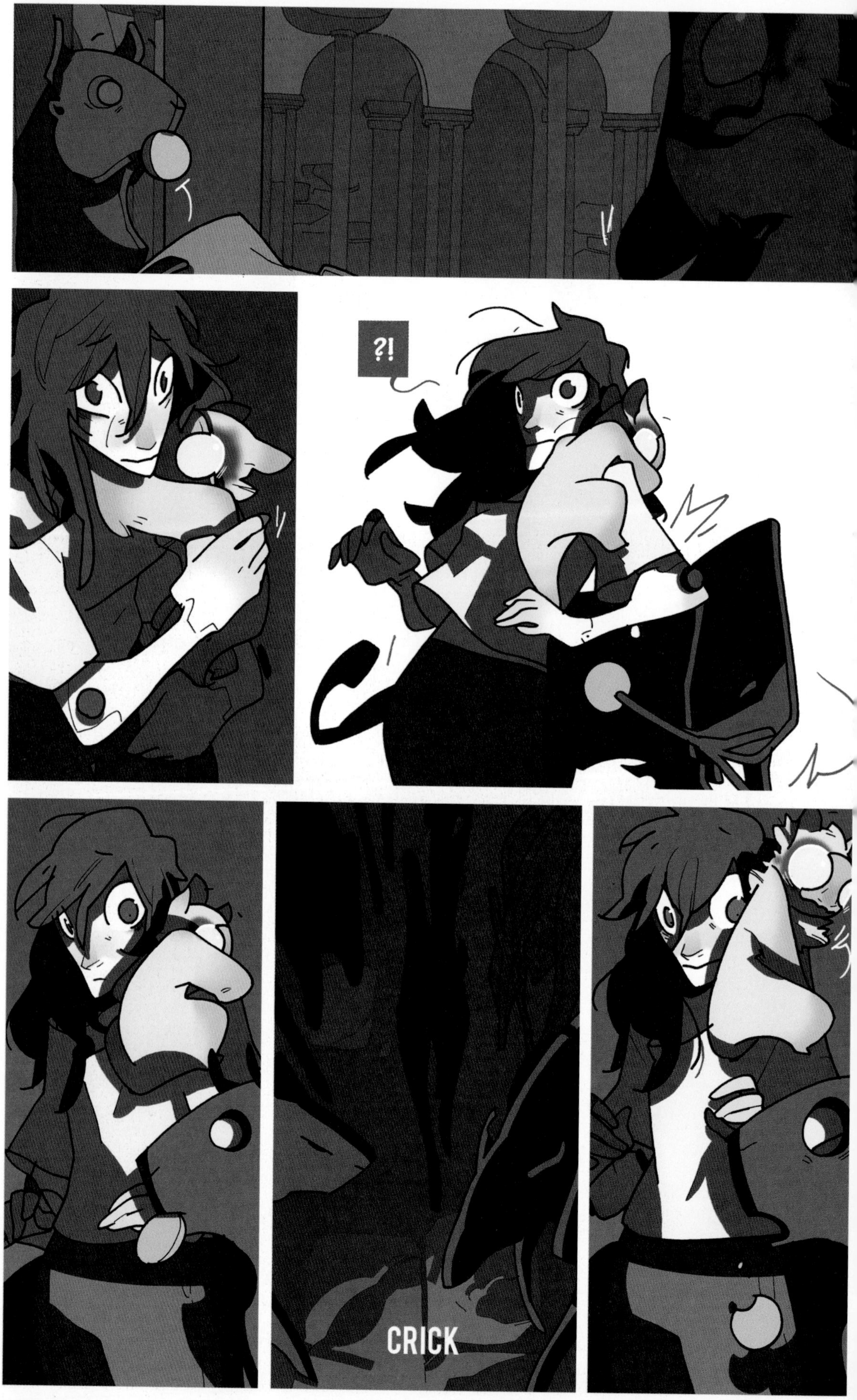
?!
CRICK

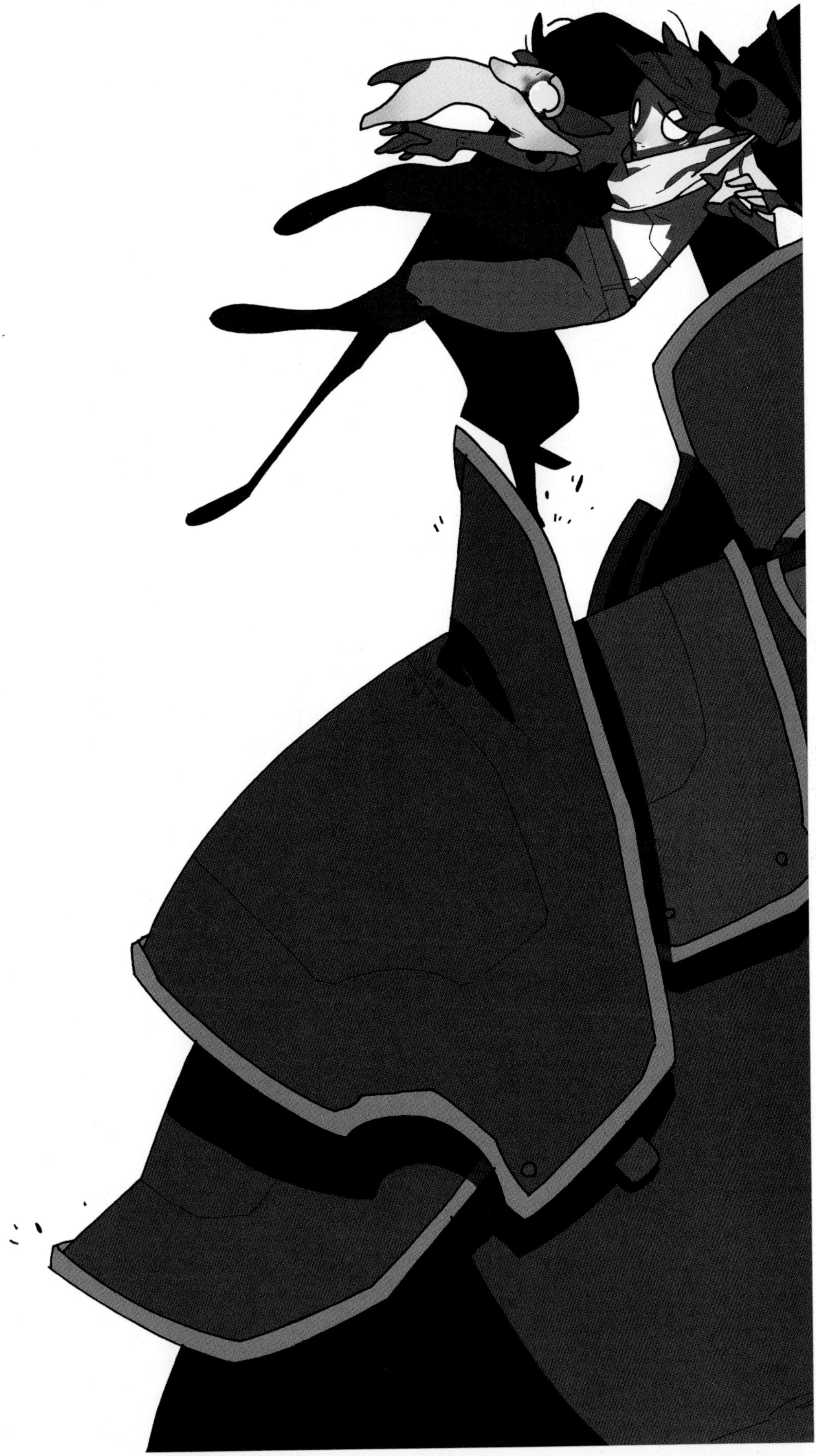

THAT'S US LEAVING THEN.

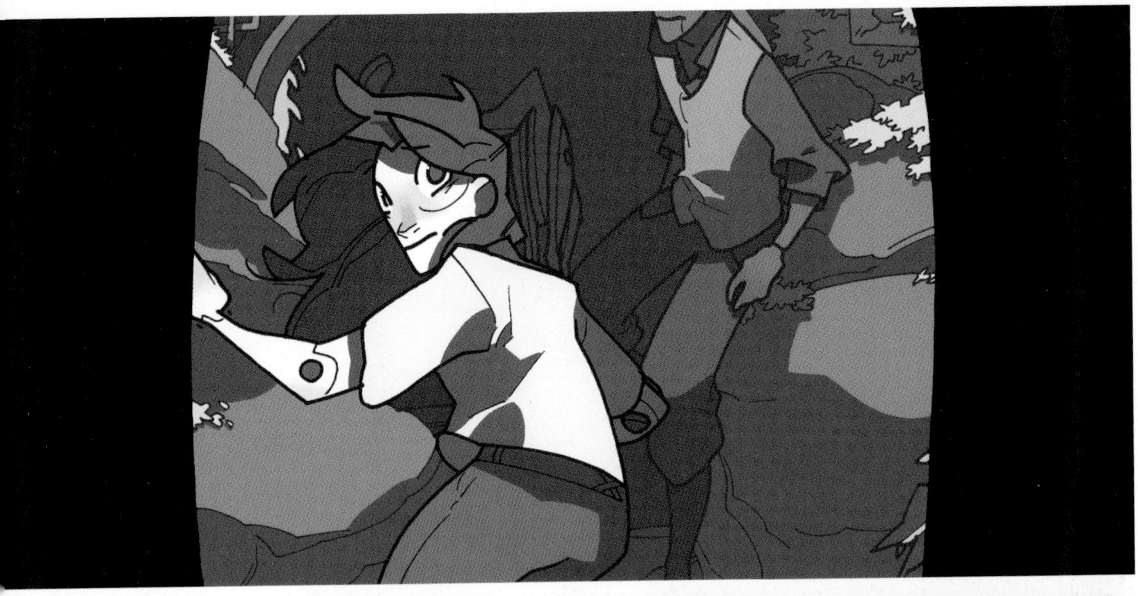

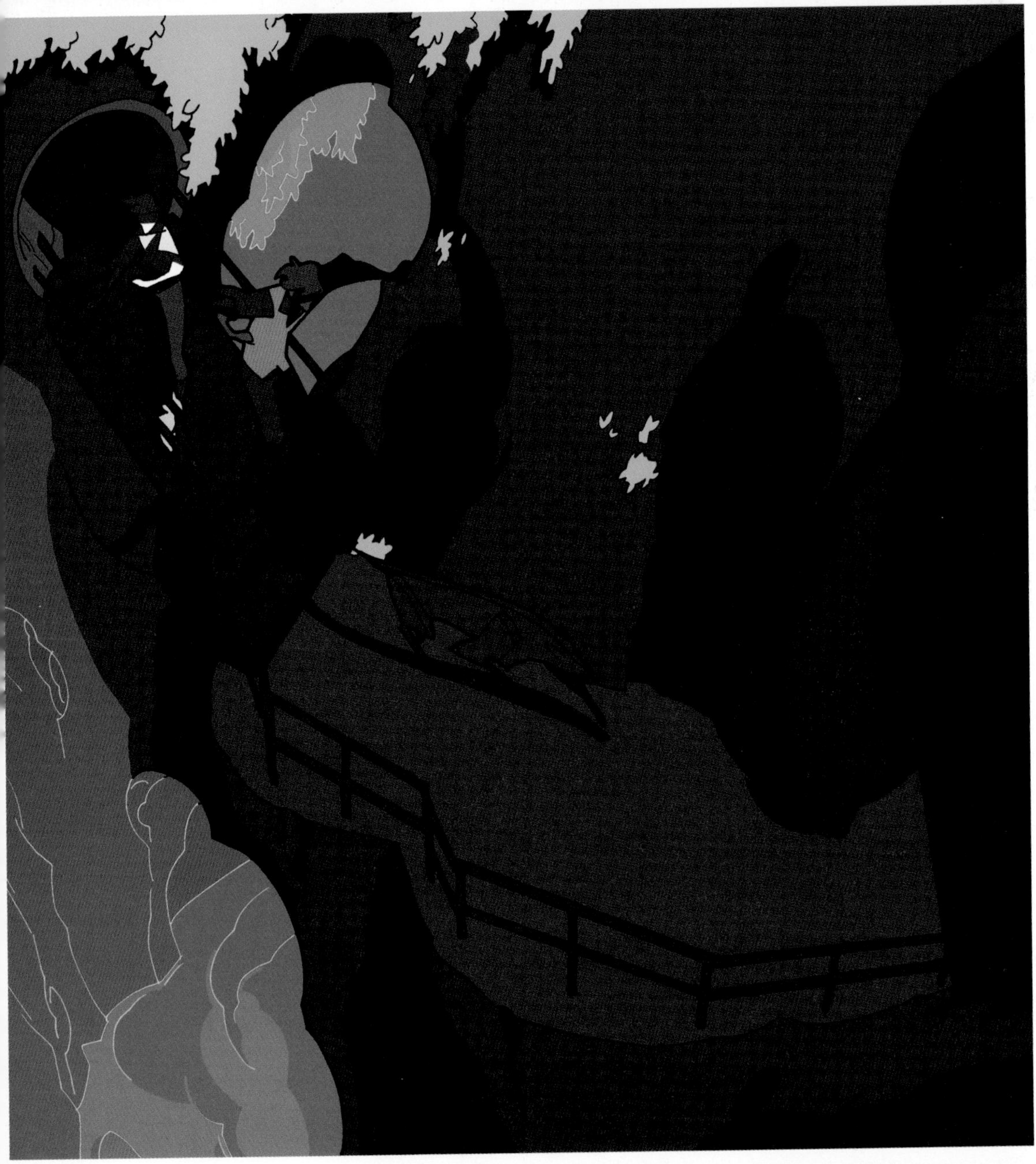

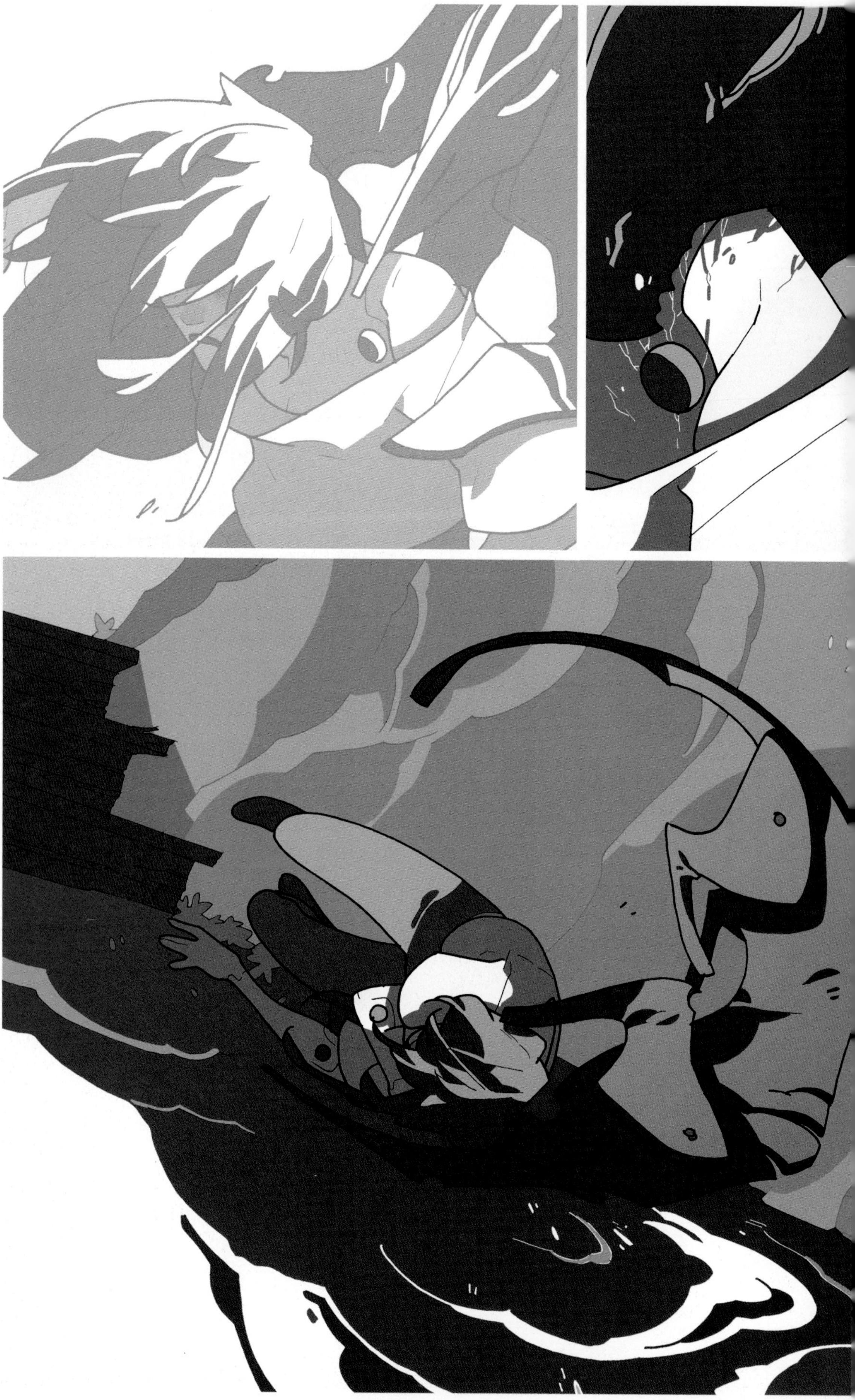

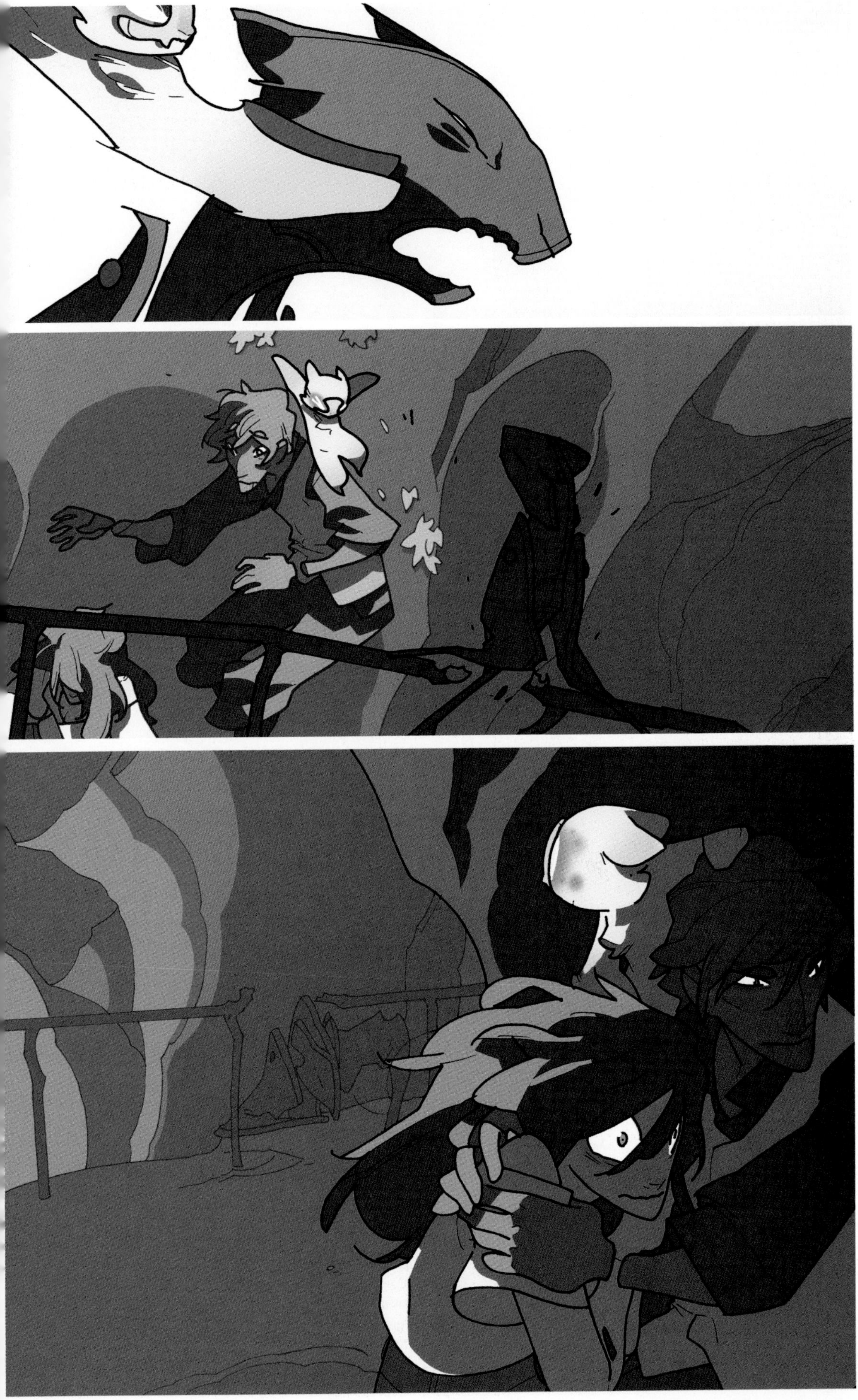

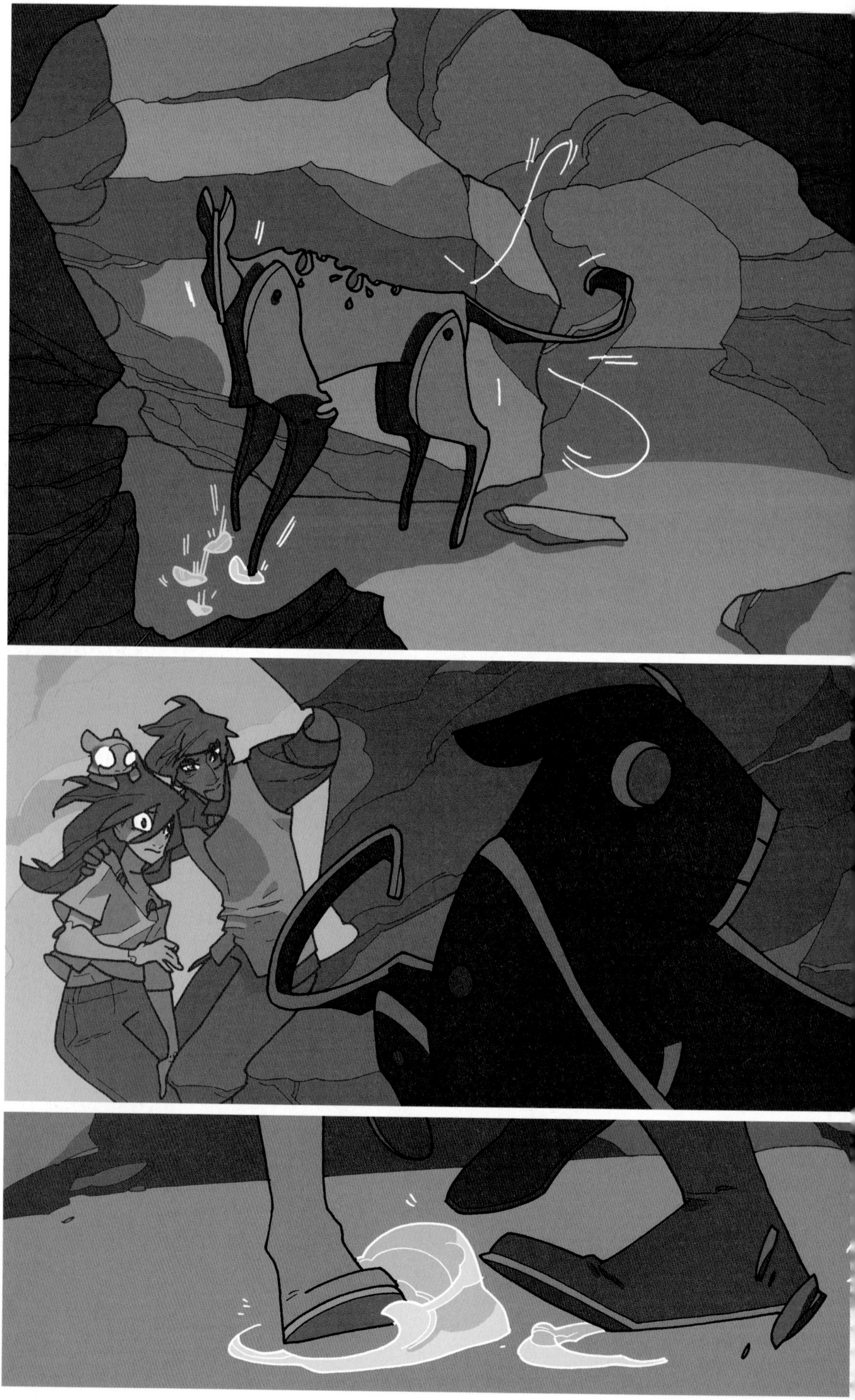

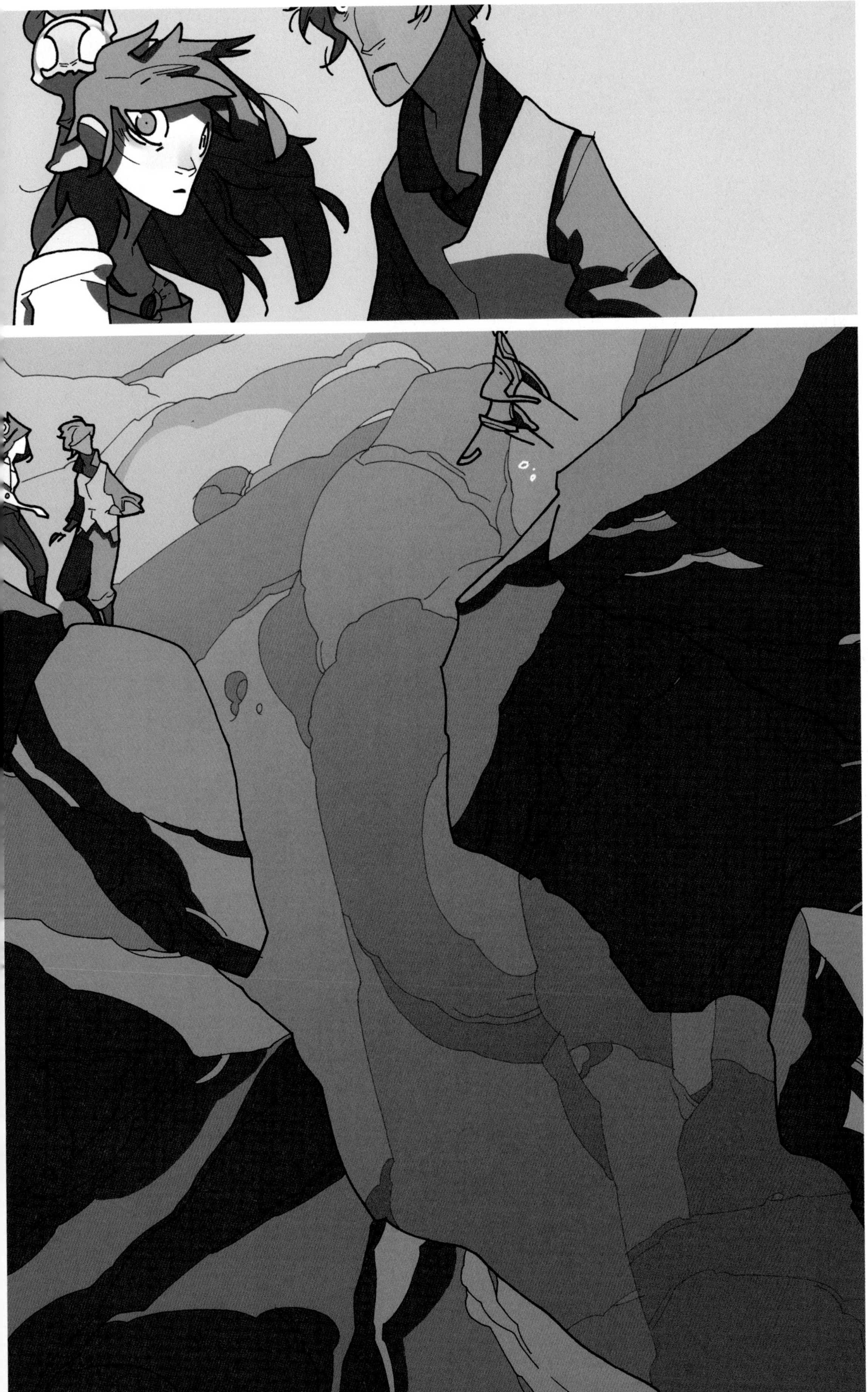

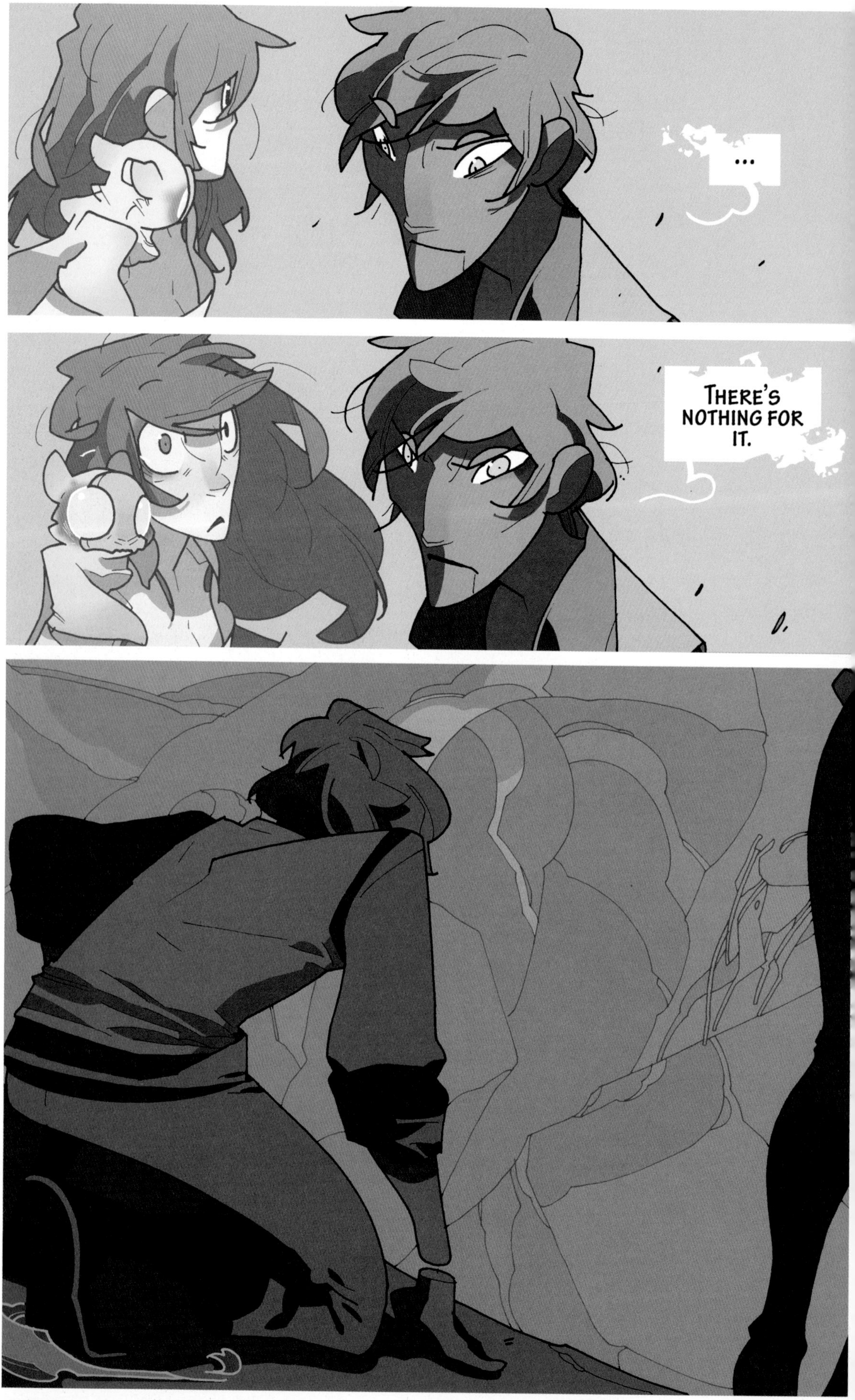
...
THERE'S NOTHING FOR IT.

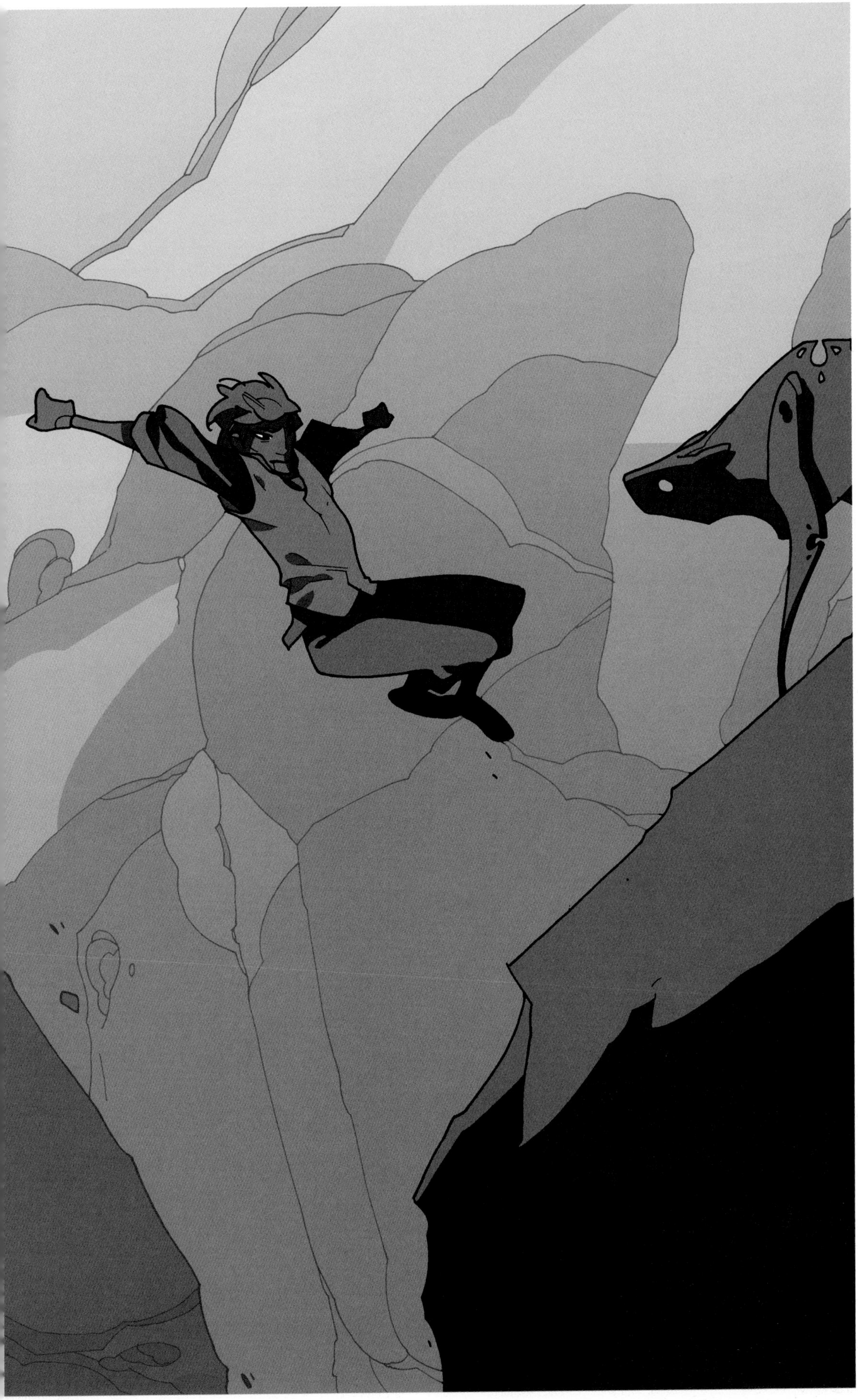

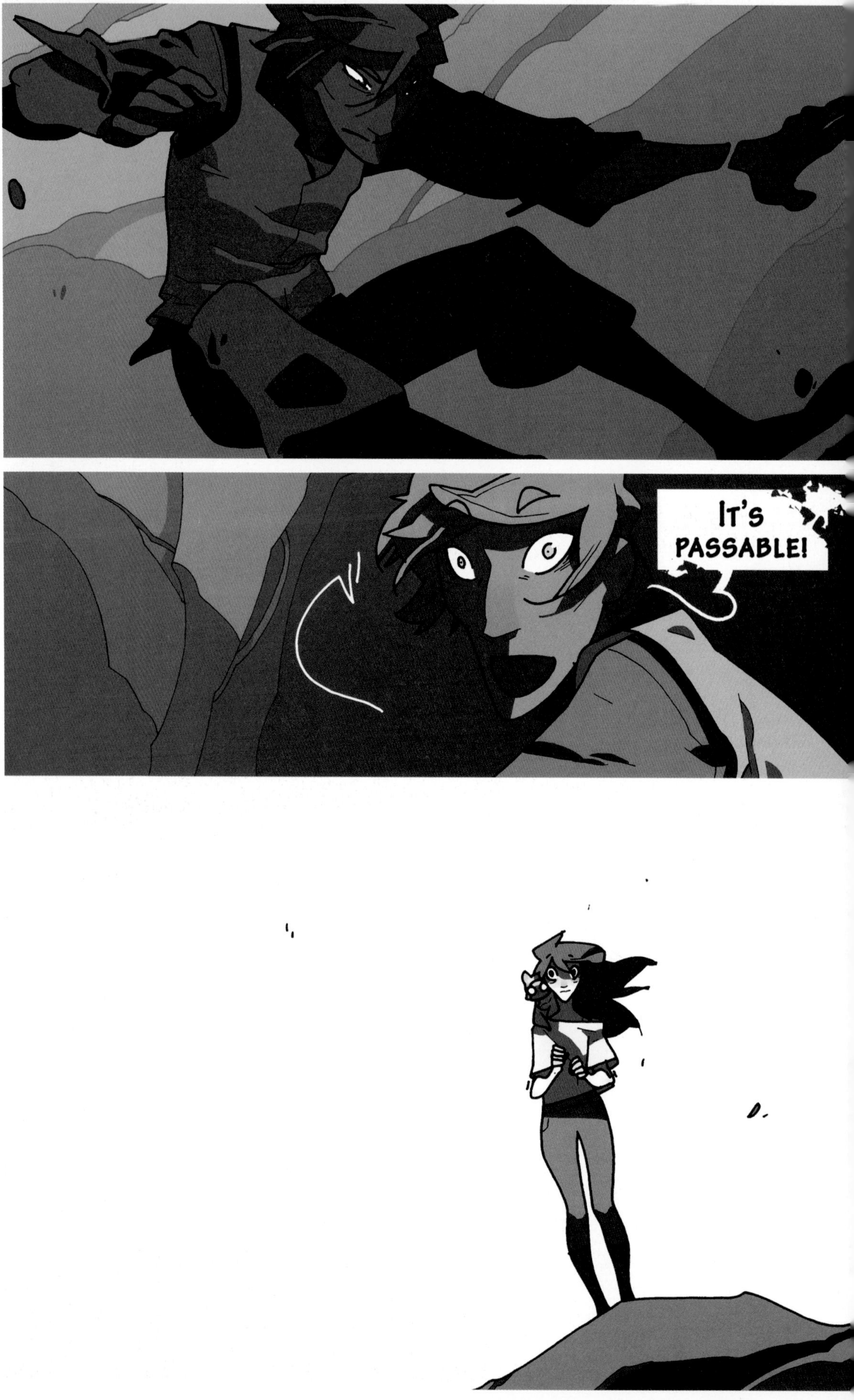
IT'S PASSABLE!

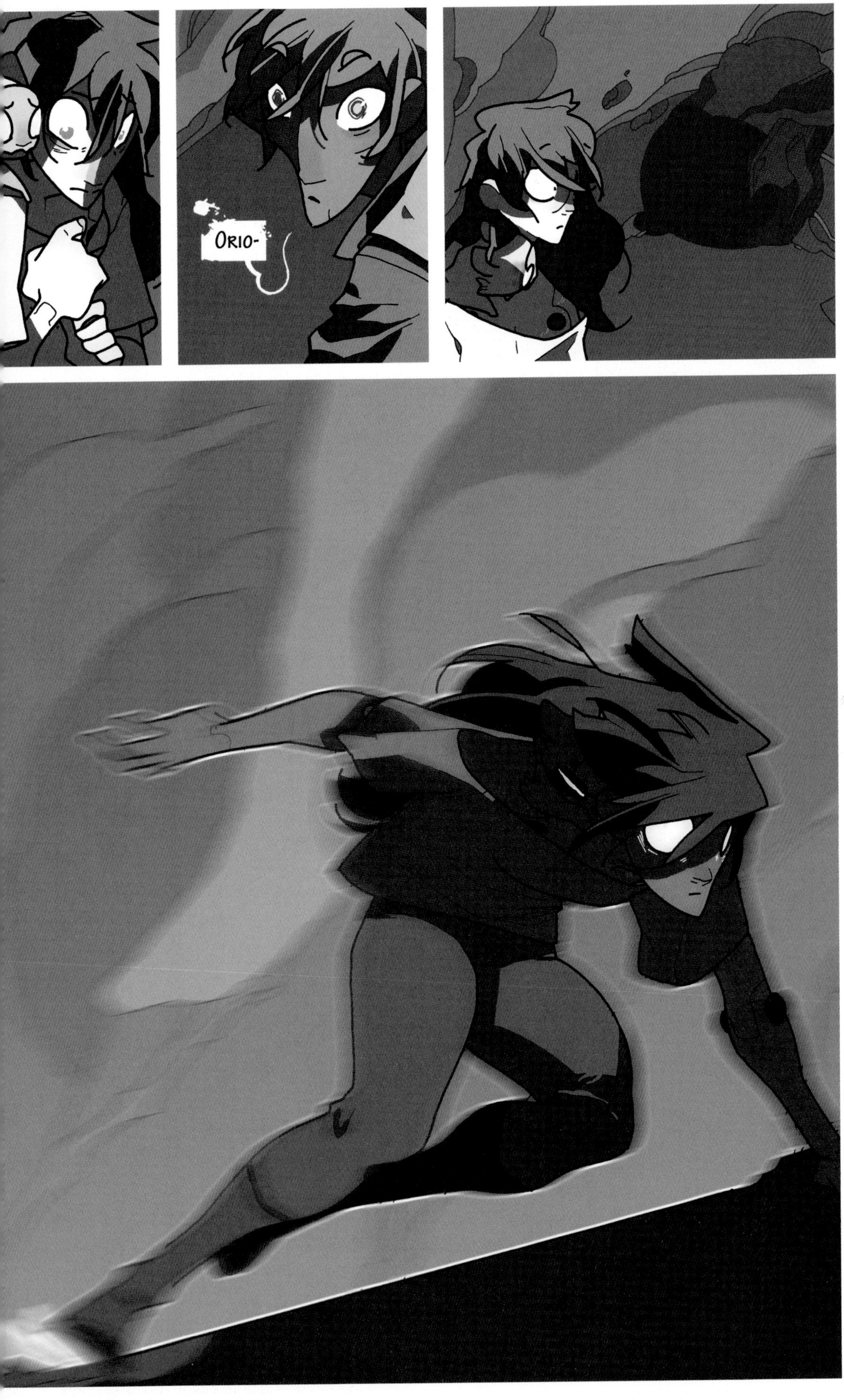
ORIO-

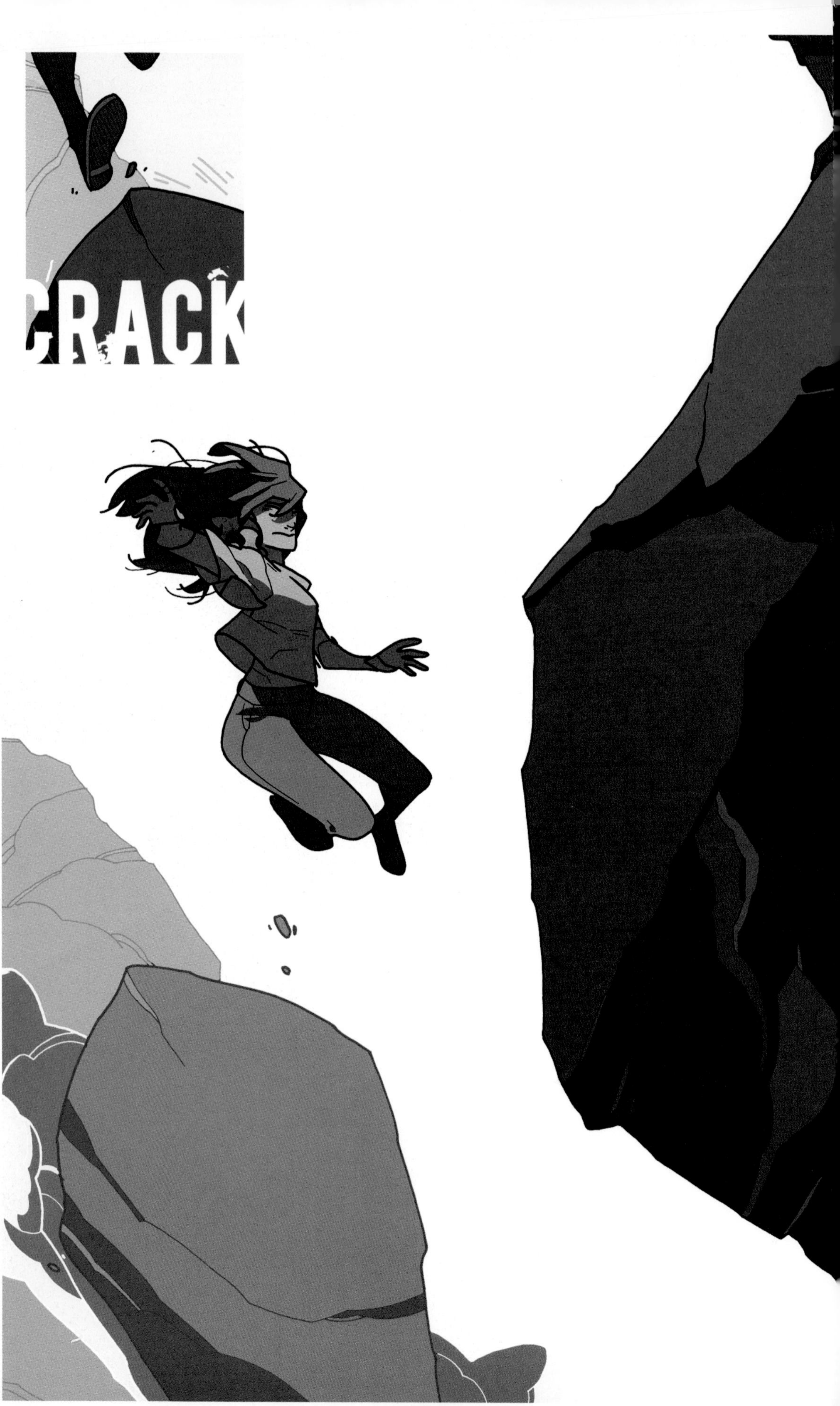
CRACK

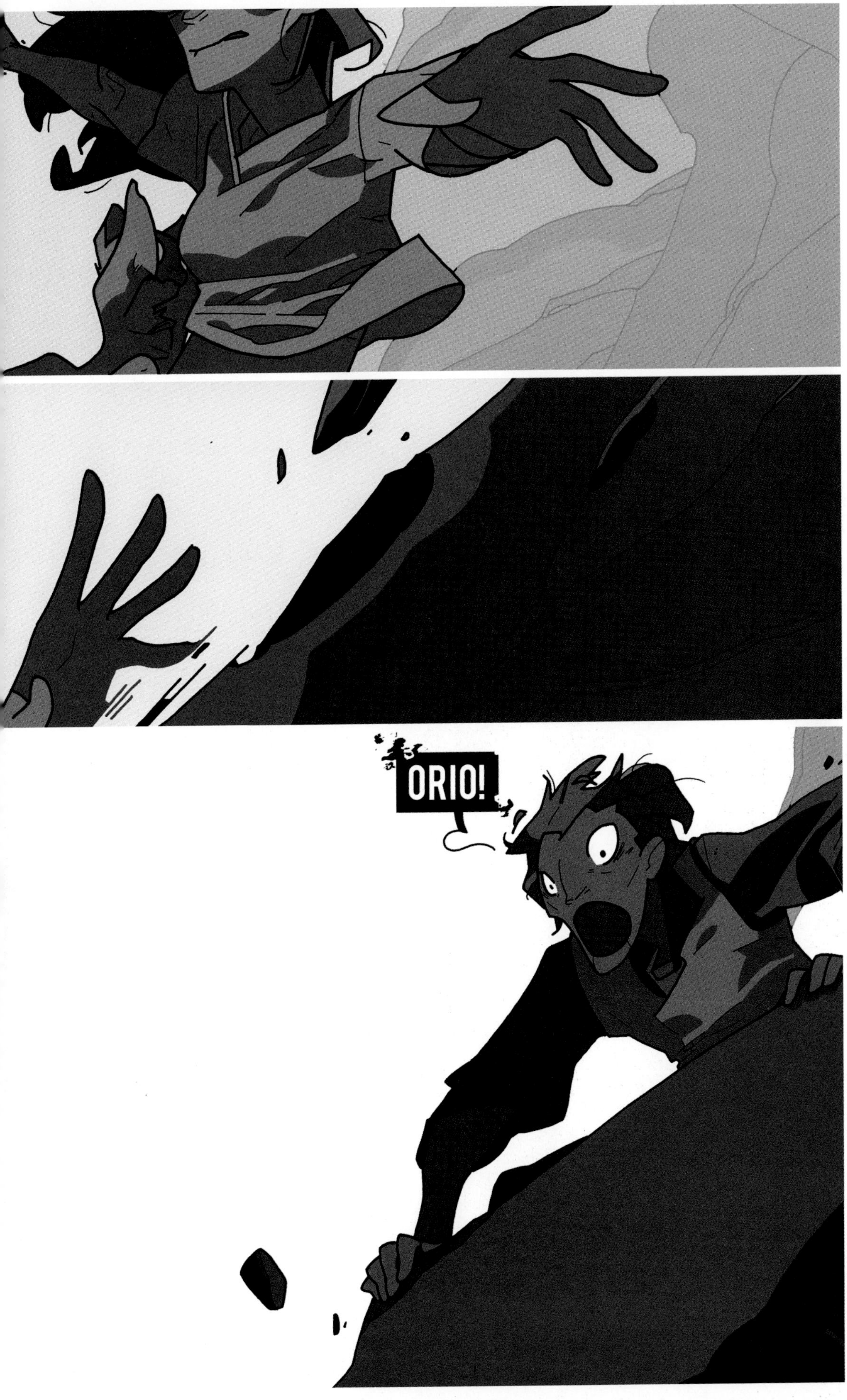
ORIO!

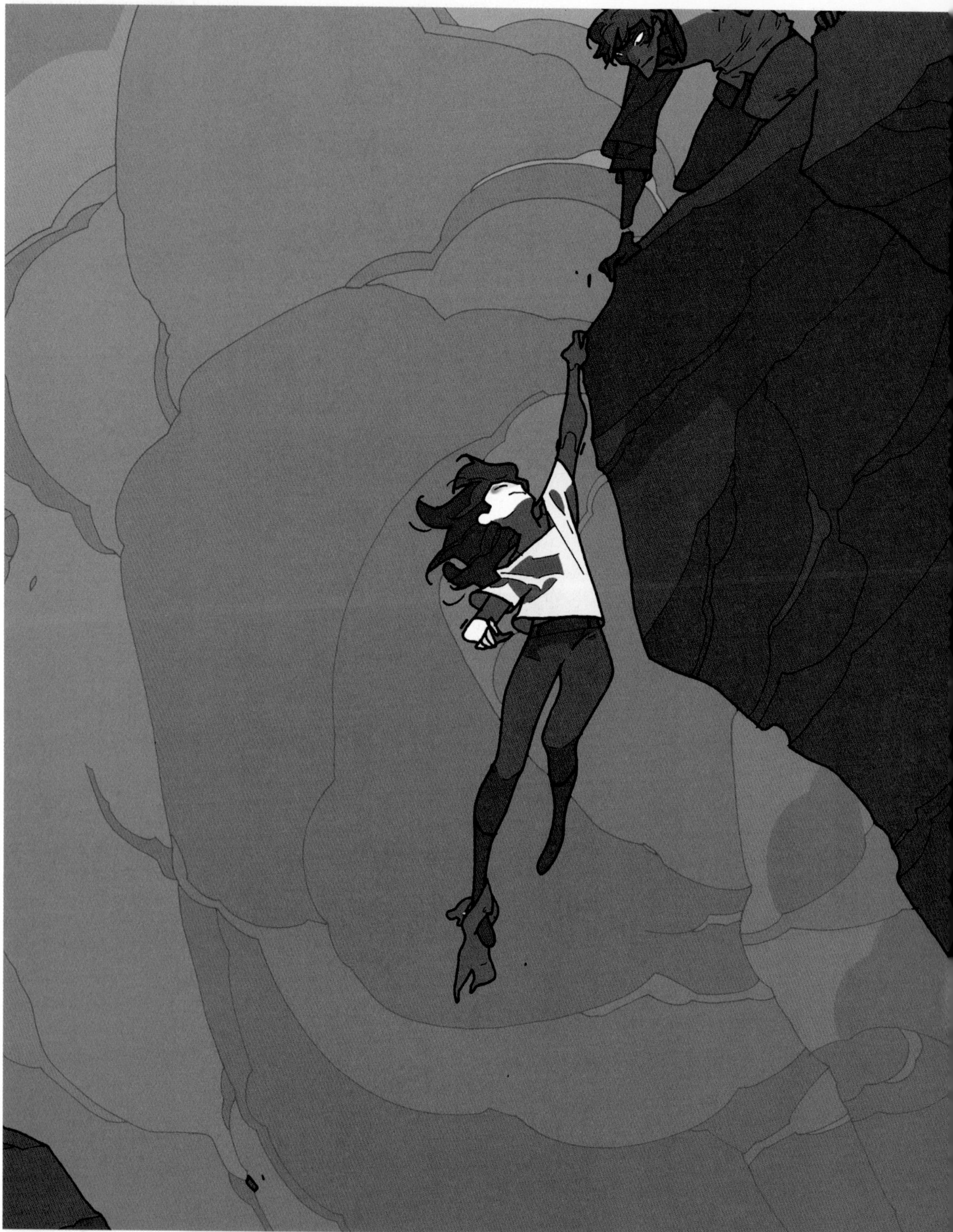

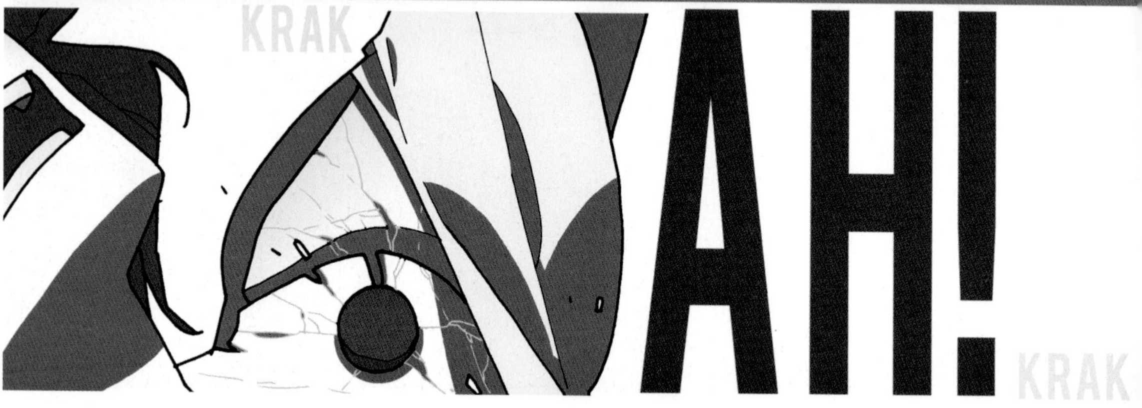
KRAK
AH!
KRAK

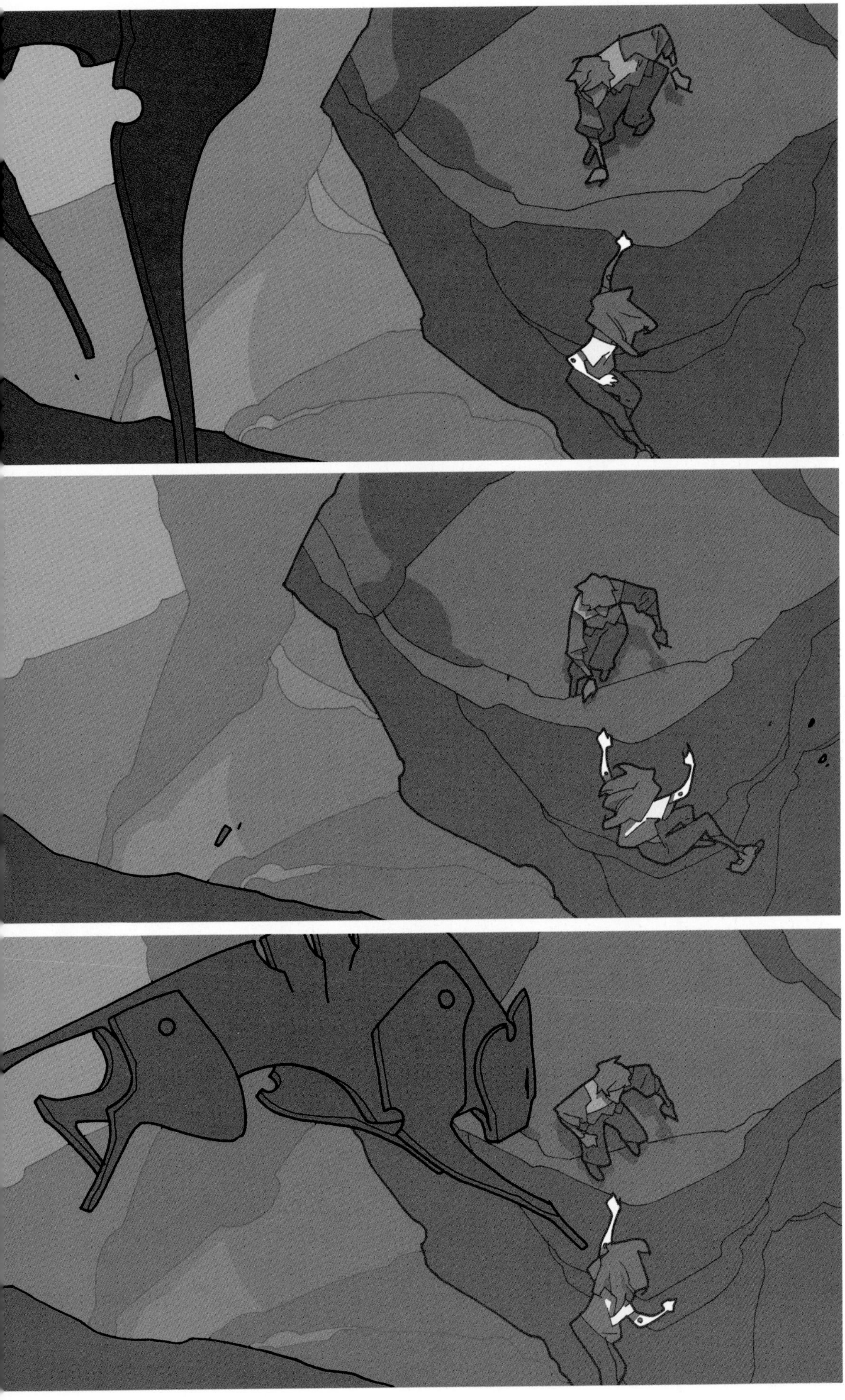

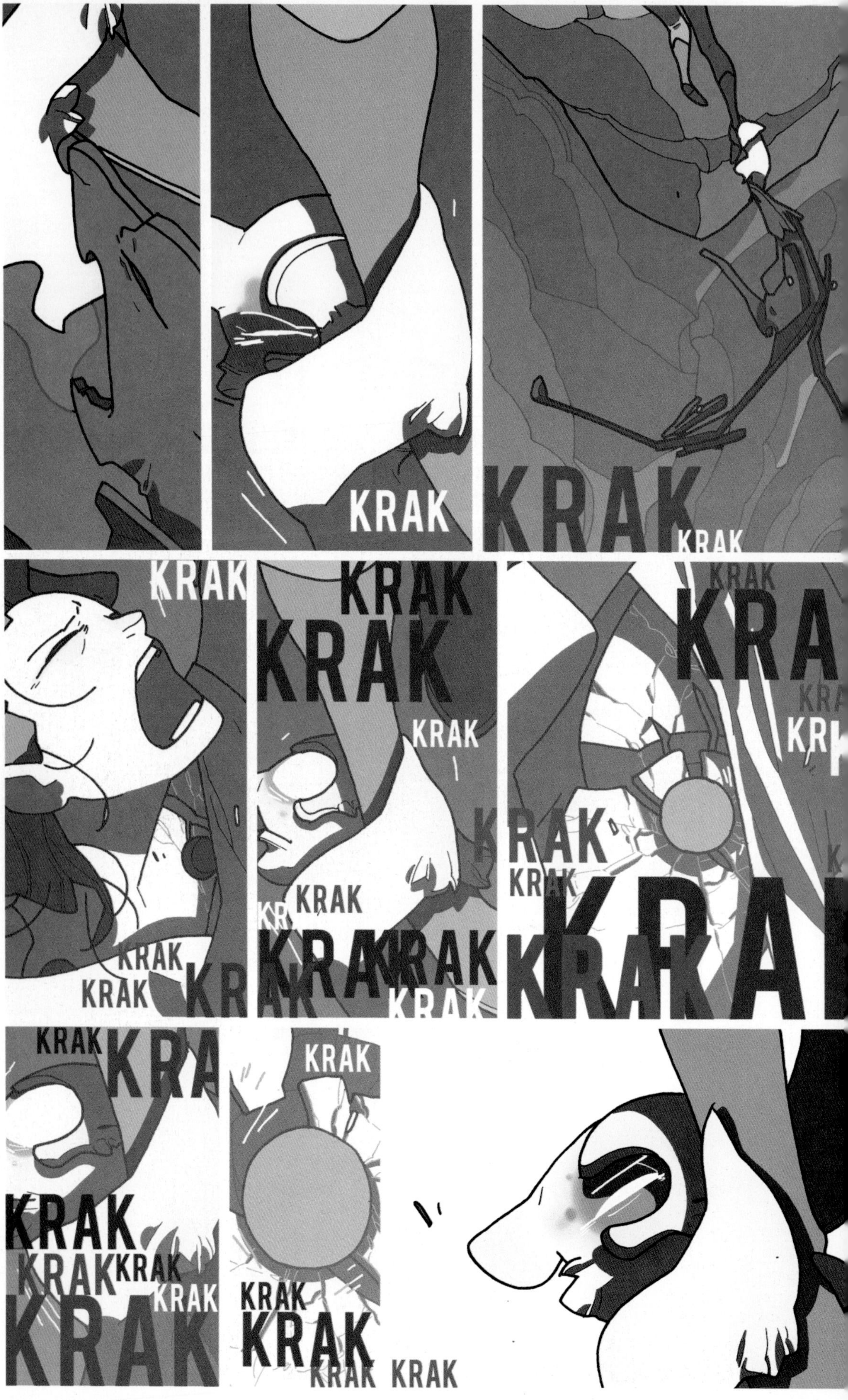
KRAK
KRAK
KRAK
KRAK
KRAK
KRAK
KRAK
KRAK
KRA
KRAK
KRAK
KRAK
KRAK
KRAK
KRAK
KRAK
KRAK
KRAK
KRAK
KRAK
KRAK
KRA
KRAK
KRAK
KRAK
KRAK
KRAK
KRAK
KRAK
KRAK
KRAK
KRAK

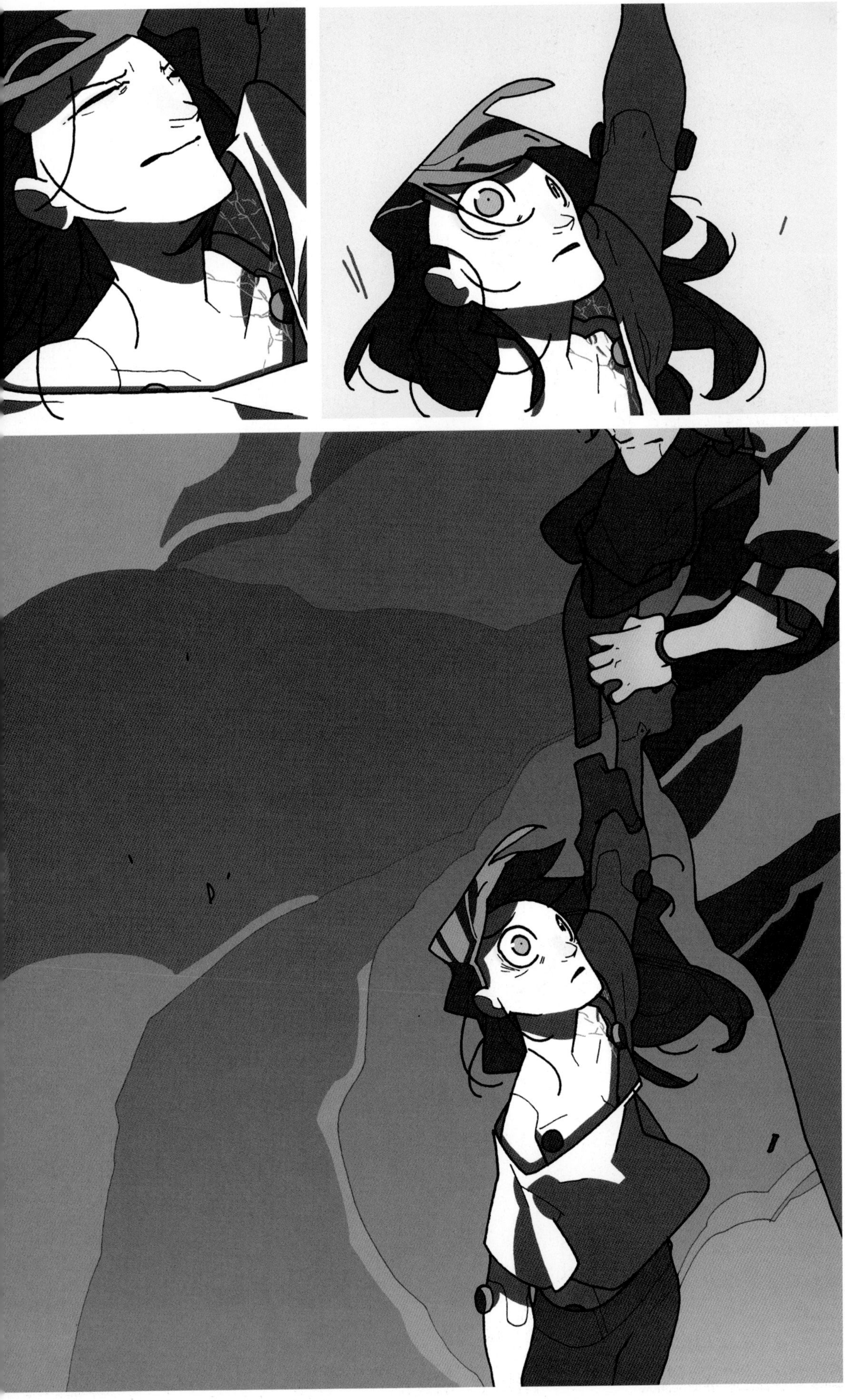

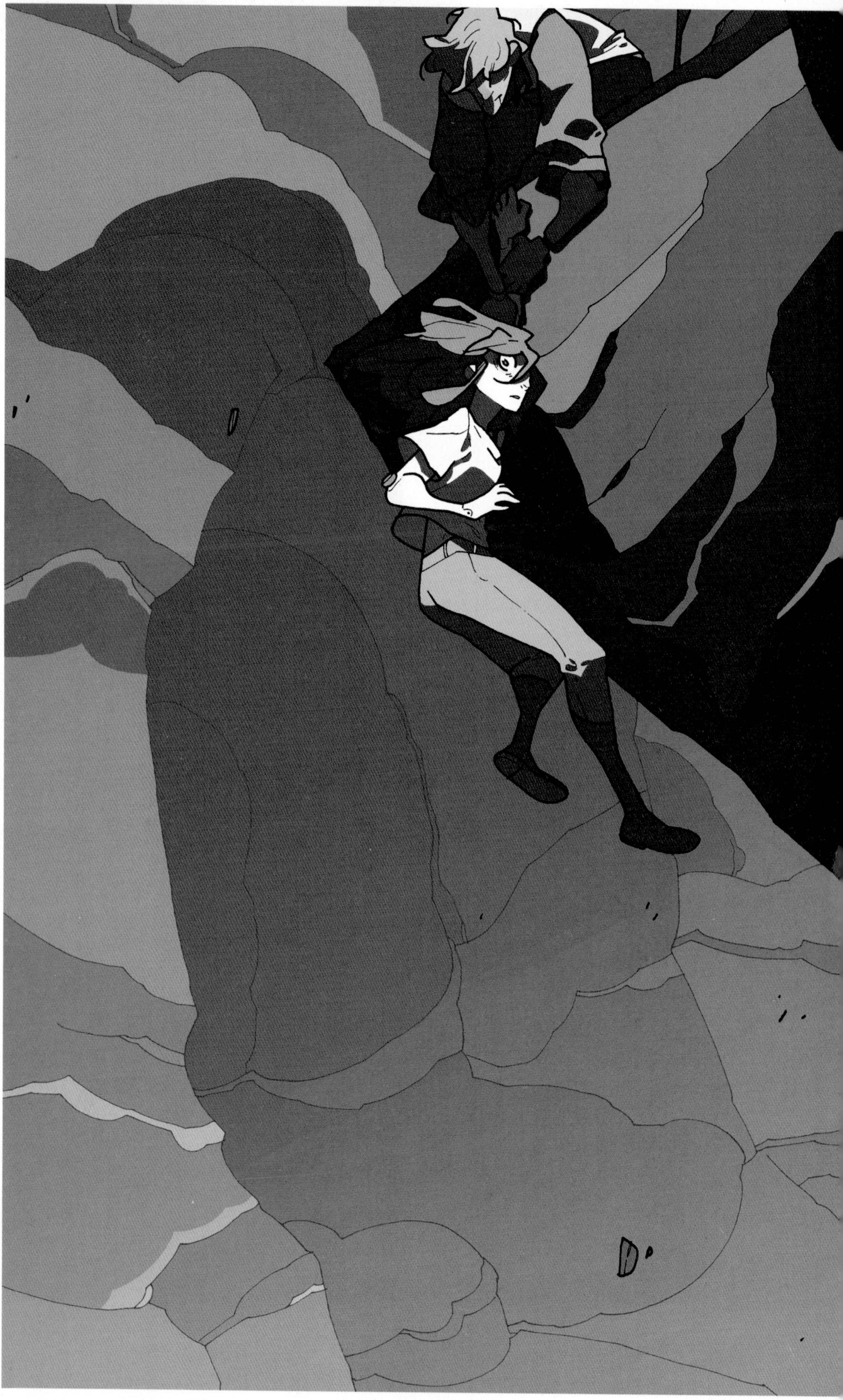